The Seer

Ariel MacArran

The Seer
By Ariel MacArran

©2014 Ariel MacArran

Cover Design: Steven James Catizone

Published by Here Be Dragons
ISBN-13: 978-0615965192
ISBN-10: 0615965199

Also available in eBook publication

PRINTED IN THE UNITED STATES OF AMERICA

One

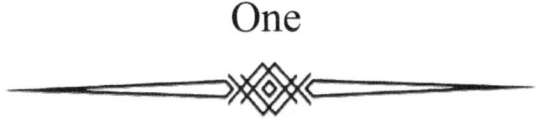

I should just let him die!

Arissa shrank deeper into the shadows. A few quick steps and she'd be out of this filthy alley. She'd disappear into the capital's twisted streets and leave the officer to his fate.

He was a fool for venturing alone into the gathering darkness, for wandering into this desolate sector of the city—and she more the fool for following after.

He'd brushed by her without even a glance—as he likely did the countless other wretches scraping to stay alive here. Certainly his crisp, red uniform and polished boots had no place in *this* neighborhood. Tall, broad-shouldered and possessed of striking blond good looks, he could have graced a fleet recruitment poster.

He felt like wealth, like abundance, like privilege.

Arissa hated him on sight.

She'd watched with narrowed eyes as, with the easy confidence of one assured of his place in the universe, the officer strolled away, heedless of the furtive, cloaked man trailing him.

The afternoon rain had stopped but a bitter gust of wind stirred her hair. Arissa pulled her thin jacket tighter and continued on. Ahead the garish lights of the marketplace were flickering to life as the suns slipped lower. Soon the market would be filled with people milling between the taverns, chemists and pleasure houses and her own evening's task was dangerous enough.

But the gut-wrenching menace kept dragging at her, slowing her steps until she stopped, her fists clenching.

By the time she caught up it was too late.

Forced into the alley, the officer glanced at man's blaster, now pointed squarely at his chest.

"Hands up." The cloaked man's back was still to Arissa, his Utavian accent harsh as the desert world from which he hailed.

"I've got money, friend," the officer said, complying with the man's demand, his palms showing. "If that's what you're looking for, no danger. I'll give you all I've got."

"I am no thief," the man fairly spat. "But you—you are Jolar d'Tural?"

The officer blinked. "Might be." He sent the blaster pointed at him a meaningful glance. "If I offended you, I didn't mean to. I don't come down here much. I met a friend for a drink. I didn't take any of the women so I couldn't have touched yours."

The Utavian's face remained hidden from her by the hood of his cloak but Arissa's breath caught as the set of his mind turned to ice.

This man had killed before. He was going to kill now.

The officer—*Jolar*—knew it too.

The Utavian hadn't noticed her yet. Her heart hammering, Arissa took a step back and the officer's vibrant blue eyes suddenly picked her out in the darkness. She froze there, her body pressed to the dank duracrete wall.

The waves of his fear and horror reverberated through her mind. He didn't understand why, even as the man extended his arm to fire, he was being cut down like this. Arissa couldn't hear his thoughts as words but his desperation roared like a thunderclap through her mind.

Help me!

Arissa threw herself at the Utavian, making a clumsy grab for his blaster. His surprise pulsed and he jerked back just as her fingers closed on the weapon, ripping it from her hand. His arm whipped around and he struck her with the butt of his blaster. Pain exploded behind her eyes and she hit the cold duracrete hard.

The Utavian shrugged his cloak back. Time slowed as he leveled the weapon at her, every detail perfectly clear: the glint in his fierce dark eyes, the sharp planes of his thin face, the street dimming to ash gray as the last light of Tellar's suns faded from the sky—

Blue flashes lit up the alley as energy bolts drilled through him.

She scrambled back as the Utavian collapsed, the pavement scraping her palms. He lay unmoving near her feet, faint wisps of smoke from his wounds rising into the cool evening air.

Arissa's breath shuddered in her throat. Her palm to her breastbone, she pressed hard against the aching hollowness she sensed, the sudden stillness where there had been life just a moment before . . .

"Fucking hells," Jolar gasped, his own blaster gripped so tightly his knuckles were white.

He kept his weapon on the Utavian's still form, his movements cautious as he approached. With a swift, sharp kick Jolar sent the man's blaster skidding across the pavement. Keeping his weapon trained on the Utavian, he nudged the man's ribs with the sole of his boot.

The burned stench made Arissa twist away. Other sensations suddenly intruded: her scraped palms stung, her feet were cold and aching in her worn slippers, the icy puddle beneath her had soaked through her thin clothes.

"Oh," she murmured, her hand going to her head. Her fingers came away bloody.

"Let me see." Jolar squatted beside her, his square-jawed face set grimly as he holstered his blaster. He cupped her chin gently to tilt her face and met her gaze for an instant. Up close his eyes were an even brighter blue.

She flinched as he touched the sore spot.

"Yeah, I bet that hurts. He hit you hard," he said, his voice faintly honeyed with the cool tones of affluence. "Do you feel dizzy? Like you might pass out? Or throw up?"

Arissa shook her head and immediately wished she hadn't.

He brushed a stray black curl from her face. "What's your name?"

"Ar—" She caught herself. "Tianna. Tianna Hayer."

"Well, Tianna, I'm Jolar d'Tural and you just saved my life." His mouth curved into a half-smile. "I'm Zartani, you know, in case my name didn't give it away. What you just did means a lot to the Zartani. It means a lot to me." He took her hand in his, looking at the abrasions on her palm and shook his head a little. He dug in his pocket and pulled out a comm unit. "I'll let TelSec know to send a medic too."

Arissa yanked her hand back and shoved him hard. She was on her feet and out of the alley at a dead run before his backside hit the pavement.

The few lights that still functioned here offered only scant pools of sickly yellow against the gathering darkness. At this hour the pathetic denizens of the area had withdrawn indoors to sink into chemical induced dazes and Arissa's footfalls echoed against the dilapidated buildings. Startled voles, their whiskers twitching in alarm, flashed glittering black eyes at her before scattering to wriggle their tiny, furred bodies into cracked walls and garbage piles.

"Tianna!"

She risked a glance back at the officer; her breath caught at his determination and how quickly he was gaining on her.

She was running full out now, scrambling to think where she could lose him. She couldn't turn off this street without being trapped in one of the side lanes. The abandoned shop she'd intended to spend the night in was off to the right but she couldn't possibly duck inside before he saw where she'd gone. The lodgings she hadn't made rent on were on the other side of the market and she didn't dare return *there* without the means to pay.

She sure as hells couldn't let him catch her.

She bent her head trying to gain more speed, her feet pounding against the worn duracrete. If she got enough of a lead maybe he would just give up. He'd just killed a man; he'd have to report in or—

He slammed into her. She cried out and stumbled, taking both of them to the wet pavement. He twisted, taking the brunt of the fall as they rolled across the ground.

Then he had hold of her wrists, pinning her down.

"Let go!"

"What the hells' is the matter with you?" His face was flushed, his vivid eyes furious. "Why'd you run off like that?"

"Get off me! Fucking son of a sular cow!"

He gave a short, disbelieving snort. "Well, that's some impression I've made on you. But watch what you say about my mother."

"Get *off!*"

He shifted his weight to let her sit up but he kept tight hold of her wrist, his grip tightening when she tried to scramble away.

"Not so fast. You saved my life," he said impatiently. "I owe you."

"Yeah, you're welcome! Festering hells, let *go!*"

He pushed up to stand. "Come on."

He was taller and stronger than she, his grip like tarasteel around her wrist. Dragging her feet wasn't even slowing him down.

"What do you think you're doing?" she cried.

"You need medical attention and I just shot someone," Jolar returned, not breaking stride. His hands and uniform had gotten dirty from their struggle and smudges showed on the fabric over his elbows, knees and back. "We're going back to wait for TelSec and then I'm going to—"

"Gods, let me *go!*"

Arissa punched him with her free hand. He twisted to catch hold of her other wrist.

"Damn it, stop hitting me! What the hells is—Tellaran security. That's it, isn't it? You're afraid of TelSec. Why? What have you done?"

"Nothing!"

He took in her forest green tunic with its embroidery fraying at the hem, matching trousers and light jacket, her scuffed slippers. "You're a scrawny little thing and your clothes have sure seen better days. You hardly look like the criminal type."

Scrawny? Her eyes stung but she couldn't deny it. Her face was so thin and wan these days and these clothes, which had fit so well before she fled her homeworld, now hung on her like sacks. Her always unruly black curls must be utterly wild now.

"I know you aren't from Tellar by your accent," he continued. "Apovian, right?"

Her mouth went dry.

"Well, come on, Apovian girl," he said impatiently. "Are you going to tell me?"

She blinked up at him. His mind felt hard and set as glass.

"Fine," he snapped, turning to continue the way they came and pulling her along. "I'm sure TelSec will be happy to."

"I'm an ornament!"

He stopped. "You're an ornament and—?"

"I haven't— I don't have a place to work. Uh, anymore."

His eyes narrowed. "Go on."

"I signed a year's contract with a pleasure house in return for transport to Tellar. But I— I didn't like it there so I ran away and now—" She gave a half-shrug. "I work on my own."

His glance went over her face, her breasts, her body. "You don't look much like an ornament."

"Well," she hedged, her cheeks hot, "some men like a girl who doesn't look like a whore. Tastes and all—"

"How much?"

Arissa frowned. "How much what?"

"Do you charge? You do charge, don't you? The pleasure house explained the idea that you get *paid* for sex, right?"

"Oh. No, sure. I mean—yes, I get paid."

"So how much?"

Sella, the hard-faced whore who rented the room next to Arissa's, charged differently depending on the service. She'd certainly heard enough of Sella's negotiating through those thin walls.

"Well, how much for what, exactly?"

"For me, exactly," he gritted out. "How much for *me* to fuck you?"

She blinked, her breath picking up speed. Negotiating wasn't the only thing she'd heard through those walls. His eyes seemed almost aglow, his heat vibrating against her mind. She glanced at his body, the broad shoulders, the slim hips.

Would he kiss her?

Would it hurt?

"I don't—I guess a hundred?"

"For the whole night or just the once?"

More than once? "Uh, I-I don't—What do you want?"

He reached into his pocket and glanced at the bills in his hand. He pushed them at her. "There. Five hundred credits for five nights."

She stared at the rainbow hued bills he held out to her, the breath rushing out of her lungs. Five *hundred*? She couldn't remember the last time she had seen so much money. It would pay five months' rent at her run-down rooming house. She could sleep in a bed tonight.

She could *eat*.

"Well?" he demanded. "Five hundred and you're mine for five nights. Do we have a deal?"

Numbly her fingers closed around the bills, the reinforced paper crinkling as she clasped them.

"Great," he muttered. "I'm looking forward to it."

He pulled her along, the money gripped tightly in her hand. Clearly he didn't trust her enough to let go of her wrist.

What did I just do?

She didn't even have any rooms to take him to! She glanced at the money clutched in her hand. Well, she could certainly pay her rent now. But he wanted to—

She swallowed. And he really *did* want to. She could feel the heat of desire, of hunger, from him.

"Just let me do the talking when TelSec gets here." Jolar said.

"You've already called them?" She stopped. "No, I'll meet you after, okay?"

He gave her an impatient look. "No, it's *not* okay. Once we're finished with TelSec, I'm taking you to the medcenter."

They'd want an ID scan before they treated her. An ID check would show her real records, her name, how out of date her information was.

A medical scan would show *why*.

"No, I—I don't need a doctor."

"Yes, you do, Tianna. Why don't you want to go to the medcenter?" He glanced at her belly. "Are you pregnant? Is that why you ran away from the pleasure house? I can buy you out of your contract if I need to. I can set you up somewhere else."

Buy an ornament out of a year's contract from a pleasure house? Set her up somewhere? That must be a staggering amount of money. Who had money like that?

Why would he even *want* to buy her out?

Colored lights suddenly flashed down into the street as the TelSec vehicle came to hover over them. A second shuttle continued on, going in the direction of the alley.

Arissa twisted her wrist sharply to break his hold. She made it only two steps then he caught her from behind.

The money scattered at her feet as she clawed at his hands, the chill breeze sending it fluttering away. "Oh, gods! *Please!*"

He hesitated, then pulled her to the shelter of an overhang. Lights from the security vehicle flashed in the alley in a nightmarish green. Her breath came in quick shallow gulps. The shuttle paused, hovering over the street. The shadows sharpened as the security vehicle directed its searchlights down. Arissa whimpered, shrinking into the scant safety of the overhang's shadow.

"This isn't about a broken employment contract, Tianna," Jolar growled in her ear. "Tell me before they get here."

"I can't!"

"Whatever it is, I promise—I *promise*—I'll help you. But I need to know what I'm dealing with!"

"No!"

"Damn it, come on! They're landing!"

He was right. The TelSec shuttle was touching down. The officer inside was looking right at them.

"I'll help you," he insisted. "Just *tell* me."

Jolar was warm against her back, his strength curled around her as he held her, the roughness of his cheek brushing her temple.

"I'm—" Her voice cracked. "I'm a telepath."

Two

He froze, his sense reverberating with shock and horror. "You're a seer?"

"You said—I helped you!" Arissa's eyes stung. "Just let me go!"

He wavered, indecisive, fearful.

"No," he said hoarsely. "It's too late."

The TelSec officer was out of the shuttle now.

"Damn you!" Arissa's fists clenched. "I should have left you back there. I should have let you die!"

Jolar gave her a shake. "Shut up, godsdamn it! I need to think!"

Arissa flinched as the TelSec officer shone his handheld light on them.

"Hands where I can see them!" The officer took a few steps toward them, his blaster in his hand. "Both of you!"

"It's all right!" Jolar shouted. "I'm the one who called you."

The brightness made her eyes water and made the pain in her head double.

"I'm going to let go of you," Jolar hissed in her ear. "*Don't* run, understand? He'll shoot you if you do. Just put your hands up. I'll handle this."

Handle it? Didn't he know she could feel his fear?

He eased his hands off. She hadn't realized how tightly he'd held her, how cold the night air was, until he moved away.

He faced the TelSec officer, his hands held up.

"Tianna," Jolar prompted and Arissa shakily raised her hands.

"Either of you armed?" the TelSec demanded.

"My blaster is holstered," Jolar pointed out. "And I don't have any other weapons."

Arissa cringed as the TelSec's light fell on her again.

"You?"

"She's not armed," Jolar said.

"I'm not asking you, am I? I'm asking *her*," the TelSec officer snapped as he approached. "You, miss—you armed?"

Her mouth dry as dust, Arissa shook her head.

The TelSec looked over Jolar's uniform. "Fleet, huh?" He threw a derisive glance at Arissa that made her cheeks hot. "Guess I don't need to ask what you're doing in this part of the capital. Don't you fleet types like to keep to the upper city pleasure houses for downtime?"

Jolar narrowed his eyes. "I came here to meet a friend."

The TelSec glanced at Arissa again. "Right." He flicked off the light and hooked it to his belt, lowering his blaster but keeping it unholstered as he pulled a scanner from his pocket. "Let's see who you are, Fleet."

He passed the red light over Jolar's right eye.

The officer glanced at the display. "d'Tural, Jolar, Commander. Zartan," he read. "Looks like you are cleared for that weapon you're carrying." The TelSec smirked. "Guess I'll let you keep the blaster after all."

"Thanks," Jolar muttered.

"You can put your hands down, Commander." The TelSec holstered his blaster and turned to Arissa. "Now, you."

Arissa gave a tiny whimper as the scanner swung her way.

Jolar blocked the instrument with his hand. "You can't scan her. She's injured, see? Her eyes are hurting too."

The TelSec's mouth tightened. "I need a scan."

"I'm telling you, you *can't*. Not if she's got a retinal injury." Jolar shifted his weight, now partially shielding her from the TelSec. "She needs medical attention, damn it. The fleet medcenter can give you her info later."

Why does he want so badly to take me there?

There was a tense pause.

"I'm marking down that I'm delaying the scan for medical reasons," the officer grumbled finally, pocketing the scanner. "But the doc's gonna need to—Wait, the fleet medcenter? You're telling me *she's* fleet too?"

"No," Jolar gritted out. "*I'm* fleet but *she's* pregnant so that's where I'm taking her."

The man snorted. "Sure it's yours, Fleet?"

"Yes," Jolar growled and Arissa blinked at his lack of hesitation. "Are you going to put *that* in your report?"

"Bit more interested in why there's a body back there." He jerked a thumb toward the alley. "You want to tell me what happened?"

"I met a friend for a drink," Jolar began. "I was walking back to—"

"She didn't go with you?" The TelSec speared Arissa with a look, his mind darkening with suspicion.

"No," Jolar said coldly. "We met up afterwards."

The TelSec narrowed his gaze. Finally, he gave a short nod.

"The man pushed me into the alley, he didn't see Tianna behind him. He pulled a blaster. Tianna distracted him and I shot first. Then I called TelSec."

"Why didn't you stay with the body?"

"Tianna was frightened. She ran off, I went after her. We were on our way back to meet you."

"Did you know the man?" He glanced at Arissa. "Either of you?"

"If I ever met him I don't remember it," Jolar answered.

The TelSec looked at her. Arissa shook her head and pain shot through it..

"You say he pulled a blaster," the man continued. "What did he want?"

"Money for chemicals probably. He had his blaster pointed at me, he was going to fire. I didn't have any choice. I need to get her to medical," Jolar said straightening. "You know where to find me."

The TelSec gave a nod in the direction of the other shuttle. "I'll get our medic to—"

"She needs a *doctor*, not some Sec officer with a first aid kit. Take us to the fleet medcenter."

Something about Jolar's glare—or maybe the clipped aristocratic tone of someone used to being obeyed—got the Telsec to pull out his communicator.

"Let me clear it," the man muttered, stepping away.

Arissa was trembling, her breath coming in short, quick bursts.

"Hold on," Jolar murmured, taking her cold hand in his strong grip. "Just a couple more minutes, okay, Tianna?"

His hand was warm around hers, his thumb lightly stroking her skin. She suddenly remembered he'd wanted her before he knew.

The TelSec turned back and nodded. "I'm authorized to take you to the fleet base."

"No!"

"Yes," Jolar said deliberately, glaring at her. "We need a ride to Fleet Sector Xan. To take you to the medcenter."

Voluntarily get into a security transport? Is he insane?

He still held her hand, his pull gentle but insistent. "Come on, Tianna. He's taking us to the fleet medcenter. It'll be all right."

He meant it.

"Jolar, I—I can't—"

His vivid eyes narrowed. "Do you want me to carry you, sweetheart? I will."

He *really* meant *that*.

She took clumsy steps forward and the TelSec slid the shuttle door open. Jolar put his hand on the small of her back and gave her a gentle push inside. Arissa wrinkled her nose. The shuttle's interior smelled artificial, heavily fragranced with some awful fake floral scent. She scooted over on the seat as Jolar sat next to her.

The TelSec slid the door shut, trapping her inside.

"Please—"

"*Quiet*," Jolar hissed.

The TelSec was already taking the controls. He spoke into his comm unit looking towards the other shuttle. "Yeah, lifting off now. Should be back in twenty or so. Right, thanks."

Arissa gripped the seat as they rose, her stomach lurching at the sudden movement. It had been nearly eight months since she'd ridden in a shuttle. Not since—

Jolar frowned. "Tianna?"

The TelSec glanced back at them. "She's not going to throw up back there, is she? I just had it cleaned."

"My head hurts," Arissa said faintly.

Unexpectedly gentle, Jolar pulled her close against his big body, drawing her head to his shoulder, encircling her in the warmth of his arms.

"Hang on," he murmured. "We'll be there in a few minutes." He stroked her hair, his hand cradling the back of her head, his cheek against her temple. "It's going to be okay."

She closed her eyes. *Gods, he smells so good.*

A tingle of desire.

Quickly crushed.

She could feel the sudden tension in his body as he turned away to look out the window. The city was speeding by below as the TelSec officer joined the airlanes, the neighborhoods showing more green space as they became more respectable.

It was a silent trip, neither man interested in small talk. The shuttle ride roiled her stomach but it was far too soon that the TelSec decreased speed.

"I'm going to drop you at the gate and—"

"No," Jolar said. "Send them my ID scan. Tell them to clear us through to land at the medcenter."

The TelSec glanced back, then shrugged and lifted the communicator to hail the gate.

Jolar's tense vibration uncoiled a bit when the gate gave clearance. He pulled away from her before the shuttle touched down and was out of the vehicle as soon as the door opened.

It was full dark now and the well-lit neat square around them was a study in straight lines and uninspired landscaping.

A military base? How is this better than a TelSec station?

Jolar looked at her sitting frozen in the shuttle. "Come on, sweetheart."

He's afraid too.

He held his hand out. "Let's get you taken care of." His eyes narrowed, his anxiety buffeting her. "Come *on*, Tianna. The officer wants to leave."

Arissa swallowed and put her hand in his.

Jolar nodded his thanks to the TelSec officer as she climbed out. He urged her back as the man closed up the shuttle and lifted off.

She clutched his arm. "You can't let a doctor examine me! My records—I never had the full medical scan. They'll do one and—they'll find—"

"I know," he said tightly. "Just be quiet."

Even with her senses crying out that he was committed to protecting her Arissa couldn't get her feet to move. Jolar fairly had to drag her into the gleaming white and silver medcenter.

The fleet emblem shone on the doors, on the walls, on the blue medtech uniform of the young man who greeted them.

"Commander." The medtech's eyes flicked toward Arissa and his eyebrows raised, just a touch. "How can I help you?"

"Call Doctor de'Sar," Jolar said. "Tell her it's urgent."

The medtech's glance took in her threadbare clothes, her face, where she'd been hit.

"Doctor de'Sar is not on duty tonight, sir." He was already looking at the datapad in his hand. "But Doctor Yuseh—"

"I know she's not here," Jolar interrupted. "That's why you're going to call her, Lieutenant. *Now*."

The man blinked and his mouth tightened. "Yes, sir." He tapped on his screen, his eyes scanning the response. "I've relayed your message. Doctor de'Sar has confirmed she's on her way. Would you care to have a seat?"

Arissa glanced uneasily at the bright, clean, empty waiting room.

"No," Jolar said. "Jensah has an exam room off her office. We'll wait for her there."

The man straightened. "I really don't think that—"

"What part of this conversation makes you believe I'm interested in your opinion?" Jolar's eyes were blue ice.

The man's nostrils flared, his tone clipped. "Follow me."

He came around the desk and led them through double doors into the main part of the medical building. The place was like a shiny white labyrinth, the lift, the doors, *everything* required the medtech to use his security pass to open.

How could she get out again?

Would she ever get out again?

The medtech led them into a cold, antiseptic-smelling room. Medical equipment was neatly laid out beside the exam table. The sharp lines of the well-lit military base below were visible through the room's one-way windows.

"All right," the man began. "Let's get a look at your records then we can—"

Arissa darted back, twisting away to cover her face as he brought the scanner up.

Jolar instantly moved to stand in front of her. "Doctor de'Sar will treat this patient. You're dismissed."

"Sir, if you let me get a scan then the young woman can change into—"

"You're *dismissed!*"

The medtech's face tightened. "Yes, *sir!*" He tossed the scanner back on the table then turned on his heel and left, the door sliding shut behind him.

Jolar blew his breath out and ran his hand through his hair. He glanced back at her. "You can sit down now."

Arissa shifted her feet. Standing made her feel safer.

"Suit yourself." He dropped into a chair and rubbed a hand over his eyes. "What a day." He looked at her, his anger sharp and hot, his fear like cold spikes. "Guess I don't have to tell *you* about it, do I? You already know."

"I can't read your thoughts," Arissa flared.

Anger darkened his face. "You said you were a—"

"It's not like that!"

He glared at her for a long moment then a puzzled frown replaced the scowl. "You didn't hear any of that, did you?"

"You were trying to *think* at me? I just told you I can't do that."

There was a pulse of surprise from him. "I just thought—"

"What?" she demanded. "That I was lying?"

"Well, what *can* you do, damn it?"

She folded her arms. "You're angry, embarrassed, suspicious, probably wondering if I'm just crazy. When you were staring down that man's blaster, you were afraid but more outraged at the unfairness of it, that you were going to die without knowing *why*. When you shoved that money in my hand, you were angry at yourself because you wanted very badly to fuck me, knew you shouldn't, and knew you were going to anyway."

His lips were colorless. "Gods," he breathed. "You really are a—"

The door slid open and Jolar shot to his feet.

The white-haired woman took a surprised half step back, catching the edge of the doorway. "Good evening, Jolar." She tilted her head. "I didn't mean to startle you."

"No, I'm—" Jolar cleared his throat. "Good evening, Jensah."

She offered Arissa a warm smile. "Well, now, is this my patient?" She shrugged out of her jacket and laid it over the back of a chair, then raised the light level over the exam table.

"This is Tianna," Jolar mumbled. "She's, uh—hurt."

"I can see that lump from here." Jensah ran sanitizing cleanser over her hands and dried them. "Come sit down, Tianna. Let me take a look at you."

The woman's compassion, her patient curiosity, was like a balm. Arissa edged closer and perched on the edge of the exam table.

She started when the woman's gentle fingers touched her chin to tilt her face up.

"I just want to see a little better," Jensah soothed. "Well, that *is* quite a lump, young lady. Did you black out?"

Arissa shook her head.

"Any nausea? Dizziness? No? Headache? Yes, indeed," she smiled kindly at Arissa's nod. "I'm not surprised. Well, let me take a quick look at your records while you go change into an exam gown and—"

Arissa flinched away as Jensah brought the scanner up. Jolar took a quick step forward.

"Jensah," he said. "You have to treat her without an ID scan, without any record made."

Jensah frowned a little, lowering the scanner, her curiosity rising in pitch. "Ah, well, I'm sure you know that whatever happens here is confidential." She glanced at Arissa. "Jolar, whatever your relationship with this young woman, you can rely on my discret—"

"No, she's not—" Jolar colored. "You can't scan her."

Jensah shifted her weight. "Jolar, it would be irresponsible of me not to access available medical records before I treat her."

"You owe me, Jensah." Jolar's said sharply. "You owe my family a great deal."

"Yes, Jolar." Jensah's sense cooled. "I haven't forgotten."

He glanced at Arissa. "Well, this is enough to wipe out that debt and put me firmly in yours."

There was a pulse of surprise and her interest reverberated. "I see. What exactly are you asking here?"

"That you treat her but make no record of it. If you have to access her ID—" He held his hand up to cut off Arissa's protest. "You do it in such a way that the request is encrypted. There can't be any record she was here."

"What you just asked me to do is highly suspect." Jensah folded her arms. "I'm beginning to wonder if this will cross into illegal."

Jolar nodded. "Yes, it will. Very, very illegal."

"Goodness, Tianna." Jensah looked round at her. "What have you done?"

"It's Arissa," she whispered. At his surprise and hurt she met Jolar's eyes. "My name is Arissa."

Three

"Oh, my *gods*," Jensah breathed as the results of the full scan displayed on the screen.

"It's true then?" Jolar asked tightly. "She's a seer?"

"If I hadn't . . . Look there, the activity in the pineal gland, the development in the front portion of the corpus callosum. Yes. Yes, it's true."

Arissa shrank back. They were looking at her like a bug under a microscope.

Jensah shook her head, tapping at her datapad. "I've got to show this to Doctor Gardi in Neurobiology! Gods, when he sees—"

"No!" Jolar grabbed her wrist. "You can't show this to anyone."

Her head came up. "Jolar, I don't think you realize—I mean, the opportunity to study one of them—a *live* subject, not a postmortem or preserved brain!"

Arissa caught her breath.

"She's a person, not a specimen!" Jolar flared.

"But the opportunity to—" Jensah shook her head. "I know a number of others in the scientific community would welcome this chance. I'm sure an exception could be made for just *one* to be kept alive for research purposes. I'm sure there's a way . . . Navik Station. Yes, the sealed research facility orbiting the outpost at Rusco. Surely if we can keep blood plague samples sealed there, we could certainly contain a seer!"

Arissa gripped the edge of the table to keep upright.

"Are you even listening to yourself?" Jolar demanded. "What kind of life would she have?"

"She would *have* a life," Jensah said sharply. "Look at her now, in tattered summer weight clothes and suffering from malnutrition. Wouldn't you—*Arissa*—rather live in a comfortable, safe facility where all your needs were seen to? Where you would be fed and cared for?"

"Like a lab animal?" Arissa cried. "No, I festering well *wouldn't!* I'd rather fuck strangers in the back alleys of the marketplace!"

Jensah's mouth thinned. "Well, I don't think you are being very sensible." She scowled up at Jolar. "Or you either. What do you intend to do with her now? Give her some money and throw her back into the street? Sooner or later TelSec is going to pick her up, you know. And what do you think *they'll* do to her?"

"I don't know what I'll do," Jolar said tightly. "But I'm not going to let them execute her and I didn't bring her here so you could turn her into a science experiment." He glanced at the clock. "I need to see Dacel. I'm already late."

"Dacel?" Jensah frowned. "You're not thinking of sending her to Zartan?"

"I just said, I don't know yet." He glanced at Arissa. "Give us a minute, Jensah, okay?"

The unhappy doctor left, letting the door of her adjacent office slide shut behind her.

Arissa tucked her hair behind her ears. The doctor had already treated her head injury, and her bruises and scrapes. They had given her some jinja juice and a protein bar but she had insisted on changing back into her own clothes.

"I have to go for a little while, Arissa," Jolar said gently.

Arissa rolled her eyes. "Yeah, I heard you. And really, you don't have to use such small words, Jolar. I'm telepathic, not stupid."

His face flushed. "Sorry. Gods, I really don't know how to talk to you." His blue eyes were anxious. "I *do* have to go now. Will you be okay here till I get back?"

"Sure. Maybe I'll make Doctor de'Sar happy and run some mazes for her."

He gave a short laugh then brushed a ringlet away from her face with surprising tenderness. "I won't be long. We'll figure this out, I promise. Okay?"

He was worried about her. His fingers lingered on her cheek and she realized at some point her resentment of him—his easy, secure existence—had simply wisped away to nothingness.

But she couldn't trust him.

She couldn't trust anyone.

Arissa looked away. "Sure."

"You look tired." He pulled a folded blanket from the shelf. "Why don't you lie down for a while? I've got a house not far from here. I have to—But maybe we'll go there just for tonight."

"I dropped your money," Arissa said sharply. "Back in the alley."

His mouth twitched. "Don't worry about it. I've got more."

Arissa toed her shoes off while Jolar shook out the blanket. It smelled faintly of sanitizing soap. She spread it over her legs, then scooted back on the exam table and pulled the blanket up.

He lowered the light levels, self-conscious and awkward as he tucked the blanket around her. He laid his hand on her shoulder for a moment. "Get some rest, Arissa. I'll be back for you as soon as I can."

"Jolar?"

He stopped in the doorway, his hair a brilliant gold in the light streaming in from the hall.

"Thanks," Arissa said. "You know, for helping me."

He gave a quick smile, dazzling in its genuine warmth. "Jensah is right next door if you need anything. I'll wake you when I get back."

Arissa curled up on the exam table and closed her eyes. She heard the door slide shut behind him.

She focused on Jolar, felt him pause to speak with the doctor, followed as the crackles and spikes of his worried rushing grew distant . . .

Arissa's eyes snapped open.

She slid off the table and in quick order had her feet back in her slippers.

With her concussion treated and food in her stomach she was thinking clearly again.

She'd bet a princess's jewels she couldn't break *into* this place in a hundred years. But getting out should be easy. Fire, gas leak, attack on the base, they wouldn't risk locking people in the medcenter. The lift needed a pass but the stairs would probably have to stay unlocked for emergencies.

But just in case. . .

Arissa pulled the security pass from her pocket. Her lip curled. Easy enough, slipping it from the jacket Jensah had tossed aside while they argued about locking her up on a space station with the fucking blood plague.

Dacel's gray eyes were pained. "Do you have any idea what you're asking of me, Jolar?"

At least he hasn't said no.

From where he stood before the Zartani councilor's desk, Jolar looked out the window of the office at the lights of the fleet base below.

"I owe her a life debt," Jolar said. "You're Zartani, you know what this means to me, what my obligation is to her."

"And you're sure she's a seer? I don't think there's been one detected in almost sixty years. If there's any chance she isn't . . ."

Jolar's thoughts flashed to her, her frightened eyes, her thin, worn clothes. She was too delicate, too innocent looking to be—

What she is.

"I was there when Jensah read the test results. There's no doubt. She's a telepath."

Dacel rubbed his hand over his face and Jolar felt a stab of guilt at adding to Dacel's many burdens. He couldn't help but notice his friend's hair had gone all silver in the last few months. He showed every one of his sixty-odd years tonight and his dark, formal shirt was too loose, as if his worries were affecting his appetite as well.

Jolar closed his eyes briefly. "I gave her my word. It's a matter of honor."

"Perhaps if you provided her with some money," Dacel suggested, spreading his hands, "I could arrange to have her taken quietly off-world . . ."

Jolar could almost see her, apprehended, sobbing, her eyes squeezing shut in terror as a TelSec placed the muzzle of his blaster against her forehead to fire.

"There's nowhere in Tellaran space she'll ever be safe," Jolar said hoarsely. "Money, sending her off-world—it'll just delay her inevitable execution. And you know it doesn't satisfy my debt, Dacel, not by a long shot."

Dacel tapped his fingers on the top of his desk, like he always did whenever he was weighing something carefully.

"The mission to Sertar—this is vital, Jolar. Your cover has been established, the house on Aylor has been purchased, all the pieces painstakingly put in place to make your role convincing. I don't have to tell you what's at stake."

"Someone tried to kill me tonight," Jolar reminded. "This wasn't a robbery, this wasn't some biter scrambling for money to get his next sartac measure—this was an assassin. I was up against a wall with a blaster pointed at my chest before I even knew he was there." He met his friend's eyes, willing him to understand. "She came into that alley *after* we did. She could have kept going, even slipped back out and left me to die, but she didn't. A seer, subject to termination on discovery, and she still didn't walk away. She almost got herself killed in that alley tonight—for *my* sake. She's the only reason I'm standing here now. She saved me, Dacel, and risked her life twice over to do it."

"This man, the Utavian—he knew you by name?"

"And I can't remember the last time I went to that section of Xan-Tellar. Which also means he knew where I would be and when."

Dacel's mouth tightened. "Who else knew you would be there?"

"Half the staff near my office knew I was meeting Tasan for a drink tonight before he shipped out," Jolar said shortly. "That's not counting anyone who could have sliced in to my files and checked my calendar."

Dacel shook his head. "I hope Tasan didn't have a hand in it. I know he's a friend."

"Tasan's not that careless," Jolar said dryly. "Once he has a job to do, he follows through. Tasan would double check to make *sure* I was dead and, if I wasn't, he'd take care of it personally."

"Maybe sending you to Sertar is too dangerous now," Dacel murmured. "If someone knows where I'm sending you and why . . ."

"She can help me." Jolar leaned forward, his hands splayed on the surface of the desk. "She's a godsdamned *seer*, Dacel! If Kav had her with him he might still be alive. Think of the advantage I'll have!"

Dacel raised his eyebrows. "You sure she'll be willing to help you?"

"She doesn't have much choice, does she? If I can offer her an ID, a non-telepath one in exchange . . ."

Dacel slumped back in his chair. "I'm having trouble keeping track of just how many laws we'd be breaking. Concealing a seer from the proper authorities, forging an ID, deleting official records . . . I'm not even sure I have the resources to make this happen."

"I can help with that," Jolar said grimly, straightening. "I'll pull in every favor I'm owed to put this together." His stomach wrenched as he regarded the Zartani councilor. Dacel was more than a mentor; the man was almost a second father to him. "I know asking this of you strains the limits of friendship."

Dacel waved it away. "Our friendship isn't on the line here. But I wouldn't *be* a friend if I didn't remind you of the very real danger to you."

Jolar gave a short laugh. "That she'll fuck with my brain, scramble me so I don't know what's what."

"It's not a joke."

His life debt to her made it an imperative he help her. Tradition—and sacred honor—demanded her life for his and his debt wouldn't be satisfied till he knew for certain she was safe. Everything in him was screaming at him to protect her. He could almost still feel the soft skin of her cheek under his fingers . . .

Jolar sank into one of the chairs in front of Dacel's desk, the leather creaking as he sat. "No," he said quietly. "It's not."

"The New Order eradicated the seers for a reason. The damage they do to a person's mind is serious, Jolar. It can be irreversible."

He should be afraid. In the two centuries since the Tellaran royal house fell, every historical accounting, every novel and holo, depicted seers as ruthless, mind-devastating monsters.

So why can't I believe that of her?

Jolar suddenly recalled sitting cradled at his father's side as a boy, the comforting scent of his father's study, of polished dalsawood and leather around him, the weight of the ancient book of paper and binding spread across his lap. Zartan's bright afternoon sun lit dust particles suspended in the air and, to his young eyes at least, echoed the lost magic of the old Realm. Over and over Jolar would trace the smooth parchment under his chubby, child's fingers, looking at the gilded illustrations, captivated as his father recounted stories of the princes and honored seers of the court and a king who ruled over a golden age . . .

Jolar sighed inwardly.

Maybe it's just Father and his fanciful tales.

But maybe I just want more than anything to believe that she's really just a frightened young woman, lost and alone.

Jolar passed his hand over his eyes at the protective impulse. *Oh, hells, I really should be afraid.*

And she's not the only obligation I have to honor.

"I understand the risks," he said quietly.

Dacel made one final tap on his desk. "All right. She'll get the non-telepath ID, a good amount of money and her freedom, but *only* if she helps you—truly helps—or she gets nothing. Make sure she understands." Dacel's gray eyes went hard. "Make sure you do too, Jolar. If she impedes your mission in any way—"

"She won't." Jolar hardened his jaw. "My first duty is, as always, to the Realm."

And whatever crazy thoughts I'm having about her, whatever this insane attraction is, I can push them aside. I can focus on what I need to do.

She doesn't get to me.

Not ever.

His comm unit signaled and he pulled it from his pocket. "This is d'Tural."

"Jolar," Jensah's voice was grim. "We've got a problem."

Four

Arissa drew her legs to her chest and rested her cheek on her knee. Her cell contained the lumpy cot she sat on, a 'fresher unit and a sink. She'd been locked in here for hours. It was long past midnight now—maybe even the wee hours of the night. Exhaustion was dragging at her but she couldn't sleep.

Fleet Security had taken the stolen badge, her clothes and her shoes. The FleetSecs gave her too-large coveralls of cheap, itchy material to wear but they wouldn't give her a blanket against the chill. She was barefoot; the floor was too icy to rest her feet on and the overhead lights were annoyingly bright, but at least the FleetSecs took the wrist restraints off before they locked her in here.

The beige walls were bare and there were no windows to the outside. The cell door had a single thick window and every now and again one of the FleetSecs would appear there and peer at her through the plexisteel, but none entered or spoke to her. They wouldn't respond to her questions either. She wondered why they bothered to do a visual check at all. Surely she was being watched via security eye.

She wondered bleakly if the reason she was still alive was to give that doctor a chance to study a real live subject.

Execution or a lifetime of rooming with the blood plague? Hard to say which sounded worse, really.

Arissa raised her head.

Someone was coming for her. Someone with a mind as hard and cold as plexiglass in winter . . .

She swallowed back tears. She'd done a lot of that in the last eight months. Her parents had worked so hard, given up so much, just to keep her alive. She hadn't been able to survive alone for even a year.

She closed her eyes briefly. *I'm sorry. I tried.*

The door lock released and the heavy door slid open.

Arissa blinked.

"Surprised a seer," Jolar said from the doorway. "Guess not many people have ever gotten to say they did that."

He was alone and she couldn't sense the guards anywhere nearby either now. "What—what are you doing here?"

The anger in his sense glowed in his blue eyes. "You were supposed to wait for me. Did you think I wasn't coming back?"

"I knew you would," she said tightly. "I just wasn't sure what you would do when you did."

"Did it occur to you that whatever I was going to do, I might've wanted to do it *quietly?* You made a real mess for me tonight."

"I wasn't *trying* to get caught, you know. Your doctor friend must have found me gone and called the gate to stop me."

"I called the gate." His glance went over her. "Did they hurt you?"

"*You* called them?" she cried, on her feet now despite the frigid duracrete floor. "*Why?*"

"Because tracking you down if you got off the base would take more time than I have. What the hells were you thinking?" he demanded. "Running like that?"

Arissa narrowed her gaze. "I was thinking, *I need to get the fuck out of here!*"

"And then, what? Where were you going?"

She threw her arms out. "To the market! Who cares?"

"Why? Is someone waiting for you there? I know it's not your parents. They've been dead for months."

Tears stung her eyes. "Yes."

"So, is there someone? Someone you were going back to?"

"Why? So you can send TelSec after them?"

His jaw worked for a moment. "Does anyone else know about . . . about you?"

"My uncle on Apovia knows." She pushed the wild curls behind her ears. "Feel free to hurt *him* all you want."

"I take it you aren't close."

"Close!" She gave a bitter laugh. "He came to tell me my parents were dead and in the same breath gave me 'til morning to clear out. No heirs, of course, except him."

"Because you're supposed to be dead too. I saw the ID scan the FleetSecs took—Kassar, Arissa. Apovia. Died fifteen years ago, at age five."

She closed her eyes briefly. "Yes."

"Why?" he asked. "Why falsify the records to make you deceased?"

"Because I couldn't go to school. Because I couldn't have the telepath screen. No *child* means no *scans*, means no *questions*."

His expression echoed his appalled sense. "Your *parents* did that to you?"

"What were they supposed to do, Fleet? Hand me over to TelSec? Let me be dissected by people like your doctor friend?"

He ran his hand through his hair. "All right. Your uncle, but he won't be looking for you. Anyone else? Anyone on Tellar who will miss you? Who will come asking questions?"

"Why do you care?"

His nostrils flared. "I don't have time for this! Answer the question or I leave you here right now."

She studied him for a moment then wiped her nose with the back of her hand. "I owe my landlady back rent on the room," she said sullenly. "She's probably already sold everything I left behind and re-rented it."

"Anyone else? Someone who—A friend, maybe?"

"I don't have friends," she said hoarsely. "There's no one."

"No one to pay off." He gave a nod, his tension easing a bit. "No one to keep quiet."

Arissa gave a short, bitter laugh. "Glad I could neaten everything up for you, Fleet."

"You should be. I'm leaving for Sertar in an hour and you're going with me." He gave a humorless smile. "You're going to help me."

Arissa stared. "Help you? Help you do *what?*"

"We really don't have time for this." He indicated the door with a nod. "Come on."

"And I'm just supposed to believe you? Just go along with whatever this is? How do I know you're not going to lock me up with the blood plague—or something worse?"

He pulsed with anger. "Arissa—pretty name by the way, I like it better than Tianna—the plain fact is this: you're going with me and you're going to help me because if you *don't* they're going to haul you out of this cell in a few minutes and put a blaster bolt though your brain."

Her mouth parted.

He held her gaze. "So I need your answer right now—are you coming with me or not?"

She wrapped her arms around herself. "Why? You know what I am. Why do anything for me? Why help me?"

"If you were Zartani you'd understand but to put it simply: you gave me my life and I owe you yours. But I've bought you much more than that." Jolar reached into his pocket and pulled out an ID scanner. "Come here."

Arissa recoiled. "What's that for? You already have my scan."

"Here's the first rule if you want to live, Arissa: you do what I tell you when I tell you. Now come *here*."

She took a few reluctant steps closer, watching him warily.

He held the scanner up near her eye and caught her chin before she could turn away. "Don't flinch. It's a simple ID scan. People do it every day, several times a day. It doesn't hurt and no one is afraid of them."

Arissa willed herself not to move as he flashed the red light in her eye.

He glanced at the reading. He turned the scanner so she could see the display.

She blinked. It was her face, her as she was now, not as a little girl, and there was no black stripe above her image to mark her deceased.

"*Legan*, Arissa?" she breathed. "What is this?"

"That's your new name. Hope you like it, though doesn't much matter if you don't."

"My new—?" The breath rushed out of her lungs. "I have an ID? Will it—Will that show on all the scanners?"

"Oh, yes. System wide, absolutely authentic and official."

An ID, a real one, a non-telepath one? The possibilities, the safety, the *freedom* of it made her dizzy.

"You did that?" Arissa managed.

"No, I called in every favor and debt owed me to *make* that happen. I just burned through every bit of influence I've built up in the last ten years—goodwill that was intended to land me Zartan's place on the Tellaran council after I retired from the fleet. And," Jolar's eyes were blue ice. "For giving up my future I expect to be well paid in return."

"Oh." She glanced at the cot. A real ID in return for letting him have her? She couldn't afford to refuse, it didn't even occur to her to try. "You want—I mean, here or—?"

He burst out laughing and Arissa's face went hot.

"You couldn't fuck me enough to pay for this!" Jolar sobered. "No, that's not what I want from you. There's something on Sertar I have to do. Something important. Having a woman with me is actually a liability—unless she has a unique talent to bring to the table. *Your* talent."

She searched his face. "You need a telepath."

"*Want* one," he corrected. "I don't *need* one. Which means you do as you're told or your best hope is that Doctor de'Sar gets her longed-for opportunity to study one of you. Are we clear?"

Arissa swallowed. "Yes."

He held up the scanner. "This is a solid ID—unless something happens to me. Make sure *nothing* happens to me. Still clear?"

Her cheeks were burning. "Don't kill you in your sleep. Got it."

His sense was as cold as his eyes now. "Don't misunderstand me. If I think for a moment you've betrayed me, I'll put that blaster bolt in your head myself."

He was such a jumble of emotion she couldn't sort it all but just the words hurt. She blinked away the sudden sting of tears. "Sorry. I was—I was joking."

"Don't joke like that again."

She dropped her gaze.

"All right," he said finally. "You're going to shower and change. I have clothes for you. They might not fit perfectly or be what you like, but put them on anyway. Fix yourself up as best you can in twenty minutes."

Arissa frowned. "Why?"

"Because that's how much time I'm giving you," he said impatiently, turning away.

She pushed the curls out of her face. "Whatever you say, Commander."

His sudden anger hit her so hard she gasped.

"Don't *ever* call me that again," he snarled. "Understand?"

"I don't—I thought—" She shook her head. "Well, isn't that what you are?"

He gave her a narrow look. "Are you fucking with me? Or have you forgotten I know you're a seer?"

Arissa seethed. "Are you expecting me to read your every thought? Because it doesn't work like that. I *told* you. And if you want me to help you, you're going to have to tell me what you need me to do."

He huffed a sigh. "Fine. Part of our cover story is I never rose above lieutenant. I left the fleet five years ago when we moved to Aylor. Can you remember that? Because it's time to go."

She frowned. "We? Our cover story?"

"Yes, *we*. I'm Jolar Legan." He nodded toward the open door of the cell. "Your husband."

Five

"Stop fidgeting," Jolar hissed, his annoyance grating against her mind. "Damn it, what's wrong with you?"

Arissa gripped the arms of the seat, struggling not to give into panic. They had been on the transport for an agonizing half-hour already, she wasn't sure how much longer she could hold herself together. "I just…" she said faintly. "I don't like shuttles."

There was a pulse of dismay and then unexpectedly he softened. "Listen, just hang on, okay? We'll be docking in a few minutes. There's dozens of safety protocols the spaceport has to follow for a transport ship like this. This is safe."

"My parents' shuttle was supposed to be safe," she whispered hoarsely.

Her stomach rolled, her face felt numb. Any moment she was going to bolt screaming for the door. Everyone aboard the shuttle would look. Jolar would be furious. Maybe angry enough to send her back to her cell. And then they'd—

"Slow your breathing down. You're hyperventilating."

"I can't." Her throat was closing. "The other people onboard—It's too much. I can't shut them out!"

"All right." He took her hand, his skin very warm. He leaned his head against hers to murmur in her ear. "Try this. Can you concentrate just on me?"

She centered on him, so calm and confident beside her. *He* felt perfectly safe sitting here. She followed the pattern of his breathing, matching hers to his. Arissa felt her tense shoulders starting to fall.

His thumb stroked the back of her hand. "That's better." His warm breath against the delicate skin of her ear made her shiver. "Just relax."

"Okay." She closed her eyes. "Okay."

She felt a jolt of desire and his breath quickened against her ear.

She met his eyes, blinking at him.

His gaze was hot, hungry. He glanced at her mouth.

Suddenly he jerked back and dropped her hand.

Arissa directed her gaze straight ahead, still very aware of him beside her, the heat of his body, his still-quickened breath.

"We're docking," he muttered, getting to his feet.

The *Queen's Light's* pretty transport attendant hurried down the aisle to where he stood. She gave him a disapproving look. "Sir, for your safety, all passengers are requested to remain in their seats until the transport is fully docked."

He looked at her impatiently. "Even if the pilot's too drunk to fuck these transports are set for automatic link. I'm fine."

The attendant blinked. Her sense made it plain she wasn't used to men dismissing her so brusquely. A few of the passengers looked scandalized by his language and sharp tone, but one of the men across the aisle snickered.

She was supposed to be his wife. He was adamant that no one doubt that they were married.

What would his wife do?

"Jolar," Arissa said softly, reaching towards him but too shy to touch. "Maybe you should sit down."

His disbelieving stare was his only response. She shifted awkwardly, her cheeks warm under the gaze of the other passengers and the attendant.

Abruptly his nostrils flared and he fell into the seat next to her. He sprawled with his long legs stuck out and every line of his posture echoed the prickles of his annoyance.

"Women," the man across the aisle said jovially to Jolar as the attendant went back to her place. "They keep us tethered pretty tight, don't they?"

Jolar's gave the man a half-smile. "That's the truth." He gave her a narrow look. "Wouldn't have it any other way, though."

Arissa turned toward the window to avoid that hard blue gaze. The *Queen's Light* looked huge but Arissa had no experience by which to judge this cruiser. The shuttle that brought her to the capital from Apovia was one her uncle had gotten her transport on. Little larger than the vessel she was on now, that one had been meant for cargo. Her uncle's bribe had gotten her on and made sure she wasn't scanned.

She glanced uneasily at Jolar as they docked.

Is he regretting bringing me?

Arissa understood now what he meant when he said having a woman along would be a liability for him.

The pretty, pert attendant's attention lingered on Jolar as they disembarked. He drew admiring glances everywhere they'd been; Arissa was like a mud sparrow next to the iridescent beauty of a firehawk.

The clothes he'd brought her, a long, belted tunic and pants in a dull tan color, were new but did nothing to flatter her, and the top bagged noticeably at the chest. Before she'd left Apovia her breasts had been the one thing that had drawn plenty of male attention—they seemed tiny now with how thin she'd become. The new brown slippers were a little too big and she felt clumsy and graceless walking in them.

A porter offered directions but Jolar shifted his weight before the man finished speaking and nudged her toward the lifts.

They got on with other passengers and briefly Arissa threw her focus at them. Most were impatient to get to their quarters, irritable as if all this luxury were not enough to satisfy. Only one—a young girl, possibly twelve or so—regarded the ship with the same wide-eyed awe she did.

Ducking her head, Arissa followed Jolar off the lift. He stopped at one of the suite entrances and, with a press of his palm to the reader, opened the door.

"Lights," he said.

Instantly the cabin was bathed in soft warm light. A large arched window filled most of the far wall and framed a breathtaking view of Tellar and two of its moons. The living area, ringed by cream colored semicircular couches, made a cozy conversation space. To the left lay a small dining room with food station and drink bar.

"We're staying *here*?" Arissa breathed.

Surprise and annoyance bloomed in his sense. "Something wrong with it?"

"*Wrong?* Gods, are you kidding?"

Her fingers trailed the smooth wall as she went down the short hall to explore. The bedroom was done in dark, rich greens. Another viewport showing Tellar dominated the wall next to the wide bed. Through a doorway lay a small neat dressing room with a vanity table, mirrors, and valet-closets to keep all the clothes in it clean and ready for wearing. Jolar's luggage had already been delivered and sat just inside the dressing room door. She didn't have anything but the clothes she was wearing.

Swirled in white and green Novician marble, the bathroom gleamed. A wide shower had showerheads on both sides and above. Folded towels waited stacked into warmer shelves.

"What's the matter?" Jolar asked when she returned to the living area.

"Is there another bedroom?"

"No," he fairly growled. "Because we're *married*. Married people sleep together, Arissa. I'm sure you've shared a bed before."

"Of course."

She looked out the viewport, at the plush carpet, at the wall.

Anywhere but at him.

He sighed. "Are you hungry? There were some selections ready in the food station so I put those out. I wasn't sure what you might—"

As soon as the mouthwatering smell reached her she was at the table and lifting the covers away to reveal the steaming contents.

She attacked the first dish, not even bothering to use a fork. Savory and hot, with some kind of cooked dough in the gravy. Gods, when had she had tasted anything so good?

She stood there, her fingers stinging with the heat, closing her eyes as she chewed. Her fingers were already dug into the second platter when his stunned sense filtered through her ravenous hunger.

Jolar's face was white and shocked.

Mortified, Arissa dropped her gaze and wiped her mouth with the back of her hand.

"Sorry." Fumbling she grabbed a napkin to clean the sauce from her fingers.

"No, it's—" He cleared his throat. "It's all right. Go ahead and eat, Arissa."

Shaky and embarrassed, she sat at the table, put a clean napkin on her lap and, ducking her head, used the utensils to fill a plate for herself, her cheeks burning.

He took a seat across from her but took nothing for himself. She kept her head down while she ate.

She wished he would stop watching her.

She scraped a plate clean in minutes and glanced longingly at the serving dishes.

"It's all right," he said quietly. "Take all you want."

She tucked a curl behind her ear and filled her plate again.

"Thank you," she mumbled when he put a glass of ice water next to her. She took a couple swallows. She finished another plate and only stopped because she couldn't manage another bite. She put her hand to her stomach, shifting a little against the fullness.

"You okay?" he asked.

She gave a quick embarrassed smile. "Just ate too much too fast. I haven't—It's been a long time since I've seen so much food."

"Do you want anything else?"

"I do. I can't right now." It took an effort to meet his eyes. "I'm really sorry."

"No, *I'm* sorry. I should have gotten you something hours ago back at the spaceport." His gaze was serious. "Listen, whenever you're hungry—whenever—you tell me. You can eat whatever we have here any time. If we're out, I'll get you something and I'll make sure you have money to buy food for yourself if I'm not with you. I won't let you go hungry again. Okay?"

A rush of tears blurred her vision. "Okay."

He searched her face. "I know you must be frightened, wondering why I've brought you here."

She gave a short laugh. "A full meal and a real bed to sleep in? No vermin, no feeling someone weighing if it's worth it to rob me or rape me or kill me? You think this is frightening?"

"Yes, actually I do." He rubbed his hand over his eyes. "I have a lot to tell you but it's ship's afternoon; we've been up all night already. You look exhausted and I know I am. We should get a few hours' sleep at least before we go over it."

Arissa's heart sped up, but she could catch no sense that he felt at all awkward about them sharing the bed. Nor did he show any reluctance to strip off his clothes once they were in the bedroom.

Broad shouldered, Jolar seemed all warm golden skin and muscle. There was glimmer of blond hair over his chest and a darker line below his waist. On either side of his abdomen, the muscles of his groin created a vee before disappearing into his undershorts and her gaze dipped to follow the shape of him under that thin material.

He already had the blankets thrown back, one knee on the mattress to get into bed, when he noticed her standing awkwardly by the door.

"What's the matter?" he asked.

"Nothing." She found it very hard to look at him.

And very hard not to.

"I'm not going to fuck you if that's what you're worried about," he said sharply. He got in bed and pulled up the covers. She stayed where she was and he threw her an impatient look. "I need some sleep and so do you. Get in bed, Arissa."

She sensed he wouldn't hurt her, would never force himself on her. That wasn't the problem.

"I don't—" She crossed her arms over her chest. "I don't have a nightgown."

"So?"

Her face went hot. She couldn't just take off her clothes in front of him.

Could she?

"Damn it," Jolar muttered, then louder: "Lights off!"

The room went dark. Light reflecting from Tellar gave some illumination but barely enough for her to see the way to the bed.

"There," Jolar grumbled. "I'll buy you a pile of nightgowns after I've had some sleep. Now come to bed."

Arissa crept forward. Feeling along the edge, she got to her side of the bed. She toed her slippers off, lifted the tunic over her head and folded it, placing it on the floor beside the bed. She undid the fastening on the trousers and felt along the floor to put them on the tunic. That would leave her with only her underwear and her halter.

She slipped under the fresh, sweet smelling sheets. The bed was soft and cool as she settled the blankets over her. She curled up under the blankets, her heart hammering.

She jumped when he rolled toward her.

"Are you warm enough?"

"Yes," she whispered. "Thank you."

He sighed. The blankets slid as he shifted again.

She had never shared a bed with anyone and warmed the bed just by being in it. The turmoil of his mind gradually slowed, calmed. It was soothing just to be so close to him. After a time his sense settled and smoothed into sleep. She wished she'd had the courage to take off her clothes in front of him.

She closed her eyes and, after a moment, scooted a little closer.

Six

Arissa started awake. Panic sent her heart racing at the sight of the dark, unfamiliar room. She cast about with her seer's senses. Blue eyes flashed in her mind.

Jolar.

Feeling his presence in a room nearby, memory came rushing back. Arissa put her shaking hand over her face. She was in the bedroom of their suite on the *Queen's Light*, not cowering in a filthy rooming house in Xan-Tellar waiting for TelSec to track her down.

She stretched her awareness a little farther toward the living room, to Jolar, shyly touching the weight and heft of his mind—his pensiveness, his determination—drawing comfort from his shimmering depths.

A flutter came back at her.

Probably wondering how long I'm going to sleep.

She withdrew the contact and rubbed her eyes, wondering what time it was. They'd left Tellar's orbit sometime when she was sleeping and the viewport showed nothing but distant stars and empty space now. He felt like he'd been awake for a while, and the space next to her was cool to the touch.

Shower or eat first?

It was pure luxury to have the option at all.

The rooming house had a shared 'fresher and a weak shower with tepid water, and she'd gotten five minutes to wash yesterday before they'd left the fleet base. Food had become more scarce when she'd had to choose between eating and rent. Driven by desperation when the money she'd brought from Apovia ran out, she had seized on a drunken man's inattention and swiftly had his billfold secreted in her own pocket.

It had been a dizzying risk to take and made her ashamed too, imagining what her parents would think.

Maybe it would have been better to offer herself as an ornament. At least that was something for something.

And whatever Jolar's task for her, it was better than execution, better than starving in Xan-Tellar. She was safe, for now at least, with delicious food in the dining room and plenty of hot water in the marble bathroom.

After so many months of fear and hunger and filth, it was like a dream.

Shower first.

She reached out again, trying to gauge how impatient he was for her to get up, and yanked the blanket up to her neck just as he came in.

Jolar stopped in the doorway. "You're awake."

She tried to smooth her hair. It must be a wild mop now. "Yes." She cleared her throat. "What—how long did I sleep?"

"It's ship's morning now."

"Oh," she said, sitting up. "Sorry. You should have woken me."

His chagrin rippled. "Yes, well, why don't you get dressed? I've gotten you something to eat, then we can talk."

"About what you want me to do?" she asked quickly before he could go. "You said yesterday you would explain."

He hesitated. "Yes." He took a step back. "Tea or caf?"

"Oh, uh, tea, please."

The door closed behind him. Grabbing her clothes Arissa went into the bathroom, and winced when she saw her reflection. Her dark curls were as wild as she feared. Her skin looked as thin and pale as parchment, her black brows arched like frightened birds in flight.

She cleaned her teeth and washed her face, rubbing her chapped lips a little with a damp cloth in hopes of making them look better. She'd worn balm on her lips at home but had run out of it months ago.

A quick search of the bathroom yielded a lucky find and she was able to make her bare nails neat and presentable again with the complementary manicure tools. She smoothed her hair but didn't have any way of styling it or pinning it up. She put the tan tunic and pants back on, tied the belt, and examined the results in the mirror.

She sighed. Scrawny and still plain as a mud sparrow, but at least she was tidy.

Jolar's expression was pensive. His long legs stuck out in front of him as he sprawled in one of the dining room chairs, but he straightened and offered a smile as soon as he saw her.

"I thought you might be hungry again," he said with a nod at the dish-laden table.

She flushed, remembering her appalling manners yesterday.

He was already pulling off the covers. "I didn't know what you'd like so I ordered a bunch of different things."

He certainly had. The table was nearly full. Some of the selections were meat dishes, some traditional evening fare, some more usual for breakfast. A number of the selections were Apovian—including one of her favorites, fried hoss. A quick, nervous brush against his mind showed he was intentionally trying to put her at ease. Abashed by his unexpected thoughtfulness, she sat down and filled her plate. Jolar sat across from her but took nothing for himself.

She stopped, fork in hand. "Aren't you having any?"

"I've already eaten."

She frowned. There was a lot of food. "I can't eat all this."

"You don't have to. Eat what you want and we'll have the rest cleared away."

She fingered her fork for a moment. Throw all that away? It was enough to keep her for a week if she could save it.

"There's plenty to eat on this ship, Arissa," he said gently. "I promised, remember? I won't let you go hungry."

She nodded, embarrassed that so much of her thoughts showed on her face, and started on her meal.

He was watching her eat again.

"Why don't you tell me what you need to do?" she suggested, ducking her head.

"It can wait till you're done."

She finished a plateful in minutes. He poured her a cup of tea and catching the aroma she smiled widely.

"Gods, I can't remember the last time I had white tea." She took the cup he offered and inhaled the spicy, sweet fragrance. She took a sip.

"How long were you on Tellar?"

Her smile faded, the cup cradled in her hand. "I left home right after—almost eight months. My uncle put me on the first transport offworld he could get."

"I'm sorry about your parents," he said quietly.

"Thank you." Her eyes stung. "No one . . . You're the first person who's said that to me."

His sense grew heavy.

"I didn't mean—" she stammered. "I don't want you to regret saying something."

His blue eyes were guarded now. "I don't know how I feel about you being able to sense my emotions all the time."

"You feel vulnerable," she blurted, then flushed.

He went still. "Yes. Yes, I do."

"And uneasy," she added carefully.

"What a diplomatic way of saying you scare the piss out of me."

"I'm sorry." She looked at the cup in her hands. "I wish I didn't. I wish I didn't scare anyone. I wish there were no reason to be afraid of me."

He gave her a searching look. "What about your parents? They knew you longer than anyone. Were they afraid?"

"No." Hot tears blurred her vision. "They felt—but they were my parents, I guess it's just natural that they'd feel that way."

"What way?"

Her brow creased. "Proud."

He gave a half-smile. "Of course. When did they figure out that—well, that you're . . .?"

"*I* didn't even know," she said hoarsely. "I didn't understand other people couldn't feel things the same way I did. But my parents learned the truth shortly after I started primary. It was autumn, just turning cold, and our class was in the playpark when my teacher discovered her necklace missing. It was a tiny gold sercat amulet with bloodstone jewels for eyes. I thought the thing was hideous but she wore it every day. An heirloom, I guess. When she ordered us to look for it, I stomped over, said it wasn't fair that we weren't allowed to play when everybody knew the assistant instructor was only pretending to look, that she already had the necklace. I made such a scene that the teacher finally insisted the woman empty the pockets of her coat just to shut me up and—anyway, my father was called. He took me aside to speak to me, far in the corner of the park so no one could hear and questioned me. I told him that I'd known—*how* I'd known. That I didn't understand why everyone was pretending they couldn't feel it too. He—he was so afraid I started to cry. He insisted I tell the school administrator I'd *seen* the assistant put it in her pocket, even though I hadn't. The adminstrator tried to apologize but he shouted her down, told them he would not have his child educated in a place where they didn't properly screen their staff. He took me straight to my mother's office, she ran tests and—" She looked down at her hands. "They never let me go back to school."

"So, you know when someone is lying?"

"Sure. Why is that so important to you?"

He looked away.

"Sorry," she mumbled into her tea.

"No." He took a deep breath then squared his shoulders and met her eyes. "I need to get used to this."

"If there's—" She stumbled over the words, rushing to get them out. "If there's anything I can do to make it easier, tell me, okay? I don't want you to be afraid of me."

"I don't want to be either." She felt him weighing his words. "And I really need to trust you, Arissa."

"Because of what you need my help with? Because of what you need to do?"

"Yes." He leaned forward, his gaze steady. "And in return for your help you'll get a new non-telepath ID—one in your real name. You'll be provided for too, well enough to keep you comfortable for the rest of your life, if you're sensible with it. You'll be free to travel to wherever you please, to work or train for a profession if you like . . . once our work is completed."

"It sounds wonderful. Too good to be true, really," she admitted, her throat tight. "But what do you want me to do?"

"Right now I just want you to become Arissa Legan. Learn your role, make it automatic. Once I know you can handle that we can talk about the rest."

It was more than needing confidence in her playacting abilities—he didn't trust her. He was holding so much back but it wasn't as if she could refuse, no matter what he asked of her.

She gave a short nod. "Okay."

He stood. "I have some information for you to memorize."

She followed him the few steps into the living area, standing beside him as he retrieved the datapad he'd left on the table there.

He hesitated. "Can you read?"

"What the fucking hells is that supposed to mean?" she demanded, scowling. "Of course I can read!"

His face colored. "You said you didn't go back to school."

"That doesn't mean I wasn't educated! My mother was Director of Medical Arts at the university in Galt-Apovia. My father was a professor of comparative literature. I would put the depth and breadth of my education against yours any day. If had an ID I would have earned four advanced degrees—two in literature arts, one in neurochemistry and one in biomolecular engineering—before I was seventeen."

"I see."

She folded her arms. "So a *smart* telepath makes you *really* uneasy."

"I barely managed to earn one degree in contemporary arts by the time I was twenty." He gave a short, self-conscious laugh. "Maybe I'm just a little intimidated."

"By me?" But he was and she frowned. "Gods, why?"

"That you're better educated? Apparently brilliant? That you know what I'm feeling as soon as I feel it? Take your pick." He shook his head. "You say you can't hear my thoughts but damn, it sure seems like you can."

She shifted. "I can't."

He searched her face. "What's it like?"

"I don't know how to answer that." She gave a half-shrug, embarrassed. No one had ever asked her before. "I've never been any other way."

"Right," he said, shaking his head again. "Never mind."

"No, I—" She nipped her lip. "Have you ever swum in the ocean?"

He rippled with curiosity. "Yes."

"Well . . . it's like when you're in the water; it surrounds you and you can feel it moving. When the emotion is really strong, like anger, it's like the breakers hitting you hard. But happiness is like when you're past the breakers and warm water is moving around you, buoying you up. But some feelings, like anticipation, rustle instead, like the way leaves sound but you *feel* it. And they're all around you."

"But how can you tell which emotion it is?"

"You just—Here, give me your hand."

He put the datapad down and put his hand in hers. She turned it, holding it palm up.

She rubbed the fingers of her other hand over his palm

rapidly. "This what anticipation feels like."

Understanding lit his face. "Okay."

"And this," she said, lightly drumming the pads of her fingers on his palm. "Is a lot like curiosity."

She tapped her fingers quickly against his skin. "This is impatience." She used her nails, rubbing rapidly but not hard enough to scratch. "Annoyance." She stopped, considering. "Fear is jagged, sharp, fast and—It *feels* sour."

"What about other emotions? What do good ones feel like?"

She leaned down to flick a lock of her hair against his skin. "Shy but friendly." She stroked his hand to soothe and comfort. "Friendship." She thought of her parents and tenderly cradled his hand in hers. "This is what love feels like."

"Gods, it sounds amazing," he breathed.

"Desire is tingly, hot waves rolling around you." Her face warmed as she realized what she'd just said, how she still cradled his hand, how close they stood. She let go. "Good laughter is like tiny warm bubbles bursting against your skin."

His eyes were alight, his mind blooming with interest. "And that's all around you? All the time?"

She nodded. "But not usually one by itself, usually they're mixed or—I guess *layered* is probably the best word for it. And they often shift quickly."

"From the same person?" His brow creased. "Doesn't that get confusing? What if there's more than one person in the room? How can you tell who's feeling what?"

"How can you tell who's saying what?"

His mouth curved. "Fair enough. What about crowds then?"

"Crowds are hard. If I'm scared or tired or upset I have

even less tolerance. Sometimes it's too much." She tucked a curl behind her ear. "But you saw some of that on the shuttle."

"What was—" His shoulders tensed. "What was Tellar like for you?"

Arissa gave a short humorless laugh. "*Really* hard. People, at least where I lived in Xan-Tellar, were usually miserable. Hopeless. Angry. Lonely. Some of the men were even—"

A stab of—

He wouldn't meet her eyes now.

Anger and . . . what? Pain? No, something sharp *like* pain. "Jolar?"

He handed her the datapad, his gaze steady, cooler. "Here's the information you'll need to memorize. This is who you need to be."

She glanced at the screen. "Grew up on Apovia? That's convenient."

"Your accent."

"Right," she murmured. "No children. No family."

"Easier to keep straight."

She scrolled through the information and frowned. "This house, the one we're supposed to live in, was purchased only a month ago. Isn't that a little odd?"

"If anyone contacts the neighbors they'll hear that the house was purchased by someone from the southern continent. Furniture is being moved in now. Anyone contracted to go in or out will be told it's been bought by a young couple who'll move in shortly. It explains why none of the neighbors know us."

"I hope I'm a good decorator." Arissa gave a wry grin at the emotion she caught. "I'm kidding."

He gave a faint smile.

She scrolled through the rest of the information and offered the datapad back to him. "Okay."

Jolar made no move to take it, sending out little spikes of annoyance. "Arissa, I need you to memorize this."

"I did."

"You couldn't have. You looked at it once."

She extended it a little further toward him. "Test me."

"I don't—Fine." He took the datapad. "Where you were born?"

"Nethara Province, Apovia."

"Where did you go to school?"

"Ikkat Academy. I received Distinguished Distinction there before attending the First University on Aylor."

He shifted his weight. "Where did we meet?"

"At a fleet dance on Aylor, you were a sub-lieutenant then. I was on my final field studies for my university degree."

He scrolled through the information, asking her tiny details, the address of their first home, his mother's second name, the date he'd resigned from the fleet.

"Gods," he muttered, passing his hand over his eyes.

"It wasn't Ponga?" she asked, frowning. "The pet sercat you had growing up? I was sure it said 'Ponga'."

"No, you got it right. How did you do that?"

"What do you mean?"

"I mean, you read this *once* and you had it memorized. Can you always do that?"

"No, but this was easy. It took me a week to memorize the comparative biostructures of the Plantae genus."

"Okay," he said slowly, lowering the datapad. "I just . . . I didn't know you could do that."

Arissa's frown deepened. "Is it a problem?"

"Not at all." He ran his hand through his hair. "It's

great, especially for—it's *amazing*."

"Then why are you looking at me as if you're worried I'm going to sprout wings and fly around the room?"

He gave a short, unsteady laugh. "Because right now I'm not sure you can't."

"It's nothing special," she insisted. "My parents gave me schoolwork to get through and I couldn't watch any holodramas or read for entertainment 'til I was finished. I learned how to connect things to other things I already knew to get through it all faster."

"Handy skill to have."

"Well, how do you memorize things?"

"Festering slowly, I guess." He nodded at the datapad. "It took me a week of drilling to learn my new history. I still don't know all of yours yet, I'm going to have to study to get it down by the time we get to Sertar." He shook his head. "I can't believe how fast you learn."

"That's not learning," she objected. "That's memorization. Learning is when you can apply knowledge in a useful way." She gave a half-shrug. "That's what my father used to say, anyway."

"Smart man." His gaze flicked to the datapad in his hand, then around the room. "All right, well—" His glance went over her. "Since you got through everything I had planned for this morning in about five minutes, let's go get you some clothes."

Seven

Arissa let her breath out slowly as the saleswoman made a tiny adjustment to the skirt.

"What do you think, my dear?"

I think I feel ridiculous. I think the price of this thing could pay six months' rent in a much better neighborhood than the one I had in Xan-Tellar.

I think I am not going out there to stand in front of him with my breasts half uncovered like this.

"I don't know," Arissa hedged, pretending to consider the deeply plunging, nearly backless silver dress precariously held up by the tiniest of straps at her shoulders.

"Oh," the saleswoman cooed, gathering Arissa's hair and twisting it in her fingers. "With your hair up to show your neck. Oh, isn't that lovely?"

"I'm not sure this is . . . it's a little much for me to carry off."

"You know, there are excellent salons onboard," the woman said, smoothing Arissa's hair back down and pretending to be absorbed with the beaded detail on the skirt. "Maybe a haircut, perhaps some new cosmetics? A little eyebrow shaping to bring your eyes out?"

Arissa's face went hot. Her mother had always cut her hair, but it had been nearly nine months since the last time and her curls had gone shaggy. She didn't even own cosmetics and had never worn any besides a little tinted lip balm. Her whole life had been about hiding. Enhancing her appearance and trying to be attractive would have just made it harder to stay invisible. Arissa's mind went to all those holodramas she'd watched, the clothes, the make-up, how she'd longed to be like other girls while she was growing up . . .

Tears stung her eyes. "I'd *like* to. I mean, I always wanted to be pretty."

The woman met her gaze in the reflection, a tiny frown touching her brow. "You *are* pretty. And with just a little effort, you could be beautiful."

Jolar's blue eyes flashed in her mind and Arissa blinked the tears away. She reached out to find him growing ever more impatient in the little sitting area outside the boutique's dressing room.

Arissa swallowed. "Would you—I mean, I don't even know what to ask for—"

The woman gave her shoulders a gentle squeeze. "I'll make an appointment for you, shall I? I know one of the ladies just adores this sort of thing; she'll take you in hand."

She didn't have any money of her own so she'd have to ask Jolar, but—"Okay. Yes, please."

"I'll take care of everything. Your husband asked especially to see this one. Are you ready?"

Arissa took one more look at her reflection. She regarded her skinny, pale arms, the bones of her chest showing, her now tiny breasts half revealed by the plunging gown, and tried not to groan.

Jolar had to be nearly ready to quit. They'd been here for almost two hours now, working their way through dresses and tunics and pants for casual day things, and now eveningwear.

And it might have been fun if Jolar didn't insist on seeing everything on her. The saleswoman selected clothes and Arissa put them on to show Jolar, who would glance up from his datapad and give her a quick once over. Usually he gave a short nod of approval but a handful of times his eyes widened and she caught a sense of—not admiration, exactly, but appreciation?—before he tamped it down. Sometimes he would frown and demand to know if she liked what she was wearing—which even a non-telepath would be able to tell plainly meant that *he* did not like it at all.

Still, considering how high the pile of ones he liked was growing—and the prices—Arissa was beginning to feel very much that they were now wasting the saleswoman's time. They couldn't possibly buy all the ones he'd picked already. The saleswoman led the way and Arissa dragged her feet.

Jolar's head came up.

"What do you think?" the woman asked brightly. "The silver color is absolutely lovely against her dark hair."

Arissa felt the blush go across her chest and up her neck under his hot stare.

"It's too long," Arissa mumbled, more than ready to escape back into the dressing room and away from those piercing blue eyes.

"Well, you'll need heels to wear with it, my dear." The woman laughed lightly. "And proper underthings of course."

Jolar's looked back at his datapad. "No."

The dismissal was so abrupt, so sharp that Arissa blinked.

"Oh," the woman said. "Is it the color? There's one more of this design in black but it would need to be altered to fit—"

"I said no," Jolar snapped, not looking up.

Arissa frowned. She could barely parse the jumble of

generosity and tenderness, irritation and eagerness—the mix of emotion came off Jolar in waves.

Arissa felt the saleswoman bite back her anger.

"Of course," she murmured.

Jolar seemed to be growing more agitated by the minute. Of the next six evening dresses she modeled for him, he only liked two. He sent her to put the tan clothes back on and she threw a discouraged look at her reflection. After seeing herself in the other outfits, what she was wearing now seemed doubly unflattering.

"Well?" the saleswoman asked, smiling. "What will you be taking?"

Jolar gestured toward the tall stack of things he'd approved. "Those."

"You mean . . . *everything*? Jolar, really, I don't need all this."

"Don't you like them? If you don't—"

"No, I like them." How could he even ask? Everything was beautiful.

He held her gaze for a moment. "Give us a minute," he said to the saleswoman.

"Of course," the woman murmured, gathering a few of the things from the rejected pile and moving to the back of the store.

"What's the matter?" he asked when the woman was out of earshot.

"Did you see the prices on those things? Jolar, it's too much."

He frowned. "I can't tell if you're joking."

"Jolar," she whispered. "One of those dresses costs *eleven hundred* credits."

He folded his arms. "I'm confused. You want the clothes but you're worried about how much they *cost*?"

"That dress costs more than twice as much as you agreed to pay me for five nights," she hissed. "And it's just a festering dress!"

She sensed his inner flinch and he took a quick step back.

"Purchase whatever you want with an ID scan, there's plenty of funds available to you. Go ahead and buy those," he said with a nod at the clothes. "And buy anything else you want, shoes, nightgowns—whatever you like. Just meet me back at the suite at nineteen hundred hours for dinner. I've got to focus on work."

It was clear there was no point in arguing with him and he was striding away before she could even try.

The saleswoman edged closer, reverberating anxiety at the possibility of losing such a huge commission.

"I guess I'm taking all of it," Arissa murmured, her stomach tightening as she did a quick mental calculation of the total.

"Wonderful!" The woman beamed. "We'll get you all set here and then I'll make that appointment for you."

Arissa eyed her reflection in the bathroom mirror of their suite and tried to calm the flutters in her stomach. Even with no limit to her spending she'd swallowed hard at the salon bill. Still, she couldn't complain about the results.

She scarcely recognized herself.

The facial took the dull look from her skin and left it glowing. Her hair had been trimmed and shaped, the mad curls layered into pretty, glossy black ringlets that framed her face and cascaded over her shoulders and upper back. The woman at the salon was both dismayed that Arissa didn't know anything about cosmetics and delighted at the opportunity to effect such a transformation. She oversaw the whole process as Arissa's eyebrows were shaped, her lash line darkened, her naturally thick black but stick-straight lashes permanently curled.

Arissa's inexperience made the woman press for lasting enhancements. The cheek and lip color as well as the dark lining around her eyes would stay perfectly in place and vibrant for several months then gradually fade. The semi-permanent color that reddened her lips, naturally such a pale shade made her mouth look twice as full. Over it she wore a plain balm to keep her lips soft.

The full, red mouth made her eyes look more balanced in her face. Now they looked okay instead of big as a frightened sercat's.

The wash-away eyelid colors Arissa would change for day or night looks and the woman wrote out detailed instructions for her on how to use the shadows. Arissa applied the evening shadow palette with painstaking care, though it still didn't look perfect. She finally decided on a gown she had chosen herself at another store after Jolar left. It was a deep green with an over layer of semi-transparent material. Sleeves of that same material were slashed from shoulder to wrist but four pieces of horizontal trim held the pieces together—at the bicep, at the elbow, mid-forearm and wrist. The effect left her looking like she was showing more skin than she was. The semi-transparent layer over the solid one had the added benefit of filling her body out and made her look a whole lot more like she used to.

And not scrawny like she was now.

I'm going to have to leave this bathroom sooner or later.

Jolar, while not back yet, would soon collect her for dinner.

The woman at the salon had been delighted with the

result of her work. Even the tan clothes that had so washed her out before the cosmetics looked better, and Arissa had drawn the eyes of a number of men on her way back here.

This is ridiculous. I certainly look better than I did. I'll just open the door and go wait in the living area.

She squared her shoulders.

I look okay. I look nice.

Blue eyes flashed in her mind.

Jolar was back.

She anxiously smoothed down a curl and with one final glance at the mirror went out into the living area to meet him. His back was to her when she came in, his emotions heavy and troubled. He tossed the datapad onto the couch and ran his hand through his hair.

"Are you ready for dinner?" he asked absently.

"I think so."

Jolar turned toward her and went very still.

His sense was as stunned as if she had actually grown those wings after all.

Arissa felt the blush creeping up her neck as his gaze ran over her. She expected him to say something—a compliment maybe or a terse order for her to change—but he didn't.

Her cheeks were burning now. She had a sudden fearful thought that with the combination of demi-permanent make-up and her own reddening face she must look like she'd come down with a raging case of vermillion fever.

Maybe I should have worn one of the ones he picked out instead . . .

She cleared her throat, nervously fingering the skirt of her green gown. "Is it all right?"

He looked away. "Give me a minute to get ready."

"Sure," Arissa mumbled.

He was careful not to come close enough to touch her, his emotions like a maelstrom, and she drew inward telepathically. This was hardly a date, but it was the closest she'd ever come to one. Arissa swallowed back disappointed tears.

He could have said something kind, even if he didn't mean it.

She certainly didn't want to pick up on whatever he was feeling now and distracted herself with the audio system, scrolling through to see the music selections. The whole thing had her wondering what would happen after she helped him with whatever he needed to do. She didn't even care if it turned out to be illegal, although she would prefer it were not immoral. She was very much hoping it didn't involve hurting anyone.

But once she helped him and had that permanent ID, there could be a whole life of possibilities. A career, a home, friends, maybe even someone to share that life with . . .

"Let's go."

He was dressed in a black shirt, trousers and boots, and he'd shaved too. The dark color of his clothes made his light hair more striking, but their style was only a little more formal than what he'd been wearing earlier.

Arissa chewed the inside of her cheek.

Maybe I'm overdressed.

Jolar looked anywhere but at her and stood no closer than necessary, even on the crowded lift. The lift door opened, and she started when he touched the small of her back to urge her out. He sent out prickles of annoyance at her reaction.

Arissa followed the other passengers to the dining

room, her glance darting about to take it all in. A large room, it was already full of diners. The clinking of glasses and the hum of conversation floated over the instrumental music.

The ceiling was aglow with soft blue light, slowly deepening to purple. A crystalline sculpture in the center of the room kept pace with the color change, and the table lights themselves shifted

"It's so beautiful!" Arissa exclaimed.

Jolar shot her a surprised look. "It's nice," he allowed.

A few guests nearby were led by one of the hosts into the dining room. A quick glance found no one else in earshot.

"Do we just wait here?" she whispered.

"What?"

"For them to take us to our table," she said. At his perplexed pulse, she added, "I mean do we go up or what?"

"We give them our name and then they seat us."

"Do we pick where we sit or do they?"

His brow creased. "They do."

"Okay." The host had come back and timidly Arissa stepped forward.

The man was already feeling tense and overwhelmed, though none of it showed in his expression. "Name?"

"Arissa."

"She's joking." Jolar shot her an annoyed look. "The name is Legan."

The host gave her an uncertain smile. "Please follow me."

Her face was hot with embarrassment but it was a thrill just to be here, to be able to go in, to sit down with all the beautiful artwork and elegantly dressed people around her. She smiled at the host when he gave her a menu. She looked around at the other diners, at the décor, at the dresses the other women wore, at how the lights were now a rose pink and changing to red. It was like being in a holodrama.

Jolar's bewildered glance followed hers. "What are you looking at?"

"Everything," she murmured.

Their waiter appeared tableside to fill their glasses with ice water and welcome them. He spoke quickly about the menu's offerings, describing the chef's dish in glowing terms before asking for their drink orders.

The man looked at Arissa expectantly, harried beneath his polite expression.

"I don't . . . I want a shooting star!" One of her favorite holo characters growing up always drank them. Arissa had never even tried one. "Do you have those?"

The waiter nodded, his face emotionless. Arissa wondered what he found so amusing.

"Two?" he asked Jolar with a raised eyebrow.

Jolar gave him a narrow look. "Wine. One of the Niman vintages if you've got it."

"Dry or sweet?"

"Dry," Jolar said shortly, his eyes on his menu.

"Thank you," Arissa called after the waiter as he hurried away.

Jolar stared at her, oscillating spikes of annoyance and confusion.

Arissa ducked her head and scanned the menu. "Everything looks wonderful," she said shyly. "I don't even know how to choose."

Jolar put his menu down. "The chef's dish sounds good."

"Oh, uh," Arissa pitched her voice very low. "I wouldn't."

His eyebrows went up, his annoyance rustling. "Why not?"

"Because our waiter wouldn't. Like it's—" She considered, frowning a bit. "Like it's cobbled together to get rid of something that's going bad. They're probably making him suggest it."

Jolar's glance darted about around them.

"No one's listening, I che—"

She broke off at his sharp, warning look.

The waiter returned with their drinks. Arissa looked at hers for a long moment, enjoying the fizzling pale pink color of it, the pretty, feminine, frosty glass. She took a sip.

"Oh," she breathed at the fruity-sweet, light taste. "It's wonderful." She beamed up at the waiter. "Thank you so much!"

The waiter's smile was his first genuine one of the evening. "I hope you enjoy it."

Jolar lifted his menu again. "Well, I guess I'm skipping the chef's dish."

"Wise," the waiter said under his breath, placing the wine glass on the table.

"What would you recommend?" Jolar asked him suddenly. "If you were going to eat here?"

The waiter hesitated, throwing a glance back where the hosts dawdled.

"The sular steak or the spring medallions are excellent," he murmured as he poured the wine.

Jolar gave her a questioning look.

"Both sound great," she agreed. "I'll take the medallions."

"The steak," Jolar said, handing over his menu. "Done medium well."

Jolar took a swallow of his dry wine as the man moved

off.

"Maybe the sweet is better," Arissa offered.

"Yeah," Jolar said, looking into his cup. "I was just thinking the dry is—"

He broke off, the knuckles of the hand holding his wine glass suddenly showing white. Nipping her lip, Arissa moved aside her cutlery, smoothed the napkin over her lap.

Jolar put his glass down.

"How was shopping?" he asked at last.

"Fine. How did your work go?" she asked as he was putting his napkin on his lap. "Well, maybe after dinner I could help you with whatever you found so frustrating."

He went still. "Do you mind letting me be part of this conversation too?"

Arissa looked at her clasped hands. "Sorry."

Jolar nodded toward her nearly full glass. "Is your drink all right?"

"Oh, yes. It's perfect."

"But you aren't drinking it."

"I just want to keep it as long as I can."

His brow creased. "Why don't you just order another one?"

"Can I?"

He stared and Arissa shifted in her seat as the waiter placed the salad course in front of her.

Jolar shoved his wine glass at the waiter. "Bring me the sweet. And bring her another shooting star."

"Should I take—"

"No," Jolar cut him off. "Just bring her a second one."

Well, with two she could afford to drink more of this one. Arissa took a longer taste, smiling into the glass.

Jolar immediately downed half his wine when the waiter brought it. Arissa sampled her salad and found the citrusy vinaigrette very good.

"I was thinking about the new house," Jolar said with a meaningful look. "Do you think it's large enough?"

She shrugged, spearing more of the greens. "I thought so when we saw it. With the two extra bedrooms we could even make one into a study for you."

He relaxed a little and picked up his fork. "You aren't worried about the move?"

"You'll be there this time. Not like the last time when you were on patrol at the border and I was on my own. It was exhausting."

"I'd forgotten about that," Jolar murmured, then his voice took on a brighter note. "Well, we should do something onboard tomorrow. If, of course, you're finished shopping for now."

She threw a smile at the waiter as he placed the medallions in front of her. "Like what?"

He shrugged. "There's an airskating rink, three casinos, a pool, and several gardens onboard. What do you want to do?"

Arissa froze, her fork hovering over her plate. "Everything," she said, her voice low and fierce. "I want to do everything."

His blue eyes were a little alarmed and she dropped her gaze.

He took another deep draft of his wine then turned his attention to his dinner.

"Good steak," he said quietly.

At meal's end he gave her his dessert after she finished her own. He settled up with the waiter while she scraped the last bit of tararoot mousse from the dish.

He stood and helped her from her chair. "That was an interesting dinner."

She bit the inside of her cheek. "Can we take a walk?" she asked as they left the dining room. "I'd love to see more of the ship."

He avoided her eyes. "Let's go back to the suite first."

Disappointed, she followed him back.

He leveled his gaze at her as soon as their suite door slid shut behind him. "Here's the thing, Arissa. It wouldn't hurt for us to be seen onboard and talk to a few people. I had planned that we'd dine at a table with other passengers in the ship's main dining room starting tomorrow."

"Oh." She wasn't sure how she felt about having to sit and converse with strangers. She'd never spoken to anyone she didn't know longer than absolutely necessary. "That wasn't the ship's dining room?"

"No," he said slowly. "That was one of the restaurants. And since we'll be sitting with other people for the rest of this journey," he folded his arms, "I really don't want a repeat of tonight's dinner performance, okay?"

"What do you mean?"

"I mean you acted very oddly," he said, throwing out little spikes of annoyance.

"Oh." She clasped her hands. "I'm sorry. I've never eaten in a restaurant before." Her fingers twisted together. "Maybe if you tell me what I did wrong, it would help."

His shock rippled. "Are you serious?"

She gave a half-shrug, her cheeks warming. "It was dangerous for me to go anywhere on Apovia so my parents never took me. I bought food from stands when I got to Tellar. There was one restaurant I got food from but I never ate there. I've seen people eat at restaurants in holos," she offered. "Of course that's usually just before something dramatic happens like someone runs out crying or the place is robbed or something. But," she said, smiling tentatively, "tonight was wonderful. I'm so glad I finally got to go."

"You're serious."

"Did I do that badly?" The waiter had been amused, but she would bet her life none of the other patrons even noticed her. "I'll do better next time."

"I just need—I need to think about this for a minute." He took a step back. "No, I need more than a minute. I'm going out."

"You could stay here and I could go," Arissa offered quickly. "I'd love to go for a walk." Her shoulders fell in disappointment. "You don't trust me to go about by myself now."

Jolar blanched. "Stay here," he said hoarsely. "Just—stay here. I'll be back in a couple hours." He took another step back. "I just need to figure this out."

Eight

Blue eyes flashed through her mind, and she started to wakefulness.

Jolar was watching her from the bedroom doorway, still dressed in the clothes he'd worn last night. "Good morning."

She'd waited for him for hours and finally gone to bed around midnight. She sat up, rubbing at her eyes. "What time is it?"

"Eight hundred hours." He took a step back. "Come on. It's time to talk."

Fear gnawed at her insides and her hands trembled as she dressed. The table was filled again with food, and he was pouring white tea for her when she joined him in the little dining area. He handed her the cup.

She wrapped her shaking hands around its warmth. "Are you sending me back?"

"No." He met her eyes squarely. "I can't. I convinced the Zartani councilor that I needed your help. I can't send you back. And I can't just send you off on your own. The deal I made with Dacel was that you'd help me on Sertar or no ID." He shook his head. "I don't think we have any choice now but to go forward. I think we still can if I can teach you how . . ."

"How not to be so odd."

He gave a reluctant nod. "You have to play this part now and you need to do it well."

"Okay." Arissa nipped her lip. "What did I do wrong at

the restaurant?"

"Not wrong." He rubbed his eyes. "I understand now why you would be so . . . *enthusiastic*. It just never occurred to me that this would be a problem." He sighed. "Sit down. You've got to be hungry."

She looked over the dishes. Now that she knew he wasn't going to send her back to Tellar, her appetite was returning. She picked up a plate, noticing again that he took nothing but caf for himself. She wondered where he'd been all night.

"What do you know about Sertar?"

She paused, the serving spoon in her hand. "Lots. I can tell you about the planet's typography, its weather patterns, the mass—"

"No, sorry." His mouth quirked upward. "About the *government* of Sertar."

She finished scooping the fried hoss onto her plate, then added grimp toast next to the vegetable. "Uh, Sertar once had a prince and lords who held various territories, but now it's a republic of elected officials." She glanced at him. "Like Zartan."

He nodded. "But, unlike my homeworld, Sertar's struggle to move from an aristocracy to a republic has been—I don't want to say unsuccessful—let's just say things didn't change much under the new system. It's really just an oligarchy now. Of all the worlds in the Realm, Sertar is the most corrupt."

Arissa washed down the grimp toast with a sip of juice. "Okay."

"And Sertar has one thing that the entire Realm needs."

"Astuk crystals," Arissa said automatically.

Jolar nodded again. "Without that power source there's no *Queen's Light*, no fleet, no Tellaran Realm—because all shipping, all interplanetary trade comes to a stop." He looked into his cup. "The lords fought for control, princes rose and fell, but as long as the crystals continued to be mined they were left to settle things in whatever blood-soaked way they wanted. Sertar—the government there—has always been weak, corrupt. Enough money can make the officials there look the other way on anything. Even murder. Even treason."

"You're going there to end the corruption?"

He snorted. "No, that's a task beyond anyone. I'm going there because the Zartani councilor no longer knows who else he can trust."

"You're afraid."

His gaze met hers, the skin beside his eyes tight. "Someone on Sertar is gathering a lot of power, using a lot of money to move people into new positions. With that kind of control over the energy supply they could devastate trade, they could bring the Realm to its knees. I need to find out who, or we might find our entire economy, even the fleet itself, crippled."

"That's why you're going there? That's what you need my help to do?"

"I'm not the first Dacel sent." He hesitated. "I've read over that agent's reports."

She blinked. "He's dead, isn't he? The one he sent before you."

"Yes." His blue eyes were grave. "That's why you're here, why Dacel agreed to let you come. I told him you could help me stay alive long enough to complete this mission. From what I've seen already, I know you can." He searched her face. "Will you?"

"You're afraid that a seer can't be trusted. That because of what I am I might give you away." Funny how much that hurt.

"I don't want to think that you would. And I need to know—now—that you won't."

She chewed her lip. "How do I know that ID is really there for me? You could kill me after I help you and no one would care."

Shock and horror rippled from him. "You saved my *life!* As a Zartani— I owe you your life in return and this is the only way I can get it for you. Help me and, on my soul, Arissa, that ID and your freedom are yours."

She probed the weight, the heft of his mind. He meant what he said. She gave a nod. "I'll help you."

"This is our lives now, Arissa. We have to be able to trust each other. We have to have each other's backs. Can I trust you?"

"Yes," she promised. "You can."

He searched her face, and whatever he saw there made his tension fall a bit. "Then for the next few days we're going to concentrate on getting ready for Sertar. Whatever it takes, we have to make sure that by the time we're planetside no one will doubt we are who we say we are, understand?"

"Yes."

"I only have a few days to get you ready," he warned. "I don't have time for niceties. Whatever I do, I'm doing to try to keep us alive."

"Okay." She swallowed. "Jolar, what did I do wrong at the restaurant?"

His sense wavered then hardened. "You didn't know how to be seated. You were too friendly with the waiter. Overwhelmed by the kind of beverage preteen girls drink. Too impressed with a not terribly impressive eatery."

"Oh," she said, blinking back tears. "I'm sorry."

"There's no time for that." His face was grim. "No time for 'sorry' or hurt feelings. If we fail there, we die. I'm going to—*we're* going to do whatever it takes to succeed. Understand?"

Her mind suddenly flashed to the Utavian man he'd shot. He hadn't wanted to kill but it hadn't stopped him. "Will we have to hurt anyone?"

"I hope not," he said. "But if we have to, we have to."

She closed her eyes for a moment. "Less friendly, more reserved. Okay."

"I also don't want you to think you didn't impress me last night. You did plenty right."

She blinked. "I did?"

"Yes. The way you could pick up what the waiter was thinking for instance."

"What the waiter...? Oh, right. The chef's special. But that was easy."

"That was incredible."

She ducked her head and took a quick sip of tea. "I made you uncomfortable."

"Yes, you did. And I was worried you would be overheard."

"Oh, no. I knew no one was paying us any attention. The waiter was too harried to care and the other patrons were focused elsewhere."

"I see." His sense oscillated as if he were trying to steady himself. "I guess I don't need to tell you to be careful about keeping your—talent—quiet."

Arissa thought of the years her parents had hid her, the months she'd spent staying out of sight on Tellar, of using that split second of inattention to lift a billfold or slip away with some bauble she could hock to feed herself for a few more days. The awful risks. "No, you don't."

"You also fell right into the role when I prompted you and you remembered good details. It sounded natural."

"Maybe I'll become an actress after this is over." His surprise rippled. "I'm joking. Go on. I like hearing about what I did right."

His mouth curved. "Of course you read me very well." His smile faded. "It makes me wonder how much you know about me."

"You're not what you look like."

His brow creased. "What does *that* mean?"

"You're—" She looked down at her tea. "You're just not what I expected."

Even with likely little sleep, his blond hair mussed from running his hand through it, and a day's growth in beard, Jolar was astonishingly good-looking. With those striking blue eyes, full mouth and his tall, lean strength it was no wonder women's eyes followed him everywhere.

He certainly had her—as little used to men as she was, let alone any who looked like him—practically stumbling over herself.

But beneath that golden exterior his mind was serious, very deeply responsible, so committed to doing the right thing, so guarded against anyone getting too close . . .

"I never got a chance to ask you." He leaned forward, his arms on the table, his shirt pulling tight over his broad shoulders. "Why did you help me on Tellar? You could have kept out of it but I saw you slip into that alley after he'd pulled the blaster. You risked your life to save mine. Why?"

"I wasn't going to," she admitted. "I looked at you and all I could see was someone who had everything I never would. But you're a good man, an honorable one." She tucked her hair behind her ear. "You didn't deserve to die like that."

"A good, honorable man," he echoed with a sudden flash of bitterness. He stood abruptly. "Let me grab a shower and get changed. Then we're going out."

"Where?"

"You wanted to see and do everything–I can't think of a better way of letting you practice."

"Jolar, I'm not sure this was a good idea, after all."

Arissa had yet to gather the courage to let go of the rail around the airskating rink. Jolar glided easily beside her. *He* was perfectly comfortable floating four inches above the floor. He even managed to look graceful despite his great height, handsome even in airskating boots that were clunky and unflattering on *everyone*.

The rink was empty now save for the two of them. There had been a family here when they first arrived. Seeing how much better even the little ones were at this than she proved so profoundly disheartening she was relieved when they left.

He held his hand out to her. "Come on. I won't let you fall."

She was less worried about falling than she was looking ridiculous in front of him.

But she didn't want to look a coward either.

Shakily she let go of the rail.

His grip was strong and sure, his long fingers wrapped around hers. "Come on, sweet,–give me your other hand."

Flushing with pleasure at the unexpected endearment, she let go of the railing and reached her hand out to take his.

Jolar smiled down at her, eyes shining, her hands in his warm grip. For a moment she couldn't breathe.

"Turn your feet a little toward me."

She got her feet pointed in the right direction. She knew she should try to move forward but her legs felt wooden; standing there, gripping his hands in terror was all she could manage.

"I'm going to pull you a little, okay?"

Her eyes flew to his face. "I don't think so."

"You don't have to do anything. Just hold on and I'll pull you." He gave her a reassuring look. "Very slowly."

She suppressed a whimper, her legs wobbly as he tugged. He skated backwards, drawing her along. She leaned forward awkwardly at the hip, her bottom sticking out a bit, trying to keep her balance.

He skated her to the rail on the other side of the rink. "Still okay?"

Trembling, she nodded and tried to let go of his hand to grab the rail.

"Hey, not so fast," he said, keeping hold of her. "We're going across again. This is the only way you learn."

She was never going to be able to do this. She was too terrified even to move her feet as he pulled her across the rink. "Why does it look so festering easy in the holodramas?"

He laughed. "Because they make up a professional airskater to look like the actress and let *her* do the skating instead." He tugged on her hands, pulling a little faster now. "You're getting better."

"It took me twenty minutes to be able to stay upright with both hands on the rail."

"And now you're moving across the rink. See? Better."

She gave a shaky laugh. "*You're* moving across the rink. I'm just holding on."

Jolar got her to the other side of the rink and turned, pulling her in semi-circle to take her across again.

"You're so good at this," Arissa complained. "It's so easy for you, you can do it backwards."

"But I learned when I was a kid so I've been doing it for a while. Believe me, I fell plenty of times. You'll get good at it too. Ready to try with just one hand?"

"No," she said quickly, tightening her grip before he could let go.

"I'll be right here if you need me."

Reluctantly she released his hand. Hers hovered over his, ready to grab him again but she kept her balance and started feeling comfortable enough that she risked pulling her free hand back a little.

"See? You're doing great."

"Thanks." She smiled back at him. "I think this is fun too."

He blinked. His glance darted around the empty rink, then his smile came back full force. "Good. Ready to try again?"

Still wobbly, she followed his instructions on how to push off and move by alternating her feet a little. He even got her to lift one foot and then the other.

On the next time across the rink he convinced her to try on her own.

She lasted less than three seconds, and gasped as she lost her balance.

Jolar caught her in his arms.

Enfolded against his broad chest, his smiling mouth only a few inches from hers, Arissa could do nothing but look wide-eyed up at him as they floated slowly across the rink. It felt so good to be held against him and she was so aware of his body, the warm male scent of him, that her skin tingled.

"You okay?" he asked, bending down a little more to look into her face, his blue eyes amused.

Her hands were resting on his strong shoulders. She wished more than anything he would lean down just a little bit more and kiss her.

Gods, I'm going to make a complete fool of myself.

"Yes," she said, quickly dropping her gaze. But that had her looking right at the hollow of his throat and she had an impulse to touch her mouth to the warm golden skin there. She twisted her head away.

"I think," she began, unable to meet his eye, embarrassed at how breathless she sounded. "I've had enough airskating for today."

He laughed. "Okay." He got her steadied and helped her out of the rink. He took his airskates off and knelt down to unfasten hers. "We should probably go get ready for dinner now anyway."

"Right." She was nervous about having to eat with strangers, having to hold a conversation without revealing herself.

"You did much better at lunch today," he assured, accurately reading her expression as he helped her get the skates off. "You were perfect."

"That was different. That was just you."

"You're going to do fine." He stood. "Come on, we don't want to miss our seating."

The dark clothes he changed into were more formal tonight, and she wore one of the gowns he'd chosen for her. This dress showed more skin than the green one she'd worn the night before but she liked how the shimmersilk went from orange at the hem, then subtly changed in color up the skirt to a light, then dark blue, reaching indigo near her shoulders. Dozens of tiny jewels decorating the low-cut bodice caught the light and sparkled like stars. She put her hair half up and half down and clipped some tiny stones into her curls to continue the sparkle effect. She took her time to apply the shadow to her eyelids and was pleased how much better it looked this time.

Jolar smiled when he saw her.

"You look wonderful," he said and offered his hand.

In her mind she suddenly saw him pull her against him, his warm, broad palm against her bare back to press her closer, his mouth hot and hungry on hers.

The image came out of nowhere and was so unexpected, so vivid, it sent a tightening rush of desire through her center.

Her face felt hot. "I think I'm pretty steady now that we're out of the rink."

His surprise pulsed and he dropped his hand. "Well, let's go then."

She wasn't supposed to look impressed, but it took a lot of effort to appear jaded as she took in the dining room of the *Queen's Light*. The room was done in dark colors but elegantly so, with little pools of light over and around the tables. The musicians played softly enough that she could hear the murmur of conversation, the clinking of glass and silverware. Located in the bow of the ship, the transparent plexisteel walls rose three stories above her head and swept outward to an absolutely breathtaking view of space.

"Wow," Jolar murmured, craning his neck to see the view.

She shot him a narrow look. "Legan," she said to the hostess.

The woman nodded and led them into the dining room.

There were eight already assembled at the table—she and Jolar would be taking the last two seats. Jolar held her chair for her and then took his place on the opposite side, farther down the table. The slender woman beside him instantly brightened, vibrating with interest. Jolar gave the woman a slow smile and Arissa pushed down a sudden impulse to hurl her soup spoon at the woman's head.

"I'm Lian," the man at her side said, offering his hand. He was an attractive man, with dark hair and eyes to match. He nodded to the striking redhead across the table. "That's Kemma." The woman gave her a friendly smile. "That's, uh—"

"Kelm," the young man said with a smile and nod.

"Hi, I'm Sona," the dark blonde girl next to her offered. She couldn't be more than seventeen, a pretty girl with a pert, freckle-covered nose and a cute overbite. She nodded to the man on Kemma's other side. "That's my dad."

"You can call me Parlen," the man said dryly, putting his napkin in his lap, his thinning hair obvious even in this light. "Rather than 'Dad'."

"I'm Arissa."

"First time to Sertar?" Kemma asked. "Or have you been before?"

"No, this is my first time." Arissa shifted in her seat. "What about all of you?"

She scarcely heard their answers and took a quick sip of water against the sudden dryness of her mouth. She was too open, and it left her feeling like she was lost in a tumultuous sea of emotion. Their conversation was buzzing around her.

Focus. Just pick one of them and focus.

Arissa looked up to see the redhead, Kemma, regarding her with a puzzled look.

"That's a lovely gown," Arissa said, narrowing her attention to just Kemma.

"Thank you." The woman oscillated with surprise. "I just said the same about yours."

"Oh." Had she? The whole conversation was proving hard to follow around the jumble of emotions she sensed and the nervousness knotting her stomach.

Kemma smiled kindly. "I guess we both have great taste."

"I guess so." She let her breath out when the waiter handed her a menu, happy to have something to do with her hands. It also occupied everyone else at the table and gave her a few moments to collect herself.

The waiter was taking drink orders.

"Niman wine," Arissa mumbled. "Uh, sweet."

"I'm from Nima," Kemma gave a self-deprecating shrug. "As if it weren't obvious."

"I've never been there," Sona put in. "What's it like?"

Sona's father threw her a disapproving look.

"I'm just talking about the weather, Dad."

Kemma's smile didn't falter, but her green eyes cooled a little. "Lovely. The beaches of the southern continent are the most beautiful in the Realm."

"Where are you from?" Lian asked Arissa. "You sound Apovian."

"I grew up there but I live on Aylor now. I mean, my husband and I do. Actually, we just purchased a new house."

"How exciting," Kemma said. "Personally, I hate to move."

"I don't mind so much," Lian said.

"That's because you leave everything to me," Kemma said, her fond smile accompanied by ripples of amused exasperation.

"Oh," Arissa said, looking between them. "Are you married?"

There was an awkward pause.

"Lian is," Kemma said, giving a nod to the waiter as he placed her drink down. "I'm not. I'm an ornament, under exclusive contract to Lian, actually."

Then he was her protector. Arissa, who had spent her life hiding, who would have been hated and hunted on any world in the Realm, simply couldn't summon any outrage or even disapproval.

And damn it, I like her.

"Well, I had to move us on my own once," Arissa said. "I vowed never to do it again. It was exhausting."

Kemma's smile returned. "Good for you."

An ornament from a planet known for its hedonistic, pleasure seeking ways—that explains why Parlen didn't want his daughter asking her about it.

"So what do you think of the *Queen's Light*?" Lian asked.

"I'm happy to be here," Arissa said. "Actually I had my first airskating lesson today so I'm happy to be anywhere outside the medcenter."

The warmth of their laughter, their approval, encircled her. She smiled around at them.

"Hey, I love to airskate," Sona protested. "It's great exercise."

"So is running from an enraged sular bull," her father said wryly. "It's not something everyone wants to do."

"Great comparison, Dad," Sona returned, rolling her eyes.

Blue eyes flashed in her mind. Arissa glanced down the table at Jolar to see him looking back at her. She was suddenly so filled with longing to be alone together, just the two of them, far away from this ship, from everything, that she could hardly breathe—

Blinking and disconcerted, Arissa tore her gaze away. The waiter had brought her drink, but she had never sampled wine before. She took a cautious sip and crinkled her nose a little. It wasn't awful, but it had sourness to it that she didn't care for. She couldn't imagine finishing the whole glass.

It was a juggling act, but she managed to keep up her part of the conversation, eat, and play her role. As she was finishing her baneberry sorbet she realized she'd actually enjoyed at least some of dinner. It made her think about what her life would be like after this.

To have friends, to make a home . . .

Parlen and Sona had already excused themselves but Lian turned a friendly smile to her as the waiter cleared away her dessert plate.

"Kemma and I are heading down to the Lightside casino after this. Would either of you like to join us?"

Kelm nodded. "Sure. I'm not much of a gambler though."

"Just do what Kemma does," Lian said with an affectionate look her way. "The woman has the damnedest luck you ever saw."

"What do you think Arissa?" Kemma asked. "Ladies against gentlemen? Loser buys breakfast tomorrow?"

"Some other time," Jolar answered for her. He was standing at the back of her chair. "I've promised Arissa a walk around the ship."

Jolar put his hand on her shoulder, and the feel of his warm palm against her bare skin made her gasp.

Her face went hot at the surprised attention she drew to herself from the others at the table. She fumbled with her napkin and almost knocked over her wine glass in her hurry to rise. His big body, radiating heat, was a scant inch from hers. She was so flustered by his nearness she barely managed a mumbled good-bye.

"Good evening," Jolar said to their dinner companions, then quite deliberately took a step aside and motioned for her to precede him.

She turned toward the main decks. He put his hand out but didn't touch her.

"No," he said quietly. "Back to our suite."

Determination pulsed from him. Anxiety rustled too and an undercurrent of something she couldn't quite catch. She quickly went over the evening in her mind. It hadn't been easy and it hadn't always been fun but she thought she'd managed well enough tonight.

"What's wrong?" she asked as soon as the door of their suite slid shut behind him. "Was it the way I acted at dinner?"

"No, dinner was fine," he said shortly. "But there's something else we need to deal with, Arissa. And I don't think this can wait any longer."

"Oh," she said, confused by his rapidly shifting emotions. "What is it?"

"You get rattled whenever I touch you, whenever I get near you. The tension is distracting, it's obvious, and it's a problem. We need to look comfortable with each other. We have to look like husband and wife." Jolar gave her a nod. "So we're going to take care of this and fuck right now."

Nine

"What?' she breathed.

Jolar's hot anticipation tingled around her. "Rule number one, Arissa, remember? What I say, when I say. Come on, now's the time to let your ornament's skills shine."

Her glance darted over him. She remembered the feel of his arms around her today, how desperately she wished he would kiss her, how much she had wanted to kiss *him*.

"You want to—?"

"Fuck," he said impatiently, already unfastening the collar of his shirt. "You know, join. Bedding. Sex."

She knew.

Gods knew she wanted to.

She just had no idea *how*.

"Okay." She swallowed, her heart thumping. "Um, what do you want me to do?"

"I don't know." His confusion and aggravation crackled. "Why don't you start by kissing me?"

She took a step closer to put her hands on his broad shoulders. The heat of his body radiated under her palms and through the fabric of her dress as his hands came to rest on her waist. Shyly she leaned forward into his warmth, into his wonderful scent, and lifted her face. She touched her lips to his. They were soft and parted as his breathing quickened, the hot waves of his desire curling around her. She closed her eyes, her mouth against his, and stayed there a moment before drawing back.

His frustration rustled, suspicion that she was toying with him like little spikes within it. "No, *really* kiss me."

She had certainly seen kisses done in holos, seen couples entwined in Xan-Tellar. She'd read about them. She tried again and tilted her head more, pressing her mouth against his more firmly, parting her lips a little. She stayed longer this time, hoping he'd take the lead.

He scowled when she drew back. "What are you doing?"

"I'm trying."

"*Trying?* Damn it, you've done this before, haven't you?"

Arissa shook her head.

"What?" His head snapped back. "Hold on. No, wait, you said—In Xan-Tellar you agreed to let me—You took the money! You *aren't* an ornament?"

"N—no."

His shock reverberated as he stared at her. "What the hells were you going to do if I'd decided to collect that night? Just wing it?"

"Well, you've done all this before," she burst out. "I figured you would—would just *do* it."

"All this? You mean you've never—" He searched her face and blanched. "Nothing?" he asked hoarsely. "Not even *kissed?*"

Her throat tightened. She shook her head again.

"I never thought—" He let go and took a quick step back, looking badly shaken. "Arissa, I'm sorry. I can't believe the way I just—" His eyes closed briefly, shame staining his sense. "Look, you don't have to worry about this. You have my word—I won't do anything like that again. And we'll just . . . we'll work around this some other way."

Her lower lip trembled. "You don't want to now?"

"That doesn't—" He ran his hand through his hair. "Gods, do *you?*"

"Yes. I mean—" Her face went hot and she stumbled over her words under his shocked gaze. "I know I'm not pretty and no one's ever—It's just I might not get another chance and you—Yes, I want to."

"Is that what you think?" He cupped her chin gently, tilting her face to look at her, his thumb lightly tracing the skin of her cheek.

"You're very beautiful, Arissa." He let her go, his regret deep and heavy. "And you need to wait 'til the time is right for you. I promise there will be plenty of chances and many men who will want you."

She gathered her courage. "Do *you?* Do you want me, Jolar?"

The heat in his eyes echoed his hot rush of hunger. "Yes, of course I do."

"Then I don't want to wait." She wet her lips. "I want it to be you first. Tonight."

His desire tingled around her. "Are you sure?"

She nodded. "Will—will you?"

"Yes," he said huskily.

Her brow creased. "You're nervous now. You weren't nervous before."

He gave a short, shaky laugh. "Gods, I keep forgetting you can do that. Yes, I'm nervous. And even more now that you know I am."

"But why?"

He brushed a curl away from her temple, his fingers gently touching her cheek. "Because this is important. Because I want everything to be perfect for you."

"I don't need it to be perfect. I just—I want the first time to be with you. You—you know the truth about me and you aren't afraid anymore."

His eyes were raw.

She gave a quick smile. "I'm nervous too. Will it hurt?"

"It's, um—" He cleared his throat. "I'll go real slow. Okay?"

"Okay.

"So," Arissa said after a long moment. "What do you want me to do?"

"Well, I think—I'm going to kiss you, all right?"

He lightly cupped her face in his hands and brought his mouth over hers, his lips soft and very gentle. He stayed like that for a moment, then pressed forward just a little more, his tongue lightly touching, parting her lips a little, flicking the tiniest bit. Arissa clung to him, the currents of his arousal, his nervousness, his hunger moving around her.

He drew away a little to look into her eyes. "Was that all right?"

The question didn't even make sense. His kiss was likely the most amazing thing she had ever felt. Her mouth was tingling from it. She couldn't even form words to describe it.

He was still looking down at her questioningly. Mutely, she nodded.

"Do you want to keep going?"

She nodded again and looked at his mouth as he leaned closer, tilting her face up to meet him. She wrapped her arms around his neck and this time she let her lips part easily when he deepened the kiss. She clung to him as he explored, his arms going around her to draw her close.

He never stopped kissing her, her face, her eyelids, his touch gentle as he drew her into the bedroom. He carefully took the clips from her hair, threaded his fingers through her curls, his heart hammering under her hand when she put her palm to his chest. He coaxed the straps of her dress over her shoulders.

The shimmersilk dress, heavy with beading, slid quickly to the floor. She tensed, using her arms to cover her breasts.

He sat down on the bed, and she realized he was concerned his height might be intimidating. He looked up at her, his fingers lightly tracing her sides, waiting.

She knew if she drew back, turned away, reached for her dress, he would let her go without a word of rebuke or disappointment.

This was her choice.

Shaking, she lowered her arms.

He held her gaze for a moment, then lowered his eyes to look at her.

"They're usually bigger," she blurted. "I mean, they were before I left home but I'm so skinny now—*oh!*"

She broke off as his mouth covered the peak of her breast. The moist heat of it tightened her center, her own heat thrumming now through her. He drew the nipple into his mouth with gentle suction, his tongue moving over the peak.

"You're beautiful," he murmured, his lips tracing across her chest to the other breast. He took longer with this one, nuzzling a bit before his mouth lightly touched her nipple. He held her by the waist again, and her palms pressed down on his shoulders, her knees so weak now that he was helping her stay upright.

When he drew back his eyes were big with desire. He held her gaze as his fingers found the edges of her underwear and slowly slid them down.

She was bare before him now, and his eyes softened as they went to the dark hair between her legs. His hands rested on her hips for a moment before sliding over her hipbones, touching the dark hair with the pads of his thumbs. His thumb touched the very apex between her legs, his stroke sending jolts of pleasure through her.

She felt tight, tingly there now, looking down at him with wide eyes. Something in her expression made his mouth take on a tender curve.

He reached for the fastenings of his shirt. "Do you want to do it or do you want me to?"

By way of answering she reached for the closures. It wasn't easy to undo them with her fingers shaking so, but after a time she managed. She pushed at the shirt and he shrugged it away to let it fall to the floor. He got his boots off and stood to bring her hand to the waist of his trousers.

"Me or you?"

Her heart was hammering in her chest. The pants were harder to undo, maybe because she could see the curve of his arousal there. In the end he had to help her.

He was in his undershorts now and cupped her face to press another kiss to her mouth. He deepened the kiss as he urged her back onto the bed, and the warmth of his body covered hers as he lay her down on its soft surface.

Her hands ran down the smooth skin of his muscled back to his hips. He drew away, poised over her, waiting. She urged the shorts down and nipped her lip when the soft material caught on his hardness. She freed him from the fabric, the heat of his shaft startling against her fingers. With the shorts off, he shifted to lie beside her.

His mouth quirked up a bit. "You can look."

Arissa lowered her gaze to see him hard and ready, the curve of his maleness jutting out, the darker blond hair, the softness below. She reached for him shyly but stopped, unsure, and looked to find his gaze hot.

"It's okay." Jolar took her hand and brought it to him, his hand over hers as she wrapped her fingers around his hardness. His skin was velvety soft and as she ran her hand down his shaft his breath caught, his eyes fell shut, and the tingles of his arousal surrounded her. His lips parted, and he showed her how to stroke him, his hand closing over hers to squeeze. His breath was coming faster, and he moved his hips under her touch until his hold suddenly tightened on her hand.

"Better stop now," he said with a shaky laugh. "Or this will be over before it starts."

He drew her hand away and with a wild thrill she saw he was trembling a little. He turned so he was against her side.

His hand slid over her hipbone to her lower belly, resting just above the thatch of dark hair there. "I want to touch you too. Tell me what you like."

"I don't know," she managed.

"What do you like when you touch yourself?" Her face went hot and he gave a soft laugh at her stunned mortification. "It's okay, everyone does it."

"Do you?" she demanded, embarrassment giving her voice an edge.

"Yes."

She caught it then, how much knowing she sought her own pleasure aroused him.

"Tell me what you like," he said, his voice huskier now, his hand slid lower resting now at her center. "I have an idea." He gave a soft, breathless laugh. "I know exactly how I want you to tell me."

His fingers slid against her, tracing the lips there, then lightly touching her where she was most sensitive. Her mouth parted. He drew little circles over the spot, and her breath caught at the tightening pleasure of it.

He drew back a little to watch her again, his fingers moving rhythmically. "Like it?"

"Gods, yes!" she gasped.

He pressed closer, his hardness hot against her hip, arching his body over hers, his breathing coming faster. She moved against his touch, her eyes opened to meet his, her lip caught between her teeth as the tightness grew. His glance ran over her face, his pupils large. He gave a quick, almost feral smile before he brought his mouth to hers again. His tongue darted in and out between her lips, a taste of what he wanted next.

He slid a finger inside her, then two, his thumb moving against her, and groaned.

"You're so wet." Jolar's eyes were nearly glowing as he searched her face. "Do you want this? Do you want me inside you?"

"Yes!"

He moved between her legs then, his big warm body covering hers as he positioned the tip of his shaft at her center. He touched his mouth to hers.

"So beautiful," he murmured, then slowly began to sink into her folds.

Arissa watched his eyes shut briefly as he entered, his pleasure surging through her mind. She made a soft sound at the pinch of pain when he filled her. He stayed there, his body tight. The sensation of having him inside was a wonderful shock.

"Are you okay?" he asked, his voice ragged, rough. "Do you want to stop?"

"No," she whispered. She wrapped her arms around his neck. "No, please don't stop."

Relief and heat burst around her and he started to move. For a moment it was as if she were in two places at once, feeling him hot inside her, her every nerve echoing the pleasure of his movements and feeling him so aroused, holding back when he wanted to move faster, harder, trying not to hurt her, not to lose control.

"So good. Feels . . ." His hold on her tightened, his body so taut he was trembling now. He moved faster, deeper then, every stroke moving against her most sensitive spot. "Can feel you," he panted, curled over her. "Gods, I can *feel* you."

She cried out as the pleasure hit her, her insides contracting hard with it. He bent his head, his thrusts deep and fast now. Another stroke and he gave a cry, shuddering as he spent himself within her.

Jolar's eyes were still shut; he was trembling in her arms. She touched the softness of his golden hair, so fiercely glad, so grateful it had been him first, that tears blurred her vision.

Ten

Jolar drew away to look at her, his blue eyes half closed, his breathing still quick, a smile curving his mouth.

His brow creased instantly. "Oh, no. Oh, sweet, I thought—"

Tears ran down to dampen her hair but she laughed too. She shook her head. "No, no, I'm fine! I didn't—That was amazing! Is it always like that?"

"No," he said hoarsely. "No, Arissa, that was special."

She took his face in her hands. "Thank you, Jolar. For making it so wonderful for me."

He closed his eyes and bent his head. "Gods, don't *thank* me." He pulled out, shifting to lie beside her and gathered her against him, cradling her. "You're okay, though?"

"Yes, I'm fine." She put her hand on his chest, feeling his heartbeat under her palm. "I'm so glad you wanted to. Fuck, I mean."

His arms tightened around her. "Don't call it that."

"Why not?" she asked, frowning. "What do you want me to call it?"

"Call it joining. Call it lovemaking." He pressed a kiss to her temple. "But it wasn't—Look, just don't call it that, okay?"

"Okay." She ducked her head. "Did you like it?"

He gave a short laugh. "Yes. Couldn't you tell?"

"Yes," she admitted. "Was it as—as nice as other times for you?"

Such a storm of emotion tore through him that she raised her head to look at him. His eyes were shut tight.

"Jolar?"

He looked at her, his blue eyes wild, his emotions a jumble. Stinging pain, blossoming joy, pulling sadness, rolling determination, fierce and sharp . . .

She frowned and touched his cheek. "Jolar?"

"Even better." The storm of his mind calmed and he kissed her with an air of possessiveness he hadn't before.

"Do you think you'd want to do it again sometime?" she asked shyly. "With me, I mean?"

"Yes, I do. Again and again." He chuckled. "As soon as I can."

She frowned. "But not for a while?"

"It takes a little while for a man to be ready again. Another of the gods' many jokes. They never seem to tire of them." He sobered and searched her face. "But you're really all right?"

"Yes. Yes, I'm fine." She laughed. "You're so relieved."

His face flushed. "I can't do what you can do. I have to guess what people are feeling from what they say, their facial expressions, their body language. You must feel like you're explaining colors to someone who's never been able to see them when you talk to me." His blue eyes shone. "I wish I could do what you can do."

"Don't say that." Her throat felt like it was closing, and hot tears stung her eyes. "I wouldn't wish it on you. I'm already afraid I'll—"

"Contaminate me? Influence me?" He twirled one of her ringlets around his finger. "Manipulate me with your wicked powers?"

"Don't joke about it," she cried. "You don't know that I won't. *I* don't know that I won't, even if I don't want to, don't mean to."

He leaned on his elbow, looking at her frankly, his palm resting on her stomach. "You're really worried about that."

"I do everything I can not to be telepathic, to dampen it down, to turn it off. I've read about the trials, the harm seers are capable of. That's why they made the laws. Because people like me hurt people like you."

"Two hundred years ago people like you supported the royal family," he said a little sharply. "They fought on the side of the crown during the civil war. Maybe being on the losing side had more to do with those laws than any harm seers ever did."

"I didn't realize you had such an interest in history."

"My father was the one with the interest in history. The lost legacy of our family, the fall of the Tellaran royal house . . ." Jolar shook his head. "He could go on for hours about it. He said that the seers kept their loyalty oaths, that they died with honor while the Zartani lords caved to the New Order."

"My father found some records hidden in archives on Apovia—records that should have been destroyed during the purges—information about seers, how they were once sought out to be trained in the temples, when they were trusted with important positions. My father—" She hesitated. But her father was dead, he couldn't be prosecuted now. "It was an awful risk for him to smuggle those out for me but he wanted me to see them. He didn't want me to be so—so ashamed."

Shock reverberated through him. "Gods, is that how you feel? Ashamed?"

She couldn't look at him. How could she explain how much it hurt to know that she could never be like him? Never really be part of the life she saw around her? Never be anything than other, different, frightening?

How much she hated the part of herself she knew would always keep her from him?

"Arissa, if you've been actively trying to clamp down on your abilities then you don't even know what you're capable of! We need to find out what you can *really* do if you try." He stroked her cheek. "You can practice on me."

Her gaze flew to his face. "No," she breathed. "No, I can't. What if I hurt you? I could—"

"You won't," he said firmly. "How can we use your abilities to the fullest if we don't even know what they are? They may make all the difference. They might keep us alive." He traced her cheek with his fingertips. "Do you trust me, sweet?"

"It's myself I don't trust.

"I want to learn what you can do. I want us to learn together." He leaned his forehead against hers. "Don't you?"

She closed her eyes, concentrated on the feel of his skin, the warmth and comfort of his big body around hers, the precious acceptance . . .

"All right. If that's what you want, Jolar."

She couldn't read him when she was sleeping.

She was resting easy now, safe in his arms and Jolar finally allowed himself the luxury of relaxing control over his feelings. When she slept was about the only time he had to let the full impact of this mess fill his mind. Distance seemed to keep her from reading him too.

But he didn't want to be away from her. Not at all.

Gods, I am so absolutely fucked.

There were novice priestesses at Seleni's temple who were less sheltered than she was. She'd been hidden away, a virtual prisoner her whole life, watching others make friends, go to school, forced to learn about life through books and holos . . .

Just looking into those wide green eyes, so frightened, so guarded, even as her gaze darted about to take in some of what she'd been denied, made his heart ache. The whole thing made him wish for a stun pike and ten minutes alone in a room with whoever enacted the whole anti-seer laws in the first place.

He covered his eyes with his hand as shame rushed over him. Shoving money in her hand like that. The growing frustration of wanting to kiss her at the airskating rink, tonight before dinner, longing to be alone with her, the wanting that had started since the moment he'd seen her on Tellar and had grown completely out of control, the hunger that drove him to make that stupid 'let's-fuck-for-the-sake-of-the-mission' demand. . .

I'm the one who deserves ten minutes under that stun pike.

I just blindly accepted her story on Tellar. I should have known better, asked more questions, been gentle with her.

He'd no idea *how* sheltered she'd been. It had never occurred to him how much of life she'd missed. How innocent she was.

How could take her to Sertar? The place was a snake pit. But he couldn't send her back to the capital either. There was nowhere to hide her; nowhere he could be certain she'd be safe in Tellaran space without that ID.

Not pretty? He could hardly take his eyes off her.

What the hells am I going to do?

For one heartbeat, just as she hovered at the edge of her pleasure, the barriers between them fell away. *He'd felt her.* Her excitement, her nervousness, her arousal—but so much more. He traced the sharpness of her intellect, the depth of her compassion, the warm innate joy that her enforced isolation could dampen but not destroy.

For that single instant too he became alert to other minds in her awareness and unguarded, found himself swept along pools of sorrow, buoyed over swells of joy . . .

A flash of the universe through her eyes.

It was the most precious moment of his life.

He smoothed away a sable curl from her face.

My sweet one. His eyes stung. *How am I ever going to let you go?*

A good man? An honorable one?

Hardly.

And when she knew the truth, it was going to end everything.

Eleven

Jolar pressed a kiss against her temple, his arm around her waist. "We should have had breakfast in our suite."

From their place in the line outside the Twin Suns restaurant, Arissa judged it would be several minutes before they even reached the host station. "We can go to the dining room."

"Oh, we long ago missed our breakfast seating." His hand slid lower down her back to just the edge of where it could decently rest in public. "I don't know what I was thinking when I chose the early one."

"We can go back to our suite and eat there instead."

"Don't tempt me," he said huskily, his other arm going around her too. "You're lucky I let you get dressed at all."

A few curious glances turned their way and her face flushed. His words weren't far from the truth; he'd kissed her awake and let her have a single cup of white tea before sending her to dress for breakfast. But once she'd dressed and joined him in the living room, he soon coaxed her right back to their bed, her clothes tossed to the floor and breakfast forgotten again.

He gave a soft laugh. "I guess I shouldn't have said that so loud."

She ducked her head as the line shuffled a few steps forward. Her cheeks burned but she sensed that, while he hadn't meant to embarrass her, Jolar didn't really care if everyone within earshot knew how they'd spent their morning.

"Hello, Arissa."

"Oh." Seeing who it was exiting the restaurant, Arissa smiled. "Good morning, Kemma, Lian."

Kemma turned her smile on Jolar. "We didn't have much chance to meet yesterday."

Jolar looked as if he were trying to place her.

"We were seated at your table last night," Kemma reminded.

His face lit with recognition. "That's right. I didn't even introduce myself. I'm Jolar Legan." He unwrapped one arm from around Arissa to shake Lian's hand.

"Good to meet you," Lian said.

"I'm sorry we intruded," Kemma said, smiling between them. "I didn't realize it was your honeymoon."

"It's not," Jolar said. "We've been married for almost four years."

"Really?" Puzzlement rippled off Kemma. "I'm sorry. You two are just so—" She laughed lightly. "Well, you're happily married anyway."

Jolar shifted his weight. "I have a lot to be grateful for."

"Remember that." Kemma glanced at Arissa. "Your wife is charming. She deserves your best."

"Yes." Jolar's tone cooled a bit. "She does."

The odd tension between them was making Arissa's stomach clench. "How's the food here?"

"Wonderful," Lian said. "The onka cakes with the gravy were delicious. Kemma had the fruit platter like she always does."

"Occupational hazard." Kemma said with a wry smile. "Constant dieting."

Jolar's smile was puzzled. "Are you an actress?"

Kemma smirked up at him playfully. "It's a sad day indeed when you fleet types don't recognize a Niman ornament."

"How did you know I was in the fleet?" Jolar asked sharply.

"I thought—" Kemma looked at Arissa, confused. "Didn't you say the last time you moved he was on patrol?"

"Yes," Arissa agreed immediately. "At dinner we were talking about moving and last time I had to do everything because you were—"

"At the border," Jolar finished with a smile as his tension fell. "She had to handle it all alone. I'm not sure I'll ever live it down."

"So who bought breakfast?" Arissa asked. "They had a bet that the last night's winner would buy breakfast today," she explained to Jolar.

"Kelm and I split the cost of the fruit platter. My only good luck is that Kemma's such a light eater." He shook his head. "I don't know why I ever let you goad me into betting with you. I always lose."

Kemma gave him a fond nudge. "Not always."

The line moved again, and Lian glanced toward the host's station. "Well, looks like you're up next so we'll let you go."

Kemma nodded to Jolar and gave Arissa a warm smile. "I hope to see you again."

Arissa grinned back. "I'd really like that."

"An ornament?" Jolar murmured in mock-reproof as the pair moved off, sliding his hands around her again. "I'm not sure I want you keeping company with someone like that. Might be a bad influence."

"Funny. What was that about Niman ornaments and fleet types?"

His face colored. Suddenly the humor of it was gone. He'd had other lovers; of course he'd had. Women as beautiful as Kemma had heated a bed with him—women whose soft limbs sought to hold him a little longer when the sun rose, whose lips parted with sighs of regret when he'd left them . . .

"Name?" the hostess chirped.

Arissa turned, breaking Jolar's hold. "Legan."

The woman noted it and, smiling, led them to a table for two.

Caf, juice and tea were served by a rushed staffer who promised to return for their order. The restaurant hummed with activity, many of the nearby tables occupied by families.

"Place is swamped," Jolar observed. "I hope we get breakfast before it's time for dinner."

Arissa kept her eyes on her menu, upset yet still ravenous enough to finish off half the offerings.

When the staffer returned Jolar ordered sular steak and eggs. Arissa choose onka cakes with warmed syrup, a plate of crispy grimp toast and two sides of sliced fruit.

She threw a narrowed look at the waiter's raised eyebrows. *Spend a few months starving on Tellar and then talk to me about the size of my breakfast.*

"What do you want to do today?" Jolar asked, lifting his mug of caf. "There's still lots on board we didn't try yesterday."

She shrugged. A toddler at the next table howled as his exasperated mother tried again to get him to drink his juice. "Whatever you like."

"We haven't been to the pool or the gaming center. We could try our luck at one of the casinos."

"You choose."

The boy continued to fuss. Arissa rubbed her forehead with the pads of her fingers.

"Are you angry with me?" Jolar asked quietly. "You're hardly looking at me."

"I'm sorry." She stirred nectar into her tea as the boy whimpered. "I don't have any right to be upset."

"Sure you do." Jolar gave her a searching look. "If you think you're only one of dozens."

She winced. "Only dozens?"

"Sweet," Jolar said softly, his blue eyes serious as the boy arched away from his mother. "This is different."

"Festering hells!" Arissa twisted to glare the boy's mother, her hand pressed against her temple. "Take him to the medcenter, his ears hurt!"

The woman blinked, her mouth parting. Shock rippled through the restaurant.

Arissa's gaze darted from one set of staring eyes to the next.

Run! Oh, gods, have to run before they—

Jolar's hand closed over hers.

"Our nephew does that," Jolar said a little too loudly. "Poor kid's had so many ear infections I'm not sure my sister slept a whole night last year."

The woman looked down at the boy in her arms. He was tugging on one of his ears, his big brown eyes filled with tears.

"Oh! Oh, I didn't even think of that! He's been so cranky that I thought just the schedule change but—" The woman gently touched her son's ear. "Oh, numkin, is that what's wrong?"

Jolar's thumb stroked the back of her hand as Arissa sought to control her trembling. The conversations and clatter of silverware on plates began to fill the restaurant again as the woman carried her child out.

"Good," Jolar said brightly to the waiter who arrived with their meals. "I'm starving."

He poured himself more caf. "It's all right," he murmured.

She raised frightened eyes to his.

"It is." He glanced around. "Check for yourself."

Wetting her lips, she did but found no hint of lingering interest or suspicion.

"You're not going to make me eat this all by myself, are you?" he asked.

Their little table was full of food, most of it her order.

Last night and this morning were the happiest times of her whole life and she'd just ruined it all. Swallowing hard, she lifted her fork.

Jolar kept up the conversation but she could scarcely manage a few mumbled replies. He told her a story about his first time on a fleet patrol, how the captain had a special shuttle run made when he found out that the caf in food stores had gone moldy.

"Two things you don't mess with," Jolar said, standing at meal's end. "Their pay and their caf. The fleet will put up with just about anything else."

He took her hand as they exited the Twin Suns. "Where to?"

Arissa avoided his gaze. "Back to our suite."

"Nope," he said cheerfully. "How about the Lightside casino? You didn't get to go with them last night. We could try our luck at tongo."

She pulled against his hold. "I want to go to our suite now."

He sighed deeply. "Arissa, for gods' sake, I'm just one man. You have to give me some time to recover before you take me back to bed."

"Are you trying to be funny?" she burst out.

"Yes," he said solemnly. "How am I doing?"

Hot tears stung her eyes.

"All right," he said quietly. He led her out of the foot traffic and beside one of the fountains. Surrounded by greenery and the few unoccupied benches nearby, it was a private spot in the middle of the busy deck. He took her hands in his and leaned forward to look into her eyes. "You can't let this throw you."

"Jolar," she whispered, "you saw what I did."

"Yes. You helped a little boy who was in pain, a mother who was exhausted and a room full of people have a much more pleasant breakfast."

Tears blurred her vision. "I gave myself away. If you hadn't been there—"

"I *was* there," he reminded. "I mean it, Arissa. You can't ruminate on one misstep. It happened, we dealt with it, now we move on."

"My kind of missteps hurt people."

He shook his head gently. "You didn't hurt anyone. You helped that boy and his mother. You *helped*."

"But—but if I hadn't said anything—"

"That poor kid would still be howling in pain. You think that would have been better?"

Arissa hesitated. "Of course I didn't want him in pain."

"So you did something about it."

Arissa swallowed. "I shouldn't have. I should have more control."

"Well, maybe you didn't have to shout," he allowed. "And the colorful language might be something to phase out. I think it was more that you were trying to pretend like there was nothing wrong, trying to ignore a problem you knew damn well was happening."

Arissa shifted her feet. "What do you mean?"

"Look, maybe instead of trying *not* to be a—what you are—maybe it's time to *be* what you are." His fingers intertwined with hers. "Sweet, the time for you to hide is over. Like it or not, you're going to have to learn to live out here with the rest of us screwed-up people now. Put what you can do to good use. It's that simple."

"Jolar, it's not that easy."

He shook his head again. "I didn't say 'easy'. I said 'simple'. You've spent your whole life fighting against what you are." He rested his forehead against hers. "It's time to learn how to make the most of it."

She swallowed hard but his warm acceptance was impossible to resist. "By playing cards?"

"Yes, among other things." He leaned down to kiss her; his mouth was light over hers, then deepened. He broke away, a little breathless. "Casino or activity center?"

"I don't know how to play tongo," she mumbled.

"Then we're evenly matched because I don't know how to play *well*." He pressed a quick kiss to her forehead. "Come on. Let's lose some money."

Folding his arms, Jolar threw her a mock exasperated look and muttered: "'Oh, but Jolar, I don't know *how* to play tongo!'"

Arissa spared him a glance, then counted out ten chips from the growing pile in front of her and moved them into the pot.

The Utavaian across the table fixed her with dark eyes as hard as duracrete, as if he could glean the values of her cards by glaring. He was a heavy-set man, and like so many from his homeworld, he was dark haired with an olive cast to his skin. Jeweled rings adorned his fat fingers, the stones flashing as he examined his cards. Judging by the tightness of the gold bracelets against his wrists and the too-small necklaces under the rolls of his neck, a good deal of that jewelry had likely been purchased when he was a younger, and much slimmer, man.

He drank Utavian desert spirits straight up. Either his girth or his annoyance had him grunting every few minutes. With heavy dark brows pulled low over his glittering black eyes, he had the ill-humored look of a man who was dangerous when crossed.

And he couldn't bluff to save his life.

But then again apparently neither could anyone else—at least not against her. Jolar had thrown in his last hand two hours ago, declaring that there was no point in continuing to lose to his own wife. A number of players had come and gone in the time she'd sat there, and all the poorer for it.

She didn't win every hand; sometimes her cards just weren't good enough to stay in. But she followed the elation, disappointment or angry discouragement of her competitors and played accordingly, folding at their sudden confidence, driving the bet insanely high when another player's bravado wasn't backed up by the cards he held.

I can't believe I was lifting billfolds in the market, running from place to place, terrified, when I could have been sitting in a nice comfortable casino instead.

The Utavian pursed his thick lips. Grunting again, he leaned forward and counted out ten chips. Feigning nonchalance, he threw them into the huge pot.

The Sertarian to Arissa's right, the only other player at the table with them, took another look at his cards and shook his head. "Nope, I'm out."

The Sertarian put his cards in front of the dealer and handed the woman a couple chips as a tip. He collected his drink and headed off, leaving just Arissa and the–Utavian in the game.

The Utavian lifted his hand and extended his sausage-like fingers in invitation. "The bet is to you."

Arissa looked at her cards. It wasn't a great hand. Three ladies, a mage and two of the lesser suit.

She kept her eyes on her cards and *reached* . . . past Jolar's amusement, the dealer's growing fatigue, and just brushed the Utavian's mind . . .

She counted out twenty chips.

Jolar's surprise rippled. "You're going to bet that?"

She placed the twenty in front of Jolar. "No." Arissa shoved the rest of her little mountain of chips into the pot. "I'm going to bet *that*."

There was burst of shock from all three and they all, the dealer, Jolar and the- Utavian, regarded her in stunned silence.

The dealer cleared her throat. "Will you see the bet, sir?"

The Utavian's jowls were shaking as he stood. He threw the cards on the table and stormed away.

"Damnedest luck I ever saw." Jolar grinned, then kissed her cheek. "Sweet, I think you could break the bank."

The dealer began to push the pile toward her but Arissa held up a hand. "No, I think I'm done."

"Hey, I don't mind," Jolar protested. "I mean, sure, my manhood is threatened but I could get used to my wife supporting me."

"No," Arissa demurred. "I'm done for today." She reached-for the stack of twenty chips and put them in front of the dealer. "For you."

The woman blinked, then gave a wide smile. "Thank you, ma'am. Do you want to cash out or shall I get a basket for your chips?"

"More like an anti-grav unit," Jolar said, eyeing her winnings.

"I want to cash out," Arissa said to the dealer.

It took a few minutes for the dealer to count it all. "Shall I add it to your shipboard account?"

"No," Jolar said. "Cash."

Arissa's lips parted at the sight of the stack of rainbow hued credits placed in front of her. There were nearly twenty-five thousand credits sitting there.

For an instant she was back in that alley, ready to sell her innocence to Jolar for a hundred credits and a chance to sleep in a bed . . .

"Arissa?" Jolar brushed a curl away from her face. "Are you okay?"

"Yes. It's just a lot of money." She looked down at her expensive new clothes and gave a short laugh. "I don't have any pockets. Will you carry it for me?"

"I think my own winnings have left me a little room," he joked, scooping it up.

She took his hand as they left, a little surprised when the lights and the noise of the casino came back into her awareness. She could feel the sea of emotions around her now, a turbulent ocean of disappointments, anger, elation and loneliness. It was astonishing that she had been able to shut them out and focus for so long.

"What now?" he asked as they exited the casino. "Are you hungry or do you want to wait till dinner?"

"I'm surprised they didn't offer us anything to eat in the casino. They certainly were generous with the drinks."

"Eating might help sober you up. They don't want players thinking straight if they can help it."

"I can't believe I'm saying this, but I'm not hungry." She smiled. "Not yet anyway."

"Well, let's spend time somewhere a little more wholesome than a gambling den. How about the activity center?"

She brightened. "I'd love to! I've never—I haven't been to the one onboard."

"Well, then." Jolar smiled. "Let's go play with the other kids."

"What about this is supposed to be fun?" Arissa demanded, the room pitch black around them. "I can't see a starblasted thing."

"Actually, this could be a whole lot of fun," Jolar murmured, his hands going around her waist to pull her against him. He was warm against her back, and the timbre of his voice sent a tightening between her thighs.

"I know you're teasing." She caught her breath as his hands slid lightly over her.

His mouth touched the side of her neck as he cupped her breasts. "It *is* awfully dark in here . . . Maybe if we were quiet too . . ."

"Jolar," she warned breathlessly as his tongue traced her skin. "There are dozens of people here."

He gave a low frustrated half-growl. "And not even a door, just a curved passageway into this game room. Couldn't you warn me if someone were coming our way?"

"I'm not sure. Ordinarily I could, but I might not if I were – uh . . ."

"Busy making those sounds you make when you find your pleasure?"

"Oh." Her cheeks went hot. "I didn't realize I did anything like that."

"You do. The sweetest little cries . . ." Jolar gave a soft groan. "Gods, this is *not* helping. We need to start the game *now* or risk getting put off the ship."

He wasn't the only one who was wondering if they might actually be able to get away with it. "How do I play?"

"Give me a sec. I'm not sure I have any blood left in my head to think with," he said, laughing a little. "Game—set up!"

Arissa gasped at finding herself hurtling through space.

There was no floor under her feet, no walls, no ceiling above, just light-years of open space around her. She gripped in terror at Jolar's arms.

"Are you okay?" Jolar's surprise and concern vibrated against her mind.

"I didn't know that would happen!"

"Haven't you ever played a—" He broke off and his sense grew heavy. "You've never played a hologame. Just like you'd never been to a restaurant. Like you never went to school."

"No." Her throat was tight. "I'm sorry."

"Why should *you* be sorry? It's the rest of us that should be sorry, everyone who forced you to—" He broke off, his anger humming. His sense calmed as if he were forcing himself to it. "Game—level one."

The view shifted. Two warships, each miniaturized to the size of a man, now flanked her. It was utterly disconcerting to have everything change and not even to be able to see the floor beneath her feet, even though her eyes registered plenty of light.

"How does it do that?" she asked, turning her head towards where she knew Jolar was. "I can't even see you right behind me."

"The sensors track your eye movements and adjust the holoprojectors to fool your perception." He hesitated. "I guess you haven't been in a holotheater either."

"No. We had holos at home but it wasn't as . . . immersive as this." If it weren't for Jolar's arms around her, the familiar feel of his mind, she would be completely undone. "And this is your favorite game?"

"Yeah, well, you spend a lot of downtime on a fleet cruiser trying to stave off boredom. The quarters are made up of a bunk, a private 'fresher and a shower if you're lucky, and a table with a chair bolted to the floor. You hit the gym, read whatever you can get your hands on, bet on stupid things like how much radiation a particular asteroid will give off. *Star Quest* here got me through a four-month rotation with my sanity intact. Are you ready?"

"Wait! What do I do?"

"The game responds to your body movements." Jolar took her by either wrist and lifted her arms in front of her. Her flying speed increased. He turned her a bit and her direction changed. "Now, just fight the bad guys."

"Fight? Oh!"

A ship came hurtling right at her, energy cannons blasting.

"What the hells!" She ducked; instinctively throwing her arms up to protect her face. "Ships just *attack* me?"

"You *are* a ship."

"Why the hells is it so starblasted loud?" she demanded trying to be heard over the cacophony of firing ships. "Why is it making any noise at all when we're supposed to be in a fucking *vacuum*?"

She could feel his body shaking with laughter but the sound of it was drowned out by the holoships roaring past and firing.

Suddenly the ships were gone and she was flying through space again alone.

"What happened?" she asked, startled by the sudden quiet.

"Level reset."

"How do I shoot back anyway?"

"Raise your hands in front of you and curl your fingers into a loose fist."

She did, this time prepared for the increase in speed. "Okay."

"Now you just kind of flick your fingers."

She tried it and gave a start when a bolt of blue energy blazed from her palm. "So they fly in and shoot at me and I shoot at them?"

"Yes. Ready?"

This time as the ship came from her lower right, she managed to fire back. It came around for another pass, spattering blue light all around her, and the level reset again.

"It would take me months to get good at this game," Arissa complained.

"It took me a while too. But I'm right behind you and that doesn't leave you free to move like you need to. I'll step back and you can try it again."

"No," she said quickly. The noise and flashing lights were giving her a headache. "I think I'm good for now."

"All right. Game—end."

The starfield vanished, replaced by the soft beiges of the hologame room and Jolar grinning at her. He was so stunning smiling down at her like this that she could almost believe the holoprojectors had created him too.

"I'd say I miss the dark but now I get to see you, pretty girl."

"You mean that," she managed.

He blinked. "I spent most of last night and this morning telling you how beautiful you are. Did you think I didn't mean it?"

"I don't—I just—"

He pulled her close then. His mouth hovered over hers for a moment.

"Beautiful," he murmured then covered her mouth with his own. He deepened the kiss, his hand cupping the back of her head.

"Come on." His eyes were dark with hunger. "If I don't get you back to our suite soon they really *are* going to have reason to put us off the ship."

Twelve

They made it as far as the lift, but Jolar's mouth was on hers as soon as the doors closed. He leaned down and she gave a surprised cry as he lifted her, his hands under her hips. He pressed her back against the side of the car. Her arms wrapped around his neck as he kissed her.

Her casual day clothes of long tunic and pants allowed her to wrap her legs around his waist. He held her balanced, her back against the wall of the lift. He groaned into her mouth, his hand cupping her buttocks now as he held her against him.

A jolt against her mind alerted her. A sharp, deliberate cough came from the doorway. Jolar, flushing, also became aware that the lift had reached the next level and another couple stood waiting to enter.

"Now that's a lucky girl," the woman murmured.

Jolar, red to the hairline, set Arissa on her feet.

"Honeymoon?" the man asked, amused. "We can take the next one."

"No, it's all right." Jolar cleared his throat. "Sorry."

"Congratulations," the woman said warmly as they got on. "Were you married on-board?"

"No we—" Jolar mumbled. "Second honeymoon."

The woman lifted an eyebrow. "*Very* lucky girl."

"I heard that," the man said dryly.

Jolar was so bashful at having been caught he wouldn't meet anyone's eye. He took Arissa's hand and ducked his head when they exited on their deck.

"I'm really glad I didn't let you talk me into anything at the activity center," she said at the door to their suite. "You're still blushing."

He swept her into his arms the instant the door opened. He had her in the bedroom and on the bed in a few strides.

He was already shrugging out of his shirt. "I've never been so close to making a complete fool of myself," he said roughly. "If they'd gotten on a minute later I'm not sure I would have been able to stop."

He was naked in moments, already fully aroused as he pulled her clothes from her. He kissed his way over her breasts and belly, and urged her wider to settle himself between her legs. His skin was warm and smooth against the inside of her thighs.

Startled, she sensed his intention. "Wait—What are you doing?"

He leaned his weight down, easily holding her thighs open with his elbows. His fingers gently parted her folds, revealing her most sensitive place before his vivid gaze.

"Kissing you." His breath was hot and moist against her center.

He pressed his mouth there, his lips warm and gentle. A moment later his lips parted and his tongue leisurely traced the spot. Her breath drew in sharply and her eyes fell shut. Her hands threaded through his soft hair as his tongue teased her higher, gasping at the thrumming pleasure he took in doing it.

He sank a finger into her folds, pressing the sensitive place inside, stroking her higher still. She cried out as release broke over her.

As he caught her sated expression, a grin of pure masculine satisfaction flitted across his face. She was still trembling from her climax as he covered her body with his.

Caging her with his arms and too roused to wait, Jolar quickly positioned himself to enter her. She placed her palms on his chest to hold him away.

He searched her face. "Sweet?" he asked, his voice husky. "What's wrong?"

"I want to do what you did," she said. "To make you feel like you made me feel."

He was taut and tense with wanting, the tip of his shaft already poised at her center and plainly reluctant to relinquish his place. But he let her move him so he was lying back on the bed.

Jolar watched her, his gaze hot, his eyes half closed as she knelt over him and traced the warm, golden skin of his chest down the muscles of his stomach. His mouth parted as she slid her hand around his shaft, feeling it jerk against her hold as she stroked. She scooted back and knelt between his legs. She leaned forward and caught how the feel of her curls against his thighs sent his arousal and anticipation soaring.

She pressed her mouth against the tip of his shaft in a kiss and flicked her tongue to taste the bead of moisture there. He groaned when she took him into her mouth, her hand moving along the length in tandem.

She let his sense guide her to what gave him the most pleasure, how fast to move, how much pressure to use.

She used her tongue against the underside of his shaft, and the rising waves of his pleasure echoed through her mind. It was a thrill to be able to rouse him so powerfully. His thigh muscles were quivering now; she felt him wild with it. She cupped him where he was soft.

"Gods," he ground out. "*Arissa—*"

His eyes were squeezed shut, his body taut and trembling, poised just at the brink now. She changed the pressure just enough to delay it, keep him there at the very edge for another moment, then another . . .

He cried out hoarsely as his climax tore through him. The salty taste of his seed burst into her mouth, his whole body quaking with his release. She held him there as the aftershocks pulsed through his shaft.

She sat back to look at him. He was shaking, his eyes shut, his hand half covering his face, the sweat gleaming on his chest.

She grinned. "So, that was okay?"

"That was—Gods!" he rasped. "The best *ever*."

"Really?" She expected that was the kind of thing men said to women all the time, but he genuinely meant it. "I just kept my awareness on you, followed what you were feeling, and whatever you really liked I did more of."

His eyes snapped open. "You can do that?"

"Apparently." She smirked. "Maybe I *should* be an ornament." She blinked at his sudden, scalding rush of possessiveness. "I was just joking."

"You better be. I have no intention of sharing you, sweet." He pulled her down to cradle her against him. He cupped her face and kissed her, then gave a wide grin. "In fact, I may never let you out of this bed again."

"What if I get hungry?"

"Hmm, I guess I will have to let you eat," he murmured against her hair.

He held her there while his breath slowed and she rested her cheek against his shoulder, enjoying the safe warmth of his embrace.

His fingers threaded through her curls, and his sense grew pensive.

"There's something I've been meaning to ask you. Something I need to know, Arissa." He searched her face.

"If you weren't an ornament, how did you manage on Tellar without an ID?"

She shifted against him, finding it hard to meet his eyes now.

"Arissa?"

He was not going to let this go.

"I, um—" She cleared her throat. "I was a thief."

"What?" he breathed, his shock reverberating.

"I had some money when I got to Tellar but it ran out after a few months." The words came out in a rush. "One day I was in the market in Xan-Tellar, I hadn't eaten all day and I didn't have any way to pay my rent and this man—I knew he wasn't paying attention, that no one was and I just . . . took his billfold."

He stared.

"Gods," he got out. "Do you have any idea how dangerous that was? For *you* of all people? What if TelSec had picked you up? Hells, steal from the wrong person and they wouldn't *bother* calling TelSec, they would have just beaten the hells out of you!"

"I didn't have a choice." She sought his gaze, pleading for understanding. "I couldn't work. I couldn't even register as an ornament. I mean, I could have tried it on my own without the license but—anyway I didn't think I could do that." She put her hand on his chest. "I could now, though."

His blue eyes were horrified. "Because of me? Because we—"

"No! I just . . . I could do it now because no one can take this time—*our* time—away from me. I'll always have it. I gave myself to someone I wanted. If I have to trade myself later, well, that'll just be my body, not *me*."

"You won't need to." His arms tightened around her. "Not ever. I'll take care of you. I promise. I just—we have to succeed on Sertar. We have to."

And what will be between us after Sertar?

"We'll be there tomorrow." She wasn't even sure why she said it. He knew when they would arrive. Something about just admitting their time on the ship was almost over put an icy knot in her stomach.

"I wish I could send you back," he said quietly. He must have seen the hurt on her face because he quickly shook his head. "I don't mean I don't want to be with you. Sertar is . . . it's not a place for someone like you."

"A seer, you mean."

"No," he said. "I mean someone as innocent as you are."

"I'm not innocent anymore," she protested with an arch look.

"Yes, you are." He gave her a rueful smile. "If I had my way, I wouldn't take you within five parsecs of that festering planet."

"You've been there. What's it like?"

"Polluted, dangerous, corrupt." He let one of her ringlets wrap around his finger. "I never went planetside unarmed. I never drank more than two lums in an evening because even a blaster won't keep you from being beaten half to death for your billfold if you don't have your wits about you."

"The whole planet can't be like that." She frowned. "There must be some nicer areas."

"That *was* one of the nicer areas."

"Funny. It can't be that bad." She traced the line of his jaw. "You're so worried about me. I survived without even an ID in Xan-Tellar for eight months, Jolar."

"Well, humor me and let's pretend you need me, okay?" he mock grumbled. "It makes me feel useful."

Despite the warm feeling in her chest that he wanted to take care of her, she didn't want him to feel he *had* to.

"All I need is an ID and I'll be fine," she insisted. "I'm a seer, remember?"

"I know. I'm still going to take care of you, sweet." He pressed a kiss to her shoulder. "That reminds me. We have practicing to do."

"Practicing?" she wondered, then quickly shook her head. "Oh! Oh, no, Jolar, I really don't think—"

"Come on, Arissa," he said with a fond pat on her bare rump. "I can't believe I'm saying this, but I want you to get dressed."

Thirteen

Jolar was insistent, and in short order Arissa found herself dressed again in the tunic and pants, sitting with him in the living area of their cabin.

"All right, go ahead." He gave a nod. "Read my mind."

She cringed. "I told you before, I don't know how to do that."

"Okay," he allowed. "Tell me what you can do and we'll go from there."

"Mostly I know what people are feeling. I know where their attention is but I don't know what they're actually thinking. I don't hear words."

"Ever tried?"

"No, and I don't want to now. I would shut this off, tear it out of my head if I could. My mother was even quietly researching if there were any surgical remedies that she might try."

His eyes widened. "Your mother was going to cut into your brain?"

"She was a surgeon, not a butcher! She was looking for some way to make me normal."

"There's nothing wrong with you," he said, his face reddening. "You're gifted, not abnormal."

"You didn't think so in Xan-Tellar." It still hurt to remember. "You recoiled from me like I had the blood plague. You threatened to put a blaster bolt through my head."

"I didn't mean it," he said quietly. "I wouldn't have hurt you. I'm surprised you didn't know that." He let his breath out slowly. "I owe you an apology for it, though—for the way I acted. For scaring you the way I did. I had so little time to convince you to come with me. I bargained everything I could to get them to agree in the first place. Honestly, I don't know what I would have done if you'd refused, but I swear I wouldn't have hurt you or let anyone else hurt you either. As to the rest, I didn't know you then. All I knew about seers was what I'd heard. I'd never—gods, I can't get close *enough* to you now. I can hardly keep my hands off you long enough to get you from the lift to the cabin."

Sudden tears stung her eyes. This is what she'd wanted, always. What she'd dreamed of—someone who wanted her. Wanted her just as she was.

Why was it so hard to accept?

"And I want to know everything there is to know about you," he said, brushing a curl from her cheek. "So let's figure this out together, okay?"

She swallowed back her tears. "Okay."

He studied her for a moment. "Remember when we were on the shuttle and you focused just on me? Let's try that to start. Just focus on me."

He was the only one here and she was getting used to feeling him. "Well, you're a little nervous. Curious. Excited, too."

He smiled a little. "It's a unique opportunity. I don't think anyone in more than half a century has had this experience."

"I didn't do anything I don't usually do."

He gave a nod. "Let try this. Try to focus more on what I'm thinking than what I'm feeling."

That first morning she'd woken up so frightened she'd sought him out for comfort, the same way she had with her parents when she was very young. But that morning she recalled almost, but not *quite*, being able to catch the thread of Jolar's thoughts. Her brow creased as she tried now.

"I'm sorry." She shook her head. "It's no different."

"You're tensing up." He cupped her cheek in his warm palm for a moment. "This isn't a test. Just try."

"Okay," she said uncertainly.

She sent her focus to him just as she had on the shuttle. Her breathing caught the rhythm of his. She skimmed along the ripples and eddies of his mind. She brushed past his interest, his nervousness, his warm attraction to her, and extended her awareness a little *deeper* . . .

She gasped.

"What is it?" he asked instantly.

"I—I don't know. For a moment, in my mind, I saw me airskating."

Jolar's eyes widened. "That's what I was thinking, about yesterday at the rink."

Arissa shot to her feet. "I don't want to do this anymore."

"What?" He stood, catching her before she could flee. "*Why?*"

"*Why?* This is wrong! I shouldn't be able to do this. No one should! I could hurt you. I might have *already* hurt you."

"Arissa, I'm fine."

"You don't know that! *I* don't know that!"

He held her by the shoulders. She could feel him weighing it but abruptly he relented.

"All right." He pressed a kiss to her forehead. "We'll stop for now. Will you tell me about it?"

She looked away.

"It couldn't hurt to talk about it," he reasoned.

She didn't want to; she didn't even want to *think* about it. "What do you want to know?"

"Gods, everything! What did it feel like?"

She shifted her weight. "Like for a moment I was in someone else's body, looking out someone else's eyes."

"Mine."

"Yes." She tucked a curl behind her ear. "I didn't realize you thought I was so . . . short."

He gave a quick, startled laugh. "Not short—delicate maybe."

"I *looked* short," she insisted.

"What else?"

If that's really how she looked to him, what he saw was far different than what she saw in the mirror. If that was indeed what his eyes showed him, he saw her as far more beautiful than she ever imagined she could be to anyone.

She wasn't about to say anything about *that* though.

"Well . . . you don't think I'm much of an airskater."

He frowned a little. "I'm not sure I was thinking that."

"You were thinking about me getting hurt. Worrying about it." She gave an uncertain half-shrug. "Maybe worried I'd fall?"

"Oh," he said quietly. "Yes, perhaps I was."

She searched his face. "Are you okay? Do you have a headache or anything from it?"

He shook his head. "No, nothing."

"Could you . . . *feel* anything?"

He considered her question carefully. "I'm not sure. I thought for a moment—"

"What?" she asked anxiously.

He touched the center of his forehead. "Something light, like a tickle. So light I wouldn't have noticed if I hadn't been trying to feel something."

"We really shouldn't do this again."

"Why not? I'm not hurt."

"But what if you are next time?" Arissa closed her eyes briefly. "And what if doing this makes it worse? What if I can't pull back at all? What if I get lost in other people and can't find my way back to myself?"

"Arissa, I think practice will *help* you control it. I think we're going to learn a lot by doing this together."

It would much easier if he weren't so fucking happy about the whole thing. "Jolar, this is dangerous. We have no idea what will happen to you if we continue."

"You know what I think?" he asked, folding his arms. "I think *nothing* will happen. I think the damage they said seers caused was propaganda. I bet nothing like that happened at all."

"There was more than enough proof during the trials—"

"And you don't think that 'proof' could have been manufactured when the New Order took power? Victors write the history, Arissa. I bet if Jensah had her chance to study you her tests would show that you aren't a danger to anyone."

Her brow creased. "Is that what you want? For Doctor de'Sar to study me?"

"No, of course not! Besides, any conclusions she might make in your favor would either be altered or quietly suppressed."

Arissa shook her head. "Jolar, my mother was a scientist. You can't alter test results like that. The scientific community wouldn't stand for it."

"It's just as well Jensah didn't get to study you. Knowing her, she would shout her results from the rooftops and the government on Tellar would have had to shut her up."

"They do things like that?" It had never occurred to her that non-telepaths—normal people—had anything to fear from the government.

His mouth was a thin grim line. "Oh, certainly. Jensah's already gone against the grain a couple times or she wouldn't have owed me so big. Her ethics are skewed toward doing what's right, not necessarily what's in her best interest."

"Like you," Arissa said with a slight smile. "Maybe it's a Zartani trait."

His vivid gaze sharpened on her. "Maybe." His smile came back. "Well, if I can't convince you to try again, we might want to think about showing our faces at dinner."

"I guess we haven't done a lot of socializing."

He shrugged. "I only wanted enough of it to enhance our cover a little. People who might have seen us onboard, that sort of thing." He pressed a quick kiss to her forehead. "Let me grab a shower, then I'll run out while you get ready. There's an errand I want to do."

Arissa let her breath out in relief when dinner had ended. It took an enormous amount of energy to keep to her role, hold her telepathic focus to the people around her, and eat at the same time. It was like performing in a theater in the round.

Worst of all, it made it nearly impossible to enjoy the meal.

The food was exquisite and beautifully presented. Vegetables arrayed in bursts of color highlighted the entrées; fruits cut in the shapes of exotic flowers decorated the sweet mousses; layered desserts glistened in Aylorian crystal glasses.

Her few precious moments of peace during the meal were spent in seeking the familiar comfort of Jolar's mind. Sitting across and down the table from her—why did they never seat married couples together?—his moods showed him anything but awed by the meal.

The blatant attempts at flirting from the Sertarian at Arissa's side won him Jolar's glare, though. Jolar sent out tiny barbed flicks of anger and annoyance at the man from his end of the table.

Still, the Sertarian couldn't miss the dark, warning look on Jolar's face when he came to collect her at meal's end. His broad, possessive hand was at Arissa's waist to urge her ahead of him and away from the man as soon as she stood.

"How was dinner?" he asked, taking her hand when they reached the busy corridor.

"Fine."

"Good," he said. Then after a moment, he continued casually: "So, I couldn't hear much from my side of the table. You seemed to be getting on pretty well with your dinner companion though."

"I guess so."

"You hardly talked to anyone else at your end."

"Oh," Arissa said, adjusting her wrap. "It just worked out that way."

"And the two of you found a lot to talk about?"

"Hmm."

"Anything you'd care to share with me?" he asked, a definite edge to his voice now.

Arissa burst out laughing.

His blond brows rushed together in a scowl. "What the hells' so funny?"

Arissa beamed up at him. "You're *jealous*."

He stopped short.

"Gods, you're right," he whispered hoarsely.

He blinked down at her, his emotions churning wildly. seer that she was, she honestly couldn't tell if he were about to burst out laughing or hang his head and sob right here in the middle of the busy corridor.

It was the most extraordinary and complex shift of emotions she'd ever encountered.

"Jolar?" She creased her brow, placing her hand hesitantly on his chest. "Are you okay?"

"Yes," he said as if that answer surprised him. "Yes, I am."

"Do you," she tried to think of something that might help, "want to sit down or something?"

His glance darted about as if he were startled to find that they were still standing outside the ship's dining room with dozens of people around them.

"No." He continued their walk and, just like that, he seemed like himself again. "Let's go to the gardens. You wanted to see them, didn't you?"

"If you're all right," she said uncertainly.

Jolar checked the directory and found the gardens' location to be two decks up.

Arissa glanced at him as they rode the lift—the strong line of his chin, the long straight nose, the fullness of his mouth. She felt the core of grave responsibility beneath his striking blond good looks. She could well imagine him rising to the rank of admiral or gaining that council seat he'd talked about. He had the charisma of a born leader and the easy confidence to lead well.

But his oddness tonight was troubling. *Had* she hurt him?

He seemed determined to keep testing her seer abilities. Even her parents, who'd loved her so, had actively discouraged her from using them. The whole idea of it made her feel queasy. Somehow she had to dissuade him from experimenting further.

Jolar took her hand again when they exited the lift. His long fingers did indeed make hers look positively delicate.

The gardens' entrance was pretty enough, but not very impressive—and with casinos, bars and dancing available onboard, clearly not very popular at this time of the evening.

A dozen paces in, they turned a corner and Arissa caught her breath.

Broad ever-moving red leaves rustled softly under a perfect lavender sky. The treetops seemed to coil high above them—even though she knew that was impossible; the ceiling of this deck *couldn't* extend up that far.

"How—" she managed. "How did they *do* that?"

"Same way the *Star Quest* game works—but I'll bet some of the plants are real." The air ruffled his hair. "The breeze is a nice touch."

"This is Novic, right?"

His good spirits dampened at the reminder that without an ID she had been unable to travel. "You've never been there."

"No," she breathed. "Have you? Have you been there?"

"Yes. Many times."

"What's next?" she demanded. The urge to see all of them quickly, before the opportunity could be snatched away from her, made her pull him along the path. "What world's next?"

"Uh, I don't know. I mean it could be any of—"

She stopped short upon stepping into a tropical world of lush green and blue. The warm, humid air caressed her face.

"Gensoy," she said, recognizing it from her studies. "This is Gensoy."

Tropical plants crowded around them, their scent heavy and rich. Beside her stood a tree thick with shiny indigo leaves. Jolar caught her hand before she could touch it.

"Gendara tree. Their leaves have a nasty sting." He touched the leaf lightly, and rubbed his forefinger and thumb together. "Though these seem to have been altered to minimize it."

"They don't sting you?"

"I have a tolerance now but damn, they stung me all right. I was stationed on Gensoy after Basic. Our shuttle blew an engine relay on the way there and fried the comset. Tasan and I had to set down and go on foot."

"Tasan?"

"A good friend. In fact I had a drink with him the day we met." He shook his head. "Two days through a Gensoy rainforest."

"Was it as beautiful as this?"

"Oh, it was beautiful all right. Until I brushed against one of *those*." He nodded at the dark leaf. "They sting every time you touch one, then you start to itch. Poor Tasan, he never did develop a tolerance. Gods, it was miserable."

"I wouldn't mind," she said, continuing along the path. "I wouldn't mind at all if I could see it for myself."

"Right," he said dryly. "I don't know if you've noticed, but the ground is covered with these leaves so there's no place to lie down. You can't even sit. Believe me, you'd mind. But this," Jolar said as they stepped into the next garden. "No one minds."

"Nima," she murmured, breathing in the salty air, the sun warm on her face. The water was clear as blue glass, the fine white sand absolutely pristine. In the distance beyond the beach, she could see flowered trees and waterfalls. "I'd love to really see it. I'd do anything to see it."

His arms wrapped around her waist, his body warm against her back. "There's no reason you can't."

"Would the ID—" she broke off. They weren't really here, alone at a beach on the paradise of Nima. They were onboard a vessel with thousands of passengers; someone could enter this 'garden' any moment.

He pressed a kiss to her temple and rested his cheek against hers. "Yes," he murmured. "Anywhere you want."

Arissa smiled and leaned back against him. The ocean breeze lifted her hair. "I wish we could go for a swim too."

"Well, that might be a little more than these projectors can handle," he said with a laugh.

Delighted, she pulled him along the path. But the sight as she stepped into the next world brought stinging tears to her eyes.

"Oh, gods," she whispered. "It's home."

The zanti trees were in bloom, their purple flowers giving off a sweet perfume. The Apovian sky was as blue as Jolar's eyes. She could almost hear her mother calling her in for the evening meal—

"Arissa?"

She was shaking. "I can't stay here. I *can't*."

"It's all right, sweet. Come on. It isn't far to the next

one."

Arissa was still trembling when she stepped into the rolling green hills of Lema.

Jolar cupped her cheek. "Are you okay?"

She focused on the dark red hardwoods of Lema, the rich country scent in her nostrils. "It was so real. It even *smelled* like home."

"You'll be able to go back there when—when we're finished."

"I don't want to," she said instantly. "I don't ever want to go back."

He gave a rueful smile. "You may want to someday."

She wouldn't, she thought, turning to continue along the path. She would take her new ID and whatever name they gave her and choose a new world. One without grief, one without memories of hiding and loneliness and guilt.

She felt his jolt of recognition before he even stopped.

"Speaking of home . . ."

Verdant and bright with clear blue skies, the Zartani vegetation was carefully cultivated, elegantly shaped as if the wildness of nature was thought to be in poor taste. Trees with fragrant white flowers bloomed around them and holographic gossamerflies glided on currents of warm, sweet air, their colorful wings shimmering in the sunlight.

Arissa's eyes widened. "Is this really what Zartan looks like?"

"This is it, all right."

"Oh, Jolar, it's so beautiful!"

He threw her a smile. "I'm glad you think so."

"How long has it been since you were here? Well, not *here*. Zartan."

He considered. "A year? At least that long."

"I'd love to see it."

"Would you?" His vivid eyes were intent now. "I'll take you. I'd love to take you, to show you my home."

Her heart picked up speed. They'd never talked about what would happen between them after she helped him. She'd been afraid to think too much about it.

"I have something for you." He fumbled in his pocket and brought out a small wooden case. His face colored and unceremoniously he shoved it at her. "Here."

She took the case from him, the honey-colored dalsawood smooth in her hand, and opened the lid.

"Oh," she breathed at seeing what the case contained.

"Is it all right?" He shifted his feet. "I mean, do you like it?"

The center jewel of the bracelet was a Zartani firestar, and the surrounding gems sparkled in the light, the gold setting astonishingly delicate. "It's lovely."

"You don't have one. If we're married you'd have a betrothal bracelet." He cleared his throat. "You *should* have one."

"Oh," she mumbled. "Right."

He took the bracelet from its case then slipped the box into his pocket. He fastened the bracelet around the wrist of her left arm, like a married woman would wear it after she were wed, not on the right as a betrothed woman would.

The delicate floral design of the golden cuff encircled her wrist for a perfect fit.

It was the most precious thing she'd ever had.

"Thank you." The words seemed silly, inadequate, far too banal for what she was feeling.

"I'm glad you like it," he said a little stiffly.

"Of course I do. It's absolutely beautiful."

His sense churned with anxiety. "Good."

"Jolar?" She rested her hand on his chest, his heart thumping under her palm. "Is everything all right?"

"Yes." He swallowed. "No." His face reddened further. "I have to say it?"

"Say what?"

His blue eyes were raw. "I love you."

Her breath caught. "You—?"

He gave a short, embarrassed laugh. "You didn't know?"

Blinking, she shook her head.

"Probably from the first moment I looked into your eyes in that alley on Tellar, I just didn't realize—" He searched her face. "But I thought *you* knew."

Her vision blurred. The intensity, the shifting emotions—she hadn't the experience to recognize what he felt. But he meant it, truly meant it. Beautiful, intelligent Jolar, whose presence lit up a room . . .

Loves me!

"Well, then if . . ." He cleared his throat again. "If you don't feel the same way, then that's all right, you don't need to—"

"I love you too."

Jolar blinked and then his face fairly glowed, wild joy bursting like a million beams of light around him. "You do?"

"Gods, of course I do." She tucked her hair behind her ear. "How could *you* not know?"

He cupped her wrist, the firestar of her betrothal bracelet catching the sunlight. "I didn't even realize why I had to buy this for you until we were standing outside the restaurant tonight. What I've been hiding from myself."

"This was your errand today?" she asked, indicating the bracelet.

"Actually I saw earrings that I thought you would like. But when I went to buy them I saw this, and all I could think about was putting it on your wrist." He traced the delicate gold of the bracelet. "I want to marry you."

Her mouth parted, but then her brow creased at the sense she caught. "But you aren't asking me, are you?"

He closed his eyes briefly. "After Sertar, we can talk about a life together." He touched his forehead to hers. "After you have that ID, after I know I've made you safe, then we can plan."

"Okay." She smiled at him through tears. "Okay."

He smiled back. "Does that mean I get to kiss you now?"

Fourteen

Arissa folded her arms. "I'm telling you, Jolar, I'm not comfortable doing this."

After the words of love spoken last night she was even less eager to attempt reading his mind. If she did harm him—no matter how unintentionally—she wouldn't be able to live with it. But she just couldn't seem to convince him that probing into his mind was *dangerous*. Certainly her stern posture now was having no effect.

She relaxed her arms and tried a wheedling little smile instead. "You know, maybe we should—"

"No," he said firmly. "You have charmed and sweet-talked and generally befuddled me with lust all morning, but now I'm insisting."

She'd delayed this by asking to be taken to breakfast, suggesting they pack, begging for a cup of white tea. She had wrapped her arms around him, tracing kisses along his jaw and ran her hand down his hardened length until he groaned and carried her back to bed.

"You can't order me, Jolar," she said, sulky now. "I'm not in the military. I'm not even technically a Tellaran citizen."

"I know. A very convenient way to deprive you of any civil rights." Jolar sighed, leaning back against the sofa in the living area of their suite. "We need to practice just to discover what you can do. I know you're afraid—"

"Because this is terrifying!"

"Is that what you're feeling from me? Fear?"

"No," she admitted. "I'm not saying you're afraid. I'm saying you *should* be. I know I am."

"And I know you won't hurt me. We are *going* to practice, Arissa. We're headed planetside soon and I don't know how the rest of today is going to shake out, so that leaves now."

"I don't even know what to do!"

"Let's try what worked yesterday," he suggested. "I'll think of a place and you describe it to me."

His sense was set, unyielding. Finally she gave a defeated sigh. Closing her eyes, she brought her focus fully to him as she had the day before. She reached past his eagerness, his stubbornness, past the peaks and valleys of worry that seemed to crowd his mind lately, reached a little deeper . . .

She caught her breath at the sudden flood of images.

"Arissa?"

She struggled to calm her breathing. "I need a minute."

He stroked her hair, his concern swirling around her.

It was stronger this time, easier to reach into his mind. *Terrifyingly easy.*

After a few moments, she gave a shaky nod. "I'm all right."

"What did you see?"

"A city, I think. No, that's not right . . . *like* a city. There were buildings all around but I knew they were empty. There was shouting, running, other people in uniform all around me with weapons, but I wasn't in any danger. It was exciting but I was worried too, trying to think of everything I needed to do—"

"*I* was trying to think of everything," he corrected. "I was remembering some of my advanced training on Lema. It was a mock combat drill. We were being evaluated on performance." Jolar shook his head, his eyes wide and awed. "Oh, sweet, what I wouldn't give to do what you can do. It's—Gods, it's amazing!"

A lump formed in her throat.

He frowned. "What's the matter? Did doing that hurt you?"

"No." She swallowed. "You make me feel . . . *better* about what I am."

"You should feel proud of who you are. Proud of what you can do." He touched his forehead to hers. "I am."

Tears overflowed, and she ducked her head against his shoulder. He held her close, stroking her back. She drank in the comfort of it, the warm familiar feel of his mind.

Anxiety suddenly stained his sense.

"What is it?" she asked, wiping at her face. "What's wrong?"

His arms tightened around her. "We'll be planetside in a few hours."

"And you have more to tell me now, don't you?"

He closed his eyes briefly. "Yes."

He went into the bedroom and returned with a datapad. He offered it to her. "This is the information the other agent was able to get to Dacel before he was killed."

She took the datapad and scrolled through the information slowly. "It looks like he was there for months," she murmured. "He did a lot of work."

"I doubt we have even close to that long," Jolar said grimly.

"So you think he was right about these five individuals? That they're the only ones with enough influence on Sertar to take control of the energy supply?"

"Four," Jolar said.

Arissa glanced at the datapad. "I thought—"

"One of them is dead now. But Dacel trusted his agent, and these findings, implicitly. Which is good because we don't have time to start over."

"I'm guessing that one being dead made it easier for the remaining four to solidify their power."

Jolar nodded. "And whoever figured out who Dacel's agent really was will be twice as cautious about who he—or she—trusts now."

"And we need them to trust *us*." She frowned. "But why would they? I mean, we're just supposed to be a married couple from Aylor; you were a lieutenant in the fleet. We're outsiders."

"They'll trust us for two reasons—one, we have a contact on Sertar who *is* an insider. He'll be hosting us, taking us around. Lending his—I guess you could say 'trustworthiness', though that term is pretty relative on Sertar—to us."

"Did he take around the previous agent?"

"No," Jolar said quickly. "And if those two ever met, it's not in the reports. But we need his help to enter Sertarian society quickly. Kav had a lot more time to cultivate those relationships than we do."

"Kav?"

"Kav de'Reaven was the agent Dacel sent before us. He and I weren't friends but he was a good man." Jolar's mouth tightened. "He deserved better."

"You said there were two reasons," Arissa prompted, hoping to draw him from his dark thoughts.

"Yes. I'm supposed to be the representative who will be purchasing the crystals for the military for the next five years."

"That must be a valuable contract."

"Very," he agreed. "And even a cursory check will reveal our finances are at the breaking point. I'm also plainly not above bringing my wife along for a business vacation on the government's tab." He gave a faint smile. "It seems we're a couple of spendthrifts living beyond our means."

"To make you appear more amiable to corruption. Smart. All right," she said looking at the notes again. "Tell me about the four that are left."

Jolar took the datapad and brought up the image of a man in his middle years.

"Larner Tovic," he said with a nod at the screen. "Native Sertarian, in fact there's no record he's ever left the Sertarian system, not even for a vacation. His family has been involved in crystal mining for generations. He has abundant wealth and connections and he's . . . aberrant."

Larner's was an unremarkable face, and he had dull brown, closely cropped hair. His gaze was remote, as if all his focus remained on his inner world.

"Aberrant?"

"No wife, no children. No lovers, past or present. No criminal history. No scandals. His life is . . . *tidy*."

Arissa raised her eyebrows. "And *that* makes him suspicious?"

"You don't wield that much power, amass that much wealth on Sertar, without getting your hands bloody. Either Larner really has managed to live like one of Seleni's novices—on the most corrupt world in the Realm—or all evidence of his wrongdoing has been scrubbed. According to Kav, a number of Larner's competitors have vanished over the last year. The details in Kav's report imply that Larner is just very proficient at cleaning up his messes."

Jolar brought up another image, this one of a woman in her thirties with dark, elaborately styled hair and brown eyes. Her jewels were beautiful and her makeup perfect—though she was wearing far too much of both. "Carlea Renn. Niman heiress who inherited a shipping empire that spans from Utavia to Lema. She's married but she and her husband seem to spend far more time out of each other's company than in it. He has an established mistress back on Nima, and Carlea seeks out a variety of men to pass the time with. Kav's last report linked her to the bribing of an official on Sertar—an official who was found dead shortly after Kav was."

Arissa frowned at the image. It was a posed picture, taken at a party or a fundraiser perhaps. Carlea's deeply plunging dress revealed much of her smooth, taut, lightly tanned skin. She was smiling broadly, but there was something about this woman's eyes that showed her well capable of cruelty.

"Danlen Mirat," Jolar said, changing the image. Danlen had a very young looking face for one whose hair had gone all silver, and his hazel eyes were hard and cold. "He's Gensoyan. He was arrested on his homeworld a number of times starting in his teen years, mainly for assault and property damage—bar fights and the like. He even served prison time for weapons smuggling on Gensoy before he left. He relocated to Sertar about fifteen years ago. He's now owner of the largest crystal refining operation in the system, and somehow he's managed to rise to what the Sertarians would deem respectability. He's married to a Sertarian woman, but he seems to keep her out of sight."

Arissa went to the next file. "Broc Atarr."

Jolar nodded at the swarthy man's image. "Like Larner Tovic, he runs a mining operation. He's amassed a great deal of money and influence very quickly. Two years ago he didn't have a credit to his name, and now he's Larner's direct competitor."

"Couldn't they all be working together?" she wondered, looking at the information again. "Larner and Broc run mining operations, Carlea is in shipping, and Danlen is in crystal refining."

"It's possible," Jolar allowed. "But with their current public alliances, their interests seem to run counter to each other."

She shook her head a little. "But gaining our military contract wouldn't be of any interest to Carlea Renn, would it? She doesn't have anything to do with mining or refining crystals, does she?"

"True, but we'll have enough clout to meet her socially at least. And she should try to steer a plum contract like ours to one of her friends. One of those friends might well turn out to be Larner, Danlen or Broc."

Arissa hesitated. "Broc Atarr is Utavian. Do you think—?"

Jolar nodded. "Yes, that Utavian in Xan-Tellar you saved me from came specifically to kill me."

"Do you know why?"

Jolar blew his breath out. "We don't even know who he *was*."

"But a scan—"

"No," Jolar said shortly. "No ID, no genetic profile. No record anywhere in the central system that this man ever existed—a wraith."

Arissa stared. "I thought 'wraiths' were a holodrama thing. I mean, I know you altered my ID, but to erase someone—"

"Oh, it's possible. Just very illegal and very, very expensive. If you hadn't been there I'd be dead now—killed by a ghost."

"Expensive . . . " She looked at the datapad. "If one of these people tried to have you killed—Jolar, what if someone recognizes you?"

"You'll tell me."

"That's how you got the Zartani councilor to agree," she said. "That's what you meant when you said I would keep you alive. Because if you were recognized, a seer would know."

He searched her face. "Would you?"

"Yes," she said confidently.

A quick smile touched his mouth. "I knew I was right."

She shot him a fond glance. "No, you didn't."

"Well," he allowed. "I *hoped* I was. Dacel will do his best to investigate, but without an ID there's not much hope. The man carried only cash and the weapon was reported stolen in Xan-Tellar three hours before he tried to kill me. Dacel had the TelSec reports on the Utavian locked down and the body removed. The TelSec officers who saw him were told the blank ID was a glitch and ordered not to discuss the case. He was Utavian, but right now that's all we know about him. Still, if anyone is looking for that wraith they won't find him."

"What about you?"

"Commander Jolar d'Tural you mean? He's still alive and well in Xan-Tellar. I complained to everyone who would listen that I was going to be buried in weeks of report writing for the council."

Arissa's brow creased. "Could someone have wanted to stop you from taking this mission? Is it possible that was why he tried to kill you?"

Jolar shook his head. "If my cover's blown from day one, they're better off letting me take the assignment. Kill me, and Dacel would just find someone to take my place, someone they might *not* know about. And after Kav . . . We were very careful. Dacel didn't even share the plan with his staff." He studied her for a moment. "That Utavian—did you sense anything from him?"

Arissa cast back in her memory to that night, to the feel of the man's mind. "It wasn't personal to *him*," she said slowly. "But it was a matter of honor for him to succeed." She shook her head. "I'm sorry. I wish I could tell you more. It all happened so quickly."

The empty space, the sudden wrenching silence of the man's mind . . .

Jolar's fingers intertwined with hers. "Are you all right?"

"Yes." She brought her focus back to Jolar, to the warmth of his hand in hers, the feel of his thigh against hers. "So who are we staying with? The insider?"

"Bruscan Milin."

"You know him."

His mouth quirked upward in an appreciative smile. "I do. Our parents had mutual business interests. I've known Bruscan for a long time. That's something we have going for us that the previous agent didn't."

She tilted her head. "You don't trust this man—Bruscan."

"He's a businessman on Sertar and he isn't dead yet—those two facts speak a lot to his character. You'll be able to tell me more about him, I'm sure."

"He knows who you are already. Does he know who I am?"

"He'll know you're Arissa Legan from Aylor."

"But he won't know—"

"No," Jolar warned. "No one can know. You'll have to be very careful."

She shook her head, puzzled at the sense she caught. "Are you worried *I* can't keep a secret?"

"They killed Kav, Arissa," Jolar said sharply. "And they weren't quick about it either. We're sitting here calmly talking about wraiths, and how many people who knew our suspects have already been found *dead*, like it's—" Jolar suddenly stood, twisting away and scrubbing his face. "Gods, I hate this! I hate taking you into this!" He folded his arms, his nostrils flared. "Arissa, there's no time to fret about what might or might not be true about the seers. If there's *any* edge we have, we're using it. We practice. Every day. At least once a day. Agreed?"

She gave a reluctant nod. "All right, Jolar."

He held her gaze, his sense churning. "I still hate this."

Fifteen

"Well, the architecture doesn't seem that different from Xan-Tellar," Arissa commented. Jolar's quiet confidence at the controls of their private shuttle calmed her fear of flying enough that she could attend to the hurly burly sprawl of Tano-Sertar below. In stark contrast to the neat squares and restrained development of Xan-Tellar, Sertar's capital was a mass of twisting streets with no thought for convenience, future impact—or likely even public safety. "But Tano seems a lot less planned."

"Civic duty is not at the forefront of most Sertarian officials' agendas," Jolar said dryly. "More like how fast they can line their pockets. The Sertarians call it 'giving consideration'—and believe me, *nothing* happens here without a bribe. You don't even want to call SerSec if you've been robbed. If they took your billfold, you won't get an officer to fill out a report because they know they won't get the expected bribe."

"So I don't want to call SerSec if I'm in trouble?"

"You *can* get swift justice if you're prominent, or under the protection of someone prominent. I'm sure Bruscan gives enough 'consideration' that someone harassing one of his guests would win a wicked beating and lengthy imprisonment."

Arissa's lips parted in horror. "That's awful."

"That's Sertar."

"I guess it's not worse for me, though." Arissa looked out over the city. "I don't even have the right to a trial, no matter what world I'm on."

"I know." His mouth was a grim line. "I'm sorry."

"Sorry?"

"To ask you to help people who would treat you like that. Especially when the best I can offer right now is that you'll be given a falsified ID. You have the right to live openly."

She shuddered. "I can't even imagine. Even if they gave me a pardon, allowed me to live, I wouldn't be welcome anywhere."

"You would on Zartan. I'd make sure of it."

"How?" she wondered. "How could you make people there accept me?"

"Because I—" he started sharply, then broke off. "I don't know," he continued, his voice steadier. "But you'd have at least one person who would welcome you there."

She threw him a warm smile. The green space below was growing more pronounced, the residences larger. "This area looks nice."

Jolar raised an eyebrow at her. "And each house has a security shield and armed guards and privately paid street patrols . . ."

At this speed she couldn't see guards or any street patrols, but the high walls and redundant pulse gates encircling the estates made each a veritable fortress.

"Where is not so nice," Jolar continued. "Is Tano-Sertar itself. The city is crime-ridden and dangerous as hell. I should have asked before—how are you with a blaster?"

"You mean firing one? Gods, I've never even *held* one."

He tensed beside her. "Okay. How about self-defense?"

"I'm a fast runner," she said lightly. Her throat closed. "You're angry."

"Yes, I'm fucking angry!" he burst out. "I was showing you how to play festering *Star Quest* and carrying you back to bed when I should have been—" She felt him take control of himself, but his grip on the shuttle's yoke was tight. "I can't go back and do what I should have done. I'll get you a blaster. I'll show you how to use it and how to defend yourself."

She hunched her shoulders. "All right."

He spared her a glance. "This is my fault, not yours. I'm not angry with you."

"I know. I just . . . I'm not sure I can hurt anyone."

"Promise me," he said sharply. "Promise me that if it's ever you or someone else that you'll do whatever it takes to survive."

She hesitated, thinking of the rush of emptiness she felt when Jolar shot the Utavian.

His eyes were intent. "If you love me, Arissa, promise me this."

"All right, Jolar," she said faintly. "I promise."

Her vow set his mind at some ease as he set the shuttle down on a large, beautifully landscaped estate. The landing was a gentle one, but after he powered the shuttle down Jolar went very still.

"Gods, without an ID—" he began hoarsely. "You can't fly one of these things, can you? Or operate a groundcar?"

"No," she said, surprised. "Of course not."

His jaw hardened. "Okay, we'll add them to the list." His attention shifted to outside the shuttle. "That's Bruscan. What do you think?"

Arissa stretched her senses toward the tall, well-dressed man wearing a pleasant expression as he walked out to greet them.

"Quick, sharp mind," she said. "Ruthless but very self-disciplined. He finds all this amusing, but he's wondering if he can get paid more. Surprised." She sent a questioning gaze at Jolar. "He wasn't expecting anyone to be with you."

Jolar threw her an unapologetic grin. "Amazing," he murmured, then pressed the control to open the shuttle doors.

Arissa kept her focus on Bruscan as she stepped out of the shuttle. She flushed a little as his glance darted over her and lingered.

Bruscan's attention swung to Jolar. His smile and embrace of welcome was sincere.

"Jolar Legan!" he said, plainly aware he was being observed by a gardener. "It's good to see you again."

"It's been too long." Jolar agreed and nodded at Arissa. "I'm glad you finally get to meet my wife. Of course, even after four years I'm not sure Arissa's forgiven you for missing our wedding."

"Let me say again how sorry I am I missed it, Arissa." Bruscan took her hand. "I hope while you're here I can earn your forgiveness."

He was tall with dark hair and eyes. Not a particularly handsome man—but with his wide smile and easy confidence, he was very much a charming one.

His vibrating interest hummed through her even as his warm fingers wrapped around hers.

She managed a flustered smile. "Of course."

Jolar nearly snatched her hand out of Bruscan's grip. "I like the new house," he said, a little loudly. "How long have you been here again?"

"Three years. Yes, it's worked out quite well for me. But please, come in out of the sun."

Nothing in her experience prepared her for the opulence of Bruscan's home. It was a mansion of gleaming Novician marble and soaring domed ceilings. Arissa spied an immense landscape by Jol Dethara—lush swirls of color built one upon another, each brushstroke fine as a human hair—hung, as if placed offhandedly, in the vestibule of the house. The palatial foyer was dotted with almost primitive looking carved birds, and her mouth parted when she recognized them as kanta idols of the early monarchal period.

The kanta's oversized eyes looked out at her with the same dispassion that had watched a thousand generations come and go before their jeweled gaze; their dark blue, glazed bodies glossy in the afternoon sunlight of Bruscan's front hall.

Just one of these sculptures was worth more than the house she'd grown up in.

Bruscan led them past the curved staircases and down the hall. Plainly garbed, the servants' interest in her and Jolar was unnervingly intent. Arissa reached out to one of them . . .

And grimaced at the chill sourness.

A quick seer's inventory of the staff nearby showed them at best unethical and at worst unmerciful. Clearly there were none inside these walls that could be trusted either.

"My office," Bruscan said over his shoulder by way of explanation as he led inside. Done in soft shades of cream, the room featured a whole wall of plexisteel overlooking the sunny landscaped grounds and swimming pool. A woman dressed in a yellow quilted jacket of Xeltan design followed them in, pausing expectantly just inside the door.

"Nela," Bruscan said. "These are my guests, Jolar and Arissa Legan. Jolar, Arissa, this is Nela, my estate manager. She oversees—well, pretty much everything. Feel free to ask her for anything you need while you're here."

Nela sent them a friendly smile but Arissa was very glad that Jolar had encrypted his datapad and put an ID lock on it. A mind touch showed Nela already cataloguing everything about her and Jolar in case it was information she could sell.

"Your suite is ready," Nela said. "I'll have your luggage brought to your rooms right away. Can I get you anything else now?"

Bruscan glanced over the refreshments that already awaited them on the low table then threw them a questioning look. Jolar shook his head.

"That's all for now, Nela," Bruscan said. "Please close the door after you."

When the woman had gone, Bruscan saw them settled on the sofa with iced fruit drinks and urged them to help themselves from a tray of fanciful sweets.

Bruscan leaned back against the cushions, a glass held casually in his hand. "So, how can I be of service to you, Jolar *Legan?*" His mouth quirked infinitesimally upward at the last word.

Jolar sent him a narrowed look. "I've had the good fortune to be chosen to select the next supplier of the fleet's crystal needs. It's a five year contract."

"How lucrative," Bruscan said. "I'm sure a number of people will be interested in acquiring such a rich opportunity for themselves—or their friends."

Jolar gave him a tight smile. "I have a few people in mind already. Can you introduce us?"

"Of course," Bruscan said. "You know, I'm in the security business. My home and grounds are quite shielded from eavesdropping, Jolar. And my private guards are the best."

"That's good to know." Jolar glanced at Arissa. "I still have every intention of showing . . . care."

Arissa weighed it, but it was a question one wouldn't have to be a seer to ask. "What about your staff? Do you trust them?"

Bruscan's mind sparked with amusement. "Oh, hells no."

Arissa's brow creased. "Why have them in your home then?"

"Because they're as trustworthy as any on Sertar," Bruscan said off-handedly and gave a nod toward the refreshment tray. "And they do their jobs superbly." His mouth curved, his brown eyes warming. "Your accent is quite charming, Arissa." Jolar's flare of jealousy seared her mind even as Bruscan's gaze shifted to him. "And your husband is *very* protective."

Jolar's eyes narrowed. "You baited me."

"We all have vulnerabilities and weak spots. It's good to know your own." Bruscan raised an eyebrow. "You can stop glaring at me, Jolar. I see the boundary line."

Jolar's jaw worked for a moment. "Clearly I need to watch that."

Bruscan shrugged. "It makes you a more believable married couple. So, to whom am I introducing you?"

Jolar gave him the names.

"Tovic and Mirat I know," Bruscan mused. "I've seen Carlea Renn here and there but Broc Atarr is recently come to Sertar. I've only met him once."

"Do business with any of them?" Jolar asked.

Bruscan shook his head. "They're wealthy even by Sertarian standards. They have their own private security staff and code slicers. But I know Larner Tovic and Danlen Mirat as friendly acquaintances. I should be able to track them all so we can bump into them."

Arissa frowned. "I thought they had private security staffs."

"Yes," Bruscan said. "But whoever will be hosting them might not."

Arissa blinked. "You're just going to hack private transmissions till you find where they're going to be?"

"Of course," Bruscan said, surprised.

"Heartwarming place, Sertar, isn't it?" Jolar said to Arissa.

"You want warm? Go to Nima," Bruscan retorted. "Wait—Carlea Renn is Niman, isn't she? I'll need to find out if she's even planetside right now. Anything else you're going to need from me?"

Jolar glanced at her. "Arissa needs some small arms training and self-defense instruction. She needs to learn how operate a groundcar and shuttle."

Bruscan blinked, and Arissa could feel his unspoken questions. That she might not be accomplished with a blaster or close combat could be expected, but not to know how to operate a groundcar or a shuttle was odd.

"Well," Bruscan continued. "I'm sure all that can be arranged. But try not to scratch the groundcar, will you, my dear? It's new."

Sixteen

No less extravagant than Bruscan's, the villa was already filled with guests. Sensing the easy confidence of those around her in their polished evening attire, Arissa's stomach dropped. She'd chosen what she thought was the most cosmopolitan of her new wardrobe for this first night out, but now she felt awkward in her low-cut evening gown and strappy high-heeled shoes—a little girl playing dress-up in a room of sophisticates.

The floor of the mansion was plexisteel and water—tinted pale blue—was visible beneath its clear surface. The lining beneath the water was reflective, deepening the visual depth so that guests appeared to move across the shimmering surface like naiads. Fat, iridescent-scaled momu fish, each with fins spread out and billowing like the wings of a gossamerfly, swam lazily beneath the floor and made Arissa, unused to heels—and a floor that appeared made of water—step even more gingerly.

She had been excited at the prospect of attending her first party but now her stomach was churning. Unused to crowds still, already the flood of emotions from the revelers was a growing rumble in her mind.

She began to wish she'd stayed behind at Bruscan's house.

"You look beautiful," Jolar said, taking her hand. He leaned over to murmur in her ear. "Just focus on me if you start to feel overwhelmed, all right?"

She gave him a quick, grateful look and, narrowing her focus to him, felt her nerves begin to settle at the familiar feel of his mind. Bruscan warmly greeted their hostess—a regal, dark-skinned Novician woman whose height rivaled Jolar's—and introduced them as his friends, the Legans from Aylor.

Bruscan stopped here and there, introducing them to his friends and acquaintances. The Sertarian was plainly an accomplished charmer and conversationalist, and Arissa was relieved to find that she hardly had to do anything but stand next to Jolar and smile. A short time later, and with a meaningful look at Jolar, Bruscan parted company from them and wandered off into the crowd.

Small groups had formed into circles of conversation and laughter floated over the soft music. Tentatively Arissa widened her focus, catching snippets of emotion—amusement, desire, excitement, boredom—

Boredom?

Curious, Arissa tightened her focus. The man was pudgy; his high-necked gray evening tunic highlighted the roundness of his face. He leaned in an archway, wine glass in hand as he surveyed the room. His mouth was tucked a bit at the corner, the only outward sign that he regarded the setting and other guests—so extraordinary to her—as uncultured and crass.

The bright tones of Novician liternwood pipe music had enticed more than a few couples nearby under the soft glow of the lantern lit dome to dance. Arissa chewed the inside of her cheek, recalling her wide-eyed awe the first time Jolar had taken her to a restaurant onboard the cruiser.

"I think it's a lovely party," Arissa ventured quietly to Jolar as they crossed to the bar. "The house is beautiful."

To her relief his smile of agreement was sincere.

"I keep worrying I'm actually going to step on one of those things," he said with a nod at the momu fish gliding beneath their feet. "What would you like to drink?"

"Nothing for now," she said.

Jolar raised a hand to summon one of the bartenders.

A gorgeously dressed woman nearby—pouting as she waved away a servant offering sumptuous looking tidbits on a tray—adjusted her light, sheer wrap so it lay over the inside of her elbow and exposed her left shoulder. Draped so, the fabric floated behind her as she walked and the effect was very alluring.

With a glance at herself in the rose-gold reflective surface behind the bar, Arissa quickly readjusted her own shimmersilk wrap the same way before Jolar turned back.

He regarded her with a warm smile. "You know, sweet, I've never even seen you tipsy."

"I've never been."

His eyebrows shot up. "Really? Well, now that's something I have to see. Maybe a few glasses of sparkle wine on a Niman beach?" His eyes went hot. "A private beach, of course." His smile widened as she felt her face warm. "Gods, you blush beautifully."

The bartender brought his Aylorian brandy. Jolar nodded his thanks, and twenty credits vanished discretely into the man's palm.

"You have to pay for refreshments? I thought—" Her flush deepened; what did she know of parties outside of books and holodramas? She lowered her voice. "Doesn't a hostess provide those?"

"She is. That was just some 'consideration' for the bartender." Jolar drank from the snifter and made an appreciative sound then offered the glass to her. "Want a sip? It's very good."

Arissa took a scant swallow to find the brandy held the mellow overtones of verum with a hint of spice.

"It's wonderful," she agreed.

And strong. She could already feel the brandy's warmth spread through her chest.

"Do you want to keep it?" he asked, a mischievous glint in those blue depths. "I can get another for myself."

"I'd better not." She handed the snifter back and touched Jolar's arm lightly. "Let's go talk to Bruscan."

Jolar rippled with surprise as he followed her nod to the other side of the room, where Bruscan spoke with a slender man of middling height.

In just that moment Bruscan's glance sought them out and his eyes flashed with urgency. Jolar took a quick, final swallow of the brandy and then caught her hand. More guests had arrived and even with Jolar's formidable physical presence it took time to cross the room to where the two men stood.

"Larner, these are my friends Jolar and Arissa Legan," Bruscan said. "This is Larner Tovic."

Jolar shook his hand as Arissa reached out quickly to brush Larner's mind. Her lungs suddenly felt as if they were filling with icy air. The man's cool, placid gaze was echoed by the chilly and methodical nature of his sense.

Larner smiled at her like someone who had learned to do so from a holodrama character. "A pleasure, I'm sure."

"It's always nice to meet new people," she said evenly. "What do you do, Master Tovic?"

"I own mining operations on the third moon."

Larner's voice and expression were pleasant, but Arissa suddenly saw an image of him practicing this demeanor in front of a mirror over and over to get it right.

"I don't know much about mining," she managed faintly.

Larner frowned a little, as if he didn't know how to answer that.

"Well," Jolar said into the awkward pause. "Has that been a long-standing career or are you new to it?"

"Oh," Larner said, his face going a little blank. "I inherited the operation. My family has been in crystal mining for generations."

Then he smiled, as if reminding himself to do so.

"You might want to talk to Jolar, then," Bruscan said genially. "He's been tasked with choosing the next crystal supplier for the fleet."

"The current contract with CenCorp ends in three months," Jolar said to Larner. "Maybe you can give me the best price. We should schedule a time to discuss it."

Larner's blankness returned. "I'm in mining, Master Legan. The law forbids me from also owning a refining plant."

"It does?" Arissa asked, surprised. She hadn't thought the law would stop anyone on Sertar from doing anything.

He turned to her. "To prevent a monopoly, of course."

Looking into those flat gray eyes and feeling the equally cold-blooded mind behind them was utterly unnerving.

"Of course," she managed.

"Perhaps you might suggest someone." Bruscan gave a self-deprecating shrug. "I'm afraid my business interests lie outside the crystal consortium."

"I will consider the matter," Larner said.

Then he smiled again.

Subsequent conversation was equally strange and ungainly, and Arissa didn't feel capable of drawing a deep breath again until the man excused himself.

"Now I wish I'd finished that brandy," Jolar muttered. "I don't know that I've ever met anyone so odd."

"He's an excellent businessman," Bruscan said lowly. "He never forgets a conversation or a detail, no matter how small."

"He's your friend?" Jolar asked. "How do you talk to him for more than five minutes?"

"I never said he was a friend," Bruscan returned. "I said I knew him. I don't believe Master Tovic *has* any friends."

"I can see why," Jolar grumbled. "And frankly, right now I wouldn't mind another drink."

Arissa pressed her palm against her forehead to cool it.

Jolar frowned. "Are you all right?"

"I will be," she said with a quick smile and dropped her hand. Feeling off balance after the encounter with Larner Tovic, the crowd's emotions rose to a roar in her head. "Can I meet you at the bar? I think I'll find the 'fresher first."

His protectiveness spiked but Jolar gave her a chagrined smile. "I guess I can let you go to the 'fresher by yourself."

"I'll be fine," she promised.

But making her way through the partygoers was harder for her than she expected, and not just because of the crush of the crowd. Emotions too crashed around her, leaving her feeling as if she were treading a stormy sea, struggling not to be pulled under.

The male guests were well dressed and all seemed possessed of the same cunning, sharp gazes. As their glances lingered on her, to her surprise Arissa realized a number of them found her attractive—but right now the attention was far from welcome. She was forced to twist her way through the crowd, and her teeth clenched as more than once a man's hand lingered 'accidently' on her rump.

The smell of so many expensive perfumes and colognes mixed in such close proximity made the air gaggingly sweet. Some of the women seemed pampered, even sheltered—mistresses, wives, and daughters—but beneath their expensive gowns and elegant coiffures most were as hard hearted as the men. Too far from Jolar now to narrow her focus to him, she pushed more urgently to escape the crowd. She hadn't sensed such ruthless self-absorption even in the most run-down streets of Xan-Tellar.

She reached the main corridor of the house, where a maidservant, seeing her hesitation, led the way. Arissa's face warmed as she realized she didn't have any money in her tiny evening purse to tip the woman. The attendant gave her a brief, annoyed glance when no credits were forthcoming and quickly moved on to better prospects.

Drawing a shaky breath, Arissa gratefully shut and locked the 'fresher door behind her. The bathroom's appointments included Utavian star lilies in the fresh flower arrangements as well as an array of perfumes, creams and cosmetics all displayed in pretty, individual packages.

Arissa wetted a cloth and pressed it to her forehead. Leaning over the cut crystal sink, she steadied and slowed her breathing, consciously drawing her focus inward to regain her inner balance.

After a few minutes she felt calm enough to go back to the party. Surveying her appearance in the mirror, she took a moment to adjust one of the combs holding up her ringlets, again very, very glad that she'd had the demi-permanent make-up done. She scarcely knew how to act at a party and couldn't imagine the added anxiety of worrying about smeared lip color as well.

Squeezing her way along the edge of the crowded room back to Jolar, she accidentally elbowed someone in the crush of bodies.

She turned to offer her apology and blinked. "Oh, hi."

Kemma smiled. "Arissa, hello."

"Kemma, I'm sorry I—" Arissa began, but Kemma waved it off.

"It's crazy crowded here. Lian," she said, reaching out to touch her protector's shoulder, "you remember Arissa?."

Lian's face lit with recognition. "Of course. How are you?"

"Arissa was on the *Queen's Light* with us," Kemma explained to the man they had been conversing with. "Arissa, this is Danlen Mirat."

Arissa's breath caught, then she smiled.

But not quickly enough.

"Do I know you?" Danlen's words still bore the echo of his Gensoyan heritage, his silver hair bright under the party lanterns light as he regarded her cooly.

Arissa cleared her throat. "Oh, I think I heard my husband mention your name."

"I know your husband?"

Danlen's hazel eyes were narrowed but she sensed he'd judged her too naïve, too young to be threatening.

She gave a half-shrug, hoping to look even more girlishly artless. "I'm afraid I wasn't really paying attention. But he's over at the bar and I'm headed that way now. Even if you don't know one another," she nodded toward his nearly empty glass, "you could get a fresh drink."

A young woman—the worse for wine and sadly lacking any skill—stood on a nearby sofa to regale her fellow guests by singing a popular tune.

"Sounds good to me," Lian agreed raising his voice to be heard over the singer. "I just realized I'm parched."

Kemma's sense thrummed for a moment, and she threw an exasperated look at the would-be songbird even as the woman's embarrassed friends sought to coax her down. "I hope it's less crowded there."

It wasn't; if anything it was more so, but Jolar's height made him easy to find.

"Arissa," he said, his expression echoing the relieved unwinding of his sense. "I was getting worried."

"Sorry. It's not easy to get around in here. Look who I ran into," she added quickly. "Kemma and Lian. And this is their friend, Danlen Mirat."

Jolar's smile hid shocked awareness.

"Your wife thought I might know you," Danlen said.

Arissa threw her focus at Danlen, probing as the man's glance went over Jolar's face.

Jolar's brilliant smile didn't waver. "Do you?"

"Oh, I'm sorry!" Arissa caught Jolar's gaze. "I guess you *don't* know each other." She gave Danlen a smile. "Master Mirat, this is my husband, Jolar Legan."

Danlen offered his hand. "A pleasure."

Jolar clasped it. "Good to meet you."

"I promised them all a drink." Arissa eyed the crowd in front of the bar. "But it looks like we're in for a wait."

"Yeah," Jolar said. "The party's really picked up."

"And a fresh one sounds good right about now. If you'll excuse me," Danlen said with a nod as he took up a place in the line.

"Arissa? Do you want a drink?" Jolar asked.

She shook her head. The last thing she wanted right now was her head clouded.

"Kemma, what about you?" Lian asked.

"I'll sip on yours," Kemma said. She put her hand on Arissa's arm to draw her along. "Meet us outside; we're going to get crushed standing here."

Arissa reached out to touch Danlen's mind but couldn't sense any suspicion or threat there.

"We'll stick close to the door so you can find us," she promised with a smile at Jolar. She gave a quick meaningful look in Danlen's direction. "I know you might have to wait a while."

She sensed Jolar, too, knew this to be a perfect opportunity to strike up a conversation with Danlen. He gave her a nod, and Arissa let Kemma lead her outside.

"So how do you know Danlen?" Arissa asked as they stepped out into the patio.

Kemma shrugged. "I don't. He and Lian just struck up a conversation about the darshball playoffs. Lema verses Gensoy, that sort of thing. How do *you* know him?" Kemma's green eyes were sharp. "Don't worry. I'm pretty sure he bought that you didn't."

Arissa bit the inside of her cheek. "Jolar is here to select the fleet's next crystal supplier. Danlen was mentioned as a possibility for the contract."

Kemma gave a knowing smile. "And so Jolar was looking to meet him, right?"

Arissa winced. "I guess I could have done that better."

Kemma gave a soft laugh. "No, it went fine. When Lian's here on business I spend a lot of my time trying to charm his contacts. Of course, being a charming companion is my business." Kemma rubbed her arms. "It's too hot in there, it's too cold out here. You know," she said, suddenly brightening, "we should leave them to charming their own contacts for once and do something fun."

"Like what?"

"Like shopping in Tano-Sertar. What do you say?"

"Jolar says the city is very dangerous."

"Well, we wouldn't be hanging around the spaceport pawn shops," Kemma returned with a laugh. "We'd stick to boutiques and shops of the upper city."

Arissa smiled. "I'd love to go."

"Absolutely fucking *not!*"

Sitting on the edge of the bed and still dressed in the gown she'd worn to the party, Arissa dropped her heels to the floor then gratefully pointed and flexed her aching feet. "Jolar, you told me to be obvious about living beyond our means. Aren't I supposed to act frivolous and spoiled?"

Arissa found the quiet and privacy of their suite at Bruscan's house a welcome balm to her overtaxed seer's senses. Done in serene blues and warm creams, their second-floor suite was larger than the central living space of the house she had grown up in. The bed she sat on was curtained, the swathes of creamy fabric drawn back dramatically to reveal the wide bed with its many overfilled pillows. The doors of their private balcony were closed against the chill night air, and the suite consisted of a combination bedroom and sitting room, as well as private dressing and bathroom beyond.

"You are *not* going alone into Tano!"

"I wouldn't be alone," she pointed out. "I'm going with Kemma."

"Right," he snapped. The formal shirt he'd worn tonight hung half unfastened, his face flushed. "A Niman ornament who just happens to know one of the most powerful crystal refiners on Sertar, a man we've come to investigate. A man who may be responsible for multiple murders. *Perfectly* safe!"

"She *doesn't* know him. They just bumped into each other at the party."

"You don't really believe that?"

"It's true!"

Jolar's nostrils flared. "How can you—" He broke off, but his mind still buzzed with worry. "Are you sure? Positive she doesn't know him?"

"I'm sure. She met him only a few minutes before I did." How could he not understand how much this meant to her? "You could send a guard with me."

"Why are you so eager to do this, anyway? You didn't seem all that enthusiastic about shopping on the ship. What's Tano got that has you so set on going?"

Arissa dropped her gaze. "It's not the shopping," she mumbled. "It's that she asked me to go. I've never done that. Spent an afternoon with someone my age. Had a girlfriend."

Jolar softened. "I never thought of that." He sat down on the bed beside her to gather her against him and pressed a kiss to her temple. "Of course you should go, sweet." Arissa gave him a quick smile, and his blue eyes went stern. "And hells yes, I'm sending guards with you."

Guards? As in plural? The hard set of his mind showed now was not the time to press the point though.

"What happened with Danlen? Did you get to talk to him at all?"

"Some," Jolar said. "He showed little interest in the contract, which is in itself strange. I wish you'd been there to tell me what was really going on in his head. I want you there next time I meet with him."

She bit her lip. "Sorry about that, I thought I'd have more time with him. I didn't think he'd leave the party so soon. I know it isn't much but—remember what Bruscan said about vulnerabilities? Danlen—there's *some* softness within him. Still, I don't bet many would think to cross him." She swallowed. "Better to cross him than Larner though."

"Why?" He rubbed her back. "Not that the man didn't give me the creeps, but I was wondering what you sensed."

"He's extremely intelligent—dispassionately so. Like he could slice someone apart and feel nothing more than detached curiosity while they screamed." She shuddered. "Danlen you could bargain with; he has enough heart that he might be moved. But Larner? No."

"And his expressions," Jolar said. "So . . ."

"Rehearsed," Arissa supplied.

"A snake pit," Jolar muttered, his expression troubled. But then he gave her a half-smile. He drew her closer and brushed a kiss across her mouth. "That Niman beach is sounding better and better."

She smiled. "So we'll go there, and then you want to take me to Zartan?"

"I want to take you everywhere," he murmured, his mouth quirked upward. He hooked the straps of her evening gown with his fingers and slid them down over her shoulders. His thumb traced the peak of her breast as he eased the gown off, the nipple pebbling under his touch. He urged her back to lie in the center of the bed, and his voice went husky. "But I have a particular image in mind of you under the Niman moons, lying back on a blanket in the sand, open and ready for me."

"It may be a while before we get to Nima," she said breathlessly as his mouth moved lower.

"Well then." She felt him smile against the skin of her chest, his palm against the inside of her thigh to spread her wider. "I guess I have time to get some practice in . . ."

Seventeen

Any enjoyment Arissa might have had riding to her first-ever afternoon of shopping with a friend was obliterated by the two granite-faced guards in crisp gray uniforms seated across from her in Bruscan's groundcar.

She was tempted to ditch them. It wouldn't take much effort now, thanks to the practicing Jolar had forced on her; a moment's inattention or redirection and she'd slip away.

But she sure wouldn't look forward to facing Jolar later. And she didn't think the guards would either.

In stark contrast to the other crime-ridden areas they'd sped through, this part of the city was clearly affluent. No chemical-seeking vagrants with reddened, hooded eyes sullied *this* section of the city, and SerSec officers had a visible presence. If it was duracrete under her feet, it had been disguised to look like Novician marble; if not, then the expense just of the pavement here was staggering. Greenery was pleasantly scattered about and every surface was sparklingly clean, but there was not so much as a bench or surface to be leaned on. The intent, no doubt, was to force shoppers to rest tired feet in one of the many eateries.

Patrons strolling here were as well dressed as the holoforms in the shop windows they walked past. Even in a shopping district meant to cater to the affluent, Arissa was not the only one with her own private security escort.

Arissa made it a little early to the agreed upon meeting place at one of the many lavish fountains to see Kemma already there.

"Hi—" Kemma's enthusiastic tone changed as she took in the uniformed men. "Arissa."

Arissa's face warmed. She was the only one in the plaza accompanied by more than one guard, and Kemma didn't have any at all. "Sorry. Jolar insisted."

Kemma looked past her and the uniformed guards and her frown deepened. "I think there are two other—"

"Yeah." In a wealthy commercial area like this having two guards was already overkill—four was absurd. "They're guarding me too."

"Will they at least carry our purchases?" Kemma asked, raising her eyebrows.

The lead guard gave a scowl. "We're protection, not porters."

"She was joking," Arissa mumbled. She shifted her feet. "Kemma, I understand if you don't want to—"

Kemma held up a hand. "Oh, no. We're shopping." With a mischievous grin she nodded toward the nearest store. "Come on, boys!"

Mortified despite their stoic expressions, the guards followed Kemma and Arissa into the lingerie boutique.

Kemma held a yellow shimmersilk nightgown against her body. "Ooo," she cooed, sticking her fingers through the slashed openings of the breast cups. "I like this one. Luckily for me, as an ornament I can write off all *sorts* of expenses."

The four men were well aware they were garnering glares from other female shop patrons. Wincing with sympathy, Arissa suggested they wait outside and the red-faced men made a hasty retreat.

"I'm really sorry they're tagging along," she said.

Kemma waved it off. "Oh, it's fine." Kemma held up another gown of pale blue without the slashed cups.

"Besides, it's really sweet that your husband is so protective of you."

Arissa's face warmed. "Yes, I uh . . ."

Kemma threw her an amused look. "Ornaments revere Arrena. We like to see the Goddess of Love make a happy marriage. Hey, maybe Jolar won't mind me taking you shopping if you come home with this?" Kemma held up a red shimmersilk gown with a slit up the leg. "Let's get a couple of fitting rooms."

Arissa bought the gown and, at Kemma's urging, the matching robe. Kemma had an armful of lingerie by the time they were finished. So high was the pile that Arissa wondered if she really *were* able to write them off.

Arissa sank gratefully into her chair when they finally stopped for lunch.

The café was high ceilinged and decorated in the ornate, opulent style of the late royal period, the walls covered in yellow watered shimmersilk, the furniture dark and heavily carved. Uniformed servers moved smoothly between tables as Apovian string melodies floated down over the diners. The busy restaurant was à la carte only and, scanning the selections hungrily, Arissa was now grateful that Jolar had encouraged her to spend as she wished— lunch was going to cost a fortune.

A young man and a richly dressed woman—likely twice his age—sat dining in an alcove nearby. Kemma and the young man had exchanged discreet, professional glances as she and Arissa were seated, and Arissa understood immediately that he was an ornament too. He was strikingly handsome, certainly—tall and broad-shouldered, with black hair and startling amber eyes.

Arissa winced inwardly. Deeply in love, this young man felt it keenly that his sincere attempts at wooing were being dismissed by his patron as nothing more than the consummate skill of a professional companion.

They sipped on icy fruit drinks until the food arrived, when Arissa flushed to see her order filled most of the table while Kemma was only dining on salad.

A woman with a soft blue dress that draped elegantly around her pregnant belly walked by the window. She was holding the hand of a little girl, smiling down at her. The child was neatly dressed in a quilted jacket and skirt, and her hair—the same golden brown as her mother's—was woven into pinned-up braids.

The warmth, the way the little girl's hand was tucked lovingly in hers, made Arissa think of her own mother. It also sent a sudden longing for a child of her own through her chest.

A child with vivid blue eyes . . .

"Kemma, did you ever want to get married instead of, uh…" Arissa blurted out then blushed at having asked such an artless question.

"Believe it or not, I love what I do," Kemma answered with a smile.

"I believe it," Arissa protested. The young man's patron pulled her hand from his, and his expression was crestfallen. "Why wouldn't you?"

Kemma raised an eyebrow. "You have an interesting attitude for a respectably married woman. I had the feeling your husband disapproved of you spending time with me. Perhaps he's worried I'll talk you into a career change."

Arissa hesitated, but she couldn't see any harm in it. "I seriously considered becoming an ornament. Before I was married."

"Wow." Kemma paused with the fork halfway to her mouth. "Sorry, I don't get surprised often, but that just about floored me."

Arissa gave an embarrassed shrug. Kemma was a stunning woman of obvious sensuality, beautifully dressed every time Arissa had seen her. "I'm probably not the type for it, right?"

"Actually, I think you would be an astonishingly successful ornament." Kemma shifted a bit to allow the server to refill her glass. "Let me know if you decide to, I'll sponsor you for training."

"What's it like?" Arissa asked. "Being an ornament?"

"Well," Kemma took a sip of water, considering. "I went the full route with three years of training in Arrena's temple in Laku-Nima. I was courted by a number of men who wanted to be my protector when I joined the Ornaments' Guild. Signing an exclusive contract with a protector is not that different than a marriage, really, except it's only for a limited time."

"And you don't get attached?"

"No," Kemma said softly. "That's where you're wrong. Perhaps the streetwalkers who do nothing more than make a man spill his seed are like that. I've had only a handful of protectors and I've loved every one of them."

Arissa looked away.

Kemma gave her a puzzled look. "What?"

"It's nothing," Arissa mumbled. "It's none of my business."

"Oh," Kemma said softly, leaning her elbows on the table. "Well, then it's either about Lian being married or me agreeing to be his shadow consort. Go ahead and ask," Kemma said without rancor. "Do I feel guilty about being the paid companion of a married man? How can I keep him from her and live with myself? What is it?"

"Do you ever want to marry Lian?" Lately she'd caught herself more and more imagining a life with Jolar, but no telepath had a future. She was superstitious about even dreaming of one. "Is it enough to be with him for now?"

"You *are* surprising, Arissa." Kemma gave a half smile. "Believe it or not, I struggled with that. And yes, it's usually enough, but sometimes . . . sometimes it's hard. And yes, sometimes I feel guilty because he's married even though it hasn't been a real marriage for a long, long time. She knows all about me and couldn't care less. Be grateful for what you and your husband have. I don't think I've ever seen a man so in love." Kemma tilted her head, her hands wrapped around her water glass, a frown touching her brow. "What's wrong?"

"I don't know. Maybe because everything's so new." Arissa's stomach clenched when she realized how she'd slipped. "I mean, having him home. He just left the fleet a few months ago."

Kemma shrugged. "Well, it'll work itself out. Give it time."

They window-shopped through the jewelry district. Arissa couldn't face the cost enough even to go inside, but she was surprised that Kemma didn't seem interested in doing more than looking either.

Kemma stopped at one window display and gave a low whistle. "Astuk crystal necklace. Now *that's* nice."

"They're beautiful stones," Arissa agreed. The gems shimmered in rainbow colors under the shops' lights. "But why make a necklace out of them? They must be worth a fortune as a power source."

"Not those," Kemma said. "If they've made jewelry out of them, they've got a fatal flaw of some kind. They'd just shatter in the converter."

"I didn't know it was possible to detect a flaw *before* it shattered."

"Sometimes you can. One of my protectors was a dealer on Gensoy, he was always trying out new tests to better weed out the flawed ones." She eyed the necklace. "Pretty, though."

"Maybe Lian will buy it for you."

Kemma threw her a smile. "Lian's a lot of things, but insanely, obscenely wealthy is *not* one of them. And to be vulgar, I'd rather have the same money in nice comfy investments yielding fourteen percent than a sparkly necklace worth a tenth of what he paid for it. The Ornaments' Guild retirement package is less than impressive."

"I'll take that as a compliment. I mean," Arissa said, flushing at Kemma's puzzled look. "You probably don't talk so, uh, vulgarly to most people."

Kemma smiled. "No, you're right. Just friends."

Warmth spread through Arissa's chest and she smiled back.

She sighed when the lead guard reminded her that the car would be coming shortly to take her back and despite the men's scowl, she offered Kemma, who was ready to hail a hired car, a ride home.

Kemma's purchases were packed around her legs and Arissa's few rested in her lap. The guards riding with them in the groundcar hindered conversation, but Lian's rented house was not far from Bruscan's home. One look at the house and Arissa wondered what Kemma *would* consider insanely wealthy, if this were not it.

Lian came out to help Kemma with her purchases. "Another successful hunt, I see?"

"I bought you something special in pale blue," Kemma said, her dimple showing.

Lian laughed. "I'm guessing I won't be the one wearing it. What about you Arissa?" He glanced at her small haul. "Did Kemma outpace you or are the rest up with the driver?"

"This is all I managed," Arissa said.

"She's new at this," Kemma said. "But I'll get her up to speed eventually."

"You and your husband should join us for dinner some night," Lian said.

"Maybe that Leman restaurant in the middle city?" Kemma suggested. "It's supposed to be divine." She gave Lian a sly smile. "As are all things Leman."

He laughed again. "So true."

"Excuse me," the lead guard said. "But we're due back at Mr. Milin's shortly."

Arissa's shoulders slumped as Lian and Kemma stepped back.

"I'll give you a call in a few days," Kemma promised then the guard shut the groundcar door.

Nela met her in the foyer. "The gentlemen are outside on the patio. Master Legan asked that you join them as soon as you arrive. I'll take your things to your suite."

It was unnerving how this woman was always watching and cataloguing the smallest thing anyone in the household did.

"Yes, thank you." Arissa nodded with a forced smile, relieved to be away from the woman as soon as she handed over the beautifully wrapped package.

Her awareness shifted as soon as she stepped outside. Seated with Jolar and Bruscan was a powerfully built man. His dark hair, eyes and bronze skin marked him as a Utavian.

Arissa recognized him instantly.

Jolar stood as soon as he saw her and pressed a kiss against her cheek. His blue eyes held hers for a moment. "How was Tano-Sertar?"

"Wonderful," she said.

"Let me introduce you," Jolar said. "Arissa, this is Broc Attar. Master Attar, my wife."

"Mistress Legan," he said standing, his Utavian accent unmistakable. "It is a pleasure."

Behind his dark eyes Broc was a jumble of stomach-churning anxiety. In the blink of an eye Arissa brushed his sense. An image of him fearfully scanning for danger, always on guard against attack, filled her mind. Jolar and Bruscan were serious-minded but not frightened.

Whatever danger Broc felt he was in, the other men felt secure here. Nor did Broc fear *them*. In fact, he would likely do anything to impress them.

"For me as well," she said.

"We've been talking business," Jolar said. "Master Attar may be interested in supplying crystals to the fleet."

"I would not wish to bore the lady," Broc assured quickly.

"Nonsense," Bruscan said. "I'm sure Arissa would love to sit in on our discussion."

Broc spread his hands. "But we have concluded for the day, I would say." He took a step away from the table. "And you mentioned you had plans for this evening, did you not?"

None of Jolar's puzzlement and wariness showed in his smile. "Yes, we have an engagement tonight."

"I will leave you, then." Broc inclined his head to Arissa. "I look forward to extending our acquaintance another time."

"Of course," she said.

Bruscan escorted Broc out, and Jolar gave her a questioning look.

"He's very fearful," she said quietly. "I startled him to the point of panic when I came out."

"He hides it well, then." Jolar gave her an appreciative smile. "Though not from you, of course. Anything else?"

"I can say for certain he doesn't know who you really are." She considered. "He knows himself to be in great danger. Like he has to constantly be on guard."

"But maybe that's because he's a very wealthy man from a poor world," Jolar pointed out. "And his money appeared too quickly for him to have come by it honestly. What else?"

Arissa thought. "He doesn't appear to bear you any ill-will. He's very interested in making a good impression."

"He's very interested in the contract, that's for sure. But considering his supposed wealth, he shouldn't need it. I'll ask Bruscan to make some inquiries about Broc's financial situation." He gave her a smile. "Maybe he recently lost it all playing tongo."

"So where are we going tonight?"

"Ah," Jolar said, sliding his arms around her waist. "We, wife, have procured some very hard-to-get invitations to the trade conference reception being held at the Niman embassy."

"Carlea Renn," Arissa said.

"Carlea Renn," Jolar affirmed. "How was Tano-Sertar, really?" He cupped her cheek. "Did you have fun, sweet?"

"Didn't the guards tell you? They watched every move I made."

"They told me that you spent a long time looking at a certain necklace—"

She blinked. She hadn't expected their reporting to be so thorough. It was disconcerting, really. "Did they tell you what I bought?"

"No, but considering *where* you bought it I can honestly say I'm looking forward to seeing it on you tonight." Jolar gave her a hot smile. "And then taking it off . . ."

Eighteen

Arissa adjusted the shimmersilk wrap around her shoulders as she looked over the crowd at the Niman embassy. A quieter, more sophisticated group than those at the previous night's party, a number in attendance tonight seemed to be Niman, with the fine and beautiful bone structure of that world's inhabitants. The décor inside the embassy was a lovely blend of cool ocean blues and warm coral tones. Even the chandeliers were abstract frosted glass reminiscent of sea creatures; the musicians played on traditional Niman wind flutes, filling the air with sweet sound.

The daily practice Jolar insisted on was helping her focus tremendously. Now, even at a crowded party like this, she could dampen her awareness of the emotions around her until they were a background hum instead of an agonizing din. She could concentrate on one person or group and shift her awareness quickly to another at will.

During this afternoon's practice session the images she gleaned from Jolar's mind had come easier and the experience was far less frightening. He'd delighted in sharing with her a memory of the sand under his feet, the feel of the warm crystal waters of the Niman ocean around him.

Jolar handed her a glass of sparkle wine.

She took a sip and smiled at the taste. "It's like a shooting star!"

He laughed, his golden hair catching the light. "Shooting stars don't leave you with a hangover if you drink too many. You know, usually I hate these things," Jolar said with a glance around at the formal reception. He gave her a warm smile. "Must be the company."

She felt beautiful under his soft gaze. "I think this is wonderful."

"Well," he said. "If you like this sort of party, I can promise we can go to plenty more of them . . . later."

Later. When this was finished and she had her ID. He would take her to Nima, and the other worlds, and show her the homeworld that he loved so much, Zartan.

A whole life together.

But right now they had to find Carlea Renn.

She had seen Carlea's holo, but with a change of hairstyle along with the formal attire of the party, and in a crowd from her homeworld, she wasn't going to be easy to pick out.

Wondering if Bruscan had had any better luck in finding their quarry, Arissa sought him with her eyes and seer's senses. She soon located him talking with the Niman ambassador on the upper galley.

Arissa took another quick sip of the sparkle wine and touched Jolar's arm. "Bruscan wants to introduce us."

Jolar's surprise rippled as he glanced around. "Uh, do we even know—"

"Upper galley."

Jolar glanced that way and finished off his wine before placing his glass and hers on the tray of a passing waiter.

The Niman ambassador was a portly man with silver hair. His formal high-collared black shirt seemed to be cutting a bit into his neck, but he was gracious in his welcome when Bruscan introduced them.

"I spent some time on Apovia in my younger years," Ambassador Tivan said to her kindly. "It's a lovely world."

"It is," Arissa agreed. "I'm afraid I've never been to Nima."

The ambassador's brushy gray eyebrows rose. "You must remedy that at first opportunity, Mistress Legan! My homeworld has much to recommend it."

At that, amusement rippled from both Jolar and Bruscan. While Arissa couldn't hear the words, she knew they were likely thinking the same thing: *Like the best trained ornaments in the Realm.*

"I understand the beaches on the southern continent are considered the most beautiful anywhere," Arissa said.

The ambassador inclined his head. "But natural beauty aside, I think you'll find the Niman people as devoted to learning and the arts as the Apovians."

"In fact," Bruscan said, "I was just admiring this piece. It's breathtaking."

The sculpture Bruscan indicated stood nearly a story high. Done in icy blue crystal, it very much resembled ocean water frozen in mid-spout. Interesting, but it lacked to Arissa's eye—and, she knew, to Bruscan's—that elusive *something* that took a work from attractive decoration to masterpiece. Still, it certainly would have been very expensive.

Arissa tilted her head. "From the third wave of the Niman abstractionists, isn't it?"

"Yes, I believe you are correct," the ambassador said warmly. "It was a gift to the embassy."

"Well," Bruscan said, "I should like to meet whoever has such exquisite taste."

The ambassador glanced around. "Unfortunately, I don't see . . . Ah, there she is! Allow me to introduce you to Mistress Renn."

As they followed the ambassador, Jolar leaned forward to mock grumble in her ear. "I'm starting to wonder if I'm needed on this trip at all. You two would probably do just fine without me."

Arissa gave him an amused glance, then turned her attention to the woman whom the ambassador was embracing. Carlea's yellow gown dipped too low for her large bosom, her hair very elaborately styled, her makeup expertly applied but too heavy. She had the unfortunate appearance of one who had spent a great deal of money only to look quite cheap.

And her brown eyes gleamed as her gaze raked over Jolar.

"So, you like the sculpture, Master Legan?" she purred to Jolar after the introductions were made and the ambassador moved off to mingle with the other guests. "It's rare to find a man who appreciates art."

Jolar gave her a dazzling smile. "Well, I've always had a soft spot for the third wave of Niman abstractionists."

Arissa controlled an urge to roll her eyes.

From the confused pulse and blank look that Carlea gave him, it was plain she wouldn't know an abstractionist sculpture if it toppled over onto her. Likely she had selected that artwork based on the impressiveness of the price tag, but in the next instant the woman simpered. "They're my favorite too. I wonder what else we have in common?"

Bruscan gave a soft cough. "It's terribly dry in here. I really must have something to drink." His hand went to Arissa's elbow. "Come along, let's get you something too."

She couldn't sense anything but lustful desire from Carlea. As soon as Arissa allowed Bruscan to pull her away from Jolar, Carlea took the opportunity to take a step closer.

"We were most definitely an impediment back there," Bruscan murmured as he escorted her to the lower galley.

"You intended all along to get them alone. You knew she'd zero in on him," Arissa said, her voice low and angry. Carlea was inches away from Jolar now, her face tilted up at him, an inviting smile playing on her lips. The Niman woman's hand came up to rest lightly on his chest, and Arissa scowled to see that Jolar made no effort to remove it. "And that she has a great weakness for blond men."

"Blond, *handsome* men, to be precise." Bruscan gave her a sly smile. "And Jolar's great weakness is you. And *that* my dear is interesting in itself."

Arissa flushed. Throwing her focus at him, she found a befuddling mix of amusement and regret. "What is that supposed to mean?"

Bruscan took two glasses of sparkle wine for them from a passing waiter when they reached the lower galley.

He handed her a glass and took a sip from his own. "Hmm, they brought out the good stuff. Must be eager to impress upon the local officials that what they'll lose in tariffs they'll make up in bribes with a new trade agreement."

"What did you mean 'interesting'?" Arissa persisted. She wasn't getting anything from Bruscan now but world-weary resignation, and she didn't dare risk a deeper probe.

"Just take it as assurance that you have nothing to fear from Mistress Renn." His eyebrow quirked upward. "Although Jolar might. I hope he's kept up with his self-defense training because, yes, she has quite the reputation." He tilted his head, his smile rueful now. "You love him."

Arissa flushed.

"It's obvious, really," he said when she didn't answer. "A lot of your feelings show on your face."

She looked away. Having had the life she did, being what she was, she had never learned to school her features as others had. She'd never needed to. "I didn't know that."

"It's not a bad thing, necessarily."

"But it's something I need to learn to control."

He took a casual sip of his wine. "You might be well served to do so . . . at least while you're here." His expression brightened. "The buffet looks sumptuous. Shall we?"

Arissa sighed and let him lead her over. The food looked wonderful. Dozens of offerings filled the tables, but for once Arissa had little appetite. Not so Bruscan, who ate heartily and managed to socialize and play escort to her without his considerable charm being in the least bit taxed.

Determined or not, Arissa struggled to hide her grumpiness as the evening wore on and Jolar didn't reappear. Worse, she reached out to him to find that, wherever he was, he was intensely focused on his companion and in no hurry to leave her.

After supper, she and Bruscan took a turn through the embassy's courtyard. Cleverly arranged with plantings and charmingly lit with hanging lanterns, the veritable maze of greenery provided enclaves for private conversation and afforded the courtyard, small in size for expensive Tano-Sertar, the feel of a much larger space.

She was sourly wondering if he would be gone the whole night when Jolar finally came upon them.

"I've been looking all over for you two," he said.

"We only just came outside," Arissa said, annoyed that she couldn't keep the sulky tone out of her voice.

Jolar pressed a kiss to her forehead. "I'm sorry I was gone so long."

"Well," Bruscan said, "our evening was pleasantly spent. I hope yours was . . . productive."

"It went quite well, actually."

Arissa turned away.

"Give us a moment, Bruscan?" Jolar suggested.

"Of course. I think I'll have another look at the center fountain."

Jolar waited till Bruscan was out of earshot. "What is it?" he asked softly.

She couldn't look at him; he would see in her face how miserable, how insecure she felt.

"Nothing," she mumbled.

"I'm not interested in Carlea." He cupped her face in his warm, broad palm. "You, sweet, are all I want."

Tears stung her eyes as she looked up into that tender blue gaze.

"I love you," Jolar said softly.

She swallowed. "I love you too."

He brushed his mouth against hers. "Let's go back to our room," he said huskily. "I missed you, and I'd be more than happy to show you just how much."

She managed a smile. "Okay."

Jolar took her hand in his. They found Bruscan waiting for them at the fountain.

"I think we can bid good evening to the ambassador now," Jolar said to him. "I'm ready to get out of here, that's for sure."

"Excellent," Bruscan said, pulling a comm unit from his pocket. "I'll have the groundcar brought around."

The crowd inside had thinned considerably and the reception was coming to an end. No doubt at this hour a number of guests were also making their goodbyes now.

Just as they reached the doorway, the breeze picked up and lifted Arissa's delicate shimmersilk wrap from her shoulders. She let go of Jolar's hand, hurrying to retrieve it before it could be carried off by the wind. Bruscan, a few steps behind them, managed to catch it. She smiled her thanks as he handed it back to her.

Jolar waited at the doorway to the embassy, where a young woman just stepping out into the courtyard nearly collided with him.

She was tall, elegantly so, and her red shimmersilk gown outlined a slender, graceful figure. Her hair was pale golden blonde, her fine-boned face strikingly beautiful.

The blonde blinked. Her smile was instant and dazzling. "Jolar!"

His horrified recognition made the breath catch in Arissa's lungs.

"Jasa," he said hoarsely.

The blonde gave a light laugh. "Well, I'm delighted to see you too! What are you doing here?"

His arm shot out and he took her by the elbow. "I need to speak with you outside."

Bruscan's sense went grim, and Arissa's heart picked up speed. "Jolar?"

He froze but didn't look at her.

"Hello," the blonde said, leaning around Jolar to regard her with crystal blue eyes and a polite smile. "Jolar, who is this?"

"Jolar?" Arissa said again.

The sound of her trembling voice seemed to snap him out of his paralysis, but he avoided her gaze. "Jasa, come outside with me *now*."

"Jolar," the woman chided, but the dimple that appeared at the corner of her mouth tempered her scold. She gave Arissa an apologetic smile. "I'm so sorry. Honestly, I don't know what to do with him when he gets like this. I suppose we shall have to introduce ourselves. I am Lady Jasa d'Akan." She linked her arm with his. "Jolar's betrothed."

Nineteen

Jasa's betrothal bracelet caught the light as she shifted closer to Jolar; it was of a heavier, more traditional and wider setting than Arissa's. The metalwork bore the look of an antique, the Zartani firestar at its center absolutely brilliant . . .

Jasa tilted her head. "And you are?"

Arissa's lips parted but she couldn't speak. She was vaguely aware of a couple coming up behind them from the courtyard, moving past into the embassy, murmuring apologies as they slipped by, of people inside the building, the slow drifting of guests as the evening wound down.

Jolar stood unmoving at the blonde beauty's side, his face colorless, eyes blazing as he met her gaze.

Arissa felt the stones of the courtyard pavement tilt away from her feet . . .

Bruscan's hand closed around her arm, his body solid beside her. "My apologies, but Arissa and I have another appointment this evening. If you'll excuse us, we were just leaving."

"Oh," Jasa said, blinking. "Well, it was lovely to meet you." Jasa's sense as she'd looked up at Jolar was buoyant, as if she had just been given the most precious of gifts. She pressed herself to his side with a confident sense of ownership. "And it's *very* good to see you, darling. With the wedding so close, there are still some small details I would like to discuss with you."

Only Bruscan's hand gripping Arissa's arm got her moving. He pulled her past Jolar and Jasa smiling up at him and through the doorway. The inside of the embassy was too bright now, the Niman flutes discordant.

He couldn't have lied about how he felt about me. He couldn't have. I would know!

But that woman—Jasa—was she really his betrothed? She reached out to touch Jolar's mind and then stopped short, desperately frightened of what she would find.

Bruscan was grim and determined. She could hardly feel his tight grip on her arm but knew he was the only thing holding her upright.

He never asked me to marry him.

"Please," she croaked. "Bruscan, that woman . . . Is—is she—"

Bruscan's mouth narrowed to a tight line. "Just a little farther. The groundcar will be right outside the door."

Arissa pressed her hand against her mouth. Bruscan responded by walking faster.

He must have always loved her . . .

The ambassador was ahead, standing with what could only be his wife, shaking hands, wishing everyone a good evening. His brow creased in alarm as he turned toward them. "Mistress Legan! Is everything all right?"

"Yes," Bruscan said jovially, his voice too loud. Several startled guests at the door followed their progress with raised eyebrows. "A simple matter of too much sparkle wine. Lovely reception!"

The ambassador hurried behind them. "Can I get you—"

"No, no!" Bruscan was already waving the ambassador's offer away. "My groundcar should be just pulling up—ah, there it is! Good evening! Good evening!"

"These young women . . ." the ambassador's wife sniffed behind them as Bruscan shoved her toward the groundcar, "They drink like trollops."

The driver who had come 'round to open the door threw a questioning look at Bruscan.

Bruscan shook his head. "Just get us out of here. He'll find his own way back."

Bruscan shut the door of the groundcar himself and took a seat across from her. Arissa gripped the edge of the velvet and silk seat as the groundcar started forward.

"You knew," she whispered. "You knew all along."

He didn't deny it. "I'm sorry."

He said he loved me!

"How could—? But *why?*" Arissa's vision blurred. "Please! I don't understand!"

Bruscan's brown eyes reflected his pity. "I know."

He said we could talk about life together. But only after Sertar . . .

"He wanted—he was worried I wouldn't do my part here?" She looked at Bruscan, tears overflowing. "Is that why he led me on? He wanted to make sure I wouldn't betray him?"

Bruscan seemed to collapse into himself. "I'm afraid the only one who can answer your questions is Jolar."

I thought he loved me and all along he was going to marry—

Sobs shook her body. Bruscan turned his face away as the streets and buildings of Tano sped by, the sympathy coming off him in waves.

It took everything Jolar had not to run after her.

His movements stiff, he disentangled his arm from Jasa's and nodded her toward the courtyard. Jolar followed Jasa numbly. His heart was thumping so hard he felt sick.

The hurt in her eyes . . .

"So do I get to know why you're here?" Jasa asked as soon as they reached the privacy of the quiet grove.

"This is work," Jolar said hoarsely. "This is important. And I'm Jolar Legan."

"Something for the fleet again, I suppose." Jasa said, sighing. Then with a resentful tone creeping into her voice, "Or another favor for Dacel."

"He's the elected senior councilor from Zartan."

She raised delicate blonde eyebrows. "He's a commoner and he treats you like an errand boy."

Jolar turned his face away. Arissa was a seer. She would read the truth in his heart.

She *had* to.

After a time, Jasa said: "So, are you going to tell me why you're here?"

"I can't."

"We have been betrothed for five years, Jolar," she reminded. "I will be your wife in a few weeks. Surely I have earned your trust, your respect, by now?"

"This has nothing to do with you," he said roughly. "What are you doing on Sertar anyway?"

She gave him a hurt look. "I came for the trade conference. You want a political career after we're married. It was *your* idea that I start making connections, showing interest in commerce. I've spent the last few months attending such things."

"How soon can you leave?"

She stiffened. "Well, I had planned to stay for the whole conference. But if my presence is going to impede whatever it is that *you're* doing here, I suppose I can return to Zartan at the earliest convenient time."

"Thank you." He gave a nod.

"Shouldn't you admire my new gown?" she asked, holding out the skirt of her red dress.

"*All* your gowns are new."

She let go of the skirt edges, the shimmersilk catching the light of the lanterns as the folds fell back into place.

She stepped closer. "I am happy to see you, darling. It's been too long since my last visit to Tellar. I couldn't possibly arrange to leave Sertar for another few days. Perhaps you could visit me? Tonight?" Her full mouth curved into a smile. "Or slip away to see me for a few hours tomorrow afternoon?"

He looked away. "Not this time."

"Ah," she said then continued, her voice growing cooler: "I hope I can expect you will at least do me the courtesy of appearing for our wedding."

"If my work here is completed by then." He felt his mouth tighten. "But yes."

"Of course, if you need me to change the timing *again*—I shall." She straightened her back. "But five years is quite long enough to wait, Jolar."

"I've told you before." He gave a bitter half-smile. "We can end our betrothal whenever you wish, Jasa."

She lifted her chin. "Our heritage demands certain obligations. Arranged or not, we are both bound to this marriage contract. People such as we do not have the option of disregarding tradition, Jolar."

"I'm well aware of that," he said bleakly. "I know who I am. I know what's expected of me."

She nodded. "As do I." Then she softened a bit and touched his arm again. "I am glad to see you looking so well, darling."

"I never bore you any ill will, Jasa. I wouldn't have wanted this for you either."

She was quiet for a time. "Well, I should go. I suppose it wouldn't do to have anyone see us talking if you're supposed to be this Legan person. You can be assured of my discretion. I wouldn't want to ruin anything for you." She tilted her head. "Will you kiss me goodbye?"

He regarded her silently.

He'd tried, years ago, to create something between them, make some peace with what was to come. Although the sex was more than satisfactory it had never evolved into anything else. Despite her beauty, the similarities in their background and the heat of her bed, her single-minded focus, her absolute confidence in her—in *their*—inherent superiority chilled him.

Jasa possessed charm but no joy, had wit yet lacked humor, was gracious but not kind.

He couldn't honestly say he even liked her.

She knew that, of course. And it made no difference to her. When he understood it did not, any hope of happiness in his coming marriage collapsed.

But now, with Arissa . . .

Suddenly his betrothal seemed so much more like a trap than it ever had.

She narrowed her gaze up at him then gave a half-smile. "I look forward to seeing you at our wedding on Zartan."

"I will be there." His eyes closed briefly. "As promised."

Twenty

Jolar's heart was hammering when he finally found her, sitting alone outside on the low wall in the courtyard of Bruscan's house. She was still in the evening gown she'd worn to the reception, her shoulders hunched against the chill night air. Sertar's moons had risen, and by their light he could see that she had been crying. Perhaps had been since Bruscan had whisked her out of his sight an hour ago.

"I'm sorry," he said quietly.

Arissa didn't even look at him. "Who are you?"

The illumination from Sertar's moons made her face paler, tinted the dark ringlets of her hair with their cool, blue light. Like the goddess Seleni, she seemed a being fashioned entirely of moonlight—a beautiful specter, delicate, unreachable . . .

Jolar came closer, drawn like Seleni's many ill-fated suitors toward a resplendence that threatened to remain forever just beyond his grasp. "You know who I am."

She shook her head, wiping at her face with the back of her hand. "You told me your name, but I didn't even think about it then. Tell me who you are."

"Jolar d'Tural."

"You're a Zartani aristocrat, aren't you?"

"Yes."

"You're Lord d'Tural then."

"Arissa—"

"How could you do that to me?" she whispered and the pain of it slashed his heart. "How could you not tell me?"

"I never expected this to happen, none of this," he said hoarsely. "What's between us, how I feel about you—Gods, I've never felt this way about anyone. I didn't even think I *could*. I love you, Arissa."

"You're *betrothed*!" Her voice rose, her eyes flashed with Seleni's light. A goddess wronged, a power not to be affronted. "You should have *told* me. You should have told me everything."

"I don't love her. I never did."

Arissa turned her face away.

"It's the truth," he insisted.

"I know."

His shoulders slumped in relief. Of course she would. Perhaps he could make her understand, somehow still make this right—

"When I realized I loved you I knew I had to tell you but I thought—I thought once we were finished here, once you had the ID, then together we could decide what to do."

She regarded him with wide, shocked eyes. "You're really going to marry her, aren't you?"

A lump formed in his throat. "I have to."

She shook her head. "Have to? You *have* to? You're wealthy. You're a Zartani lord. You can do anything you want!"

He gave a short, disbelieving laugh. "That's what you think? That my life is my own? It's not. It never has been. I have to live out my heritage, there's no other honorable way. I'm bound by family name, Arissa, by a thousand years of Zartani tradition. That I ever joined the military despite that heritage was only the result of years of battle between my father and me. Gods, it's the only thing in my whole fucking life that's my own, that I earned for myself. I was contracted to marry Jasa years ago. Once I made that vow, signed that contract, there was no going back."

"People break betrothal contracts all the time," she retorted. He realized she thought it only an excuse.

"Arissa, I can't break the contract. If Jasa wanted . . . but that's not going to happen. I gave my word as a Zartani nobleman to marry her. I have to do what's right."

Her shoulders fell. "And marrying Jasa is what's right."

"After my mother died, Father insisted that I make a 'suitable' match. He chose Jasa just as his parents chose my mother for him. He said she'd settle me, help me focus myself—whatever the hells that means. I didn't want to be promised to her. I didn't love her. I knew I never would. My father and I fought about it all the time." His throat tightened. "Then he got sick, weaker every day and finally, five years ago, when the healers said there wasn't much time left . . . He said it would make it easier for him to go if he knew that I was promised. So Jasa came to the house and we stood at Father's bedside . . . He pressed my mother's betrothal bracelet into my hand and—— He died the next morning."

"I know you loved him," Arissa's voice was soft. "That you still grieve for him."

Hesitantly, Jolar sat beside her on the low wall.

"I meant what I said." He touched the betrothal bracelet she wore; his finger traced the curves of metal warmed by her skin. "I want to marry you."

Tears filled her eyes. "But you can't ever do that, can you?"

"It shouldn't be like this." His hand wrapped around hers, her fingers were cold. "I can't marry you, as much as I want to, but that doesn't mean we can't spend our lives together."

Her face twitched with hurt. "Be your shadow consort, you mean?"

"It wouldn't be like that," he promised. "You are my heart, Arissa. You'll be my life."

"While you're married to Jasa."

"I love *you*."

She didn't say it back this time. She knew every feeling he had, every heartache and joy, and at that moment he wished so much that he too were a seer—that he could know if she still loved him, if there were any hope at all—that he felt sick with it.

She turned away. "How would you feel if I were going to marry someone else?"

"How can you even ask that? You know how I'd feel. Arissa, there's nothing I can do. I'm promised to her. I didn't want to be. Not ever. My father wanted this, not me."

"Did you ever join with her?"

His rush of shame must have given her the answer.

"Looks like you wanted it at least a little," she said, her voice choked.

"I haven't been intimate with Jasa for a long time, and what we did was never more than—It was never like it is between us. I can't undo what happened before we met but I can give you everything from now on. I promised to take those vows but I won't have a life with her. I won't live with her."

She stared at him. "So you'll marry her and then what? You'll kneel in Arrena's temple, take vows you don't mean at the Goddess of Love's altar and just never consummate the marriage? You'll put Jasa in a big house and me in a smaller one, stand beside her at official functions and spend your nights with me?"

"I gave my vow to my father. I made my promise to Jasa as a Zartani nobleman," he said roughly. "Tell me how to make this right and I'll do it!"

"There's only one way to make this right, Jolar," Arissa said, tears shimmering in her eyes. "I let you go."

"No." His fingers clenched reflexively around hers. "No, there has to be a way. We'll find a way."

"I can't live that like that. Being hidden away again. Not anymore."

"You *won't* be. You'll have your ID. Everyone who matters to me will know who my true wife is. People have done it for centuries."

"*Your* people—Zartani aristocrats—you mean."

His voice rose. "People who had duty and wanted happiness too!"

"What about Jasa?"

"I won't make any secret of what she can expect from this. She'll know about you—about *us*—before I marry her. Honestly, I can't believe she'll care."

"Could you really do that? Make vows you don't mean? Live a lie like that?"

"Yes," he said sharply. "If it means I can be with you."

"What about children?"

"We could have—"

"I can't risk having a child like me! That leaves Jasa."

"Then I won't have children," he said flatly.

"But you want them, don't you?"

"I'm not going to have everything I want. If I did, you and I would be at Arrena's temple right now getting married."

"So, you'll marry Jasa but not share her bed, not give her a child and she'll live out her life alone while you spend yours with me?" She searched his face. "You can't do that, Jolar."

"If Jasa agrees, then what difference does it make?"

"Would you have kept your marriage vows if you hadn't met me?"

Even now he could recall the flowers etched into the door of that tidy house in Kev-Zartan. The puzzled, polite look on the face of the woman—about his mother's age— who answered his knock, how his father had blanched upon seeing him there. How right then, swaying with the soft, spring rain dampening his face, he'd sworn never to betray his own wife the way his father had . . .

Jolar closed his eyes briefly. "Things are different now."

Arissa shook her head. "I can't let you do this."

"I don't love her. She *knows* that. Neither one of us has been faithful."

"But you were going to be after you took your marriage vows, weren't you?"

"Why are you doing this?" he demanded. "We can have a lifetime—a whole lifetime—together, Arissa!"

"Jolar, you wouldn't—you *couldn't*—respect yourself if you did this."

"Because I'm a good man," he said and the words tasted like ash. "An honorable one."

"It will eat at you," she said softly. "It's eating at you now and I can feel it. I can't live with that, feeling this, feeling what this will do to you."

"Of course you can feel it," he said, his voice bitter. "Anyone else I could hide it from."

With shaking fingers, Arissa unfastened the cuff from her wrist. She held it out to him, the Zartani firestar of the betrothal bracelet blanched of its color by the moonlight. "Here."

Tears burned his eyes. "Keep it."

"No." She extended it a little further. "It's not right. And I just—I can't wear it again."

"Please," he begged. "Even if it's all you'll ever have of me, gods, at least it's something."

Twenty-one

"Loosen your grip," Jolar advised, resetting the target. He had reserved the entire Tano-Sertar indoor shooting range to teach her in privacy. "It's important not to hold the blaster too tightly."

"Okay," Arissa said, trying to relax—no easy task with Jolar right next to her. She longed to slide her hand into his, just as at night she ached to reach across the wide silent expanse of their bed . . .

It wasn't the immorality of taking a man who belonged to another, though she imagined if she were of better character that would bother her. Even her resolve not to be hidden had quickly worn threadbare over the past three days. She'd be no more hidden than Kemma was, and Kemma wasn't miserable or ashamed. Certainly Arissa didn't condemn Kemma and Lian for what they had together.

But she knew Jolar's mind. How important loyalty and fidelity were to him. She knew once he took those final vows to another, he would forever be torn by keeping her as a shadow consort, no matter how above-board the arrangement was. She knew he would do his best to honor her, and his wife. But he would hate himself for the double life.

And every moment they had after, no matter how joyful, would be stained by that guilt.

She couldn't live with herself if she let him do it.

But her selfish heart didn't seem to care about noble intentions or sacrifice in the name of what was right. All it knew was that Jolar was beside her, the warmth of him tempting her to turn and bury her face against his chest.

"Try it now," Jolar said.

Arissa focused on the target, the outline of a person, and fired.

"That's good," Jolar said, with a nod toward the target. "You got him right through the center of the throat."

Arissa lowered the weapon Jolar had purchased for her that morning. It was a small blaster, powerful but easily hidden, its grip comfortable in her hand, firing with no trace of recoil. Each power cartridge held a charge for weeks and at full charge guaranteed no fewer than fifty shots before she would have to switch it out.

Initially it hadn't felt heavy, but her arm was starting to ache from holding the diminutive weapon in the firing position for so long. "I was aiming for the shoulder."

Jolar frowned. "Why?"

"I was trying to wound him."

"Don't," he said flatly. "Once you're at the point you have a blaster aimed at someone you need to try to kill them."

"Can't I just leave it on the stun setting?"

"Stun isn't foolproof. Sometimes it takes an instant longer than you have to take effect. And you need to hit them square to be sure you're going to knock them out rather than daze them. That's why when I shot that Utavian, I shot to kill."

"Because he wasn't facing you?"

"No, because he was facing *you*," Jolar said sharply. "And me taking that extra instant for stun would have given him time to burn a blaster bolt through your head."

Arissa rubbed her eyes. She wasn't—*they* weren't—getting much sleep. It might be obvious to Nela and all of Bruscan's other household that *something* had changed between them, but they still shared a room—and a bed.

That first night Arissa had returned to their room and found that Nela had laid out the pretty new shimmersilk nightgown set she'd bought. She'd sat on the bed holding its soft, slippery fabric against her face and cried.

The bed was used for sleeping only now, what little they got of it. They lay far apart, and Arissa could feel every time that Jolar kept himself from reaching for her. She wouldn't be able to bear it if he didn't hold himself back; one touch of his skin against hers and her resolve would crumble.

They went about to parties and luncheons, continuing the pretense of being a married couple as Bruscan's slicers gathered what information they could. Their investigation was proving painfully slow. Danlen Mirat was disinterested in all of their overtures, Broc Attar pursued them like a love-starved sluoof cub, and Larner Tovic showed only slight puzzlement each time they sought him out.

But not even Broc Attar was more focused on them than Carlea.

Focused on Jolar, that is.

"Ready to try again?"

"My arm is tired," she said.

"Try a few on stun and then we'll quit."

"Why practice the stun setting if I'm never going to use it?"

He sighed. "I didn't say it was never useful. Tactically there are a number of situations where it is a better choice. If you need to question someone, drilling a blaster hole through his chest isn't the smartest move. When you're more experienced you can make a better judgment about when to stun, but for now just practice it."

Arissa reset the blaster to the stun setting the way he'd shown her. She raised the weapon and fired off four shots.

"Much better," Jolar said approvingly. "You hit him dead on. What did you do differently?"

"I knew it was set for stun."

Jolar's mouth thinned. "Things may get to the point where it's kill or be killed—in which case, Arissa, you need to make it *kill*. Understand?"

She rubbed her forehead. His exhaustion and tension was only adding to her own. "How long do we have?"

"Do you want me to pay for another half hour?"

"I meant before you're supposed to meet Carlea," she said, more sharply than she intended.

Jolar looked down the range. "An hour and a half."

"Then we should get back so you can change." Arissa set the safety on the blaster and placed it back in its carrying case along with the extra power cartridges. "She hates it when you're late."

"I don't have any interest in Carlea." Jolar sent out little spikes of annoyance. "I'm not going to sleep with her."

"She'll tell you whatever you want to know if you do," Arissa said bitterly, slinging the case over her shoulder. "Maybe that would be best."

Jolar pulsed with anger and hurt. "So it's all the same now to you if I do?"

Arissa turned away. She had to stop this. What he did and with whom he did it were Jasa's concerns now, not hers.

"We have dinner plans," Arissa reminded. "Bruscan said Broc was very insistent he see us tonight." Jolar didn't answer. Arissa followed him out, the lights of the range powering down as they exited.

Outside Jolar settled into the passenger seat of the groundcar and gave her a meaningful look.

Biting the inside of her cheek, Arissa took up her place on the driver's side as the vehicle's anti-grav field powered up. "Maybe we should try another couple runs around Bruscan's property before I do this."

"It's a short drive back to Bruscan's," he reminded. "And almost the whole drive is through residential areas."

Letting her breath out, she took the controls and scanned the area around them, then started the vehicle forward slowly.

"You're better at this than you think," Jolar said. "You're doing fine."

"I don't feel like I'm doing fine," Arissa said, adjusting the groundcar's antigrav a little, then increased speed. "My hands shake the whole time."

Very glad the groundcar was equipped with multiple repulser fields around the body to prevent collision, Arissa increased speed. Navigation would keep her from getting lost even in the twisting streets of Tano and it would be a simple matter to set the groundcar to autopilot and ride as another passenger, but Jolar wouldn't allow it.

"Autopilot is fine when nothing goes wrong," he'd argued. "The whole point of this is to prepare you for when something *has* gone wrong."

Street after street showed nothing but high walls and intimidating security gates. "Not much of a walking city," she murmured, tilting the yoke and slowing to make the turn navigation indicated—and bit her lip as the groundcar swiveled more jerkily than she'd intended.

"Not a safe one either," Jolar returned, "if you're on this side of those gates."

"Is the rest of the planet like this?"

Another groundcar ahead, its driver far more confident, took the next turn a great deal faster. Chewing her lip, Arissa didn't slow the groundcar, this time making the turn smoothly.

"Most of it. There's too much money here, too much greed. It's spoiled what beauty Sertar has."

Seeing no groundcars nearby—and this lane a reassuringly straight one—Arissa risked a quick smile at him. "But Zartan isn't like that?"

He gave a self-conscious laugh. "If Sertar has too much greed, I guess Zartan has too much pride."

"It's natural to be proud of your homeworld."

"Is that how you feel about Apovia?"

"Of course." Arissa felt her shoulders start to relax. Talking was helping her nervousness. Talking and the very light groundcar traffic during mid-morning in a residential area.

"It's beautiful there," Jolar said. "The meditation gardens, the museums. Your world has produced most of our greatest literature, our most important artworks. You have a lot to be proud of."

"My father said the Apovians uplifted others with their art, that we helped people bear the harsh realities of life. He believed we were on the cusp of a new golden age." She gave a fond chuckle. "But he was a poet as well as a professor."

Jolar shook his head. "My father believed that Zartan's golden age ended when the Tellaran royal family fell. A man born too late to ever be happy."

The pulse energy field of Bruscan's reinforced security gate flashed once as it deactivated. A moment later the tarasteel gate itself retracted, and Arissa engaged the forward drive again.

"Too bad they never met. My father was a born optimist." Arissa brought the groundcar to a stop and set it in standby mode, thrilled with her accomplishment. Maybe she *could* try her hand at piloting a shuttle soon. "Bruscan will be happy to see us back. I think he's more nervous about me driving than I am."

"See?" Jolar said warmly. "You did great, just like airskating."

"'Great' because no one wound up at the medcenter?"

Jolar laughed and she gave him a smile. He cupped her cheek in his broad palm, already bending for a kiss. Instinctively she leaned toward him . . .

Suddenly she jerked back and wrenched her face away.

The pain she sensed slash through him left her gasping. Her fingers curled into fists to keep herself from reaching for him. From the corner of her eye she saw him pass his hand over his face.

"We should go inside," she managed, powering down the groundcar with quick, shaky movements.

"Right," he said hoarsely.

Bruscan looked anything but relieved as he came out into the courtyard to meet them; the icicles of his tension stabbed at her mind.

"We're free for dinner tonight after all," Bruscan said, his face tight. "Broc Attar is dead."

Jolar lifted Carlea's hand from his thigh, grateful again that he'd insisted this lunch take place at a public restaurant.

But he'd blundered in letting her choose the establishment. Located in a respectable enough commercial zone, the restaurant's design—dimly-lit and cozy semi-circular booths each obscured by frosted plexisteel and sharp corners—made it an ideal destination for those seeking to discreetly meet a paramour during work hours.

Their spot at the leather-padded booth seemed tailor-made for an assignation. Their table faced a window with a particular tint of plexisteel treated to provide a terrific one-way view of Tano-Sertar's skyline.

Extra insurance against any spy-cam toting hawkshaw hired by a suspicious spouse, Jolar thought dryly. He wondered if Carlea's husband bothered to have her tailed. Of course, depending on the terms of Carlea's trust fund, to have their marriage dissolved might not be in her husband's financial best interest.

Still, this table was as private a spot as clandestine lovers could hope for in a public space. Their booth had a control to signal for the waiter to come—even to refresh their drinks—so their server wouldn't stumble upon them at an inopportune moment, and the music level seemed loud enough to cover *most* sounds.

Although, Jolar reflected wryly, if he were so inclined as to couple with Carlea in a *restaurant* for gods' sake, with his height the confines of the booth might prove tricky.

But the only witness to that copulation could possibly be the white, fluffy, blunt-nosed pet snuffer Carlea had brought along. She'd cooed over the thing all through lunch, feeding it bits from her plate, its enormous black eyes regarding her in simpleminded adoration, crumbs catching in the fur around its sharp-toothed mouth. Jolar couldn't help but wonder how much it had cost Carlea in 'consideration' to be allowed to bring the creature in here.

Its belly rounded out with the culinary achievements of an intersystem-ranked chef, the beast was now curled up asleep in its carrier, huffing snores out of its stubby nose.

"I'm married," he reminded as he moved Carlea's hand off his leg—*again*—but he smiled when he said it.

Carlea gave a careless shrug. "So am I."

"Oh," Jolar said, feigning ignorance. "How long?"

"Too long," she purred.

"Does he live on Sertar?"

Carlea's mouth tightened. Plainly the subject of her husband was not a welcome one. Jolar hoped it helped to cool her overtures long enough for him to get any useful information at all.

He was uneasy at being separated from Arissa, even with Bruscan's promise to stay with her until he returned. After Bruscan's grim news that their most promising and eager suspect had been shot in a gambling establishment in Tano an hour before, it had taken every bit his discipline to leave her at all. A disagreement over cards, Broc's death had happened in front of dozens of witnesses, his killer—a Leman—had already paid a hefty fine and been freed by SerSec, only to vanish so well even Bruscan's slicers couldn't find him.

Broc had been very anxious that they meet with him privately that evening, and now he had a blaster bolt through his heart.

Larner and Danlen were positively chilly toward them.

And all of it made the meeting with Carlea something he couldn't afford to cancel.

Carlea's sexual innuendos showed her both experienced and adventurous, but he struggled not to cringe away from her. Time spent with her was anything but pleasant.

And every moment stole from what little time he had left with Arissa.

At the thought of her now, his chest tightened with longing. Since that night at the embassy she had never touched him nor allowed him to touch her. She shied away whenever he got close. He had gotten very good at directing her when they went out without once putting his hand on her.

Sharing a bed with her was torture. She kept her back to him, as far away as the mattress's width would allow. Now there were no smiles, no shared laughter, no easy talk as they lay within each other's embrace.

She practiced her seer skills with clear reluctance. He tried to make it easier on her, focusing on pleasant memories of childhood, the darshball playoffs with Tasan at the academy, Admiral Henlon's speech when he was promoted to commander's rank.

His casual suggestion yesterday that she might consider Zartan as a new home after their mission was met with stony silence, the message clear. He'd ruined everything between them. He could not even hope for the tepid position of friend.

And when this was over, he might never see her again.

"Let's not waste our lunch together chatting about spouses," Carlea said with a toss of her glossy, dark hair. "I find the topic so dull."

"Have you considered the contract I showed you?" Jolar said, shifting to take a swallow from his wine glass. It allowed him to face her better and move further away at the same time.

She gave a half-shrug, a smile playing at her lips. "Of course I'm interested in anything you want to show me."

"How interested?"

She scooted closer to him, brushing her full breast against his arm as the snuffer gave a loud raspy snore from its carrier. "*Very* interested."

This was going nowhere and Jolar had had enough.

He set his glass down. "How long did you say you're going to be on Sertar?"

She blinked. "At least another two weeks."

"That's excellent." Deftly avoiding her bejeweled and painted talons, Jolar dropped a kiss to the back of her hand as he simultaneously pushed the control to summon their waiter. "When can we meet again?"

Jolar's legs gave out and he sank down on the wide, curtained bed in their suite at Bruscan's house, the message on his coded datapad still displayed. Since leaving Carlea all he could smell on himself was the cloying fragrance of her perfume. He'd intended to take a shower and change before going in search of Arissa. But he'd had to check his messages first, and now—

He sat trembling with the datapad clutched in his hand, longing to go to her, to bury his face in the silky black ringlets of her hair. He wanted to inhale the scent of her, feel her softness, take comfort just in her presence . . .

Arissa came in and closed the door behind her.

Of course she knows. Probably sensed it as soon as I read the message.

"What is it?" Arissa asked. "What's happened?"

"Dacel—My friend—the Zartani councilor—" Just the words seemed wrong and it took such effort to get them out. "He's dead."

Her face paled. "How?"

"Shot. He was shot through the chest." Jolar shook his head. "Dacel was a good friend, one of the best I ever had,

Arissa. He was a good *man*. He worked for Zartan, for the Realm, for over thirty years. And last night someone just walked into his house on Tellar—and blew a hole through him."

"I'm so sorry." She gave a sharp headshake. "Oh, no. Jolar, no, this is *not* your fault."

"It's not? Dacel trusted me to figure out what's going on. I was the only one he felt he could trust, and I *failed* him! He's dead because I didn't figure this out fast enough. I promised—I *promised* him—"

She came closer, but not close enough.

Never close enough now.

The desire to pull her down to the bed, to bury his face in her hair, bury *himself* in her, arced through him.

Jolar forced himself to look at the datapad gripped in his hand. "This message came from Rekan d'Barat, the new acting Zartani councilor. He's ordered me to contact him immediately on our status. I have to get him apprised of our situation here. I want to know if there's—if they know who killed Dacel. The media hasn't even started reporting it yet. I suppose it will come out sometime today." His grip tightened on the datapad. "I've got to convince Rekan not to scrub the mission."

"Gods," she whispered. "Jolar, if someone's killed the Zartani councilor, then—"

"I have to do this," Jolar broke in roughly. "I promised Dacel. I have to keep my word. I *have* to." He closed his eyes briefly. "Arissa, if you want to return to Tellar or—"

"No," she said quickly. "No, if you stay, I stay too."

He hesitated. "I'll make sure Rekan keeps Dacel's promise to you."

"No, I meant—We're making progress."

Jolar shut his eyes for a moment. He could scarcely remember the last time he'd slept well. "Progress, but no answers. And Danlen Mirat's abruptly come around. I heard from him right before I got the message about—" Jolar swallowed. "Danlen has an estate in the western mountains of the southern continent, and he's invited us to be his guests there for a few days."

"His guests?"

"Alarm bells ringing?" he asked wryly. "Yeah, mine too. Considering he's been the least interested in having anything to do with us this turnaround is suspicious, but Bruscan says Danlen's just spent a great deal of money. He may just really need the income."

"What did he spend it on?"

"That, we haven't found out yet. I know it's dangerous as hells but as friendly as he's suddenly become, he won't come here. Something about his wife being not able to travel and her wanting to meet us."

"Then we go to them," Arissa agreed softly. "What happened with Carlea?"

He sighed. "Nothing useful. Bruscan says her finances are solid. Too solid."

Arissa frowned. "What do you mean?"

"She inherited her wealth, and as near as Bruscan or I can tell she has advisors to run it all. She doesn't seem to do anything but spend money and screw her latest interest. The problem is that everyone on this festering planet holds dummy corporations, puts ownerships in trusts, hides behind partnerships." He gave a short, humorless laugh. "Well, not everyone. Larner seems to claim ownership of everything he has, but maybe he's just better at hiding it all."

"We need to have dinner with Carlea—her husband too, if you can manage it." Arissa looked thoughtful. "That should give me enough time to give you some insight."

Jolar winced. "That'll be a fun evening."

"It's the only way I can—"

"I know." He waved it off. "It's a good idea. I'll send her a message after I speak to Rekan. I'll tell her my wife's getting suspicious and we need to show there's nothing going on. She'll probably like that."

Arissa hesitated. "While you were with Carlea, Bruscan and I managed to track Larner down. We 'accidentally' bumped into him as he was leaving a business meeting."

"And?"

She tensed, wrapping her arms around herself. "And . . .he has the oddest mind. It's like it's put together *differently* than any other I've ever encountered. He wasn't surprised to see us there."

She must have felt his alarm because she shook her head.

"He wasn't *expecting* us either. He wasn't angry or unhappy or startled. He told me that he would have some suggestions of who might suit the contract soon. He said it as if that were the sum total of all that needed to be said." She shook her head again. "It's like people are nothing but holoprojections to him."

"And dead or not, Broc Attar isn't off the list yet. Bruscan's going to continue working on his end to see what he can find." Jolar looked at the datapad. "As long as I can convince Rekan."

"You don't like him."

Rekan was Zartani councilor now. He had to respect the office if not the man, but still Jolar felt his lip curl. "Dacel was worth a thousand Rekan d'Barats."

She was silent for a moment. "Is there anything I can do?"

"Other than turn your abilities up to full blast?" He let his breath out. "I guess while I contact Rekan you can start packing. In an hour we'll either be going to Danlen's or headed back to Tellar."

Twenty-two

The forest blurred below them as they travelled southwest, following the sun. Arissa knew her fear of flying still lingered, though she felt completely safe with Jolar piloting. A loan from Bruscan, this shuttle was a luxurious vehicle. She wasn't sure she wanted to fly something this expensive on her first attempt, but she began to wonder if the best way to finally conquer her fears were to get behind the controls herself.

Other shuttlecraft became scarcer the further they travelled from the capital and Sertar's northern continent. Now she spied other shuttles only rarely; she hadn't considered just how isolated their destination might be when she agreed they should go.

She glanced sidelong at Jolar. There was anguish beneath his determined expression, but nothing she said seemed to ease his grief—or his self-recrimination.

A herd of tanelope bounded across the savanna below, their hooves kicking up a half-kilometer of dust as they ran and Arissa exclaimed in wonder. She had never seen wild animals with her own eyes before, but Jolar couldn't even seem to spare a flicker of interest for the herd.

The plains had long ago given way to the thickly forested mountainous regions when he finally spoke.

"We're coming up on it."

She could already feel him sinking back into his painful thoughts.

"You said Danlen was pressing about us visiting," she prompted.

Jolar began the descent to land. "Remember—this isn't Bruscan's place. We're going to have to be careful what we say even when we're alone."

She threw him a smile as they touched down. "I'm sorry we're not both telepathic."

"I'm sorry too," he said softly, his hands resting lightly on the yoke. He had his safety restraints off and was out of the shuttle before the door on his side had even completely opened.

Arissa breathed in the warm, clean country air as she stepped from the shuttle. While already late evening in Tano, it was only mid-afternoon on this side of the continent. A two-storied brown and bronze structure, Danlen's estate sat within a clearing but the land around was heavily wooded. Sporting many windows and balconies, this home possessed a style and grace that harmonized with the forest encircling it and was free of the tacky ostentatiousness found in so many of the mansions in Tano-Sertar.

Danlen looked far more at ease here; his clothing was looser, his hazel eyes brighter as he came out to meet them. The woman beside him was sweet-faced, with striking white-blonde hair and large gray eyes, but though she was far taller than Arissa, she had the air of one delicate to the point of fragility.

Danlen smiled at them. "Found the place all right?"

Jolar nodded. "No problems at all."

"Your home is beautiful," Arissa said honestly as she reached out to brush their minds.

"All Cenon's doing," Danlen said, with a loving look at the woman. "Jolar and Arissa Legan—my wife, Cenon."

"Welcome. It's so nice to have guests again." Cenon gushed, her native Sertarian accent kind to the consonants.

"We haven't had many lately." A shadow passed over Danlen's face. "Cenon has been ill."

She took her husband's hand. "I am perfectly fine now," she said firmly.

Arissa wondered if Jolar, too, could hear the lie.

"Please, come into the house and we'll get you settled," Cenon continued. "Dinner will be ready in about an hour and I'm sure you are tired from your trip."

Jolar was tense beside her as they went inside. He hid his displeasure with a friendly smile when the weapons detector flashed in the doorway and he had to hand over his hold-out blaster.

It was a fine house with gleaming wood floors, smooth plaster walls and a polished wooden ceiling. Arissa spied a number of servants both inside and out, and a mind touch revealed they lacked the single-minded ruthlessness of servants in Tano. These people had a sense of ease and belonging here, as if they considered the place just as much home as Cenon and Danlen did. The furniture seemed selected with comfort as a priority rather than style, and the whole house was worn enough to show it more home than showplace, but there was no sign of children within.

As the couple showed them to their room, two spots of color showed in Cenon's cheeks. She was a little out of breath from climbing the stairs. Danlen sent worried looks her way, but he hid his concern as soon as her eyes turned to him.

A servant brought their luggage to the room. Cenon and Danlen left with him, entreating Jolar and Arissa to rest and come downstairs as soon as they were ready.

The wide planks of their suite's floor were rich dark, rich wood. The rugs were faded but clearly valuable antiques. The beautiful oval windows were made of cut crystal, not plexisteel, and rainbow colors shimmered as one moved about the room. The windows were swung open, and the breeze smelled of sunshine and growing things. Pale green plastered walls gave the room a cool, organic feel and echoed the serenity of the woods outside.

In the little sitting area a thickly padded sofa and chairs showed soft curves and the earth-toned linen fabrics bespoke comfort. Arissa could well imagine whiling away a rainy afternoon contentedly settled in a chair by the window with a novel in her hand and a cup of white tea at her elbow.

A wide bed was tucked into an arched wooden alcove, a cozy haven that invited the joyous intertwining of bodies and Jolar's glance, too, lingered there . . .

Arissa looked over the grounds toward the surrounding forest. "It's wonderful to get out of the city. I've missed the fresh air."

"I was worried you would be bored."

"Oh, no. In fact, maybe we could explore the countryside a little tomorrow? Just pack a lunch and wander off alone?"

His glance showed he too knew that this house was no place to speak freely. "We might be able to squeeze in a walk after dinner tonight. Explore the woods a bit?"

"That sounds perfect," she agreed. "The sooner the better."

"I think we're far enough from the house," Jolar said with a look at the woods around them. From the forest he could hear only the faint hum of insects, the occasional *ah-wop* of a furred nectar glider. "It should be safe to talk."

She glanced back, the silky black curls of her hair framing her heart-shaped face. She'd learned to hide her feelings much better; he couldn't read her expressions as easily as he once had. He remembered bitterly how he'd worried Sertar would take that sweet innocence from her.

No, I'm the one who did that.

There was a sadness about her now, even when she smiled. Only in the times of their closest intimacy could he feel her too, and those were some of the most cherished moments of his life. He would have traded all he had to be a seer now. To know if there was any love left for him behind those beautiful eyes.

To know if there were any hope at all.

It was hard to be so close to her. It was hard to sleep beside her, to feel the warmth, the softness of her near him and accept that he would never know it again. But as agonizing as this was, he knew even this would come to an end.

And then he would have nothing of her.

At least right now he could see her, hear her, soak in her presence. With every moment he wanted to cry out to her that nothing had changed for him, that any part of her life she allowed him to occupy he would take with humble gratitude.

But the simple fact was that, knowing as she must that his love was unchanged, she never spoke of it.

And that told him everything he needed to know. After all the hurt he had caused her the very least he could do was spare her the burden of speaking his unwanted affection.

"I don't sense animosity from them," she said quietly. "If anything, Danlen's extremely concerned we think well of him."

"Yeah," Jolar grumbled. "He's very friendly now, very much the affable host. He was so standoffish in Tano, unmoved to the point of disinterest in the contract."

"Has he talked to you at all about it yet?"

Jolar shook his head. "He suggested I join him for a drink when we get back from our walk. I'm guessing he's going to broach it tonight."

Her brow creased a little.

"You're worried." He started to lift his hand to cup her cheek, then caught himself and clenched his fist at his side. *Don't touch her. You don't have the right.* "What is it?"

She folded her arms, looking back at the house again. "It's just *odd*. They're so welcoming, so friendly. Like we were old friends instead of barely-met business contacts."

"Maybe they're just in desperate need of the money."

"But they aren't desperate. They're very much at ease. And they feel friendly enough toward me but are anxious that *you* think well of them."

"That's understandable if they want me to choose them."

"I don't . . ." She sighed. "Maybe that's it."

"Can you—I don't know—describe what you're feeling from Danlen?"

She considered. "Amiable, friendly. Like he feels you can do each other a great deal of good, like you have the same goals." She shook her head, frustration plain on her face. "I'm sorry, I wish I were better at this."

"No, the information you're able to give me is extraordinary." He swept his glance over her, the waves of her hair in the fading sunlight as the day drew to an end, the soft curve of her cheek. "I can't imagine what it would have been like to do this without you."

She gave him a faint, fleeting smile.

He cleared his throat. "What do you think of Cenon?"

"She's very much what she appears. And he loves her very much."

As the breeze stirred her ringlets, Jolar remembered the silky feel of her hair against his cheek, his shoulder, curtained over his thighs . . .

He twisted away to face the house. In the far distance he heard a frantic rustle of leaves and the startled yelp of some tiny creature—cut short as though it were devoured by a larger, stronger one.

An omen?

He had never believed in such things before.

"Jolar?"

"Yes?" he managed, surprised to find his voice so steady.

She was silent, but if she were touching his mind he couldn't feel it.

"We should probably get back," she said at last. "Danlen must be eager to talk."

"I wish I could have you with me," Jolar said hoarsely.

Jolar took a swallow of his brandy.

We should all have been actors. We play our parts all so well.

Anyone looking in though the arched windows of Danlen's house tonight would think them only two married couples enjoying a few days of fresh air and camaraderie. Soon after they returned from their evening walk, Cenon invited Arissa to see the enclosed herbery off the kitchen while he and Danlen settled in comfortable chairs.

"You're lucky to live out here," Jolar said with a nod toward the tree line not far from where they sat. "I didn't realize Sertar's southern continent was still so unspoiled."

Danlen shrugged. "Tano is so crowded."

And our room definitely bugged. The only thing good about knowing that bed would be used tonight for sleeping and nothing else was that Danlen wouldn't hear Arissa's sweet little—

"Yes," Jolar agreed and took a scant swallow of the excellent brandy. Danlen had brought out the best. This stuff must cost hundreds of creds a bottle. But while it had just gotten dark here it was past midnight in Tano. A full glass might just have him snoring in this chair. "It's good to get a break."

"You're welcome to extend your stay with us. I'm sure Cenon would be agreeable. She really enjoys Arissa's company."

"I'd really like to, but I'm on Sertar for business." Jolar gave a regretful shrug. "There are a number of people who I put off to come here already. This is still a working vacation."

"Maybe I can help you out with that," Danlen said with a half-smile.

Jolar took another drink. "How?"

"If you and I come to an agreement about the fleet contract—" Danlen leaned forward. "Well, then the rest of your trip to Sertar would be a lot more relaxing."

"You have an offer to make?"

Danlen inclined his head. "An excellent one."

"It's a good opportunity. I'm sure I'll get a lot of good offers."

"Mine will be better."

"I'm listening."

"How much of a cut do you get from the contract?"

Jolar laughed. "Aylor isn't Sertar, friend. I get a flat fee and that's it. My job is to choose the best deal for the fleet."

"Well, what if I could offer the best deal for the fleet . . . *and* something for you?"

Jolar held up his brandy glass. "A bottle of this, maybe?"

Danlen laughed. "I can do better than that. Much, much better."

"I'm still listening," Jolar said.

Danlen rolled his glass between his hands. "I know all about you, Jolar. What your trip to Sertar is really all about."

Jolar's mouth went dry and his mind flashed to Arissa, now far away at the other side of the house.

Gods, I'm such a fucking idiot! She's there, I'm here and I don't even have a festering blaster!

"Is that so?" Jolar shifted slightly, moving so the balls of his feet were on the floor, getting ready if he needed to fight. "My wife seems to think it's all about shopping."

Danlen's smile was bemused. After a moment, he shrugged. "Beautiful wife who clearly enjoys fine things. New house." Danlen tilted his head. "It looks like you're overextended, friend."

Jolar's heart hammered with relief. "I'm doing all right."

"No, you aren't," Danlen said genially. "I'm willing to bet that you're losing sleep over it."

"Everyone has problems."

"I have a solution to those problems. I can offer you a deal that will not only end your current financial difficulties but will provide you and Arissa with a luxurious future."

"All to give you the contract?" Jolar suddenly felt as awake as if he'd been drinking caf instead of brandy. "Excuse me if I'm a little skeptical. It could hardly be worth it to you to pay me that much, uh—*consideration*. Providing us with a luxurious future would leave you without any profit at all."

"Profit isn't everything, and it's worth it to me," Danlen returned. "Worth it enough that you could likely name your price."

Jolar gave a short laugh. "Now I really *am* skeptical. And the price I'd name would probably floor you."

"Try me."

"All right." Jolar lifted his glass. "Ten million credits. And that sparkly necklace my wife's been eying in Tano."

Danlen gave a nod. "Done."

"You're joking."

Danlen stood and opened the wall safe. He counted out the rainbow-hued credits and placed the pile in front of Jolar.

"That's one million credits. You'll get another four when the contract is signed. Another five after the crystals have been delivered and accepted. I'm afraid you'll have to point out the necklace. Tano has a lot of jewelry shops."

Jolar stared at the pile of money in front of him. This contract couldn't be worth that much to *anyone*. "Are you serious?"

"Absolutely."

What the hells is going on here?

"Why is this so important to you?" Jolar asked bluntly.

"Do you care?"

"I care if you're going to leave me twisting in the wind over it," he said sharply. "I need to know why."

Danlen shrugged. "I want my crystals on fleet ships and nobody else's."

"Why?" Jolar demanded. "Are they set to detonate or something? I was in the military; I'm not going to help you kill any fleet personnel."

Danlen laughed. "You really don't know anything about astuk crystals, do you? No, of course not. Nothing in my crystals that could damage the ships or kill anyone." Danlen's hazel eyes were sharp. "Do we have a deal?"

I have to get to Arissa. We have to figure out what's going on here.

But right now I need to buy us some time.

"Well," Jolar said slowly. "I'll have to hear any other offers, just for appearance sake."

Danlen smiled. "Sounds like we can find the ladies and open a bottle of sparkle wine."

"Absolutely." Jolar stood to offer his hand to Danlen, and heard a terrified cry in his mind just as the wall behind him blew apart—

Twenty-three

Someone was screaming his name.

Jolar came to, coughing. Black smoke stung his eyes, and he could hear intermittent blaster fire nearby. He frowned, trying to recall his objective for the training simulation. He fumbled about unsuccessfully for his pulse rifle, then his hand went to his blaster but he found that weapon—and his hip holster too—missing.

Ah, fuck, that's going to cost me at the eval.

Groaning against the throbbing in his head, Jolar rolled over and started crawling toward her. Her panicked cries vibrated so loudly they were making his teeth ache.

"Give me a minute, damn it," he muttered.

She wasn't helping matters by screaming at him like that. He bumped up against someone lying in his way. Jolar raised his head and moved a little closer. Whoever it was, he was in civis.

And dead.

"Wait," Jolar murmured, frowning as he realized the blaster sounds were outside his head and her terrified screams were inside it.

Arissa!

The bloodied body was Danlen's. Jolar's gaze darted around, taking in his hellish surroundings.

Danlen's study, what's left of it anyway. She and Cenon . . . the kitchen! Which way to the festering kitchen?

He'd given over his holdout blaster, and half this room was already a smoking ruin. The wall where the windows had been was gone, leaving the room open to the warm southern Sertarian night. He'd already found the schematic of the mansion that Bruscan provided inaccurate, and the power was out. He'd been through this house all of once, and never to the kitchen.

Danlen's money was scattered around the room, some of the rainbow-hued bills blowing about.

Anyone with that much cash in his house is going to have a blaster on him somewhere!

Jolar quickly ran his hands over Danlen's body, ignoring the slickness that could only be blood as he patted the man down. He was about to give up and go without it when he found the small blaster in Danlen's boot.

The mental screams suddenly ceased and left an echoing silence that froze his heart.

Arissa?

Arissa! Oh gods, answer me!

He threw himself over Danlen's body, crawling in the direction he'd felt her. There was something else, monsters moving through the dark around her.

No, not monsters. Men with monstrous thoughts. The clean fragrance of the forest and that awful burnt coppery smell . . .

That he could even know that—was sure enough to bet his life on it—burst into his awareness and left him gasping. In the next instant he shoved the shock, the astonishing wonder of it, brutally aside.

All that mattered now was finding her.

He couldn't go through the house. Staying low, Jolar crawled forward. He had to get outside, and that ruined wall of windows was the fastest way. Jolar got to a crouching position and eased along the wall. He heard the sound of a blaster shot not far away and an agonized cry. The blaster fired several more times. He didn't have to look to know that whoever these men were, they were intent on killing everyone here.

He pushed to his feet and ducked through the opening. As soon as he was outside he ran for the tree line. Probably only the position of the house and the close proximity of Danlen's study to the forest saved him. Any other place on the estate and he would have had twice as far to cover.

Panting, he made it to the trees. Now that he was hidden by the foliage, Jolar turned back to look, and his eyes went wide. There were two shuttles that hadn't been there before and a number of cloaked figures moving around the property, blasters at the ready, hunting survivors. The woman who had served their supper broke free to run from the house and was cut down before she got five steps.

The house itself was afire. Even as Jolar watched, the fire spread.

Jolar gripped the tree he hid behind hard enough for the bark to bite into his palm. He forced himself to breathe, to think.

She could smell the forest! She's not in the house!

Jolar made his way along the tree line. He didn't bother with quiet. The screams, the blaster fire would cover his movements; it was far more important he stay hidden. He bruised his shin painfully on a rock he missed in the darkness, and it took an eternity to circle to the back of the house. There was a garden here, a little patio next to the herbery and the ruin of the kitchen behind it.

Jolar jerked back, bringing his blaster up as one of the men came around the building.

The man stopped, looking at something on the ground in the garden. He kicked at whatever it was, then almost as an afterthought lifted his weapon and hit it with two blaster bolts. The man moved on, the style of his cloak familiar from Xan-Tellar. For a moment the fire illuminated the high cheekbones and strong brow, the bronze cast of the man's face.

He was Utavian.

The man continued his search, and once he was out of sight Jolar moved to the edge of the tree line.

He swallowed hard as he recognized Cenon's bright hair. Danlen's wife was face down in the garden, unmoving.

Arissa wasn't with her.

The house was engulfed now, and he almost didn't hear the shuttles powering up. They circled over the ruin of Danlen's home once, then disappeared into the Sertarian night.

Jolar broke from the tree line and quickly reached the herbery, but there was no one inside the ruined greenhouse.

She was outside! I know *she made it outside!*

But what if she hadn't? What if he had run for the trees when he should have been making for the kitchen? What if she had died inside that inferno?

"Arissa!" he shouted.

He knew that the Utavians could have left someone here. The shuttles taking off would be an excellent ruse to draw out any survivors. His grip tightened on the blaster. Right now he wouldn't mind so much if someone had stayed behind though.

It would feel very good to hurt one of them.

"Arissa!" he shouted again.

He covered the garden quickly, crushing the plants beneath his boots as he searched.

She made it outside! Please tell me she made it outside!

She would have been with Cenon. Cenon was running for the forest. Had Arissa run too, but in another direction? Was she bleeding, dying, somewhere else? If he lost her—

Arrena, Goddess, please, I'll do anything!

He went back to where Danlen's wife lay in one of the furrows of her garden. The wounds on her back rendered any assistance hopeless, and her blue gown was gruesome with burns and blood. Her long hair spread out over the ground, golden by the light of the burning house—and, against the ground, weakly reflecting the blaze, one black curl . . .

Jolar dropped the blaster and threw himself down to roll Cenon's body to the side.

Arissa's dark hair covered her face, her skin deathly pale, the back of her dress soaked with blood.

Jolar's heart tore as he gathered her, limp and cold, into his arms.

Twenty-four

Arissa groaned. Blue eyes flashed in her mind.

Jolar.

"Arissa? You're awake?" he asked softly, his palm gently cupping her cheek. "Sweet, are you awake?"

"What the fuck happened?" she croaked and tried to force her eyes open.

She heard his breath catch. He made a choking sound, but whether he were laughing or crying she couldn't quite tell.

Her head hurt, and opening her eyes sure didn't help her headache any. The room that swam around her was unfamiliar, with a gray ceiling and walls that looked to have been cut from rock. There was a light flush against the ceiling above her, and below her was the soft-firm feel of a mattress. She was dressed in just her halter and underwear and there was a blanket over her.

But she had the answer about the choking sound. He was doing both. Jolar smiled down at her, tears running down his face.

"W-where—" she began.

"In a minute. How do you feel?"

"Like a sular fell on my head," she murmured. "What? What did I say?"

"Cenon fell on you," he said grimly. "And when she did, she saved your life."

"Cenon?" Arissa wondered then her eyes went wide. "Jolar—there are men, armed! You have to—"

"It's all right," he said quickly, cradling her hand gently. "That was yesterday. They're gone now."

"Yesterday?" She looked him over. "Are you all right? Did they hurt you?"

His eyes were steady, but there was an echo of deep pain in them. "The initial attack knocked me out, but I wasn't hurt."

He brushed a lock of her hair away from her face.

He hasn't done that in so long . . .

"I'm all right and we're safe here, okay? Now, you said your head hurts. Anything else?"

Arissa shifted carefully. She could feel her fingers and toes, and nothing seemed to be broken. She ached all over, though.

"How are my eyes?" she asked.

Waves of fear flowed around him. "Are you having trouble seeing?"

"No, I mean are my pupils different sizes? That could mean concussion."

He peered closely. "No, they're the same size. I'd bet you do have a concussion. I thought—" His pain rolled over her. "I couldn't wake you."

"I want to sit up."

"Let me help you."

He was gentle as he eased her into a sitting position, but she winced all the same. Her hand went to her temple. "Okay, I can definitely say that my head hurts."

"There's some analgesics in the medkit. Hold on."

He placed the medkit on the bed beside her and rifled through the contents. The room was sparse, with this large bed in the center of the space and a couple of storage units around the room. There were no windows, but through the open doorway she could see another room beyond this one with the same ceiling, walls and utilitarian lighting, but it had a table and metal chairs.

"Where *are* we?" she asked.

"Danlen's emergency shelter."

"Oh." She frowned. "He told you he had one?" That didn't seem like information you'd share with someone you barely knew.

"No," he said, placing the pain patch on her upper arm. "Give that a minute. If you feel dizzy or nauseous, tell me right away."

"What time is it?"

He shrugged, closing the medkit. "It was almost nineteen hundred hours last time I checked. But that was a while ago. Feeling any better?"

The headache was slowly retreating, and the pain patch was helping with her achiness too. "Is there anything to drink?"

In response he went to the other room and brought back a metal cup filled with cold water.

"Hey, not so fast," he objected at her thirsty gulps. "Just sip, okay? We aren't going anywhere for a while."

"Where are we again?"

"A shelter, not far from the estate."

"If Danlen didn't tell you about it, how did you know it was here?"

"I didn't. Our shuttle was destroyed, the house was on fire, and you were," he swallowed, "hurt. I was just sitting there with you on the ground trying to figure out what the hells to do. Cenon was lying there in the dirt next to us and I suddenly wondered why. She knew Danlen was in the house, so why run outside and not to him? Then I thought about how you said Danlen loved her. He wouldn't have left her, not in *his* business, without providing for her safety.

Maybe she wasn't just running *from* something but *to* something." He sat beside her on the bed. "So if she were supposed to just cut and run in case of danger, then that's where she was heading when she was killed." He closed his eyes briefly. "As much as I didn't want to leave you, I couldn't help you by sitting there. I managed to find a working hand light and went in the direction Cenon was headed. I didn't find anything but forest. But Danlen would have made sure Cenon could find whatever it was even in the dark. So thinking it might be easier seen in the dark I shut off the light."

"And that's when you saw it?"

He gave a half-smile. "No, that's when I tripped. I caught myself against a tree, thank the gods. Remember the gendara trees? On the ship?"

"The one you wouldn't let me touch?"

"It was a gendara tree."

She frowned. "Okay."

"A gendara tree," he repeated. "On *Sertar*. A tree that you'd know even if you were blind and deaf because—"

"Because you'd feel the sting," she finished.

He nodded. "And Danlen was Gensoyan. So I just followed the gendara trees and I found the door hidden in the side of the hill."

"The door was unlocked?"

A pained look crossed his face. "No. I needed Cenon's palm print to open it. I had to carry her out here. But as soon as the door was opened all the systems automatically came online. We have heat, fresh air, food, water. We could hold out here for months."

"You aren't planning to stay here that long, are you?" she asked, surprised.

He gave a faint smile. "If I did, would you stay with me?"

Arissa looked away. "Is there anything to eat?"

She'd hurt him. Why did it always come to this? She couldn't be any part of his life without wanting all of him. To see what she wanted before her and never have it would be agony, and staying with him as his mistress would make him despise himself. If she were gone at least he would keep his self-respect.

And maybe someday it wouldn't hurt so much.

"Yes," he said. "Think you're up to walking? I can carry you if you're not."

-"I'll walk," she said quickly. "I'm uh, going to need something to wear, and probably a shower too."

"I can give you a dress. You can have the shower as long as I'm in there with you."

"Jolar, I really don't think—"

"First off," he interrupted. "You just woke up after being out way longer than you should have been for a concussion. It may have something to do with being a seer or you could have suffered such a bad blow that you have a cranial fracture. I just don't know. I don't know much beyond basic aid and I don't have the equipment to diagnose, let alone treat you. I'm not about to let you get into the shower when you could lose your balance and suffer another injury.

"Second," he continued. "I don't think there's a part of you I *haven't* seen, so there's really no reason I shouldn't be in there with you."

"I guess I'm not going to get a shower then."

His lips thinned. "Have it your way. But I'm telling you now, until I'm sure you're all right, you aren't getting in there without me."

She choked back hysterical laughter, her hand tight on the blanket over her. Just sitting with him, feeling the warmth of his body had her breath quickening. But both of them naked, with warm water running over him . . .

Sitting here with him on the bed, when under this blanket all she had on was her underthings wasn't helping either. "Can I at least have something to wear?"

He went to a storage unit in the room and dug through it. He shook out a gown and offered it to her. It was a simple pale green dress of soft fabric. Pull-over style, the dress had a wide neck, three-quarter sleeves, and a tie belt. No doubt it had belonged to the much-taller Cenon.

It was also going to be about as flattering as a festering sack.

"Is there anything else?" she asked, looking at it with dismay. "I'm going to be swimming in that."

Hitting her head must have knocked the good sense right out of it.

He's betrothed to someone else! The last thing I should be worried about is trying to look pretty for him!

"I want something that's going to be easy to get off you."

She blinked.

"I mean if you get dizzy or sick to your stomach," he added.

"Fine," she mumbled, holding her hand out to take it. "Give it to me and turn around."

He pulled it away. "No, and don't bother arguing. I'm not going to turn my back the first time you stand up, Arissa. I need to be ready to catch you if you fall."

"Jolar, I'm fine."

"Good. I really don't want you to fall."

She glared at him.

He raised an eyebrow. "You're the seer; what would you say the chances of me giving in on this are?"

She sighed.

"All right," he said when it was clear she wasn't going to argue further. "I'm going to help you stand up. If you're steady, I'll put the dress on you."

This really was ridiculous. He helped her to her feet as if she were a complete invalid. He kept hold of her while he put the dress over her head and had her stick one arm through, then the other. He tied the belt around her waist himself.

"All right?" he asked, his hands still at her hips as he peered into her face.

"If you're like this *now*, as a father-to-be you'll be completely insufferable," she grumbled.

There was a sudden silence and her throat tightened. Just the thought of him and Jasa having . . .

"Come on, let's get you to the table," he said.

He half-carried her to the next room, despite her protests that she was perfectly all right to walk, and helped her sit.

"We have some the finest meal pack selections in the quadrant," he said with forced brightness. "What sounds good? Onka cakes? Sular stew?"

"What are you having?"

"I was going to try the stew, but it doesn't matter," he replied. "They're individual packs so you can have whatever you like. There's spring medallions, how about those?"

"Okay," she said, taking the opportunity to look around the room while he got their meal ready. It was twice as big as the bedroom and contained this table, a small kitchenette, a couple of comfortable looking sofas and chairs, and a computer terminal. What appeared to be the door to the outside was sealed. Neatly organized on the wall behind her, between this room and the bedroom, was a complete arsenal of weapons.

"Are there external security systems?" she asked.

He followed her gaze. "Oh, yes. We have infrared cameras, mounted pulse cannons, proximity detectors that will go off if anything larger than a snouse runs by."

"A man with a lot of enemies," she murmured.

He placed the medallions in front of her and, smiling, set beside it a metal cup holding a fizzy pink concoction. "We even have several months' worth of ingredients to make shooting stars."

Her throat tightened. He'd recreated their first dinner out on the *Queen's Light*.

It hadn't been an accident either.

"Is it all right?" he asked quietly.

"It looks great," she managed. She took a sip of the drink. "It's great, thanks."

Jolar sat across from her, and they ate in silence for a while.

"If the shuttle's been destroyed, we'll need a way back to Tano," she said.

"There's a groundcar in a storage room off this one. If I can get it running it will get us to Patim-Sertar. We can get transport to Tano from there."

"You don't seem very concerned."

"Getting us back to Tano has been the least of my problems."

"You mean someone just murdered another one of your suspects?"

"And I didn't learn a damn thing about Danlen. Oh, except that he was willing to pay me ten million credits for a contract that would be worth maybe a tenth of that to him."

She blinked at him. "That was his offer?"

"We shook on it right before someone blew the room apart."

She shook her head. "Why would he do that?"

"I don't know. I was hoping *you* would be able to tell me, but then—" Jolar rubbed his hand over his eyes.

"You're exhausted."

He gave a short laugh. "I've still got plenty to do." He stood. "How about some caf?"

"Jolar, you need some rest."

"I'm not going to get any anyhow," he said over his shoulder. "I need to fix the groundcar and stay awake in case you start having trouble."

"Jolar," she protested. "I'm fine now. Really."

"Good," he said, starting the caf. "Then you can keep me company while I search the rest of the place and figure out why the groundcar's power cells are empty. I need to make a real assessment of our situation and make sure everything is locked down tight before I can think about sleep." He nodded toward the computer. "That might have some interesting information for us too."

"We should start with that."

"No. We need to search the shelter. I need to figure out how to use those external weapons. Then groundcar. Then sleep. *Then* computer."

"I could do it," Arissa offered.

"That just has me standing around watching you. I already downloaded all the information on it to a datadisk. No, the computer search is for tomorrow. Let me get a cup of caf and something for this blasted headache then I'll start with this room."

Jolar was very thorough, and his search of the room took almost an hour. He took time to familiarize himself with the external defenses, but he didn't make any practice shots just in case there were anyone nearby to hear. Along with the weapons, he uncovered a substantial amount of cash as well as another medkit.

The kitchenette held only food and eating implements. The bathroom had a 'fresher and shower, toiletries and towels.

He had her rest on the bed while he searched the bedroom. There were clothes and bedding, but not much else. The storage room held equipment, a valet unit to clean clothes, and a number of tools to make repairs along with a back-up power generator.

"Well," Jolar said, sitting in the groundcar with the door open. "We aren't going anywhere in this thing. I ramped up the power flow from the converter yesterday and still no charge."

"Danlen was so careful about everything in here. Why would he leave the groundcar uncharged?"

Jolar stood and walked to the back of the vehicle. "He didn't. Look, one of the leads is burned out. *That's* why I couldn't get it to charge. The groundcar's probably fine."

"How long?"

"You mean *if* I find new leads to even get this thing charging?"

"Yes."

He sighed. "A few hours at least."

They made a search of the storage room and main shelter, but there were no spares.

"Maybe you should just do this tomorrow and just get some sleep," she suggested.

"I must look bad off." He shook his head. "Now that I know what's wrong, I don't want to leave us without a fast way out of here in case we need it. I'm going to try to either fix these or slap something together that will work. You can go rest if you're tired."

She glanced at the door to the shelter's main room. She should keep as much distance as possible between them.

But he wanted her here.

And she didn't want to go.

"Maybe I can help," she said.

Twenty-five

Arissa sat up, rubbing her eyes. Jolar had closed the door between the rooms and without a window or chrono she couldn't say how long she'd slept. She mentally reached out and found him nearby in the storage room, his mind busily occupied. From the weight and heft of his thoughts, he would likely be busy for a while.

And that meant . . .

She joined him in the storage room a short time later.

"You weren't supposed to shower without me there," Jolar said with a pointed look at her freshly washed and dried curls.

"I feel fine, and I knew you were working. How's it going?"

He sighed. "One of my improvised leads came loose while we were sleeping. I've fixed it, but the groundcar is only at a quarter charge now." He stood. "Since the shower's free I'm going to get cleaned up too. Then breakfast?" He glanced at the chrono. "Or lunch?"

Arissa smiled. "Both. I'm starving."

Arissa had the meal ready for them by the time he emerged from the bedroom.

Taking in how she'd filled the table with food, he laughed. "Breakfast, lunch *and* dessert."

"I know you're just as hungry," she countered, biting into the grimp toast.

He grinned and reached for a baneberry biscuit. "Hey, I'm not complaining."

After a few mouthfuls she gave him an exasperated look. "Stop it."

He blinked. "Stop what?"

"Watching me eat."

"I like watching you eat," he said softly.

Clearly he was neither embarrassed about getting caught nor intending to stop. Arissa put her head down, determined to ignore him and finish her eclectic meal despite his attention. At meal's end she cleaned up while he made caf for himself and tea for her.

He brought their drinks to the little sitting area. "How are you feeling?"

"Fine." She shifted her feet. It was so quiet here with no other minds humming in the background of her senses. For the first time ever, she could sense only one mind beside her own.

I know why it's harder now. Harder here. We're completely alone. No Bruscan, no servants, no fellow passengers or party guests. Just us.

Feeling just him was like being immersed in warm, bright currents—

Gods, I need something else to focus on!

Arissa's glance darted about and landed on the computer terminal. "Shouldn't we get started going through the computer?"

"I've already copied everything on that terminal to a datadisk," he reminded. "We can go through it when we get to Tano if we have to. And we're not going anywhere without that groundcar fully charged. You have time to drink your tea, I promise."

She took a seat on one of the chairs. She picked up her tea to find he'd made it sweet and with extra spice, the way she liked it.

"How are you feeling?"

"You just asked me that. Jolar, I feel absolutely fine."

"You're sure? No headache? No dizziness?"

"I'm sure," she insisted.

"Good," he said. "Because we've missed two days of practice. Since you feel so absolutely fine we can do it now."

She blinked. She was already overwhelmed by his closeness. The last thing she needed was to be actively touching his mind.

"No, wait," she stammered. "I really don't think we need to continue practicing now—"

His eyes flashed. "You mean now that we barely escaped the destruction and killing of everyone at the home we were staying at? Now that two of our suspects and the Zartani councilor have been murdered? Because any abilities you might bring to the table are now extraneous?"

"I'm a seer whether I practice with you or not," she hedged. "What I can do won't vanish. I only wish it would."

"If you can honestly tell me that our practice has not made any difference in your skills, we can stop right now."

She looked away.

"All right, then," he said when she didn't respond. "Let's start."

Her heart hammering, she closed her eyes. She reached past his worries, the calmer settled sense of him, to his core . . .

Her breath quickened and a rush of heat ran through her center, her body responding as if it were actually *against* his. She broke off and turned her face away.

"Are you all right?" he asked. Concern and worry rippled around him.

"I guess I do have a headache after all."

"You're lying."

Startled, she looked up. "No, I'm not. I'm—"

"You're lying," he repeated. "Why?"

"Maybe I just don't want to do this right now," she said, a note of resentfulness creeping into her voice. Why should she even *have* to? Why should she be forced into bringing herself so close to someone she couldn't have?

"This is important," he said evenly. "Unless you really are ill, in which case you'll spend the remainder of the day in bed resting, you should get on with it."

She certainly didn't want to spend the day in bed, with nothing to distract her from her own unhappy thoughts and the torment of feeling Jolar nearby.

It's just for a few minutes.

She swallowed. "All right."

She closed her eyes again and let her breath out. She felt him settle himself, prepare himself, and then she reached for him—

Fire and the acrid smell of smoke. *Have to find . . . please, I'll do anything . . .* The night sky spun above as the shuttles left. On the ground lay Cenon, her back a ruin of burns and blood. Arissa herself deathly pale, so cold, Jolar crying out as he cradled her. Longing that never ceased. *So close he could gather her in his arms now, feel her warm and sweet against him, kiss . . .*

"I have to stop!" Arissa gasped, standing.

"Why?" He stood too, blocking her retreat. "Because you can feel how much I want you?"

"It doesn't matter. We can't—"

His breath caught. "You want me too, don't you? You want me."

"Of course I do!" she burst out. "Did you think I *didn't*? That I could just turn off how I feel? That it isn't agony to sleep next to you every night and not touch you?"

"Do you still love me, Arissa?"

She shut her eyes. If she looked at him she would shatter. None of her good, righteous intentions would mean a damn. What little self-respect she had left would be shredded. He'd see how close she was to giving anything just to be with him, taking whatever shadowed part of his life she could have.

"I love you, Arissa." His fingers whispered over the skin of her cheek. "My sweet one. My heart."

She could feel the waves of his love, his desire hot around her.

"If you don't love me anymore, tell me. I can't hide my feelings from you, I know that, but I can promise I'll never speak of how I feel again."

She looked up at him, at his pained blue eyes, and her vision blurred.

"I have to know. Do you still love me, Arissa?" His voice broke. "Do you?"

"Yes," she whispered and tears overflowed. "Gods, yes, I love you."

He made a soft choked sound, his whole being pulsing with sudden white-hot joy. Then his mouth was on hers, and nothing mattered but to be with him.

He brought her by stumbling steps into the bedroom, clumsy with wanting too long denied. He was rough with his own clothes and shaky with hers. Arissa caught her breath at the shock of skin against skin as he brought her against him. Jolar's mouth never left hers as his fingers stoked her center, groaning against her mouth to find her so ready for him. Then the cool fabric of the blankets was against her back and he was sliding inside her, his arms braced beside her head. Her hands were on the straining muscles of his back, his lips a few scant centimeters from hers, their breath joining as she moved against his rhythm.

She bent her head as he brought her to the brink. One, two more stokes and she cried out against the skin of his shoulder.

"Sweet," he managed, losing the smooth rhythm as she felt him spend within her.

Still shaking, he brushed a kiss against her mouth, then withdrew to collapse beside her.

Arissa's breath suddenly caught with a sob, and she covered her face with her hands.

"Don't cry, love," he said, pulling her close again. "It's all right."

She shook her head. "We shouldn't have done that," Arissa wiped at her face. "It was wrong."

"No, it wasn't." His arms tightened around her. "I know what it's like to fall on my knees in the dirt and believe I've lost you forever. I looked right at the long emptiness of my life without you and, by the gods, I'm never going to see that again." He pressed a kiss to her temple. "I won't lose you. I *can't*."

"I can't be your mistress," Arissa whispered. "It would be like this. The guilt, the heartache, for the rest of my life."

"No, you can't be my mistress," he agreed, cupping her cheek in his broad warm palm, his blue eyes serious. "Because I'm going to marry you."

Twenty-six

She stared. "You can't."

"Arissa, this is a genuine, though admittedly poorly executed, offer of marriage." He raised his eyebrows. "Look, I'm not above begging, but I'd rather not put you through being embarrassed for me like that. Just say yes now so I don't have to."

"You already have a contract to marry, remember?"

Jolar traced her jaw with his fingers. "Jasa deserves a husband who loves her. So I'm going break off our betrothal and let her go find him. I want to tell her in person, though. I owe her that much at least. In Tano, if she's still there. On Zartan, if she's not."

She shook her head. "Jolar, you're a Zartani aristocrat. You can't marry a commoner, an Apovian, let alone a— You *can't*."

He gave a short, disbelieving laugh. "After all this you think I'm going to let a little thing like a death sentence stop us? You love me. I love you." He wound a ringlet around his finger, his mouth curving tenderly. "You've never seen me when I'm really determined. You might as well say yes now, Arissa, 'cause I'm *going* to marry you."

"You can't."

He put his elbow on the bed and propped his head on his hand to look at her. "I can. I will."

"You're going to break the promise you made to your father on his deathbed? Go against all Zartani tradition? What about your honor?"

"My heart, I'm going to spit in the face of a thousand generations of Zartani tradition and I'm not even sorry." He gave a rueful smile. "There *is* no honor in lying, in pretending. That's what I'd be doing if I married Jasa: lying. I'd be lying for the rest of my damned life. If my honor truly matters to me then ending a forced betrothal and making vows to the one I love is the only way to keep it truly intact. I'm going to do what I know is right, what I know is really honorable. Besides, it wasn't two days ago I swore to the Goddess Arrena I would do anything to have you back. And you can bet if I break a promise to *her* the question of my honor will be the least of my problems."

She rubbed her hand over her eyes. "You don't mean it."

"Is that what your seer abilities tell you, sweet?"

But he did. He meant every word.

"What's the matter?" He searched her face. "You don't want to marry me?"

"No, I don't."

He grinned. "Liar. Promise you'll marry me. I'm not going to give up."

"Ask me after you've broken with her."

He regarded her with steady blue eyes and drummed his fingers lightly against her belly. At last he nodded. "Fair enough. I'll break with Jasa first."

"And we can't—"

He groaned and flopped onto his back, plainly anticipating what she was going to say. "No."

"You're betrothed to someone else," she said sharply.

"Oh, *hells!*" He scrubbed his face with his hands. "All right, but if the gods have any mercy in them, Jasa's still in Tano and I won't have to go all the way to Zartan to do this. Hold on—" His brow creased. "Can I still kiss you?"

"You shouldn't."

"I'm going to take that as tacit permission." His eyes lingered on her breasts, then went lower, his smile hot. "Can I kiss you everywhere?"

She gave him an exasperated look.

He held up one hand. "Just clarifying the rules." He gave her an appraising glance. "This is going to be even harder than sleeping next to you and thinking you don't want me."

"Is that what you thought?" she asked, genuinely surprised.

"You didn't act like you wanted me."

"Because you're betrothed to someone else!"

He took her hand and gently pressed a kiss to her palm. "Not for long. And I'm already cataloguing what I want to do once I'm officially free." He grinned, his joy white hot. "You love me."

She ducked her head. "I shouldn't."

"Well, I don't deserve you, that's not even a question," he agreed. He slid closer to cradle her against him, his happiness warm and tingly around her. "I love you, sweet."

She rested her cheek against the smooth warm skin of his shoulder while he stroked her back. His lips pressed against her temple, brushed her cheek, then lightly touched her mouth. He deepened the kiss, his fingers sliding lower to trace her breast, his breath quickening.

"Jolar," she pleaded, already more than a little breathless herself.

Jolar huffed, then rolled onto his back to look at the ceiling.

"Well, lying here with both of us naked isn't helping," he grumbled. "So let's go through that computer while the groundcar finishes charging. I want to get back to Tano as soon as we can."

A short time later, Arissa settled next to Jolar at the computer terminal. She wrapped her hands around her teacup, trying to keep her mind from the feel of his thigh pressed against hers.

"The good news," Jolar began, "is the thing isn't locked down by ID scan or password. It came online along with everything else."

"He didn't lock it?" Arissa asked. "That seems pretty careless."

Jolar shrugged. "The shelter is likely only keyed to Cenon and Danlen's palm prints and well-hidden. If Cenon came here alone he wouldn't want to deny her access because she'd forgotten a password, and he wouldn't want anything to go wrong with a scan. She had immediate access to weapons, cash, medkits and a groundcar. Clearly she was more important to him than safeguarding any information he might have on this thing."

"So what can you access?"

"Well," Jolar said, engaging the screen, "I can look around outside the shelter, tell you the current weather conditions in Tano-Sertar, explore the latest fashions on Tellar, tell you the current tidal conditions on Lema . . . "

"So pretty much a whole uplink."

"Yup. And incidentally, everything you could want to know about Danlen . . ."

Arissa's eyes widened as he brought up the information. "Gods, look at that. Bank accounts held under access numbers only, passwords, company holdings—"

"Nice of him to leave it so well organized."

"He left it for Cenon," Arissa said quietly.

Jolar's sense turned grim. "There was nothing I could do for her. She was already dead. I didn't have much time, but I did bury her. I said a prayer to Bathena to guide her to her peace with Danlen."

"That's good. I liked her."

"She liked you too. Danlen told me so." Jolar shook his head as he scrolled through the information. "Looks like Danlen had most of the officials on Sertar by the throat. He practically ran the planet. But his estate here was positively humble for what he had. Why would a man that wealthy live so modestly for his means?"

"Cenon said it was her family's home," Arissa said. "I was saying how pretty the herbery was and she said it had been her grandmother's. She grew up in that house."

"Well, that explains that. But why bother with our paltry contract?"

"Maybe he was overextended?"

Jolar called up Danlen's financial records.

"I don't think that was it." Jolar gave a low whistle. "This man was insanely wealthy. His statements—"

He went still.

"What?"

He pointed to a line on the screen. "Five hundred thousand credits—Kav de'Reaven."

"Dacel's other agent?" she asked. "The one he sent before us?"

"Danlen paid to have him killed."

"So it was Danlen we were looking for."

"If he knew de'Reaven was Dacel's agent . . . Did he know about us?"

Arissa shook her head firmly. "Jolar, everything I felt from him and Cenon was friendly. He had no ill intentions toward us at all."

"He wanted to come to an agreement," Jolar said thoughtfully. "He wanted us to stay there longer. He offered me so much I couldn't possibly turn it down. Why?"

"Maybe he wanted the crystals contract too?"

"But why? He didn't need the money. Even *he* said the money didn't matter to him."

"He was in crystal refining," Arissa reminded. "He had a good portion of the market; maybe he wanted to maintain that position."

Jolar nodded toward the screen. "But he made ten times more from other revenue streams."

"Maybe for the prestige of supplying the fleet?"

"It's not that prestigious. Certainly not worth ten million credits and that necklace you were looking at in Tano. Danlen said what mattered to him was that his crystals were on fleet ships."

Arissa stared. "He knew I was looking at that necklace? That was part of his offer?"

"Actually I'm the one who brought up the necklace," Jolar said. "You liked it right?"

"It was beautiful," Arissa said. "But it cost a—wait."

"What?" he said, his brow creased.

"Kemma said the necklace had been made out of crystals with a fatal flaw. Danlen wanted his crystals on fleet ships badly enough to bribe you with a fortune. If it wasn't the money and it wasn't the prestige . . . What if there was another reason he wanted his crystals on fleet ships? What if Danlen's crystals had a flaw that would make them shatter?"

Jolar frowned. "They run tests when they swap out a crystal, Arissa. If a crystal shattered when the conversion matrix was engaged, they'd just replace it."

"But what if it worked for a while? And shattered only when he wanted it to shatter?"

Jolar's frown deepened. "You can't decide when a crystal shatters."

"But what if you *could?*" Arissa persisted. "What if you could send a signal or something? Input some kind of overload?"

Jolar was already shaking his head. "There are so many safeguards on a fleet vessel that it would take most of the crew working together to make something like that happen."

"But a sonic pulse at the right frequency can shatter a crystal."

"Well, yes," Jolar agreed. "But you would have to know what frequency that particular crystal needed in order to shatter it. The only way you could be sure to shatter more than one is if—" His face blanched. "Gods, if you had a way to alter them to fail . . ."

"Fail when you wanted them to fail."

"A shattered crystal would cripple the ship without firing a shot. You could cripple the whole fleet that way. You could bring the Realm to its knees in hours." He shook his head again. "But the new contract I was supposed to be filling wouldn't start for another three months. Even if Danlen intended to do that, it would take years before enough ships switched out enough crystals to make a difference."

"Who had the previous contract?" She started scrolling through the files . . . something she'd seen . . .

"A company called—"

"CenCorp," she finished, pointing at the screen. "Look."

"Gods," Jolar murmured looking at the company information. "He went to a lot of trouble to hide his ownership of that company. That's why he didn't care about the new contract, he has the current one. If those crystals are flawed, he's been providing the fleet with flawed crystals for years. . . .CenCorp. Cenon—his wife."

"But suddenly he cared very much about the new contract and then someone killed him."

His face was grim. "Do you think it's possible that Danlen wasn't the real target? Do you think someone knows who *we* are?"

"I didn't get anything like that from the men who attacked Danlen's estate," she said slowly. "They weren't searching for you or us. They were there for Danlen and Cenon but they were also intent on killing everyone there."

"They were Utavians. Broc Attar was murdered a few days ago. It could have been revenge." Jolar let his breath out. "Still, that's it then."

"What do you mean?" She frowned. "Jolar, someone killed everyone at that estate. We need to find out who."

"No," Jolar said firmly. "Finding out who killed Danlen wasn't our assignment. We were sent to find out who was gathering power on Sertar and get the evidence for the Tellaran council. We know it was Danlen and I have the datadisk to prove it, but I can't be sure this uplink is secure and I'm not about to broadcast our presence here. If there *is* something wrong with the fleet ships, we need to get back to Tano so I can transmit this to the council. FleetSec will have to take the investigation from here."

"So," she said. "We're done?"

"We're done here. Our task now is to turn this evidence over. They'll probably want us back on Tellar for debriefing."

"And then?"

"You'll get your ID. We'll go to Tellar and then Zartan—if I can wait that long to marry you." His smile was hot. "Then Nima for a long honeymoon."

She hesitated.

His smile faded. "Right. Jasa." He sighed. "I *really* hope she's still in Tano."

Twenty-seven

An hour later, with the shelter powered down and sealed, they used the groundcar to reach the southern city of Patim-Sertar. Jolar didn't contact Bruscan until after they had secured a shuttle rental to take them back to Tano. He paid cash for the rental and added an extra ten thousand credits 'consideration'—a staggering sum that widened even the jaded attendant's eyes—to make sure their names wouldn't show in the system for at least twelve hours, long after they would arrive in Sertar's capital.

Jolar was on edge, but their return to Tano was an uneventful one. He didn't begin to relax until they'd landed at Bruscan's estate. Their host, having come out to meet them, took in the rented shuttle and raised his eyebrows.

"You'll be compensated," Jolar promised.

"It was a very expensive shuttle," Bruscan warned.

Arissa gave Jolar a meaningful look.

"Would you accept 'expensive', rather than 'very expensive'?" Jolar asked. "The Tellaran council doesn't like 'very expensive'."

After a moment Bruscan gave a short nod. "How was the visit to Danlen's?"

Jolar took Arissa's hand. Bruscan's quick look showed he took that in too.

"I could use some caf," Jolar said. "I'm sure Arissa would like some tea. Maybe in your office?"

"Of course." Bruscan glanced over Arissa's too large dress. "Nela will get your luggage from the shuttle."

"We came without it," Jolar said.

Bruscan blinked, his only outward sign of surprise. Once they were inside with the door to his office shut, Bruscan settled back in his chair to regard them with interest.

"Carlea Renn has invited you and Arissa to a supper party tonight, Jolar," Bruscan said. "It seems you've very much tickled her . . . fancy."

"Nothing I discovered about Carlea implicates her in what we're investigating," Jolar said coolly. "I don't see any reason to see her again."

"Can I take that to mean that your investigation is concluded?" asked Bruscan.

Jolar nodded. "Danlen Mirat."

"Huh," Bruscan murmured, drumming his fingers. "I thought him the least likely of your suspects."

"He was good at hiding things."

"As one has to be—to succeed on Sertar." Bruscan tilted his head. "The rented shuttle and Arissa's present less-than-flattering ensemble speak to a hasty retreat. Can I assume that Master Mirat is onto your discovery?"

"Danlen's dead."

Bruscan frowned. "You killed him?"

"No," Arissa cried. "Of course not!"

Bruscan glanced between them. "Who, then?"

"We don't know who," Jolar said. "They killed everyone there except us."

"Fortunate, indeed." Bruscan frowned. "Mirat was married—"

"Cenon—she's dead too," Jolar said quietly.

Bruscan seemed to deflate a little. "A shame. She was . . . kind." He sighed. "Well, now what?"

"I have to go to the Zartani embassy." Jolar glanced at Arissa. "Then I have a personal matter to attend to. I expect Arissa and I will leave for Tellar at the earliest opportunity. As soon as tomorrow." Jolar shifted on the sofa. "Bruscan, I need to ask you to stay with Arissa until I return. I don't want her to leave your house and I want you to keep security tight. No guests at all. Just until we're off-world."

Bruscan frowned. "You think someone knows who you are?"

"The evidence I needed is safe," Jolar said firmly. "I don't have any reason to think our cover has been blown, and those implicated are dead." He looked at Arissa again. "But—"

"Of course." Bruscan gave a faint smile. "I'll keep her safe for you."

Jolar entered the Zartani embassy at mid-afternoon. Done in the traditional Zartani style of gleaming dalsawood and large windows, it was a mute testament to his homeworld's wealth and power. The embassy compound was made up of several buildings including offices, quarters for staff, and the ambassador's mansion. Technically he now stood on Zartani ground and the laws of his homeworld applied here.

He had intended to hand the disk over to the ambassador to transmit to the council, but found himself standing before Rekan d'Barat, the junior councilor—now Acting Councilor of Zartan—who rose from his place behind the ambassador's desk to greet him.

"Lord d'Tural," he said pleasantly, offering his hand. Not as tall as Jolar, his hair a few shades darker, Rekan still bore the stamp of a Zartani aristocrat in his bearing. "A pleasure to see you again."

Jolar gave a nod. "I prefer 'Commander' if you don't mind."

"As you like, Commander." Rekan waved him to a chair. "Please, sit." Rekan went back to his chair behind the desk.

"Where is Ambassador d'Serrat?"

Rekan looked surprised. "Attending the memorial for Councilor de'Par on Zartan."

Jolar's brow creased. "*You* aren't attending Dacel's memorial?"

Rekan spread his hands. "I am Acting Councilor of Zartan. Like yourself, Commander, I have duties that I cannot leave at the moment. I agreed months ago to present at the trade commission and I barely arrived in time to attend the final day of meetings. My schedule is overwhelmed with responsibilities. I will be returning to Zartan to pay my respects at Dacel's grave and to call on his family at the earliest opportunity."

Dacel's family. Gods, what they must be going through now . . .

Jolar swallowed. "Yes, I will do so as well, as soon as I return home."

"I wish that I had been apprised of your mission here earlier," Rekan said. "And when the councilor was lost to us—"

"Do you know what happened?" Jolar asked tightly. "Do you know—do you know why?"

Rekan shook his head. "I'm afraid we have more questions than answers. The investigation into his death is still in the early stages."

"TelSec must have some idea what happened," Jolar said sharply. "Dacel was a Zartani councilor. You'd think someone would have answers by now."

Rekan folded his hands. "Dacel's death is a great loss to Zartan, Commander. A great loss to the Realm. I'm sure TelSec will submit their findings soon. Believe me when I say that getting those findings, those answers, is one of my top priorities."

"I'm sorry," Jolar said. "He was my friend."

Rekan's face was grim. "He was mine too."

"I have the evidence he asked me to gather, along with my findings." Jolar pulled the datadisk from his pocket. "What I discovered was very disturbing."

Rekan nodded. "We should transmit the information immediately. With your permission I'd like to ask two of the ZarSec officers assigned to the embassy to step in and bear witness."

"Of course."

The uniformed ZarSecs came at Rekan's summons, and both offered Jolar respectful nods. Jolar handed over the datadisk, and the men watched as Rekan transferred the information for transmittal to the Tellaran council.

Rekan then took the datadisk and placed it in a safe in the ambassador's office before dismissing the men with a nod. "Well," he said heavily. "It's in the council's hands now, but I'm sure they will have questions for you. Is there anything else I can assist you with right now, Commander? My schedule is very full and I have a great deal to attend to."

Jolar rested his fingers on the dalsawood desk and made a sudden decision. "There's a young woman assigned to this mission with me—Arissa Legan. I think it best if she and I relocated here to Zartani soil until we return to Tellar. Can you arrange a shuttle and ZarSec officers for her protection?"

"Certainly," Rekan said. "Allow me to have a word with my secretary about living quarters. I can have him book your transport to Tellar as well."

"Yes, thank you," Jolar said.

Something was nagging at him. The sooner he got Arissa under the protection of the Zartani, the better he'd feel.

He contacted Arissa to tell her of the change of plans and spoke to Bruscan as well. The ZarSec and a shuttle bearing the Zartani emblem were already on their way to collect her. Arissa would be safely on Zartani soil within the hour. The uneasy feeling kept gnawing at him, but it was possible that the coming meeting had him so on edge he was overreacting.

Jasa had never been an easy woman to deal with.

All the same, it was a relief to find her still in the city. She readily agreed to a meeting and welcomed him warmly when he arrived at her rented house. It was a well-appointed home, as elegant as Jasa herself. Not for Jasa the trailblazing eccentricity of a plexisteel floor over languorously swimming fish, nor the tasteful but opulent soaring spaces of Bruscan's mansion. He could not even imagine her willingly occupying the rough comfort of Danlen's country home.

Highlighted by pure white trim, watered citrine shimmersilk covered the walls of the sitting room she led him to. Tall windows—high enough for a man to stand in—encircled the room and provided a dazzling view of the sunset and the gathering cool shadows of the garden below.

Chairs, sofas and tables were scattered about. It was a well-thought-out design, pleasing to the eye but not a comfortable room, nor a space that invited one to linger.

Jasa's gown today was cream-colored and hugged her curves enticingly, her light golden hair worn up with tiny pearls interwoven into it. Looking at her now, Jolar thought that the sitting room's amber shimmersilk furniture and floors of blond wood seemed deliberately intended to frame the perfection that was Jasa.

He was willing to bet it wasn't an accident either.

"Can I get you anything? I purchased some of that Niman brandy you're so fond of." A sultry smile touched her full, pink mouth as she glanced at him sidelong. "In hopes you might find time to visit me after all."

"No, thank you," Jolar said. "I'm glad to find you still in Tano. I thought you might have left for Zartan, now that the trade conference is over."

Jasa sat on one of the amber colored chairs and extended her hand, inviting him to a seat opposite.

Jolar blinked. He recognized this chair. A copy of one she'd had made upon their betrothal to accommodate his larger frame more comfortably when he visited her home. He wondered if she'd ordered the rental's sitting room redecorated to suit it.

"I'll stand," he said.

Jasa rested her arm on the round table beside her. Her immaculately manicured hand dangled in studied casualness as she regarded him. "Well, I'm delighted to see you, Jolar. How fortunate for me that my other business kept me here."

Jolar's brow creased. "I wasn't aware you were involved in any other business."

"No." Jasa smiled without humor. "But you aren't terribly attentive to me, are you darling?"

He closed his eyes briefly. "Jasa, I don't want to fight with you."

"I would prefer we didn't," she agreed.

While he had never loved her, he had no wish to hurt her either. He caught himself pacing, at a loss for the right words.

"Jolar?" she asked, brows lifting. "Whatever's the matter?"

"I'm breaking our betrothal contract, Jasa." He leveled his gaze at her. "I'm not going to marry you."

Her gaze didn't waver, her expression still one of polite interest.

He cleared his throat. "Did you hear me? I said—"

"I heard you. Actually, I've been expecting this." Jasa stood, smoothing the skirt of her cream gown. "Unfortunately, I am quite busy today. Are you sure I can't get you anything before I go? Shall I have a meal brought to you? The brandy really is excellent."

"No, I'm fine. I'm glad you—" He shook his head a little. "—took it so well."

Her full mouth curved upward. "If there's nothing I can get you, you'll excuse me, then."

The sun's final rays of daylight faded from the room and suddenly the hairs rose on the back of his neck.

"Certainly." He took a step back. "I can see myself out."

Jasa held up one graceful hand. "I'm afraid I'm going to have to ask you to stay here, Jolar. It's safer for you, darling."

"Safer?" He realized he was fighting the urge to flee the room. But this was Jasa, his former betrothed—a woman who, while he had never loved, he had certainly never feared.

Until now.

"Jasa, I think it would be better if we spoke again lat—" Jolar started, twisting around when the door opened.

Two Utavians stood there, blasters already drawn.

"Jasa, get—!" He glanced back at her to finish his warning to see that the drawer of the table she stood next to was open and she too held a blaster.

Pointed right at him.

"You were supposed to be safely tucked away on Tellar, buried in work," Jasa said with a sigh, adjusting the hold on her blaster. "Not running around Sertar on some mission for Dacel." She spared a glance at the men in the doorway. "Wait outside."

They nodded and closed the door behind them.

Her mouth quirked up a bit. "Oh, do stop looking so alarmed, Jolar. I'm not going to kill you. Although, since you just tried to jilt me, I suppose it's a reasonable assumption to make." She raised the weapon a bit. "The blaster is set on stun."

"I'm happy to hear it." Jolar eyed her warily, easing his body around to face her better. "Then if it's all the same, you can stop pointing it at me."

"I'm sorry, darling, but I don't put it past you to play the hero, even now that it's too late."

"Too late?" he demanded. "Too late for what?"

"To stop us, of course. By this time tomorrow, the New Order will be ended, the monarchy re-established, and we—" she smiled, "will be returned to our proper place in the Tellaran Realm."

"The fleet ships, the shifting of personnel, the murders. It's not just Sertar, it's wider—" Jolar felt the blood drain from his face. "Gods, you're seizing power to rule Zartan."

"Don't be ridiculous. *You're* the one seizing power." Jasa bent her head respectfully. "Prince Jolar."

Twenty-eight

Jolar stared. "What the hells are you talking about?"

"I'm talking about you taking your proper place," Jasa returned. "No council seat, no elections, just you claiming your birthright as our prince and ruler of Zartan—with me, of course, as princess."

"I'll be honest, Jasa," he managed after a moment. "I can't tell if you're joking or just crazy."

"Well, you never did bother to get to know your bed companions all that well. As a point of fact, I'm neither. You will be declared Prince of Zartan. Actually," she said, tilting her head thoughtfully. "You already have been. Your claim was acknowledged in a meeting with the Zartani lords two weeks ago. I'm happy to say that you have their full support. In a few hours, your forces will have taken control of the planet and your rule will be declared publicly on Zartan." She smiled. "Tomorrow we will make our triumphant return home together. You'll be crowned, and then we marry."

"My forces?" He shook his head. "*What* forces?"

"The loyal Zartani sons and daughters who are poised now to seize control in your name, Your Highness."

"You're serious," he breathed.

"Oh, absolutely."

He shook his head again, the sun had set, and automatic controls raised the light levels within the room. "Why would you do this?"

She blinked. "For you. For us. For the people of Zartan. For the people of the Tellaran Realm."

"For me?" he asked hoarsely, throwing his arms wide in outrage. "For the *people*? You coldheartedly plotted to overthrow their government—the government I vowed to uphold—by way of murder and you say did it for *me*—for *them*?"

She lifted her chin. "I would have preferred a bloodless return to the old ways. It wasn't possible."

Jolar stopped short, his hand pressed against the shattering pain in his chest. "You killed Dacel."

"It was necessary. I'm sorry, I knew his death would be difficult for you."

"Necessary?" His hands curled into fists. "He was the duly elected councilor from Zartan. He was my *friend*. You murdered him!"

"He wouldn't have stepped aside for you when the time came."

"Why the hells would you think I would ever go along with this?"

Jasa took a quick, urgent step toward him. "Because, Jolar, you want power as much as I do."

"I've never wanted anything like this!" He realized that unconsciously he'd put the chair—his chair—between them. "I've never been power hungry."

"Not hungry for power?" Jasa returned with a laugh. "You told me yourself you were determined to take the Zartani council seat after Dacel's term ended."

"That's an *elected* position." His hand gripped the back of the chair. "To take it I would have to be chosen by the Zartani people."

"Chosen? You don't really believe that? You don't really think that your name, your money, your *nobility* wouldn't be what brought you that seat? Do you truly think they wanted a commoner—like Dacel—representing them?"

"Other commoners have!"

"How often?" she countered. "A handful of times, for a few years, and then another of *us* takes that seat? Jolar, don't you see? I'm giving you *everything* you want! You will shape Zartan just as you wanted to, as you were meant to. Not for a few paltry years, not wheeling and dealing to keep a council seat like a common trader but as you were meant to, as our Crowned Prince." Her blue eyes were lit with inner fire. "Together, Jolar, we will create a dynasty!"

"You're delusional," he spat with a dismissive push against the chair.

"Your father was right about you. You do need to be guided and maneuvered every step of the way to the throne."

He rounded on her. "My *father?* He would never have agreed to this!"

"Agreed?" she cried, her hand on her chest. "Do you think *I* planned all this? That *my* money funded it? Whose idea was it for us to marry? Your father set this in motion before you took your first steps, Jolar. He knew that with me at your side, with my work and support, you would take your proper place! When he learned he wouldn't live long enough to see it done, he made me vow I would."

"My father couldn't—No!" He shook his head vehemently and took another step back. "No, my father came to support my joining the fleet, encouraged me to aim for the council seat—"

"You're so blind!" she said impatiently. "Of course he did! He let you go play hero so you would learn military strategy. He encouraged your political ideals to fuel your ambitions. He molded you into what you needed to be."

His throat felt like it was closing. His father's insistence on his marriage to Jasa, his infatuation with Zartani history, with the monarchy, with their lost royal heritage—

"Whatever he hoped to mold me into, he failed," he said hoarsely. "I'm not a traitor. I won't be part of this!"

"Part? You are the *center* of this. This was done in *your* name, for *you*. There's no stopping it now."

"The *center*? You sent a man to kill me on Tellar!"

She stopped short. "What are you talking about?"

"The night before I left for Sertar. You sent a man to kill me."

"Kill you?" The set of her shoulders showed for the first time a waver in confidence. "Don't be stupid, why would I do that?"

"Right," he said bitterly. "Without me to marry, you can't be princess. You need me to fuck to make your dynasty."

"You never minded fucking me before," she said coldly. She tilted her head and leaned her body forward slightly as if to remind him of its allure. Her mouth curved a little. "I'm sure you can summon the motivation again."

"I wouldn't count on it," he bit out.

She raised delicate blonde brows. "I know you Jolar, far better than you think I do. Once you see how much power you wield, once you see how much the people need you to continue your line for their safety and security, you'll do what you need to. Besides, we always got on, didn't we? You never got out of my bed disappointed, did you?"

"I don't love you, Jasa," he said bluntly. "I never have. I never will. Even if your plot succeeds you'll never be Princess of Zartan. I won't marry you."

Her white teeth flashed as she laughed. "Do you think I love *you?* Don't get me wrong, you're a beautiful man and a skilled lover, but really—" Her eyes, cool and speculative, ran over his form. "Your confidence in your appeal is quite pompous. I don't care if you don't love me. We *will* marry."

"No." He straightened and folded his arms. "We won't."

"I know who you *do* love," she said, her voice deceptively soft. "That pale little thing, Arissa. Tell me Jolar," her crystal blue eyes narrowed, "have you stopped to think what's happened to her while we've been having this conversation?"

His mouth went dry. "She has nothing to do with this. If you hurt her—"

"You love her," Jasa said simply. "Quite desperately. It's in your eyes when you look at her, Jolar. It surprised me, really. I've carefully followed every one of your many liaisons, but you've never fallen in love before. And I was never one to throw away a gift when it was handed to me. Play your part and be the Zartani prince you were born to be, or you'll watch your little whore die screaming."

He felt himself blanch. "You really are insane."

She sighed. "Once you have that power, you'll thank me for making you take it. I'll even let you keep her, provided she doesn't bear you any children to challenge my own." She paused. "On second thought, before I give her back I'll make quite certain she won't be able to."

He glanced at the blaster in her hand.

"Don't try it, Jolar," she warned, her body tensing as she edged toward the sitting room door. "I don't want you injured but we can carry out the plan with you unconscious just as easily. Maybe that would be better."

"You can't hurt her," Jolar growled. "I've sent her somewhere safe."

"Yes, the Zartani embassy." Jasa smiled. "I've been told she's just arrived."

Twenty-nine

Arissa stood outside in the late afternoon sun with Bruscan waiting for the Zartani shuttle. Nela had helped her pack the belongings she and Jolar hadn't taken with them to Danlen's, and their luggage now sat neatly piled on the paved courtyard.

Kemma called to invite them to dinner, and Arissa—feeling guilty as well as disappointed—made an excuse and promised to contact her later. According to Jolar, though, they would soon be off-world. Kemma lived on Lian's homeworld, and it was possible that she might not see her again.

"It has been a pleasure having you here," Bruscan said.

"Thank you."

He gave a faint smile. "It seems you and Jolar have come to . . . an arrangement."

She swallowed. Jolar had assured her he was going to break the contract with Jasa, that he was headed there after his call telling her to ready herself for the Zartani embassy. Still, the deed wasn't done yet.

But if Jolar asked her to marry him again, she would say yes. Despite the danger and her fears, she couldn't imagine a life without him. Perhaps she might even risk having the children he wanted so badly. That *she* wanted too . . .

"I hope we will."

Bruscan looked away. "Perhaps someday you will return to Sertar."

His attraction was unmistakable. She wondered how long it would last if he knew she were a seer. "Maybe we will."

Bruscan's dark brown eyes rested on her again. "You are welcome at my home anytime, Arissa. And if you ever have need of me . . ."

"Thank you," she said sincerely. She smiled a little. "That means a lot to me."

Bruscan nodded at the sky. "Your shuttle's here."

When the shuttle landed, even Bruscan was surprised at the number of ZarSec that were to accompany her.

"Looks like Jolar doesn't want to take any chances with you," Bruscan said.

Arissa reached out with her seer's senses. These men were genuine about their task to keep her safe.

One of them, the ranking officer, came forward and gave her a nod. "Mistress Legan, our orders are to transport you to the Zartani embassy compound immediately. If you'll get onboard?"

The luggage was already being loaded. She turned to Bruscan and shyly kissed his cheek.

He smiled and pressed her hand. "Good journey, Arissa. I hope we meet again."

"So do I," she said.

She followed the ZarSec into the shuttle and waved to Bruscan as they lifted off. The men onboard had the look of Zartani, with their height and light eyes. They were efficient and respectful, but none tried to engage her in conversation.

Despite it though, her stomach knotted in anxiety when she reached the Zartani embassy. Jolar insisted she come but despite the wall, the guards, the assurance that the grounds were as secure as any military base, she felt far less safe here than she had with Bruscan.

The ranking ZarSec officer, Lieutenant de'Rec, walked her into the embassy building. It was quiet inside—no doubt at this hour most of the embassy staff had finished for the day—and their footfalls echoed in the soaring reception hall.

"Councilor d'Barat asked me to bring you to him as soon as we arrived."

Arissa's brow creased. "The acting Zartani councilor? He's here?"

Lieutenant de'Rec's sense was heavy. "The Zartani senior councilor was killed a few days ago."

"I heard," Arissa said quietly. "Did you know him?"

The officer shook his head. "No, but he was well regarded. A good man. Councilor d'Barat has a great deal to live up to. He came for the trade summit, but I understand he intends to return to Zartan tomorrow."

Lieutenant de'Rec led her to the second floor and walked past an empty desk—one likely belonging to an assistant—to the double doors behind it. He rapped his knuckles on the carved dalsawood door and, without waiting for a response, opened it. The wall carvings of this office were masterworks of Zartani artistry, the curved desk equally elaborate.

The man seated behind the desk stood. "Ah, Mistress Legan. Do come in."

Rekan d'Barat was in his early thirties and had the Zartani height and blue eyes, but his hair was far darker than Jolar's, closer to a light brown than blond, really. He smiled in greeting, but Arissa swallowed at the contempt she sensed.

What did Jolar tell him to make him think so little of me?

Councilor d'Barat glanced at de'Rec. "Lieutenant, you may go."

The ZarSec gave her a nod and left, closing the door behind him.

The councilor's smile was polite, but the way he clasped her hand was somehow a bit too familiar. "Well, you're not what I expected."

It's like this is all a private joke to him.

"Expected?" Arissa frowned, easing her hand out of his grip. "I don't understand."

"I just thought you would be somehow . . . different." He shrugged and leaned on the edge of his desk, his pale blue eyes running over her appraisingly. "Well, certainly Lord d'Tural thinks highly of you."

What the hells is going on here?

Arissa sent a quick tendril out to touch more deeply into Rekan's mind even as she shifted her feet to move away from him.

Gods, he hates Jolar! Hates him enough to tear him apart. And he feels nothing but contempt for me . . .

"In any case," he continued, his face the soul of affable politeness. "I am very glad to have you here. I understand that you have done a great service to the Realm." That amusement reared again. "I imagine you will continue to provide excellent service."

"I should like to," Arissa said carefully. The sun had nearly set, and as far as she stretched her senses she couldn't feel Jolar nearby. "Has Commander d'Tural returned yet, Councilor?"

"He'll be here shortly, and I'm sure when—Oh, just a moment," d'Barat said as his comm unit signaled. He reached across the desk to retrieve it and took a moment to reply. Rekan stood, slipping the comm into his pocket. "I am afraid that my responsibilities call me elsewhere, Mistress Legan. But if you will come with me, I will show you to your quarters on my way out."

"Yes," Arissa said, eager to be away from him. "I would very much like that."

He indicated that she should precede him out of the office, then closed the door behind them.

"Lord d'Tural was very concerned about your safety," d'Barat said gravely as he clasped her elbow. "Is there anything I should know about? Any extra measures my staff should take?"

"No," His grip on her arm was just at the edge of discomfort, and she found herself leaning away from him. "I'm sure the ZarSec officers will make sure no one gains entry to the embassy grounds."

"Absolutely," d'Barat assured. "Our security is very tight, especially now. No one enters without an ID scan, and everyone is required to carry a security card to move about the grounds."

"Why especially now?"

"After Councilor de'Par's death we instituted new security protocols."

"Of course," she murmured.

Rekan led her down another level and across a suspended bridge overlooking the courtyard. He gave a wave to the ZarSecs waiting there next to a shuttle. He took her down a long hall and stopped before an open door.

"Here we are," d'Barat said, only releasing her arm when they were inside. "I think you will find it very pleasant."

They were actually very nice living quarters. Her things had already been brought here and the little apartment contained a well-appointed living area, small kitchen and bedroom. It even had a private balcony.

"I've had the kitchen stocked for you. You may wish to rest while you wait for Lord d'Tural's return." The councilor gave her a regretful smile. "I apologize, Mistress Legan, but there's a shuttle waiting for me. I really must go."

"I understand." Arissa glanced around the room. "I'm sure I'll be very comfortable here. Thank you, Councilor."

"Of course." He bent his head to her and left, closing the door behind him.

She held up the security card she'd palmed off his desk. "Thank you very much indeed."

Arissa stood at the doorway of her private balcony to watch d'Barat's shuttle leave. He'd locked her in, of course. The balcony was too high to jump, and there was no way to climb down.

But then again, she didn't need to.

As soon as the shuttle passed from sight she was through the living room. With a quick swipe of his security card she had the door open. A moment later she was out in the hallway, easing the door shut behind her.

Her heart hammered as she listened with ears and mind. It was quiet, and she sensed no one nearby. Clearly d'Barat had housed her where he was sure there was no one about to hear her pounding on the door. Perhaps if she had stood on the balcony and screamed long enough, someone would eventually come to her aid but that would have taken a very long time.

And wherever Jolar was now, he was in danger.

Arissa took quick stock. She was wearing casual day clothes: belted tunic, pants and slippers. She had d'Barat's security pass and her newly-honed seer senses.

She also had the nearly twenty-five thousand credits she'd won playing tongo.

They'd brought her luggage to the room, but while the cash Jolar had insisted she keep was there, the little blaster he'd given her was missing. Someone had also deactivated the uplink in her quarters so she couldn't just call for help. She didn't want to risk calling from somewhere else inside the embassy either.

She needed to get back to Bruscan.

She headed down the hall. A few moments later she was in the stairwell. She made it to the ground floor undetected—thanks to d'Barat's security card.

She sensed someone and ducked back into a doorway. A door opened further down and closed again.

Now she just had to find a way out of the embassy.

Closing her eyes, she reached with her seer senses as far as she could.

To her right, people were moving about. Slowing her breath, she counted out six of them. Their minds were occupied and they were a bit tired. She had never tried such a deep mind probe like this with anyone but Jolar. She reached out and deliberately sent her focus into one mind . .
.

Through his eyes she could see all around a large gleaming kitchen. Other workers labored nearby, finishing up for the evening. The smell of cleanser filled the man's nostrils. One woman turned and spoke to another, then swiped a card to open the door outside.

Arissa changed her focus and sent it in the other direction, toward the gate. There were a few ZarSecs on guard; one felt very familiar. She reached out and brushed his mind.

Lieutenant de'Rec, her ZarSec escort from Bruscan's house.

Even if he doesn't know I'm supposed to be locked in my quarters, he won't let me just walk out of here.

Back door it is.

This had almost worked on Tellar. She prayed it would work here.

She was just going to walk out.

There were five workers left in the kitchen, but only two looked up with questioning glances. She threw the men a smile and kept her feet moving. Her hands were shaking when she reached for the door. She swiped the security card.

Nothing happened.

Oh, gods.

She tried the card again.

Come on, come on!

She was gathering attention from the remaining staff; she could feel one of them approaching behind her. Frantically she swiped again.

"Pass not working?"

She turned around to see a heavyset man in his middle years, his eyes narrowed with suspicion. He was better dressed than the others and had an air of authority.

He jerked his chin at her. "You don't look Zartani."

"No, I'm—my husband is. He got me a job here."

"I haven't seen you before."

"Well, I just started in the administration department a few days ago." She gave a half-shrug. "I guess that's why my card keeps giving me trouble."

"Why don't you go through the main entrance?"

"This time of day? You know how the ZarSecs are. They always want to make small talk. I'm really tired and I just wanted to go home."

He searched her face.

Arissa forced a smile.

"This door's a bit finicky. You have to swipe the pass just right." He leaned forward to use his own card, then pushed the door open for her. "Just ask one of us to open it next time."

"Oh," Arissa managed. "I will. Next time. Thanks!"

Arissa plunged out into the early Sertarian evening. Intended for foodstuffs deliveries to the kitchen, this door was a few short steps from the rear wall. Her purloined pass opened the service gate. Fortunately the Zartani, hailing from such a wealthy world, had procured for themselves property for their embassy in one of the better parts of Tano.

Unfortunately, that meant a neighborhood without any shuttles or groundcars for hire. She could see a grouping of brighter lights about a kilometer north. But she'd have to get there on foot.

The sun had set, the evening breezes carrying away the heat of the day. There wasn't any foot traffic here, this street not designed with pedestrians in mind. She clung to the edge of the road, fearful that in the gathering darkness she would be struck by one of the groundcars speeding past. Likely if she were hit they wouldn't even stop.

The glow of lights was a grouping of eateries. A number of people were coming and going, and she spied a single battered-looking shuttle. The driver inside was glancing about, scanning the crowd and, hopefully, looking for a fare.

She hurried toward the shuttle, out of breath. Leaning into the open passenger side window, she asked, "Are you for hire?"

The driver's white mustache was stained yellow, and he stank of sarrat smoke. He looked her over briefly. "Where you headed?"

She gave him the location of Bruscan's house.

"It'll be a hundred—*cash* not scan. You got that much, girl? That don't include tip." His eyes narrowed. "I'll call SerSec if you try to stiff me."

"I've got it," she promised.

She could feel him weighing it, but then he nodded. "Get in."

She climbed inside and pulled the door shut behind her. "Just get me there fast."

He shrugged, powering up the shuttle. "Fast as I can."

She wrinkled her nose at the pungent smoky smell. The interior was none too clean either. She strapped in, chewing at her lip.

It was a short ride but an agonizing one, and Arissa closed her eyes briefly in gratitude when she saw the lights of Bruscan's house below. With Bruscan's connections and resources he would be able to get to Jolar.

She unstrapped as the shuttle landed in the courtyard. She held out the hundred to the driver, already reaching for the door only to find he'd locked it.

"Five hundred creds," the pilot said.

"What? You said *one* hundred!"

"One to let you in." He smirked. "Four hundred to let you out."

I don't have time for this! Furious, she counted out five hundred and handed it to him, but not fast enough. He saw that she still had more.

She peeled off more bills and pushed them at him. "That's another three hundred. Now let me out!" She gritted her teeth when she felt him weighing it. "Open the fucking door or you can explain to SerSec why you're harassing one of Bruscan Milin's guests. I'm sure they'll be happy to show you how a stun pike works!"

He jammed his finger at the door control with a snort.

She was out before the door was open all the way.

"You want me to wait?" he called.

After a five-minute ride costing eight hundred creds?

She threw him a disgusted look. "No! Go rob someone else!"

He shrugged. She heard the shuttle lifting off just as she was running across the courtyard. The pulse gate lowered; the security system must have already identified her as she approached. From the number of lights on, it was plain that at least someone was home. And Nela could summon Bruscan back from wherever he was if he'd gone out.

Arissa threw open the door of Bruscan's house to find that Nela wouldn't be calling anyone.

Her body, hideous with blaster wounds, lay sprawled in the ruin of Bruscan's foyer.

Arissa's mouth parted in horror she took in the destruction. There were blaster holes everywhere, the artwork smashed, torn or burned. This was an act of utter rage.

She took a step back to flee.

But *someone* was in the house, still alive . . .

Whoever was inside was surprised, but not in pain. Trembling, she took a few steps inside and went past Nela's body. Two other of Bruscan's servants lay in the living area. Too shaken to focus well, she reached out clumsily with her mind. One person. A man, just inside the office. And she didn't detect any anger from him, none of the fury that could have done this.

"Bruscan?"

In the hall outside Bruscan's office she had to skirt the chef's body. The woman lay face up, her eyes wide and fixed.

"Bruscan? It's Arissa."

The door to the office opened.

Her breath froze as she met his cold flat eyes.

Then, as if reminding himself to do so, Larner Tovic smiled.

Thirty

Snarling and with fists clenched, Jolar took a step toward Jasa, who quickly raised her blaster. Jolar stopped short, breathing hard, the muzzle of Jasa's weapon a scant inch from his left cheekbone.

His eyes narrowed. "So help me gods, if you hurt Arissa I will kill you."

"Hurt her?" Jasa scoffed. "As long as I have her, I have *you*." She gave a little smile. "Perhaps if you behave yourself, I'll even let you see her tonight. Step back, darling."

His heart hammered as he ran through his options. Even the most powerful of telepaths were never reputed to hear thoughts from this kind of distance, and she had scarcely started learning to focus her abilities. There was no way to warn her, no way to reach her, not telepathically.

He glanced at the weapon in his face and forced himself to ease back. In response Jasa lowered the blaster but kept it pointed at his chest.

"You must have known I was sending her to the Zartani embassy as soon as I contacted her," Jolar said. "You have people there, don't you?"

"*We* have people everywhere."

"Everywhere? Will other worlds be crowning princes?" He jerked his chin toward the windows, taking the opportunity to do a quick visual of the sitting room. No comm units that he could see, no other blasters visible. "How many?"

Jasa smiled. "Other than Zartan and Sertar? Three."

"You'll fail," he said harshly. "You can't take the whole Realm with only five worlds."

"You can if you cripple the fleet."

His head came up. "Danlen was working for you."

"*With* me," Jasa said. "Danlen's crystals are installed on every fleet ship from Utavia to Rusco. We will disable any ship whose crew doesn't pledge loyalty to us. It may be as many as two thirds, unfortunately. But as we will allow commerce to continue only to planets that accept the monarchy's return, it won't be long before the other worlds are forced to concede."

Jolar folded his arms. "You really think fleet crews are going to pledge their loyalty to you?"

"Why should they care which flag they follow?" Jasa scoffed. "Has the New Order done so much for them? For any of us? We won't destroy their ships or take their lives. They'll get their pay same as always, their retirement. Besides," she added, her gaze running over him. "The Zartani prince is one of their own."

Jolar's mouth tightened. He recalled how he'd once told Arissa that fleet people would put up with anything as long they got their pay and caf.

Jasa might just be right.

"Three other worlds." He shifted his weight, moving a hair closer to the door. "One of them must be Utavia. Who's the Utavian prince?"

"Broc Attar." Her lip curled. "Cowardly fool, always needed handholding and reassurances! The man was not fit to rule. Just as well someone killed him."

Jolar raised his eyebrows. "You didn't kill him?"

"Of course not!" She gave him an impatient look. "He was our ally, Jolar."

"*Your* ally," he corrected. "Is that why he was on Sertar? To meet with you?"

She raised one delicate shoulder. "What better place than Sertar to coordinate our efforts?"

"I imagine Broc's the one who provided the Utavian guards you've got out there."

"A veritable army of loyal Utavians in exchange for Zartani wealth to buy food and medicine for his tribe. Though Attar took more than his fair share of those credits, if you ask me. Thank the gods he did us the favor of leaving heirs. The eldest has the promise to become a great leader, and he's only seventeen. I regret it took us so long to bring this to its conclusion." She looked at him thoughtfully. "You would have grown into your own as prince by now if *you'd* been crowned by seventeen, Jolar."

His jaw clenched. "Instead of wasting my time working my butt off in the fleet."

"No," she said mildly. "I think it was time well spent. You sowed your oats on a dozen worlds before you were well known, and that will save me some embarrassment. You matured. You worked your way up the ranks without benefit of your birth; that will help win the commoners and the fleet ships to your side."

"Glad I could do my part," he fairly spat.

A rueful smile touched her lips. "In only one thing did you disappoint—myself and your father both. We were sure you would fall in love with me."

"You must have been very displeased," he said bitterly. "How much simpler it would have been to manipulate me if I'd loved you."

Jasa gave an unapologetic shrug. "It would have made things easier for us all, I think. I knew, as your father did, that when you did fall you would fall hard. And you did."

She sighed. "Just not for me. You would have accepted the crown for love. Then, having taken the throne, you would have learned how well it suited you. I think you would have been happier as prince. But we'll make do with what we have."

"That crown doesn't belong to me, Jasa," he said. "It doesn't belong to anyone anymore."

"Oh," she said softly, "it belongs to you all right. By birthright, by blood, by our hard work and sacrifice. It's yours. Maybe you can't see it yet, but you will. This is *right*, Jolar. We are going to return order and beauty to the Realm." Her eyes were aglow. "Think about it! The greatest of our achievements as a people happened under the monarchy. The New Order has only brought danger and shortsighted opportunists with no care for how their actions will impact future generations. A return to the old ways will give the Realm the stability, the care and direction it needs to flourish again."

He swallowed. In many ways she was right about the New Order, but he believed in the ideals of the republic. And while he could never agree with her methods or her goals, he couldn't help but admire her conviction.

"Do you really think people are going to support the return of the monarchy?" he demanded with a gesture toward the windows, to the billions of Realm citizens out there. "What about the Tellaran council? What about the people of the other worlds? The ones who don't have royalty ready to climb over the backs of the people to reach the throne?"

"Heirs will be found for those worlds. Even the Tellaran royal family left a few offshoots when they were wiped out. As far as the Tellaran council goes, those who oppose us won't see another sunrise. And," she said with a quick smile behind her as the door opened. "some have actually been our allies all along."

"Gods," Jolar whispered when he saw who stood in the doorway.

"You see, Jolar?" Jasa asked. "We really do have people everywhere."

Arissa took a step back. "Where's Bruscan?" she asked stupidly.

Larner's smile disappeared. "I don't know."

"Why—why did you do this?"

Larner gave a slight frown. "Do what?"

Arissa swallowed. "Kill all these people."

"I didn't." He tilted his head. "Then *you* didn't kill them?"

"No," she whispered. He really *hadn't*. She glanced around at the ruin of Bruscan's office, his home. "If you didn't—What are you doing here?"

Mild surprise crossed his face. "You asked me for my recommendations for suppliers."

"What?"

"For the fleet contract your husband is administering." Larner pulled a small datapad from his pocket. "I have researched and compiled a list of six companies that I recommend. I came to discuss my findings."

He offered the datapad to her. Shakily she took it and glanced at the list. He had included their holdings, earnings projections for the next five years, personnel profiles . . .

"That's why you're here?"

"Yes." His flat gaze went to the body of the chef in the hall. "Does she look afraid? I wish I knew what people were feeling," he said longingly. "I don't know unless they tell me."

Arissa gave a short, half-hysterical laugh. "I wish I *didn't* know how they were feeling."

He looked at her, his eyes intently focused on her. "Is it something you could teach me?"

"No," she stammered. "No, I can't."

"I study people's faces. I can make their expressions but I don't know when I ought to." His glance went over her face, his slight frown returning. "Are you afraid now?"

"Yes," Arissa said. "Very."

"Of me?"

Arissa reached out and brushed his peculiar, rigidly structured mind. He felt emotions of his own, but he was baffled by the expression on her face.

"No," she said, her shoulders falling. "No, I'm not." Arissa took in the destruction of the house. "You didn't find Bruscan?"

"No," Larner said mildly. "But I didn't search the whole property. It is possible he is here." Larner took a step back. "I have an appointment in an hour. Good evening, Mistress Legan. Feel free to contact me about my recommendations."

I can't feel anyone but Larner. If Bruscan's here, he's dead. If he's not dead I have no idea how to find him and no time to figure out how.

Larner was going to walk away from this carnage without a thought and continue on with his evening. He wasn't a man who would be swayed by her appeals for help, not using any of the means at her disposal.

She couldn't go to SerSec; the only evidence she had that Jolar was in danger at all was telepathic.

"Wait," Arissa said quickly, realizing there was something Larner would be agreeable to doing. "If you have a shuttle, perhaps you could drop me somewhere?"

There was only one other person on Sertar who could help her save Jolar now.

Someone with no reason to help me—and every reason not to.

Thirty-one

Larner's shuttle lifted off behind her. It was full dark now, the courtyard deserted around her as Arissa ran for the door of the mansion. She slipped on the marble stairs, hammering on the estate's door even as she caught herself against it.

I know you're here!

Arissa pounded again.

After an agonizingly long moment, the door opened.

"Arissa?" Kemma frowned, her alarm rippling. Her brilliant gold-red hair was loose around her shoulders. She was clad in a silver shimmersilk tunic and trousers, a dark blue wrap around her shoulders against the evening chill. "What are you doing here?"

"You have to let me in!"

"Of course." Kemma stepped aside to allow Arissa into the foyer, then closed the outside door. "Come on, come in here," Kemma urged, leading her across the foyer and into a sitting room. "What's wrong?"

Arissa barely glanced at the parlor's gold and green décor, the sinuous lines of the furniture. "I need your help."

"My help?" Kemma's frown deepened. "What do you need my help with?"

Arissa wet her lips. "You're a seer, aren't you?"

Kemma's face went white. "I don't know what you're talking about."

"It took me a while to figure it out," Arissa said in a rush. "You're so good at handling people, you always know exactly the right thing to say."

Kemma's nostrils flared. "I'm an ornament," she said tartly. "When I get paid to put something in my mouth, I guarantee you, it's not a foot."

"That could just be your ornament training," Arissa agreed. "But from what Lian says you're an amazing card player."

Kemma gave a short, disbelieving laugh. "I'm lucky! It happens."

"No You're a good ornament, a good card player because you *know* how people are feeling, maybe even what they're thinking. You knew on the *Queen's Light* that Jolar and I were new to each other, not married for years like we said. You thought we were on our honeymoon."

"Don't be ridiculous." Kemma said coldly. "You two were all over each other. It was an honest mistake."

"You slipped the day we went shopping in Tano-Sertar. You said I was new at shopping. There's no way you could have known that."

Kemma's green eyes narrowed. "I'll tell you what I *do* know. I know you've been lying about a lot. You're not who you say you are, Arissa, and neither is Jolar. He's your lover but he's not your husband, is he?"

"No," Arissa admitted. "I met Jolar a couple of weeks ago on Tellar. He brought me to Sertar. He's—we're—investigating . . . something."

Kemma was watching her warily. "So what do you want from me? Money?"

Arissa hesitated. She wasn't sure what she needed. Jolar was in danger; she had to find him but she had to rescue him too. "Maybe."

Kemma's sense suddenly became heavy with resignation.

"I'm sorry, Kemma," Arissa said sincerely. "I consider you a friend."

"Yeah," Kemma said. "I'm sorry, too."

"Kemma," Arissa began, squaring her shoulders. "Listen, I'm a—"

Someone's behind me!

Arissa didn't even have time to turn. She arched against the pain in her back as the blaster bolt hit her.

Just before the world went black she felt Kemma's absolutely genuine regret.

Jolar's stomach sank as Rekan entered and closed the door behind him, his last hope for Arissa's safety now crushed.

"Councilor d'Barat." Jolar's lip curled. "What about your oath to the Tellaran council? To the republic?"

Rekan spared him a smug glance, his own blaster holstered at his hip. "You didn't think I would side against my own kind, did you? I have every reason to want to see my birthright restored."

"What about *her*?" Jasa asked sharply. "Arissa?"

"Safely locked away at the embassy." Rekan assured as he strode into the room. "I saw to it myself."

Jasa gave a satisfied nod. "And the other matter?"

"Milin's dead."

"You killed Bruscan?" Jolar cried. "Gods, *why?*"

"I didn't have anything against him personally," Jasa replied, and to her credit she looked regretful. "But like you, he was working for Dacel. He might even have been motivated to interfere if he discovered he couldn't reach either of you. I didn't—*we* didn't work this hard to have things go wrong now." Jasa gave Rekan a smile. "Did we?"

"Just a few more hours," Rekan said softly. "And all those years of work will bear fruit."

Rekan pressed a kiss to Jasa's mouth, then stood protectively at her side.

"Ah," Jolar murmured. "*Now* I understand."

Jasa gave him a half smile. "You mean why I don't mind about your little plaything?"

"My apologizes, Jasa," Jolar said with false humor. "You didn't send that Utavian to kill me on Tellar. Rekan did."

"No, he—" Jasa glanced at Rekan and her nostrils flared. "You tried to kill Jolar?"

"More than once actually," Jolar said. "He tried again at Danlen's estate. Those Utavians he sent killed everyone. They leveled the place trying to kill me."

"They said they *had* killed you." Rekan briefly bared his teeth. "I should have told them to bring me your body—" Rekan narrowed his gaze "—or eyes, as proof."

"You—?" Jasa pushed him from her side. Rekan's face reddened and he caught himself against the chair. "What about Cenon?" she demanded.

"Our Sertarian allies will find another royal princess—or prince," Rekan said sharply, leveling his gaze at her as he straightened. "You know it was doubtful that Cenon would ever be well enough to produce an heir. We don't need the thorny question of succession coming so soon. Besides we're better off with someone easier to control than Danlen was proving to be."

"*That's* why," Jolar said, shaking his head. "It wasn't for money or power. Danlen had all that. He loved Cenon. He wanted her to be crowned Princess of Sertar. That's why he was so eager I think well of him. We were supposed to be allies." Jolar raised an eyebrow at Jasa. "Or even family, I suppose. Once everyone started producing little heirs to marry off."

Rekan gave Jolar a narrow glare, his grip tight on the chair back. "We don't need *him* any more either."

"He's Prince of Zartan," Jasa snarled. "*Our* prince. Of course we need him!"

Rekan straightened. "We can choose another to be prince."

"He means himself," Jolar said in mock helpfulness. He nodded in Rekan's direction. "He's a Zartani aristocrat too, in case you've forgotten. Kill me, take my crown," Jolar raised his eyebrows, "obviously you've already helped yourself to my betrothed."

Rekan's lip curled. "As if you were deserving of her. As if you were ever faithful."

"Not to Jasa," Jolar agreed. "Not for a moment. And you know, Jasa," he continued, folding his arms. "I'm feeling less and less guilty about breaking our betrothal contract with every passing minute."

Rekan took a step forward. "Breaking—?"

"Gods, you didn't think I *wanted* to marry her, did you, Rekan?" Jolar gave a short laugh. "I actually have Jasa to thank for making it to commander's rank. If I hadn't been so reluctant to make my vows to her I would have left the fleet years ago. But, you know, the retirement package works out to an extra thousand a month, so I guess I can't complain."

"I never did care for your so-called sense of humor, Jolar," Jasa snapped. "I suggest you keep quiet now or I will stun you 'til this is over."

"If he broke the betrothal contract—" Rekan took Jasa by the shoulders, searching her face. "I know you don't want him. Beloved, why are you doing this?"

In a moment of heart-wrenching clarity Jolar saw the way out of this. The way to end Jasa and Rekan's treason, to keep his promise to Dacel, to protect the republic from collapsing.

And the only way to save Arissa.

Someday, gods, let her forgive me and . . . let her find someone to spend her life with, to care for her as I wanted to do.

Jolar stepped beside Jasa. "Because Jasa needs me to make her dynasty. Oh, come on, Rekan. Haven't you figured out that she aims higher than even Princess of Zartan? She wants her pretty backside," Jolar threw an appreciative glance at Jasa's rounded rump, "on the Tellaran throne to rule it all. For that she needs a Zartani prince who can make claim to the Tellaran crown too and become king. And to be blunt, that's me, not you. Go on, Jasa," Jolar invited. "Explain why my seed in your belly is so much better than *his*."

"Jolar," she warned, her voice low and dangerous.

"Is that true?" Rekan demanded, his grip tightening on her, his eyes furious. "*That's* what you wanted him for? Because you thought I wasn't good enough?"

"He's our prince!" Jasa said impatiently, shrugging off Rekan's hands. "He has the best claim to the Zartani crown *and* the Tellaran throne! Or have you forgotten what this is all about?"

"You know, Rekan," Jolar said. "It's kind of fun for me to see Jasa showing her temper to someone else for a change."

"Shut up, Jolar!" Jasa hissed.

Rekan pointed at Jolar. "I didn't do this so I could bend my knee to this son of a sular cow!"

"Why does everyone always bring my mother into things?" Jolar asked. "Don't you understand, Jasa? He's been working behind your back all this time. Two days ago Rekan sent Utavians Danlen *thought* were his allies to kill him and his wife. He probably got Danlen to let them past the security grid by saying they were extra guards to protect Cenon. He wants me dead so *he* can take the crown."

"What did you expect?" Rekan demanded, his face red and furious. "That I was just going to let you get into bed with him?"

"You mean '*back* into bed with him', don't you?" Jolar asked. He feigned a frown. "Wait, he knows I've been fucking you all this time, doesn't he, Jasa?"

Rekan's face went almost purple.

Jolar smirked. "I guess not." He put his hand over his heart and gave an abbreviated, mocking bow. "Well, my word as your prince, Rekan, she was always quite sated by the time I pulled out."

Snarling, Rekan drew his blaster and took aim at Jolar's heart.

There was a brief flash and Rekan collapsed to the floor, unconscious from Jasa's stun bolt.

Jolar sighed. "Now that is a shame."

Jasa shot him a cold look. "Don't worry. It's a light stun. He'll come around in a minute or so." She shook her head at Jolar in disgust. "You think you're so clever. That you could get us to argue, try to turn us against each other."

"Oh, I wasn't trying to do that at all."

Jasa frowned, searching his face. "You wanted him to kill you."

"Hard to keep those good souls fighting in my name after you've shot their prince." Jolar gave a sardonic smile. "Without me your whole scheme is fucked, isn't it?"

"Then how fortunate I was here to save you, darling." Her blue eyes narrowed. "I'd forgotten how stupidly selfless you can be. And—just in case you think about doing that again—remember that you're leaving your little bedmate to my tender mercies when you go."

Jolar felt the blood drain from his face.

"I see. You thought that, with you dead, I'd have no use for her at all and I'd . . . what? Let her go? Oh no," Jasa purred. "If you do succeed in taking yourself off the playing board, I give you *my* word, you'll hear her screams all the way from the spirit world, Jolar."

Thirty-two

Arissa came to, groaning.

She tried to bring her hand to her throbbing head and discovered she was tied to the chair she was sitting in. She blinked rapidly, trying to clear her vision. "What—?"

Kemma stood nearby, her body half turned away, her arms folded, her brow creased with worry.

Lian's face was grim, a blaster held at his side.

"What—" Arissa shook her head. "Gods, what are you doing?"

"Actually that's a good question, Lian," Kemma said tightly. "What *are* you doing?"

"What the hells was I supposed to do?" Lian demanded. "She knows!"

Kemma ran her hands through her russet hair. "And now what? You'll kill her?"

"Wait!" Arissa cried. "Wait, please. You don't want to do this. I know you don't!"

Lian's face was taut. "Of course I don't! But your husband, or *whoever* he is, is an investigator of some kind. So who is he? Military? TelSec? You know about Kemma—that's why you came here. You came to blackmail her—or worse—because she's a seer!"

"No!" Arissa shook her head sharply. "Because *I* am!"

Kemma's head whipped around. "What? What did you say?"

"I'm a seer!"

Lian took a half-step forward and Kemma quickly put her hand on his arm. "No, Lian, she's telling the truth."

"She can't be, Kemma!" he insisted. "There aren't any other seers except you!"

"Oh, this is just fucking incredible!" Arissa choked out. "I hide my whole life and when I finally admit what I am, you don't *believe* me?"

Kemma knelt to look up at her, her hands resting gently on Arissa's knees.

"Hiding?" she asked urgently then, in a tender, sisterly gesture, Kemma brushed the ringlets out of Arissa's eyes. "Who? Who hid you?"

"My parents. They figured out what I was. They hid me."

"You really are, aren't you?" Kemma searched her face and Arissa felt the lightest of brushes against her mind. "You're a seer too," she whispered, her green eyes wide with wonder. She stood. "Lian, untie her."

"Kemma she knows about you!"

"And I know about *her*! Lian, don't you understand? She's like me." Kemma looked back at her, shaking her head. "She's like me."

"I can prove it," Arissa said to Lian.

"Okay," he snapped. "Prove it."

"Think of somewhere you've been."

Lian and Kemma exchanged a glance.

He handed the blaster to her. "Watch her," Lian warned. He gave Arissa a nod. "Go ahead."

Arissa shut her eyes. Her head was pounding and she was parched, but somewhere whoever killed all those people at Bruscan's might have Jolar too. She steadied her breath and mentally reached toward Lian.

"Snow," she murmured. "There's snow everywhere. Children laughing, racing sleds. There's someone, another boy, with you. Your brother. He's older and he takes you down the hill because you're too afraid to go alone."

"Xeltan," Lian said, shaken. "That was Xeltan. My parents took me when we were kids. And yeah, I was thinking of when Naran took me on his sled."

"Can we untie her now?" Kemma demanded.

"Yeah," Lian said. "Sure."

He bent to undo her bonds, and Kemma snatched them from him.

"My favorite silk scarves," she muttered.

"I was in a hurry," Lian retorted. "It's not like I hold people captive often enough to invest in tarasteel cuffs."

"I need your help." Arissa rubbed at her wrists. "Jolar is in danger."

"Who are you?" Kemma asked. "Really?"

"My name is Arissa Kassar," she said, standing. "He's Commander Jolar d'Tural of the Tellaran fleet. I saved his life on Tellar and he promised me a non-telepath ID if I helped him. Someone was poised to seize control of Sertar and we were sent here by the Zartani councilor to find out who."

Their astonishment reverberated through the room.

"Seize control of—?"

"It was Danlen Mirat," Arissa interrupted Lian.

Kemma blinked. "Wait—the man Jolar wanted to meet at the party?"

"But Danlen's dead. Someone killed him and everyone else at his home while we were there." She swallowed. "And I think Bruscan Milin is dead too, everyone at his house was when I went there tonight. I came here because I didn't have anywhere else to go."

"Why don't you contact the Zartani councilor for help?" Kemma asked.

Arissa shook her head. "Councilor de'Par is dead. He was murdered a few days ago on Tellar."

"That's right," Lian said slowly. "I remember hearing about that."

"And the Acting Zartani councilor is part of whatever this is. Jolar sent me to the Zartani embassy and Councilor d'Barat tried to hold me prisoner there."

Kemma paled. "How bad is this?"

"It's bad." Arissa pushed her hair from her face. "When Jolar called to tell me to go to the Zartani embassy he said he'd already given all our evidence to Councilor d'Barat."

Kemma and Lian exchanged a glance.

"So what do you want from us?" Lian asked. "We aren't FleetSec or commandos."

"Actually you're better because I don't think I can trust any of them. Besides all I've got to go on is what I know telepathically; you two are the only ones who believe me *and* won't kill me for being a seer. I think I know where d'Barat was headed. I think that's where Jolar is." She looked at Kemma. "And I'm going to need your help to get him out."

Jasa, ever the well-bred hostess, had food brought in along with the Niman brandy.

Jasa and Rekan left him in the sitting room and withdrew, intent to finish destroying everything he'd worked his whole life to defend. Legs stuck out, Jolar sprawled in the chair that Jasa had so thoughtfully had copied for his comfort, and regarded his Utavian guard.

Apparently this man was Jasa's creature, not Rekan's, and had strict orders to protect His Highness at all costs.

Protect him by being sure he didn't go anywhere.

She wouldn't leave him alone, not even with two other Utavians outside the sitting room door—he was far too valuable to her as sire for all the princes and princesses she planned to bear—but Jasa wouldn't offend his dignity with restraints.

Odd, what Jasa was willing to do and what she wasn't. It was quite a pile of bodies that Jasa was willing to climb over to place that blood-soaked crown on his head. Bruscan, Dacel, Danlen, Cenon . . .

Arissa.

He clenched his fist, his jaw so tight it hurt.

Jasa was right: as long as they had her, they had him.

How could I be so godsdamned stupid? I sent her right to them.

Rekan had said he had her locked safely in the embassy. But that didn't mean anything. Rekan had sent assassins to kill him—kill *them*—two days ago. His Utavians would have cut her down without a thought.

So many deaths, so many more to come, and all for—

His eyes burned.

Jolar thought those long talks in his boyhood had been just his father daydreaming about what could have been. Instead they had been meant as lessons, splendid tales to fire Jolar's ambition, justification for the treason he was committing.

And if his father had been working toward this since he was an infant, that meant everything he'd believed about him, about Zartani honor itself, was a big fat fucking *lie*.

All those arguments about joining the fleet, the maneuvering to gain his promise to marry Jasa, all those manipulations, all that deceit . . .

All for a crown he had never wanted—*still* didn't want.

Father, how could you have thought you were doing it for me? Didn't you know me at all?

The Realm was about to be plunged into another blood-soaked civil war, but if he survived the next few days he would be crowned on Zartan.

Jasa truly believed he would feel obligated to keep their marriage contract. That their heritage was one of sacred honor and benevolent sovereigns. She conveniently forgot about the purges by paranoid despot princes, the injustices of absolute rule, how the many labored to provide glittering lives for the few.

Jolar's mouth took a bitter curl.

Maybe we are *a match. Gods know she's as great a fool as I am.*

But he knew one thing. If that crown did touch his brow, Rekan and Jasa would be sorry they ever put it there.

As Prince of Zartan his rule would absolute. Jolar would have the power to banish those two to live out their days on that miserable research facility with the blood plague. He could order them *infected* with the blood plague if he liked. He could chain them to the wall of the palace's dining hall in Kev-Zartan and throw feasts while he enjoyed watching them starve.

If he were crowned—but he probably wasn't going to live that long. Clearly Rekan had already realized he couldn't afford to let him take the throne. And that meant someone was going to kill him very, very soon.

And if he died—

His father and Jasa had taken his faith in his heritage, in Zartani honor, and they might succeed in destroying the republic he pledged to uphold, but there was no festering way he was going to let them take Arissa too.

And to save her, I have to get out of here.

Jolar measured the guard with a glance. The man's blaster was holstered, the traditional Utavian dagger strapped to his left arm. This man, and the Utavians outside, had been tasked with both protecting the Zartani prince who they would pledge to follow as supreme king over all and keeping him prisoner.

Apparently the absurdity of it was lost on them.

"I met your prince," Jolar said, shifting to sit up. "He seemed like a fine man."

The guard gave a spare nod.

"I seems you and I are to be allies—Your new prince and I, I mean. The boy's how old now? Eighteen?"

"His highness, Prince Brotar, is seventeen." His voice was gravelly, his tone respectful as he addressed the Zartani prince.

Jolar gave a faint smile. "Oh, I guess I was misinformed. Of course I don't expect I will live long enough to meet him."

The guard frowned. "I do not understand, Your Highness. You will be Tellaran king. Even our prince must swear fealty to you."

Jolar leaned forward to look over the spread that Jasa had brought in. Meats, bread disks, vegetables cooked in glistening tarva sauce, sweet puddings.

Of course, all traditional Zartani fare.

Except the Niman brandy. Knowing Jasa, it probably was excellent. He reached across the table and poured two snifters.

"Want some?" Jolar took an appreciative sniff and held the glass of the amber liquid out to the man. "It's the good stuff. 'Course, it's probably poisoned."

Surprise flickered across the man's face.

"Oh, I beg your pardon," Jolar said politely and tilted his head. "Perhaps *you're* to kill me instead."

The guard looked shocked. "My orders are to protect you, Your Highness."

Jolar leaned back in his chair again, pretending to study the amber liquid in his glass. "Some of your people tried to kill me two days ago," Jolar said conversationally, then looked at the guard, his eyebrows raised. "Know anything about that?"

The Utavian's nostrils flared. "My tribesmen would never act so dishonorably."

"Some did. They killed the soon-to-be crowned Princess of Sertar. Her name was Cenon. She was a sweet lady. I buried her myself."

The guard went still.

"You know," Jolar continued. "It's just plain dumb luck that I survived. We have a lot in common, you know, your young prince and I. I think he, and the rest of your people, are being used to seize power for Jasa and Rekan."

The guard's face became closed and set. "We are allies. We will return to the old ways, the ways of honor."

"Honor? If I'm their prince, a man they claim they vow to follow onto death," Jolar made a casual wave with the snifter toward the closed door of the sitting room, "why am I not permitted to leave this room?"

There was hesitation in the guard's eyes.

"I'll tell you why." Jolar hooked a finger to coax the man toward him. The guard took a few steps closer and Jolar dropped his voice to a confiding whisper. "Because

Rekan wants my crown for himself. And pretty soon a few of your tribesmen, who are being used like you and I are, are going to come through that door," Jolar said with a nod in that direction, "to kill me. And since you happen to be standing in their way, they're going to kill you too."

The guard frowned.

"If you don't believe me, go ahead and take a drink. Because if Rekan got the chance, all this," Jolar indicated the meal and leaned forward to get the balls of his feet under him, "is poisoned. Either way, you and I are not going to live to see morning."

At the sound of blaster fire in the hall the Utavian guard whipped his head toward the door. And that moment of distraction was all Jolar needed.

He had the Utavian down and the man's blaster in hand before the bodies outside hit the floor.

Jolar reset the blaster to kill and shot out the window, blowing the plexisteel outward into the night in a shower of reflective shards. He was already on the windowsill, ready to jump to the garden below when the door behind him burst open.

With the muscle memory of thousands of hours of practice, Jolar turned to fire.

Arissa let her breath out slowly; keeping her own anxieties at bay was easy compared to blocking the fear pouring off Lian as they crouched outside Jasa's residence. Kemma, sleekly dressed in black shirt and trousers, her copper hair drawn back, narrowed her eyes as she looked at the mansion. She seemed to be handling this far better than her protector.

But then, she and Kemma could see in a way that Lian could not.

"How many of them are there?" Lian asked in a tight whisper.

"Four out here—" Arissa began.

"—nine inside." Kemma finished.

Even in the darkness, Arissa could see Lian blanch.

"Are you out of your godsdamn minds?" His voice rose an octave. "We can't take on thirteen armed gunman!"

"We don't have to take them on," Arissa promised softly. "We just have to stun them long enough to get Jolar out."

"Stun them all *before* one manages to hit the security alarm or knocks us all out with a wide beam scald pulse?" Lian's dark eyes snapped. "I don't know if you ladies have noticed yet, but we're also *outside* their security shield with no way *in*."

Arissa chewed the inside of her cheek. Lian was right. Above this short, deceptively decorative brick wall, the slight distortion extending over the house like a dome revealed a security shield that would surely block any blaster bolt. One touch against it and the thing would flash, alerting the guards in the yard to their location and likely setting off an alarm inside it too.

And there was also the matter of the four Utavian guards, each with a heavy duty, rapid-fire blast weapon swung over his shoulder, standing between them and the house.

"Sure Jolar's in there?" Kemma whispered.

Arissa threw her focus toward him, tears stinging her eyes at the familiar feel of his mind. "Yes."

He was in such mental anguish, flooded with anxiety—

"Oh gods, someone in there is going to kill him. We have to get him out!"

Lian tightened his grip on his blaster. He'd had three blasters at the house that they now carried; all meant for self-defense, and not one looked like it had ever been fired. He looked at his shadow consort, his face grave. "I'm telling you, this is crazy, Kemma."

Kemma's jaw hardened, the blaster she held at the ready giving her a particularly fierce demeanor. "Lian, you can stay here or come with us, but I'm *going* to help Arissa."

Arissa closed her eyes, sending her mind touch frantically toward Jolar and hoping to discern something—anything—that might help them save him.

A well-appointed room, a feast before him, possibly only one guard.

There were others inside the house, most with the rigid determination of the Utavian guards out here. Two others, a man sulking as if smarting under a rebuke, and a woman, proud and eager . . .

"We're not even going to be able to get inside the shield," Lian argued, jolting Arissa out of the mind touch.

Kemma gave the patrolling men a speculative look. "I have an idea."

"Where are you going?" Lian hissed when Kemma started to ease away from them.

"Just stay here and be ready to shoot," she whispered.

In the darkness Arissa could faintly follow as Kemma moved along the outer wall, the ornament's sense reverberating with a kind of manic glee.

In another moment Kemma had vanished from sight. Arissa felt Lian's concern spike.

"Arissa, look," he began. "I know you're worried about Jolar, but this is impossible. Maybe we should just call SerSec."

"And tell them what?" she demanded.

He shifted his weight as he squatted behind the wall. "I don't know . . . maybe that Jolar's comm unit cut out and he said he was in danger," Lian gave a weak shrug, "or something."

Her nostrils flared. "Even if we could offer up an outrageous enough bribe to convince SerSec to storm a private residence in *this* neighborhood, there isn't time to get them here! We need to get Jolar out *now!*"

Lian began to retort when he spied something past Arissa's shoulder that made his eyes widen. In the same instant the guards' attention slammed around. Arissa twisted about to see what they were all looking at and her mouth parted.

Oh, my gods . . .

There, in the warm glow of light from Jasa's house, her magnificent red hair cascading over her shoulders, Kemma stood as breathtakingly beautiful—and as naked—as the goddess of love herself.

"Excuse me," Kemma called sweetly, waving to the guards who stared at her. She swayed a little then giggled, twisting a finger in her hair as unselfconscious as Arrena, and artlessly aware of her own splendor. "I was at a party over there—" She pointed, then looked befuddled and pointed in another direction. "No, *there*. And, somehow," she gave a careless shrug. "I've lost all my clothes."

The guards' attention was locked onto her with such lustful intent it made Arissa's face go hot.

Kemma gave a little pout. "Does one of you have a jacket or—" she said, as if she just noticed their attire. "A cloak you could lend me? Just till I figure out where my clothes went?"

Drawn as if by Arrena's own power, one of the guards walked toward Kemma. Sensing his intention, Arissa quickly put her hand to the back of Lian's dark head and pressed down. She ducked as the man looked around to be sure Kemma was alone.

"You should not be about so," the guard scolded. "Come to the gate and I will let you in, foolish one."

"Oh, thank you I—oops!" Stumbling against the wall she collapsed into giggles. Kemma put her hand to her cheek and looked up at him fetchingly. "I'm not sure I can make it that far."

His gaze locked on her breasts as they quivered with laughter. His bronze skin was now dusky to the hairline.

He cleared his throat and swung his weapon onto his back. "Stay there. I will lift you over."

In the next instant the security shield glinted as it came down. Kemma smiled and opened her arms wide for the man to pick her up.

Arissa pushed to her feet and, using her seer's senses instead of her eyes, snapped off several blaster shots.

In the same moment Kemma clamped her arms around the guard's neck and yanked him toward her over the wall. With astonishing dexterity she freed his weapon from the strap around his body and pointed it downward to stun him, then lifted it to fire at another guard.

There was a roaring in Arissa's ears. It took her a moment to realize that all of the guards lay stunned, and the night was again silent around them.

Lian was already running toward Kemma, who—still unabashedly bare—had swung over the wall and now stood inside the courtyard, her heavy weapon trained on the house.

No alarms howled. Arissa threw her focus toward the house to find those within undisturbed. Probably the house's insulation, designed to spare those within from the noise of traffic and shuttles flying overhead, had also blocked the sound of the blaster shots.

Arissa scrambled over the wall. That still left security eyes plus the eight humans inside to be dealt with. Kemma was already heading around to the less populated rear of the house and Arissa followed.

Lian caught up with them as they reached the garden. There was a door to the inside here at the back of the house, and a half-floor above stood tall windows.

That was where Jolar was being held.

Arissa frowned. She couldn't see anyway to climb up there or to signal to him that she was here without also alerting whoever was in that room with him.

"They call seers *dangerous*," Lian hissed, shoving Kemma's clothes and boots at her. "But in actuality they're just fucking *insane*!"

"It worked, didn't it?" Kemma whispered, flashing a grin.

"How do you even know how to fight like that?" Arissa asked.

Kemma shrugged. "One of my protectors was an arms dealer and martial arts expert. He knew a lot, so now I know a lot."

"You took them all out before I could get off a shot." Lian shook his head. "Are you two personal friends of Jandar or something?" he asked. "Is the god of war patron god to seers too?"

"Just for that, I'm going to say an extra prayer to Arrena later—in your name," Kemma muttered, handing her weapon to Lian and shimmying into her clothes.

Apparently ornaments could dress as fast as they could undress; in mere heartbeats Kemma was fastening the last closure on her boot.

"Okay, we're inside the shield," Lian said. "Now what?"

"Get inside the house," Arissa murmured.

"Great plan," he grumbled. "And just how are we—?"

Arissa held her hand up to silence him, and raised her blaster. Sharply Kemma shook her head, and while Arissa caught the lightest touch against her mind, she couldn't tell what her friend wanted her to do.

The door to the house slid open, and in that moment Kemma sprung. In the next instant she had the Utavian unconscious using only her bare hands. Arissa helped Kemma drag him a few steps back, then they eased the man to the ground.

Kemma signaled to Lian for the weapon she'd taken off the guard. She adjusted the settings and, pressing the muzzle to the guard's belly, silently squeezed off a shot, keeping him from coming to any time soon.

"Okay, Kemma," Lian whispered, his lips barely moving. "You are really starting to scare me now."

Kemma gave him a wry look. "Thanks," she mouthed.

Arissa was careful to keep her footsteps soft on the wood floor as they entered the house. Keeping close to the wall, she crept up the stairs, Kemma and Lian behind her.

Arissa slowed her breathing, sending her focus down the hall. Two guards outside the door where Jolar was held. One inside with him.

Closer now, she recognized the feel of Rekan d'Barat's mind, his mood sullen and irritable. He was on the other side of the house with another, a distinctly strong-willed feminine presence who could only be Jasa. They had two guards of their own there too.

Oddly, the house held no servants.

She sought Kemma's gaze. Arissa raised up three fingers and pointed down the hall then pointed to herself. In response Kemma nodded, held up four fingers, pointed to the front of the house where Jasa, Rekan and their guards were, then indicated Lian and herself.

Kemma gave her a small smile then she grabbed Lian's hand, pulling him across the hall at just the right moment so the guards did not spot them.

Arissa struggled to keep her breath even as Kemma and Lian disappeared around a corner. Jolar's worry was spiking, frantic to escape.

She longed to reach for him, to try to send him a message of reassurance, but she didn't dare draw her focus from the guards outside his door. She closed her eyes and opened her seer senses to them, feeling where they were relative to her.

Her heart sank. They were next to each other on her side of the hall; that meant one was sheltered from her line of sight by the other. Shooting so precisely, for someone as unpracticed as she, was likely going to prove impossible.

The muffled sound of a blaster shot from the front of the house made both men startle away from the wall. Arissa's eyes snapped open. Without even focusing her vision she fired twice, managing to hit each of them in the back.

Her breath froze at the sudden violence inside the room where Jolar was captive.

No!

Running and throwing herself against the door to open it, Arissa brought her blaster up to fire.

Thirty-three

"Arissa!" Jolar gasped, quickly raising his blaster. He looked down at her from his place on the windowsill as she wrenched her own weapon aside, the chill evening breeze cooling his face. "Gods!"

He jumped down to the sitting room and pulled her against him with his free hand. He was shaking; with his blaster on this setting he'd come a heartbeat from blowing a hole right through her chest. He buried his face in the dark softness of her hair, inhaling her sweet fragrance.

"You're all right," he said hoarsely. "Thank the gods you're all right."

Her arms wrapped around his waist. "And you."

He drew back, scowling. "What the hells are you doing here?"

"I should think that's obvious," she said, her expression hurt. "I'm rescuing you." She frowned at the ruined window. "What were you doing?"

"I was escaping so I could rescue *you*." He looked past her to the unconscious Utavians in the hall. "Apparently you're better at this than I am."

He pressed a quick kiss to her forehead. He wanted so much more, but there was no time. He had to get her away from here.

"They said you were locked up at the embassy." He took her hand in his, pulling her toward the sitting room door. "How did you get here?"

"I had help," Arissa replied.

Blaster in hand, Kemma appeared in the doorway.

Jolar's weapon was instantly leveled at her.

"No!" Arissa caught his arm. "They helped me!"

"Evening, Kemma," Jolar said, lowering the blaster only slightly. "Not to sound ungrateful, but I'm having a little trouble today keeping track of who's on my side and why." He jerked his chin at her. "Are you republic or monarchy?"

"What do you mean 'monarchy'?" Arissa asked.

"That's what this is," Jolar said shortly. "A revolution to reinstate the monarchy."

Arissa's eyes widened. "But you're a Zartani lord."

"Yeah," Jolar muttered. "And a proud day it is to be a Zartani aristocrat." Jolar looked at Kemma. "So why are you here?"

Kemma hesitated and Arissa spoke quickly. "I went to Bruscan's, but he's . . . "

"They told me," Jolar said grimly.

"I didn't know where else I could go. Kemma's the only one I thought might help me."

Jolar nodded at the unconscious Utavians. "You pick this up from the Ornaments' Guild?"

"Self-defense training?" Kemma raised an eyebrow. "Are you kidding? Fleet, I could take you down armed with nothing but a caf stirrer."

"Now what?" Arissa asked Jolar as Lian joined Kemma in the doorway.

"Now we have to figure out a way to stop this," Jolar said. "Jasa said her forces had already been ordered to move. I have no idea who we can trust and who we can't."

"Her forces?" Arissa asked. "*She's* the traitor?"

Jolar's face tightened. "Oh, she and my father spent years playing me for a fool. He created this plot and handed it off to her to complete when he died."

"So where is she now?" Arissa asked.

"Uh." Lian cleared his throat. "Beautiful blonde, bad temper?"

Jolar gave a short laugh. "That's her."

Lian looked chagrined. "I think I just shot her."

"Did you kill her?"

"No!" Lian exclaimed. "She's just stunned. I'm doing a lot of that tonight," he mumbled. "Knocking women unconscious."

"What about Rekan?" Jolar asked.

"Councilor from Zartan?" Kemma asked, hefting her blaster. "I got him."

"Anyone else in the vicinity that we need to worry about this second?" Jolar asked.

Arissa and Kemma exchanged another glance.

"No," Arissa said. "We used the heaviest stun setting, so it should be a while before any of them start coming around."

"Still, we should get out of here." Jolar looked at the Utavians. "And there's only one place we're going to be safe now—the Zartani embassy."

Arissa blinked. "Jolar, I just *escaped* from the Zartani embassy!"

"I know," he said. "But whether I'm their lord or their commander or their festering prince, *everyone* there has sworn to obey me. And getting there is only chance we have to stop the Realm from tearing itself apart."

"I'm not going to help you destroy your father's life's work, Jolar," Jasa said coolly from her chair in the ambassador's office. Even with Rekan held prisoner in a basement room, with herself helpless and surrounded by guards, she sat with back straight and golden head unbowed.

The Sertarian communications net had been blacked out, and even at this hour the populous of Tano-Sertar were nervous. By Jolar's order no one was to be admitted to the embassy grounds and none could leave.

"Not to mention my own years of effort," Jasa continued. "It's time to graciously accept your place in history."

Jolar narrowed his eyes. "Like hells I will."

Jasa gave him a charming smile, tilting her head to look up at him. "You're too well-bred to harm a woman, darling, so you might as well stop looming over me. I am not intimidated."

"For fuck's sake, Jasa, do us both a favor," Jolar bit out, "and *stop* calling me that."

Jasa glanced at the guards, all Zartani. "Are you aware that half the staff in this building are on my side?"

"That's funny." Jolar folded his arms. "I was under the impression it was *my* side they were on. After all, you did this all for me, didn't you?"

In truth, Arissa sensed that a great deal more than half the Zartani here would bow to Jolar—if he allowed it. But bow or salute, he'd been right; they all obeyed him. Any who might have followed Jasa or Rekan would not disobey their ruler and take their side against him.

And those loyal to the republic certainly wouldn't either.

Jasa's nostrils flared. "Your ingratitude is unbecoming in a prince."

"And your treason is appalling," he snarled.

She sighed and gracefully folded her hands. "Jolar—"

"Don't you mean 'Your Highness'? I *am* your prince."

"Your Highness," she corrected icily. "This was years, decades, in the planning. All was done with meticulous and careful timing. It is flawless, beautiful. And it is unstoppable now."

"Oh, you've made a lot of mistakes, Jasa," Jolar said. "Not the least of which was assuming that you could use me to gain the throne for yourself."

"There is no one better suited to rule at your side than I." A confident tilt lifted Jasa's chin. "I'm like you, Jolar. We are forged of the same noble heritage. We possess the same innate understanding of our place in the order of things. It isn't an accident that you rose to the rank of commander, that you longed for a council seat. *This* is who you are." Her eyes glowed. "A leader born to rule worlds."

His lip curled. "You have no idea who I am. And no matter what happens, I can promise you'll never be princess."

"You'll need me, Jolar. Things will be chaotic for months, perhaps years. You'll need a strong, capable consort at your side. One who can forge alliances and inspire loyalty. One who—like you—was bred to rule. You need me to carry on your line. What else can you do? Make *her* your princess?" Jasa asked with a disdainful look at Arissa, who stood by the door. "And have a *nothing*, a commoner from Apovia, taint the blood of our next ruler?"

Jolar leaned back against the ambassador's desk. "If the Zartani crown lands on my head, Arissa will be princess, not you. *She* will sit beside me when I take the Zartani throne and—if I ever do allow you in her presence—I'll enjoy watching you bow to her."

Jasa's delicate skin flushed. "I'll kill that whore before I ever bend my head to her."

"You bow to her." Jolar leaned forward. "Or you tell me how to stop this!"

Her face was still tight and her eyes hateful, but Jasa gained hold of herself again. "The command to begin the reconquering of the Realm has already been sent out. Communications are blocked except to our forces."

"These are *my* forces. I can order them to stand down. Tell me how."

She gave him a smug smile. "Eventually you might halt the fighting. But not until Zartan is so battered and divided that you'll be forced to take control just to stop the bloodshed."

"This is our homeworld you're talking about!" Jolar snarled. "These are our own people!"

"Then save them!" Jasa spat. "Lead them! Serve them as their prince!"

Jolar's palm slammed on the desk. "Tell me how to stop this!"

"There's no way to stop this," Jasa hissed.

"That's not true," Arissa said softly.

Jolar head came up. "What do you mean?"

Arissa took a step forward. "There's something she *can* do, some way to call it off . . . A code she can transmit in case things go wrong."

Jasa was visibly startled.

"Can you get the code from her, Arissa?" Jolar asked.

"'Get the code'?" Jasa mocked. "Will your little whore torture me for it?"

Arissa closed her eyes and *reached* . . .

"What is she doing?" Jasa demanded.

"Reading your mind," Jolar said simply.

"Reading my—Dear gods! She's a *seer?*"

Arissa brushed past the shock rolling off Jasa and the Zartani guards. Past Jasa's heretofore-unshakable confidence in victory now being shaken, her scramble to remember everything she knew about the seers, her contempt for Jolar to—

A flash of Rekan's face as they discussed a plan for all contingencies . . .

Arissa broke away, swaying. "I need a datapad."

Swiftly Jolar handed her one. Arissa carefully wrote the code and the instructions for its use that she'd gleaned from Jasa's mind.

She offered the datapad to Jolar. "Broadcast this code and their forces will stand down."

Jolar's eye ran over the information. "I need to get to the embassy's emergency uplink."

"No!" Jasa shouted, rising. "No! Jolar, for the love of the gods, don't do this!"

"Keep her here," Jolar ordered.

The ranking ZarSec gave a nod. "Do you want a guard, Your Hi—uh, Commander?"

Jolar flinched inwardly, but his eyes were steady. "No. I'm armed, I'll be fine." He nodded at her. "Arissa, come with me."

"Won't the communication block affect this uplink too?" Arissa asked as soon as the doors closed behind them. She could still hear Jasa's shouting. Sella, the ornament whose room was next to hers in the boarding house on Xan-Tellar, had nothing on that noblewoman when it came to obscenities.

"Gods, I hope not," Jolar said. "Lieutenant de'Rec said that the embassy's uplink is on a separate frequency. Besides, I can't imagine Jasa and Rekan not having a way to communicate with Zartan. I think that's actually why they stayed after the summit. They needed a safe place off-world where they could monitor everything."

"Why wouldn't they do all this from Zartan?" Arissa hurried to keep up as he strode down the hall. "Wouldn't that make more sense?"

"Not when Sertar would fall so easily. From what Jasa told me Cenon was to be crowned tonight. Then she would provide a military force to accompany my transport and escort ships to Zartan. With the influence Danlen gathered and the alliances they forged here I don't doubt that Sertar would have awoken tomorrow to a new crowned princess." He opened the stairwell door for her. "And probably the Sertarians would have shrugged and gotten busy selling souvenir caf mugs with Princess Cenon's face on them."

Arissa frowned as they flew down the stairs. Before she'd come to Sertar she could have argued, pointed out the Articles of the Republic and declared that these people would be up in arms against the loss of their autonomy.

But not now. Sertar ran on putting credits in the right pocket, and most of the population wouldn't give a damn who was in charge as long as business went on and money flowed.

Jolar nodded to two of the ZarSec guards. Admiration glowed in their eyes at the sight of their prince.

"What about the Zartani?" Arissa asked.

She glanced up at Jolar's sudden flash of pain. "I'm not sure Jasa's wrong about how easily my homeworld would accept a return to the monarchy," he said tightly. "Two hundred years ago the Zartani lords struck a deal with the New Order to keep their titles and most of their wealth in return for accepting the council's rule. They relinquished the prince's crown but they never stopped thinking of themselves as—as—"

"Noble?" she supplied. "Aristocrats? Gently born?"

His mouth was a thin line. "Something like that."

"You know, I just took a quick tour of one of those 'noble' minds. Jasa barely considered you to be above breeding stock." Arissa narrowed her eyes. "You have lousy taste in women."

"My *father* chose Jasa." He gave her a quick wolfish grin as he opened the door. "*I* have excellent taste in women."

Located in the lowest level of the building and equipped with blast doors of tarasteel, this was clearly a hold-out shelter in case of assault on the Zartani embassy. There were weapons, water, food and the emergency uplink equipment in this reinforced room.

Jolar sent the two guards stationed there outside and shut the tarasteel doors himself.

"We're safe in here," he said with satisfaction. "A concussion cannon couldn't blast this thing open."

"I hope the uplink is all right," Arissa said, moving to stand in front of it. "The equipment looks untouched."

There was a pulse from him and she turned to find that he was standing with his back to the door, his gaze inward.

"Safe," he murmured. "Absolutely safe."

"Jolar? Are you all right?"

"Gods." He shook his head a little, bemused. "I'm Prince Jolar of Zartan now."

Arissa frowned.

His blue eyes were almost aglow, his hair a rich gold in this light. "Jasa and my father spent years, decades, to make this happen. They bribed who knows how many, promised gods know what. They committed murder and treason, but

Jasa is right. They accomplished their goal. The lords on Zartan have thrown their support behind me, the men outside these doors—There's a whole military force waiting to follow me." He swallowed. "All I have to do is wait a few hours and it will be done, Arissa. They'll crown me and you'll be safe."

Her eyes widened. "You're really thinking about going along with this . . ."

"My word will be law on Zartan." His jaw worked for a moment. "I have the Zartani crown, the wealth and power—the support—of my homeworld behind me. I know the military. I have the right bloodline. That's why it had to be me, because I can claim the Tellaran throne and rule it all as king."

Her breath stopped. "The Tellaran throne?"

"Arissa, don't you understand?" He crossed the room to clasp her hands, his skin fevered. "I can abolish the anti-seer laws! In just a few hours I can do it on Zartan. We can marry tonight and you'll be Zartani princess with a whole *world* sworn to defend you. It wouldn't matter if our children were telepathic—gods, it would be *better* if they were! We can have as many telepathic children as the palace will hold. You'll be able to live openly, forever. I can give you everything you deserve. All I have to do is let this happen."

"You'd be an accomplice to Dacel's death and countless others! Going along with this would be sanctioning your friend's murder. Think of the people who are going to die when Jasa's people take control!"

"People are going to die anyway," he said hoarsely. "This code will leave them defenseless. The people who vowed to follow me—when I send this I'm going to betray them, some of them to their deaths. The seers were the backbone of the monarchy. There's no reason they couldn't be again. Together no one could stand against us."

"You'd be a traitor!"

His blue eyes were wild. "You'll never have to be afraid of discovery again. I can keep you safe—*really* safe now, sweet."

"At the cost of everything you are! At the cost of your integrity—of everything you believe. This will bring another civil war to the Tellaran Realm. Think of the lives that this will cost—the suffering! These people didn't enact the anti-seer laws, those were made hundreds of years ago. What they did to people like me was wrong but, Jolar, this is wrong too."

"You're worth it." He leaned his forehead against hers. "You're worth all that and more to me."

She cupped his face. "I know."

"I love you—I will do this for you. I will never regret it."

"I love you too, Jolar." Tears overflowed then and she didn't try to check them. "And I can't let you destroy everything you are for me. Send the code."

His blue eyes were agonized. "The new ID they promised you—there'll always be a risk that you could be caught."

She swallowed. "We'll think of something."

"Are you sure, sweet?"

"Yes." She gave a teary smile. "All that matters is that we'll be together."

He closed his eyes briefly. "The Realm doesn't deserve you," he said roughly, turning to the uplink. "But then again, neither do I."

Thirty-four

"Sweet?"

Arissa blinked awake. It was a testament to how tired she was that she hadn't even felt Jolar come into their quarters. The code transmission had been only the beginning to the Tellaran council's efforts to re-establish control last night, and there were skirmishes reported as far away as Xeltan. Even hours before sunrise, Jolar was still communicating with the council. They insisted on hearing everything he knew in an effort to glean enough information to keep the Realm from falling apart.

Arissa was swaying on her feet by that time and the council insisted on conferring with him alone. Jolar sent her to the quarters Rekan had prepared for her and she fell across the bed, asleep in minutes, still fully dressed.

Jolar's face was drawn with exhaustion, his fingers gentle on the skin of her cheek.

It was mid-morning now. She sat up, pushing her hair away from her face. "What's happened?"

"The Tellaran council is declaring victory, saying the coup was a failure from the beginning," he said. "That's what the media is reporting too, but really things are a fucking mess. Half the communication grids are out. Two other council members have been implicated, there are arrests everywhere. The financial markets are badly destabilized."

Arissa looked out the balcony doors. "Things seem quiet here."

"Probably because everybody on Sertar's holed up with a pile of cash and a blaster in hand. We've been recalled to Xan-Tellar, effective immediately. They want to debrief you in person as well. Don't worry," he said, accurately reading her expression. "The ID is yours. They gave me their promise."

"When do we leave?"

"We've got a little over an hour. The fleet ships may still be compromised so they've arranged a private cruiser to take us back to Tellar. Along with some of the other personnel."

"You mean Jasa and Rekan."

"No, I'm having Jasa and Rekan moved to the FleetSec base for the time being. Just in case one of their allies pops up to attempt a rescue I want those two behind tarasteel walls and armed FleetSec guards until they can be brought back on a fleet cruiser."

Arissa looked around the room. Her luggage was sitting in a corner of the bedroom. "Do I have time to shower and change?"

"And for a quick breakfast, but then we have to leave."

She hesitated, wanting to tell him about Kemma—but it wasn't her secret to tell. "Are Kemma and Lian still here? I'd like to say goodbye."

"I didn't want to send them out with things so uncertain. I got them rooms on the other side of the embassy. Why don't you get ready first? I'll make sure they know you're stopping by."

Arissa frowned again. He really looked bad off. "Are you all right?"

"Just a headache. I haven't been put through this much since Basic." Jolar passed his hand over his eyes. "I'll be fine after a shower and some caf."

A half hour later, Arissa knocked on the door to Kemma and Lian's quarters. Jolar had reminded her before she left that she only had a few minutes before the shuttle would take them to the spaceport.

Kemma opened the door. The ornament looked tired too and was dressed again in the black shirt and trousers she'd worn last night, but a smile lit her face. "Arissa, come in."

Their quarters were comfortably done with kitchenette and living room and large windows to brighten the space. The door to the bedroom was closed.

"Lian's still asleep," Kemma said in response to Arissa's glance. "And anyway, I'm glad that we have a chance to talk alone."

Arissa gave a short, embarrassed laugh. "I don't know where to start, and we have so little time!"

Kemma gave her an understanding smile. "There's so much I want to ask you."

"Me too."

"You first then."

"Okay." Arissa considered; there was so much. "Did you always know?"

Kemma shrugged. "My mother figured it out. I was pretty young when she did."

"I couldn't go to school," Arissa blurted. "Could you?"

Kemma looked stricken. "Yes, but not 'til I was old enough to know how to hide it. 'Til then my mother undertook my education, but I was under strict orders not to tell *anyone*."

Arissa frowned. "But what about the school physical? The medical exam?"

"Well," Kemma said with a shrug, "there are certain doctors who can be paid to say whatever you want them to."

"You had your exam done on Sertar," Arissa said, understanding.

"Cost my parents a fortune, too. 'Course in my career I've more than made up for it."

"Don't you worry it'll show if you get injured? What if they do another telepath screen?"

"Pellar syndrome."

"What?"

"My medical records state that I have Pellar syndrome. According to my records I can't have that scan again without risking a life-threatening reaction, so no one ever does it."

"My mother should have thought of that," Arissa said, frowning. "She was head of the medical arts program."

"Well, you would have had to have the exam to show that you were a non-telepath, and then a reaction to reveal Pellar syndrome. Or a faked one anyway." Kemma gave a rueful smile. "The Sertarian doctor came up with the idea. Doubled the price, but it was well worth it."

"If you—"

"Slipped through then maybe others did too?" Kemma finished for her.

They both smiled, but Kemma shook her head. "Not that I know of, Arissa. It's possible, but that doctor was paid to keep secrets. He sure never revealed mine."

"So there might be others?" Arissa asked. Though why she should feel hopeful she didn't know.

Kemma hesitated. "I wanted to talk to you about that."

"Not to tell anyone, you mean," Arissa said. "I won't. Not even Jolar, not unless I'm absolutely certain it's safe. But Lian—?"

A smile lit Kemma's face, her green eyes shone. "I slipped and he caught on, but he's always loved me just the same. More, maybe." She tilted her head. "And Jolar knows about you."

"He's the one that encouraged me to use it. I was so afraid I would hurt him." Arissa searched Kemma's face. "Are you? Are you afraid you'll hurt Lian?"

"Sometimes," Kemma said quietly. "I don't know what's true. What to believe." She brightened. "You know, finding you is like discovering I have a sister."

"For me too." She hesitated. "I know you and Lian live on his homeworld—"

"Oh, no," Kemma said. "Don't even think about us losing touch. We are absolutely going to arrange to see each other again. We have a lot to talk about."

Arissa smiled in relief. "Okay. Only . . . we should wait till I have my new ID. I don't want anyone to get curious about you. I want to make sure it's safe for you to know me."

"What about Jolar?"

Arissa's face went hot, and Kemma's eyebrows rose.

"I meant to ask if you are worried about Jolar. But looks like there's more news about you and Jolar?"

"Before . . . I mean, he couldn't ask me to marry him, but . . ."

"That's wonderful," Kemma said warmly. "I love weddings!" Suddenly her face flushed. "I mean, I know I'm an ornament so maybe you don't—"

Arissa blinked. "Are you kidding? I don't mind about that! Kemma, you're my *friend*."

Kemma smiled. "Good. You're mine too." Kemma tilted her head. "Did you mean what you said, that you had thought about being a courtesan?"

"Yes. Did you mean it when you said I'd be good at it?"

Kemma laughed. "Yes, but don't tell Jolar I said so. I don't think he would appreciate it as much as you do."

"We're being recalled to Tellar. They want to question us in person."

"And Lian wants to return to Lema as soon as possible. Sounds like things are going to be scary for a while and he doesn't want us here in case things take a turn for the worse."

"A lot of people are probably going to feel that way."

Kemma sighed. "I know. The fleet has grounded most commercial ships from leaving the system. There's a few private cruisers making a run that way, but for the prices they're asking we could *buy* a cruiser."

"Do you want to stay here at the Zartani embassy until you can arrange to go back to Lema? I can talk to Jolar."

Kemma glanced back at the bedroom door. "Lian was up most of the night trying to get us off-world." She considered. "I don't want to wake him. Yes, ask Jolar if we can stay for a few days."

"I have to go," Arissa said reluctantly.

Kemma hugged her. "I'm going to miss you."

Arissa smiled and hugged back. "Me too."

Jolar looked somewhat better than he had before, but there were still dark shadows beneath his eyes, and his cheeks seemed a little sunken. Almost as if all this were draining him from inside.

He caught her gaze on him, and his brow furrowed.

"You okay?" Jolar asked, his hand on hers. Their shuttle, a larger vehicle piloted by one of the ZarSecs that accompanied them, was circling to land at Tano-Sertar's spaceport.

"I'm okay," she said. "It was hard saying goodbye to Kemma."

"You'll see her again."

The port was surrounded by traffic jams. Shuttles, plainly not permitted to land, circled above. Even from here she could feel the anger and fear of the crowds.

"It looks pretty bad out there."

"FleetSec is supporting SerSec to keep things under control," he said. "There's a lot of panic, a lot of fear that the government isn't telling them how bad things really are."

"But they aren't," Arissa murmured.

"No," Jolar agreed grimly. "And if people knew how bad things really are, not even FleetSec could keep things under control."

Guards from the Zartani embassy escorted them into the spaceport. A plexisteel barrier separated the main port from the boarding areas, now it served to hold the crowd back.

A line of uniformed, armed personnel stood on this side of the shield barrier. Arissa couldn't hear the crowd through the barrier but she could see them, could feel their fear, anger, and worry. Small children clung to exhausted parents, and the terminal was full. Many simply sat, surrounded by their belongings, on the floor. Some argued with the uniformed guards, and Arissa swallowed at the tension in that peace force. It wouldn't take much to nudge the frightened civilians into an open and violent conflict with the security officers.

This side of the barrier was not nearly as crowded. A small number of private transports were being allowed to leave, and every seat was claimed. The crowd in here was far more hopeful than those behind the barrier, but even here armed peace officers were walking through the crowd with their rifles at the ready.

The crowd's emotions were howling through her mind. Shaken, Arissa forced her focus to just Jolar and edged closer to him.

The arrival of more peace officers in the form of Jolar's ZarSec guard detail was not a welcome addition. A pair of SerSec confronted Jolar's guards almost immediately to insist they depart. Jolar was reluctant to let them go until they boarded the shuttle, but the SerSec made a very valid point that the Zartani were not part of the coordinated security effort and were acting as private guards. With the SerSec insisting that the Zartani leave and tempers already running hot, Jolar reluctantly sent them back to the embassy.

"It looks like there's more than enough security here," Arissa offered.

Jolar rubbed at his temple. "I'll feel better once we're on the shuttle. Come on, let's see what the holdup is."

The spaceport gate attendant gave him a regretful look. "I'm afraid there's a delay. No one is being permitted to board that shuttle."

"How long of a delay?" Jolar demanded.

She was tired and clearly under strain, but her voice was polite. "I haven't been told."

"Why has the shuttle been delayed?" Jolar fairly growled. "Is there a problem with the cruiser?"

"I'm sorry. I don't know."

"Is there anything you *can* tell me?" Jolar snapped.

"Sir," the woman said, cracks showing in her calm façade. "FleetSec is coordinating all the transports on and off Sertar now." She nodded over at a knot of officers on this side of the barrier. "Maybe *they* can tell you."

"Fine," Jolar muttered. "I'll ask one of them."

Arissa followed as Jolar took a few steps away from the woman's desk, searching the crowd for the ranking FleetSec.

A fleet officer in a crisp rust uniform was making his way toward them.

"Jolar," the officer called, his hand raised in greeting.

"Tasan!" Jolar smiled, his sense rippling with surprise and warm familiarity as the dark-eyed man with the wavy dark hair drew closer. "What are you doing here?"

Arissa's stomach clenched as the FleetSecs in the area swung their determined focus to her. Then they were shifting, spreading out . . .

What are they—?

"Jolar," she cried, touching his shoulder.

Jolar's glance took in the FleetSecs' change in position.

"Tasan, what are you doing here?" Jolar asked sharply.

"Jolar, I need you to step aside." Tasan's face was grim. "We're taking the seer into custody."

Thirty-five

Jolar stepped in front of Arissa, blaster instantly in hand.

"What the hells are you talking about?" he demanded.

Urged back by the FleetSecs, the crowd around them turned startled, frightened eyes to her. The spaceport attendant hurried away, and all the civilians around them fled the confrontation as well. SerSecs were moving people farther back, clearing this section of the spaceport terminal. FleetSec personnel quickly formed a perimeter around them a good dozen paces back, their rifles at the ready.

"You aren't taking her anywhere," Jolar warned Tasan.

He backed her up so that the spaceport attendant's desk was behind her.

The fleet personnel fanned out around them. They started to move in, and Tasan held up a hand to halt them.

Weapon still holstered, Tasan took a few steps forward. "I'm under direct orders from Admiral Henlon to take this woman into custody."

"Henlon?" Jolar exclaimed. "The council has ordered her, ordered *both* of us, back to Tellar. She's under the council's protection. Last time I checked, even Admiral Henlon reports to them."

"I spoke to the admiral less than an hour ago," Tasan said. "It was the Tellaran council that ordered her arrest. They've determined that she poses a clear danger to the population."

"They did *what?*" Jolar snarled. "Those lying godsdamned—! Arissa isn't a danger to anyone! A few hours ago she saved the whole Realm from destroying itself. She saved every one of those councilors' miserable fucking lives!"

"I know you're upset—"

"As I recall, my tutoring got you a passing grade in armed negotiations class, Tasan," Jolar snapped. "I would appreciate it if you didn't try that 'empathize with the gunman' crap on me."

"All right then." Tasan straightened. "You're a commander in the Tellaran fleet and so am I. It's not my place to decide which orders to follow. And it's not yours either. You are hereby *ordered* by Admiral Henlon to hand her over to our custody immediately. Step aside, Jolar."

"I don't care what the orders are," Jolar spat. "You aren't taking her. Dacel promised her—"

"Dacel is dead, Jolar. The Tellaran council has ordered her arrest."

Tasan glanced at Arissa and she shrank back under the waves of revulsion.

"When I heard—What was Dacel thinking to put you in this kind of danger? Honestly I can't believe you even went along with this."

"Tell your officers to stand down, Tasan. I'm not going to let you take her!"

"I can't believe this is you talking." Tasan shook his head. "How long have we known each other?" He held his hands out, palms up. "Jolar, I'm your friend. You're not thinking clearly."

"That's why Henlon sent you, isn't it?" Jolar asked bitterly. "He sent a friend so I'd trust you, so you could talk sense into me."

"I wanted to come. I want to help you. The admiral sent me because he hopes—*I* hope—you'll listen to me. You're ill, Jolar."

Jolar shook his head. "There's nothing wrong with me, Tasan."

"You look like hell."

"I'm fine."

"Having headaches?"

Jolar didn't answer. His jaw twitched.

"Jolar," Tasan said, taking a half step closer. "I give my word as your friend that she won't be hurt. Our orders are to take her into custody and return her to Tellar *unharmed*. I'm to turn her over to the authorities there."

"So *they* can execute her? So they can figure out some way to make her a scapegoat for all this? No!"

"She's a seer. She's hurting you; she probably has been for weeks."

"That's ridiculous," Jolar snapped. "And you need to tell your people to get back right now. I'll open fire if I have to."

"Look at what the hells you're doing!" Tasan burst out. "I've been your friend for *eleven* years and you're pointing a blaster at me! You devoted your life to serving the Realm and now you're disobeying a direct order, threatening to open fire on fellow fleet personnel. Does that seem like you, Jolar? Does that sound like something you would do?"

Arissa's throat closed when Jolar didn't answer, when she felt him wavering. "Jolar?"

"I'm fine," Jolar said, but there was the slightest hesitation in his voice.

"Jolar, I don't want to give them the order to stun you. I don't want to arrest you too, but I will unless you stand aside!"

"I can't!"

"She's a *seer*. You know what her kind is capable of!" Tasan said urgently. "Tell me—do you hear her inside your head?"

"Jolar?" she asked tremulously when he didn't answer.

"I can see it in your face, Jolar," Tasan said. "Be honest with me, with yourself. Do you hear her?"

"Yes," Jolar said hoarsely. "But it's not—"

Arissa's eyes widened in horror. *Gods, why didn't he tell me?*

"We need to get you away from her *now*." Tasan stepped forward, his hands outstretched. "You know I wouldn't lie to you. If you ever believed me to be your friend, step aside!"

Her mouth parted as she felt Jolar hesitate, the questions in his mind . . .

"Think, Jolar," Tasan insisted. "Really *think* about things you've done since you've been with her. Doesn't it all seem out of character for you? Isn't it possible that I *could* be telling you the truth? Damn it! Don't you understand? Manipulating you is what she's done all along!"

Jolar glanced back at her, his face white and tense.

"It's not true!" She shook her head, her heart felt like it was being torn from her chest. "Jolar, I love you! I would never try to hurt you!"

"What are you going to do?" Tasan demanded. "Kill one of your best friends? Open fire on fellow officers? I don't want to order them to take you down, but I will. If you don't step aside right now, you're going to be facing charges. You're throwing your career—maybe your life—away here!"

Jolar twisted his head away from her.

Tears stung her eyes. "Jolar?"

"Put down the blaster and let me *help* you!" Tasan urged.

"Jolar, please!" Arissa could feel his mind's turmoil, his indecision, how his body trembled. "Don't do this! Gods, *please!*"

Suddenly Jolar's voice rung in her mind as clearly as if he had spoken—

He's right. Tasan's right.

Then Jolar stepped aside and let them take her.

Thirty-six

Arissa's arms ached. She was bound, hand and foot, by tarasteel restraints at all times, and they were heavy.

She had been imprisoned for two days in the Tano-Sertar fleet base brig now. She was kept isolated and had not even seen another prisoner in her time here. Her cell was monitored by two guards who watched her constantly; she was not even allowed to use the 'fresher in privacy. Her physical exam had been done under guard. To bring her meals they opened the door and turned her to the wall with a blaster rifle to her head while a third guard brought her tray. She wasn't allowed to turn around again until they had all cleared her cell and the plexisteel door was closed and sealed again.

She wondered if Jasa and Rekan were there somewhere too. She doubted that they were restrained even when they slept like she was.

Considered too dangerous to be moved by commercial or private cruiser, she was to be taken to Tellar on a fleet troop carrier in a few hours.

According to her very, very nervous advocate.

She wondered why they gave her an advocate at all. Probably someone on the council—or someone responsible for their public image—thought they should at least appear to be providing her with the rights guaranteed to republic citizens, despite the fact that she was not one.

"Of course," the advocate said, not meeting her eyes. "With the telepath screen completed and the results so plain there's really no way to refute the evidence."

Pudgy and wearing an ill-fitting and painfully unflattering beige suit, he sat on the opposite side of the long table. He wouldn't even come close enough to shake her hand when he'd come in.

"What will happen to me once I get to Tellar?"

He flinched every time she spoke to him. The guards in the room—four of them at present, all with blaster rifles at the ready and armed with stun pikes as well—were almost as bad. They treated her as though she were a pulse cannon rigged to explode.

They swapped the guards out often too. She hadn't yet seen any one of them more than once; clearly they were trying to limit exposure to her so no others could be injured as Jolar had. A few of the guards who came and went regarded her with lustful thoughts, though with her hands restrained and the fleet brig coveralls she wore, how they could do so was beyond her.

There was one aspect of all the practice she and Jolar had done for which she was deeply grateful. She could now pull her awareness back—far back into herself—'til she couldn't feel the FleetSecs around her at all.

"Well." Her advocate cleared his throat. He'd done a lot of that since they'd shown him in. "Well, I imagine that they will question you."

"In other words, you have no idea."

He started. His small eyes and shaking jowls made him look like a frightened snouse. "I—I—"

"I didn't read your mind," Arissa said tiredly. "It's obvious that you don't know."

She lifted both hands—bound together as they were—to push her hair away from her face. How they thought she could make use of a hair tie to affect an escape she didn't know, but they refused to give her one.

"Will you be representing me?"

He reared back. "My practice is restricted to Sertar."

"So, no."

He blinked his snouse eyes at her.

"Will I have an advocate when I get to Tellar?"

"I really—I really could not say."

"Is there anything you *can* tell me? Other than they have all the evidence they need to execute me and I'm being transported to Tellar soon?"

"Well, uh . . ." He shifted in his chair and lifted his datapad. "I can review the laws and precedence that are relevant to your case—"

"You mean the Anti-Seer laws that make me a criminal and the cases that set the precedence for my coming execution?" Arissa asked. "No, thank you."

The door to the room in which they were meeting unsealed. Commander Tasan Rutell came in.

"That's fifteen minutes," he said shortly.

The advocate's relief was palpable. "Well, we have actually reached the limits of the legal assistance I can offer Mistress Kassar." He stood quickly his datapad in hand. "If I can be of assistance in the future, Commander Rutell, please contact me."

For the next seer they take into custody? How many seers did he expect to offer his non-existent legal help to?

In all this she could at least hope Kemma was still safe. She was so desperately glad that she had never shared Kemma's secret with Jolar.

Her eyes stung.

Jolar. . .

The FleetSecs had seized her as soon as he stepped aside at the terminal. They cuffed her as she begged him not to let them take her. She sobbed his name as they dragged her out.

Jolar never even looked at her.

"Godsdamn, you put on a good show, Seer." Tasan folded his arms. "Pretty little thing, so fragile looking. You'd probably get to me too if I hadn't seen for myself how badly you fucked Jolar up."

Her head came up. "What do you mean?"

Tasan's lip curled. "As if you didn't know what you did. He's a mess. Headaches, confusion, dizziness, nausea. He's still at the medcenter. He can barely keep it together to hold a five minute conversation."

"Commander Rutell, please—" Tears blurred her vision. "Please, is Jolar going to be all right? What—what do the doctors—"

"Save it." Tasan nodded to the two guards by the door. "Get her back to her cell."

She sat in her cell with her hand over her mouth as she cried. One of the guards, moved by her tears had offered her something to blow her nose. Tasan had relieved him of duty immediately and replaced him with another. The new guards ignored her tears completely.

Arissa now wiped her face with her sleeve.

I shouldn't have let him talk me into it. I knew it was dangerous.

How badly was he hurt?

Jolar, I'm so, so sorry.

Commander Rutell wouldn't tell her any more about him. He made a practice of ignoring her questions.

Maybe if I hurt Jolar it's better this way. Maybe I was hurting him all along even though I didn't mean to.

Maybe he never really loved me at all . . .

They loaded her into an armored shuttle a few hours later. It had taken twenty minutes for them to determine that either she needed to be carried to the shuttle or the restraints on her ankles would have to be taken off. In the end, they decided that she should walk and have her ankles cuffed for the shuttle ride, but the guards were increased and now numbered a half-dozen armed FleetSecs.

She drew into herself as much as possible. Their hate and fear literally made her sick to her stomach. She didn't even look at them if she could avoid it.

The shuttle landed. After a moment the door opened and the guards piled out. Two kept blasters on her while another handed off his weapon and got back inside to remove her ankle restraints. Under strict orders not to touch her, he retreated with the cuffs in hand.

Commander Rutell came to the door. "On your feet."

Awkward with her still-restrained hands, Arissa stood.

Tasan took a step back. "Out of the shuttle."

She dragged herself forward and, holding onto the side of the shuttle doorway, managed to get down onto the spaceport runway. There was a very large boxy transport already there.

That's why they're using a troop carrier—because it can go from planetside to space and back again. If they used a shuttle to get me up to a larger ship, that would be three transfers instead of one.

The six guards fanned out around them, their weapons constantly trained on her as they moved toward the transport.

Once inside, Tasan stopped to press the onboard comm. "This is Commander Rutell. Power up, we're going to secure the prisoner and then you can lift off." Tasan nodded to the guards. "Let's go."

Tasan led the way to the onboard brig. It seemed a small ship to have a brig, but maybe they used this to transport fleet prisoners too.

Tasan nodded at the cell. "Inside. Sit on the cot."

Arissa sat as she was directed.

"Get the cuffs back on her."

"Please, do I have to be restrained all the time?" Arissa cried. "It hurts!"

The guard kneeling to put on the ankle cuffs hesitated. He and the other guards sought Tasan's gaze.

A muscle in his jaw twitched. "I'm not interested in your comfort. Get the damned cuffs on her *now*."

The guard kneeling at her feet winced and placed the cuffs around her ankles. They instantly resealed again to fit her.

"Secure the door. Then I'm rotating the four of you out," Tasan muttered as he strode from the cell. "Apparently she's getting to you too."

This cell was smaller than the one on the base had been. The room was no more than a few paces across. Outfitted with sink and 'fresher and a plexisteel wall and door as well as cameras, she would be watched constantly.

The *Queen's Light* had made the journey from Tellar to Sertar in five days. Likely she had even less than that for the return.

She closed her eyes. She didn't even know if she could look forward to a trial. They certainly didn't have to bother with one.

She wasn't sure how long she'd sat there before she felt the engine hum under her feet. Apparently the *Queen's Light*, as a commercial cruiser, had been far better insulated against the movement vibrations than a troop transport.

She swallowed as she felt the ship lift off. Somehow it seemed as final as the first clump of dirt hitting a casket.

From the corner of her eye she saw new FleetSec guards outside the plexisteel wall. After a moment the door unsealed and one of them came into her cell, his rifle blaster in hand.

The FleetSec slung his blaster over his shoulder then knelt in front of her to reach for her ankle bindings.

She frowned. "Did Commander Rutell say the restraints could come off now?"

The guard tilted his head up to look at her from under his tan FleetSec cap.

"Jolar," she breathed.

Thirty-seven

Jolar grinned and caught her chin to press a hot kiss to her mouth.

"How—" She was too stunned to do more than blink at him, her mouth still tingled from his kiss. "What are you doing here?"

"Well, my last rescue attempt was less than impressive, so I thought I'd give it another go. How am I doing so far?"

Behind the plexisteel wall of the cell there were no other guards. She'd seen just Jolar and since there were always at least two, assumed another one was there as well.

She held up her wrists, where the restraints still bound her. "*You* let them take me! You stood aside and let them take me! You *agreed* with Tasan! I heard you!" Her voice broke. "You—you thought, 'Tasan's right'."

He blinked, his face alight with wonder. "You heard—?"

Something in her face clearly told him this was not the time for that.

"I'm sorry, sweet." His blue eyes were serious now. "But he *was* right. There were FleetSecs all around us and no way I could get you out of there. Getting myself stunned and thrown into a cell wasn't going to do you any good. I didn't have any choice. I had to give you to them to keep you safe."

"Safe?" she cried. "And what if they'd just put a blaster bolt in my head instead?"

"You know, it's a shame you won't get to know Tasan," Jolar said, directing his attention to the bindings around her wrists. "I really have known him forever, and he's a good man. When he came to visit me I could tell he was starting to question your arrest. Given time I know he would have come around. But what I've always liked best about Tasan," Jolar added as the last restraint came free, "is that he's even worse at bluffing at tongo than I am."

Arissa winced in relief as the bindings came off but it hurt too. Without them her arms felt too light and her shoulders ached.

He took her hands in his. "I knew Tasan was telling me the truth about getting you to Tellar unharmed. I know him well enough to know that *whatever* happened he was going to follow orders and make sure you got safely transported to the capital." He gently massaged her wrists where the bindings had been. "That doesn't mean I haven't been half-crazed with worry about you."

"He said you were ill." She pulled her hands away. "That I'd—I'd *hurt* you."

"I was ordered to return to Tellar, remember? Faking sick was the only way I could stay planetside."

She tucked her hair behind her ears. "You had headaches."

"Arissa, I have a head. Sometimes it aches," he said reasonably. "I didn't have any more headaches with you than before we met." He traced the curve of her cheek. "On my soul, I only told them what they wanted to hear so I could stay near you."

"You said you could hear me inside your head." Her lip trembled. "I-is that true?"

"Yes," he said gently. "I was going to tell you eventually. You were just so skittish and I didn't want to frighten you. I knew I was fine." His smile was tender. "I really like having you in my head, sweet."

Arissa stretched her arms, leaning away from him. He couldn't be telling the truth, no matter what her senses were telling her. He'd just put her through the worst days of her whole life.

She reached out, surprised to find that she couldn't detect anyone else on board. "Where—what about the other fleet personnel"

"Nobody here but us fugitives."

"But *how?*"

"We just left Sertar, remember?" He helped her to her feet. "Most corrupt planet in the Realm and there's nothing that can't be bought." He glanced down at himself. "Including a FleetSec lieutenant's uniform and security card."

"What about the other FleetSecs?"

He shrugged. "Tasan was ordered to return to the base about five minutes before we lifted off. The last bunch of FleetSecs got off the ship and none of the others ever made it on. Some found the doors to their base quarters wouldn't open this morning and their uplinks out, some got on what they thought was the right transport and it wasn't. Some got so drunk last night they missed their shift, some got stranded when their escort shuttle's engine blew out."

"You did all that?"

He laughed. "No, that's a lot for even me, and they were watching me. Or at least they thought they were. A good slicer can play havoc with surveillance records. It looks like I'm still in quarters in Tano-Sertar. Bruscan says hello, by the way."

Arissa blinked. "Bruscan's alive?"

"Wily as a river snake, twice as tough, and smart enough to have an escape tunnel out of his state-of-the-art security palace," Jolar said wryly. "Once he realized he was the only one left alive he slipped out and disappeared to one of his nearby bolt-holes. Lucky for me, he tracked me down at fleet medical. He sliced in with a security signal, got me transferred to civilian quarters, and we started on a plan to rescue you."

"Bruscan did all this?" she asked. "For me?"

"Now, don't go all gooey with gratitude to him," Jolar warned. "Bruscan was very, very well paid."

"You paid him?"

"And how."

She searched his face. "Why? Why are you doing this?"

His arms went around her waist and he touched his forehead to hers. "Because—just in case my thoughts and feelings aren't shouting it to you, my beautiful seer—I'm madly, wildly in love with you and nothing is going to keep me away from you. Not the law, not the fleet, not the whole festering Realm."

"Oh," she breathed. His love was undeniable—white hot, more unbreakable than tarasteel and the waves of it surrounded her, filling her with its warmth. "I love you, too."

He pressed a quick kiss to her mouth. "Come on—before you utterly distract me. I need to get back to the bridge."

He took her hand and led her through the empty ship. The bridge was small, with four duty stations. They had already left Sertar's orbit. Jolar settled into the pilot's chair and she stood beside him.

Her brow creased. What he'd done was more than extraordinarily dangerous—it was treason. "So what now?"

"Well, first I'm going to set the autopilot to take us toward the outpost at Rusco."

"Where Doctor de'Sar wanted to study me? There's not even a colony there."

"No matter, we won't be stopping there," he continued with a smile as his hands went over the instruments. "We are heading out to a place past the Rusco outpost."

"There's nothing past the Rusco outpost," she argued.

"That's what we thought," Jolar agreed. "But a deep space probe found something interesting a few months back. Turns out some of unsettled, uncharted space *isn't*. Light-years past the Rusco outpost there's a whole civilization. They're primitive, warlike and have limited interplanetary travel. In fact they don't have near the level of technology we do. They call themselves 'Az-kye'."

Arissa stared. "You want to go *there*? You're kidding."

"Do you want to stay in Realm space?" he asked seriously. "I believe in the ideals of the republic but I can't back the council again, not after they lied to me, not after they broke about a dozen laws themselves. They were willing to throw you to the fire even after you saved their worthless skins, and I'll follow their orders again when hells freeze over. But there's still plenty ready to raise a flag for the monarchy. You'll make a beautiful princess. Say the word and I'll change course to take us to Zartan."

"Would they still follow you?"

"You don't know the Zartani. Even Jasa would still follow me as her prince. Even Rekan would—after I was good and crowned. 'Course I wouldn't trust him near me with so much as a cheese knife till then. Actually considering the way it turned out I'm really sorry I didn't grab the fucking crown when I had the chance."

"No, you aren't," she said softly.

If they went to Zartan they would be plunging a whole world into conflict. He would do it, but he would be doing it for her.

Jolar was willing to give up a home he loved, a heritage he had been raised to revere, for her. Surely she could do this for him?

"How do you know we'll even be welcomed by these Az-kye?"

He gently pulled her into his lap. "Well, I don't," he said, cradling her in his arms. "But they aren't Tellaran so we won't be hunted as traitors or forced to the throne there." He looked around their heavily shielded and armed boxy transport. "And they might be very appreciative of some far more advanced Tellaran technology. Besides, from what the probe already gleaned about their religion they have a particular fondness for those with, shall we say . . ." He touched her temple. "Magical powers?"

"Oh, you *are* kidding," she managed.

He shrugged. "Maybe they play tongo."

She chewed her lip for a moment. "Can we make it in this ship?"

"We'll make it," he said confidently. "With only two of us on a ship built for thirty, there's enough food and power to get us there. There and back, actually." He looked at her coveralls. "The fashion selection might be a bit limited, though. Hey, that reminds me," he said, reaching into a pocket. "I paid a little extra in 'consideration' and got this back for you."

The Zartani firestar jewel caught the light as he held it out to her.

But as soon she reached for it he snatched the betrothal bracelet back.

"Hold on," he said. "Our agreement was that I couldn't ask you until I was free again. Now that my betrothal to Jasa is officially broken, I'm asking." Gently he took her right hand. "Arissa, will you marry me?"

Her vision blurred with happy tears. "Yes, Jolar, I will."

Grinning, he fastened the cuff around her right wrist. He leaned forward and pressed his lips to hers, then deepened the kiss, the heat of his hunger flaming around her.

When he broke away his eyes were dark with desire. "Now that it's official, I just realized," he began huskily, his fingers brushing over the curve of her breast. "We're free to do all sorts of things again . . ."

Epilogue

Arissa looked askance at Jolar. "Are you really going to be carrying that around all the time?"

Jolar's hair had grown out over the past several months, long enough now to tie it back like the men of this world did. Still, he was blond where they were dark-haired, and though their neighbors had grown used to him, he garnered a number of stares whenever they walked through the crowds of the Az-kye capital city.

Jolar shrugged, the hilt of the sword at his back shifting with the movement. "I'm pretty sure the empress intended me to. Zartani still wear ceremonial swords sometimes. And we decided to acculturate remember?"

"That's not ceremonial," Arissa pointed out.

"All the more reason to carry it," Jolar returned.

"I know you have a holdout blaster hidden on you."

"As if I could hide anything from you. Besides, I'm not much good with the sword yet." His palm rested on her rounded belly. "And I have a lot to protect." As if aware of being the topic of their conversation, the baby shifted under his hand. Jolar smiled. "I think that's a foot I'm feeling."

Arissa rubbed her back for the hundredth time today.

"Feeling okay?" Jolar asked. "We don't have to go to the market today."

"Since the baby dropped I can finally breathe again," she said, touching the curve of her belly and brushing the blissfully contented mind within. "Of course now I can't *walk*. But if you don't mind going slowly, I really want to go."

Jolar gave her a sympathetic look. "I'll buy you one of those litter things today, sweet."

"I can't believe they don't have groundcars yet."

Jolar laughed. "I'm just glad their empress was so eager to acquire our ship." He looked back in satisfaction at their sprawling, recently built home in the Az-kye capital city. "And you were amazing in the negotiations. I can't wait to see the lands she gave us on the new colony. Once they start production on the new Tellaran style ships we'll be able to get there in days instead of taking years in one of their ships. The technology we brought is going to transform this area of space."

Arissa gave him a warm smile. "You look pretty happy for a man who's looking at a lifetime of wearing animal skins."

"It feels good to help people who give real weight to the word 'honor'. And the skins aren't so bad," Jolar said. "In fact, they're pretty comfortable. I just wish warriors didn't have to wear only black. It's funereal."

"You look good in black. And it's a huge honor, you know."

He gave a short laugh. "Yeah, and at least they've finally stopped calling me 'Jolar Zartani'."

"You introduced yourself by pointing at your chest and saying, "Jolar. Zartani," she reminded, smiling. "Of course they thought that was your name."

"I'm not sure I'm ever going to get used to 'Jolar of the Az'anti'."

"I love the clan name the empress gave us. Really I do," she insisted at his eyebrow raise. "'Children of the Sun' . . . it's very poetic. My father would have liked it."

He nodded ahead at the spires of the palace in the distance. "If I'd known she was going to pick it as our new name I would have landed us at night."

"'Jolar of the Az'urhat'?"

He winced. "No, 'Az'anti' is better."

"Besides I think the name the empress chose has more to do with someone's distinctive feature," she said with a pointed look at his golden hair, "than what time of day we landed."

"I can't believe how quickly you picked up their language," he said. "I can barely hold a basic conversation."

"Yeah, well, being able to read their thoughts helps, but it's really two languages – one much, much older than the other."

Jolar glanced at the Az-kye around them. "Have you been able to figure out why they keep calling you 'Cy'atta'?"

She shook her head. "But every time I remind them to call me Arissa, they do. Maybe 'Stardancer' is some kind of honorific in their ancient language. Or," she said, having met one pair of dark, dark Az-kye eyes after another. "It has something to do with having green eyes."

"Or being able to read minds."

Arissa laughed. "I wish I could ask Kemma to come here. I never imagined a seer would be so warmly welcomed and respected anywhere."

"Well, what the Az-kye lack in technology they more than make up for in wisdom."

"It's wonderful for me but . . ." Arissa stopped to study his face. "I know you miss home."

"I miss Zartan." Jolar touched his forehead to hers and took her hands in his, the firestar of her bracelet catching the light of Az-kye's sun. "But home is wherever you are, sweet."

Futuristic Romance
by Ariel MacArran

Kinara's quest for revenge goes horribly wrong when she crosses into Az-kye space. Defeated and enslaved Kinara offers herself to Aidar, the Az-kye commander, in exchange for her crew's protection.

But this warrior wants more than just her body, he wants her heart . . .

STARDANCER

An excerpt follows

STARDANCER
©2013 Ariel MacArran

Tall and heavily muscled, the passing warriors were indeed an intimidating bunch. Between the arrogance of their strides, the dark skins they wore and the obvious scars of battle-hardened men, they seemed to be spoiling for a fight.

They might be strong, but she bet if something blocked their way they would probably hammer at it for hours with a sword rather than simply walk around it.

The thought made Kinara smile.

"That warrior pleases you?"

"Huh?" she said, jolted out of her thoughts to find a warrior looking back at her intently as they passed.

"Perhaps pleases you enough to share a bed with him."

She looked at Aidar to see that he was genuinely annoyed. "No, I was just thinking."

"And looking you on other warriors."

"Is there something wrong with looking? I'm curious about your people too."

"Do you look so boldly on them, they will think you wish them to join with you."

Kinara immediately dropped her eyes. She didn't want any of these warriors thinking she was making offers, and she didn't want any trouble right now either. She watched her feet and she looked at the walls. She tried to make a mental map of the ship so she could get back to her crew if an opportunity for escape came up.

They went down a passage she hadn't seen yet, but the curve of the floor was so steep she knew they were going down another level. Aidar nodded to the warriors at the door. One of the warriors stepped forward to follow them inside and the other opened the door.

The sight that greeted her was appalling. Her crew was here, dressed as she in plain white smocks, but if Barin's slave quarters were bad, these were atrocious.

They were herded together like animals, and there was not so much as a heating unit or a blanket here. Cold lights placed high on the walls gave a sickly greenish light and the room was freezing. Kinara suddenly realized that they were huddled together mainly for warmth.

Tears stung her eyes at the enthusiastic greeting they gave her. They looked so frightened, and so young. Tedah rushed forward and and pulled her into his arms.

He was dirty and the growth of his beard scratched her cheek as he hugged her.

"I'm so sorry," she whispered. "I'm sorry about all of this."

"Kinna, I thought they'd- no, never mind. You're all right." He cupped her face, and briefly kissed her. "You're all right."

"Tedah, is everyone-?" This was her fault, all of it, and the shame she felt wouldn't let her finish.

"We're all right," he soothed. "We haven't been hurt and everyone else is here."

All right for now. But in a place like this they wouldn't be all right for long.

She let go of Tedah, motioning him to stay behind.

She stood before Aidar.

"My lord—" It took a moment before she could lift her eyes. "My lord, please, my people are not used to this treatment. They will sicken and die in this cold. Please, some blankets and heating unit—"

His disbelief was evident. "They will not die. Even Tellarans cannot be so weak."

"They will. Look at them."

His dark eyes ran over them with a mixture of contempt and calculation.

"Please, some comfort for them would-"

His lip curled. "Think you I care for the comfort of slaves? Come, if looking on them upsets you so, we will leave."

She put her hand on his arm.

"Please, Ad- my lord," she said, her voice low and her eyes downcast. "I would—" She swallowed. "I would be grateful."

He looked at her face, glanced at her body. "And in your gratitude, *Cy'atta*, what do you offer?"

She wet her lips. "You wanted to bed me. You wanted me willing. That is what I offer."

Stay informed at www.arielmacarran.com

Historical Romance
by Ariel MacArran

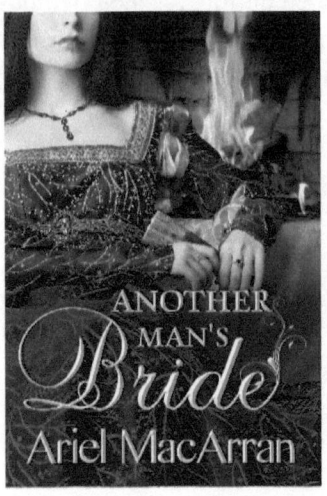

Fleeing charges of witchcraft at the English court, Lady Isabella Beaufort agrees to a marriage arranged by her cousin, Queen Joan of Scotland. Deep in the Highlands, Isabella is captured by Colyne MacKimzie, an enemy to the king and a man set on claiming a rich ransom for her return.

Even as she is drawn irresistibly to Colyne, Isabella's visions show her terrifying images of him. Colyne knows giving into his desire for this beautiful, haunted woman invites his swift destruction just as he knows he will risk anything to have . . .

Another Man's Bride

An excerpt follows

Another Man's Bride
©2013 Ariel MacArran

She might have been alone in the world, Isabella thought, as the silence deepened around her. She could neither see nor hear the others from her place by the well. There was no sound but the faint stirring of the cloths as they moved in the breeze and Isabella stood for a long time, watching them.

Offer a prayer for herself? What could she pray for? A swift end to her imprisonment? That she find her betrothed pleasing, and he, her? She had all the wealth she could wish for. Provided her husband did not squander it or deny her pin money, she should never fear hunger or cold.

Nothing she could think of seemed right somehow.

An end to her visions?

The visions retreated to haunt her nightmares but she knew they would return. She might have escaped her enemies at Bella Court by fleeing to this frozen country but they would follow her to the ends of the world.

She dipped the cloth in the water, surprisingly warm despite the frigid weather.

Isabella thought of the French girl she had seen in Rouen, the girl they called La Purcell, twisting and screaming in the flames.

Her hands were shaking as she tied the cloth to the tree.

"Please," she whispered.

Isabella looked at her tied cloth, hanging on the branch in this sacred place. She bent her head and heard a sound behind her. Seeing who it was, she quickly fanned her hair to hide her face.

"What is it, lass?" Colyne asked softly.

She kept her head turned away and her hand covered her mouth.

"Are ye longin' for home then?"

She did not reply and he continued, his voice rough, "Ye're nae afeared of me, are ye? I'd never hurt ye."

Her eyes closed when she felt him touch her hair, sliding his fingers through the strands. Just that simple touch was enough to break through her fragile self control and very gently he gathered her in his embrace as she sobbed. His body was warm, a refuge in a world of loneliness, and she clung to him. He rocked her, murmuring soothing words softened with a Scottish burr.

Isabella lifted her face as he pressed a kiss to her temple. His eyes searched her face for an instant, and then he caught her chin gently, tilting his head to bring his mouth to hers.

She clung to him as he explored, reaching up to his powerful shoulders, catching the silky strands of his brilliant hair between her fingers. His hands were under her cape now. This kiss was gentler yet hungrier than the last.

He broke away suddenly, breathing hard, his forehead against hers.

Had she done something wrong? Timidly she tilted her head to bring her mouth to his again but he would not let her. He squeezed his eyes shut, and with his hands firmly at her waist, pushed her away.

Shocked by the chill Isabella scrambled to pull her cloak closed against the cold. He was looking down at her, his mouth tight and drawn now.

"Ye're not for me."

Of course, Isabella thought. *Alisoun.*
And Douglas.

"No," she agreed hoarsely.

"Dinna fear." He took a step back, his mouth tight. "I'll nae lay a hand on ye again, lady."

With that he was gone, leaving her alone and bereft in the cold, a thousand heartfelt prayers fluttering in the tree beside her.

Stay informed at www.arielmacarran.com

Acknowledgments

I owe a great many thanks to my editor, Erin McCabe. Working with her is an amazing experience. I learn so much and my writing is so much richer for her insight, ideas and gentle guidance. I am humbled by her generosity and very grateful for her hard work.

Thanks to my cover designer Steven James Catizone for making my vision for the book a reality.

Thank you to my friends who supported and encouraged me and, most of all, to my family.

About Ariel MacArran

Ariel MacArran has had a lifelong love of books, stories and writing. Nothing makes her happier than the opportunity to give back some of the magic of being swept up into a story that other writers have given her. Ariel lives in Charleston, South Carolina.

Ariel loves hearing from readers! Please visit her website:

www.arielmacarran.com